Before We Sleep

Before We Sleep

A Novel

Jeffrey Lent

B L O O M S B U R Y
NEW YORK · LONDON · OXFORD · NEW DELHI · SYDNEY

An imprint of Bloomsbury Publishing Plc

1385 Broadway	50 Bedford Square
New York	London
NY 10018	WC1B 3DP
USA	UK

www.bloomsbury.com

BLOOMSBURY and the Diana logo are trademarks of Bloomsbury Publishing Plc

First published 2017

ISBN: HB: 978-1-62040-499-7
         ePub: 978-1-62040-501-7

LIBRARY OF CONGRESS CATALOGING-IN-PUBLICATION DATA

Names: Lent, Jeffrey, author
Title: Before we sleep : a novel / Jeffrey Lent.
Description: New York : Bloomsbury, 2017.
Identifiers: LCCN 2016029724 (print) | LCCN 2016036369 (ebook) | ISBN
9781620404997 (hardcover) | ISBN 9781620405017 (e-book)
Classification: LCC PS3562.E4934 B44 2017 (print) | LCC PS3562.E4934 (ebook)
| DDC 813/.54—dc23
LC record available at https://lccn.loc.gov/2016029724

2 4 6 8 10 9 7 5 3 1

Typeset by RefineCatch Limited, Bungay, Suffolk
Printed and bound in the U.S.A. by Berryville Graphics Inc., Berryville, Virginia

To find out more about our authors and books visit www.bloomsbury.com. Here you will
find extracts, author interviews, details of forthcoming events and the option to sign up for
our newsletters.

Bloomsbury books may be purchased for business or promotional use. For information on
bulk purchases please contact Macmillan Corporate and Premium Sales Department at
specialmarkets@macmillan.com.

For Marion, Esther, Clara
I truly couldn't have done this without you

One

Katey

IN HER MIND she was already gone and had been some weeks, months even. Half past midnight in the second week of June she slipped from her bed and pulled on jeans and a blouse and carrying her tennis shoes went soundless into the dark hall past her mother's bedroom and across from that the room where her father slept those same months. Down the stairs easing over the one third from the bottom, a tight grip on the rail as she went, on through the kitchen where the screened windows were open to the night air. The clump of lilacs a shadow against one side of the entryway, the last blooms infusing the room. She unhooked the screen door and slowly opened it, the rusty spring groaning a gentle scrape, then let the door settle back into place.

She went into the old carriage barn that had long ago been altered to a garage for winter parking although only her mother's car was there now and along to the stack of old apple crates where she lifted out her suitcase left earlier in the day. The backside of the carriage shed had been rebuilt as a workshop for her father, a place she'd spent many hours as a little girl. She went back into the drive where the truck stood, backed in from the street. She opened the driver door and set the suitcase on the bench seat, climbed in and let off the handbrake and took the truck out of gear. She stood back upon the driveway and leaned into the open door with her right hand upon the wheel and rolled the truck forward, tugging the wheel toward her until weight and gravity converged and the truck began to move. She jumped in and pulled the door to, though not yet latched, took the wheel with her left hand, turned the key to ignition and depressed the clutch and, keeping the clutch pedal down, slipped the truck into second gear as by the light of the small iron streetlights she began to roll down Beacon Hill to the village below. She used the handbrake to keep the speed down, waiting to be close to the bottom of the hill before she popped the clutch and fired the engine. The truck made a small lurch and cough and rolled along and she pulled the knob for the headlights and the dashboard lit up.

Two weeks ago to the night she'd made a practice run, more gesture to herself than need to prove it could be done. That night she'd circled the Common and then driven south a dozen miles and parked along the river with the engine off and watched the moon rise over the eastern hills and fracture and splinter among the eddies and pools of water, listening to the radio out of Waterbury and then had driven home, gliding uphill with the lights off easy as could be before cutting the engine and coming to rest back in the drive. Even that had been practiced those weekend mornings when she rose early to drive into the village where she waitressed at the Double Dot. That evening coming in she smelled tobacco smoke in the entryway and paused but heard nothing. The next morning when she came downstairs her mother was already gone and her father sat with his coffee and a magazine and said Good Morning to her and she replied as she made toast and heard his chair scrape back and he left the house for his workshop with nothing more said.

Thursday evenings after supper her father left the house for the village, "overstreet to Market" was the phrase he used, where he parked at the small VFW behind the courthouse and county sheriff's office, where he'd sit at the bar and listen to the old swing tunes on the jukebox, watch other men shoot pool and drink a single slow draft beer, this taking a little more than an hour before he returned home. He'd speak if spoken to but otherwise blew smoke rings toward the stamped tin ceiling, watching them break apart and fade together. She'd been told or overheard someone speaking of it or perhaps in the way of these things simply knew that was what he did and nothing more. And regardless if he'd driven the truck since the previous Thursday outing, he'd stop first at Sim's and top off the gas.

So this early morning she had three years of meager wages and tips gathered and saved for college in an envelope in her suitcase but also a full tank of gas. Which, along with the truck, she felt was the least he could do. No—that wasn't fair. What she knew was come morning and the discovery that she was gone, he would not allow her mother to involve the police. He'd know she was doing what she had to do, that she always had. He'd let her go. In this way he'd help her go. Even as he'd understand he was part of the reason she had to leave.

She was less sure her mother would come to the same conclusion.

In the village she turned onto the state road and went on through the three blocks of two- and three-story buildings, all dark, the houses set back from the street, the elms and maples dense canopies passing overhead and then lost to the headlights, the streetlights abrupt small flares that died and fled behind her, a wavering row of them out ahead. She drove carefully, alert to the possibility of a cruiser and had her story of sleeplessness ready and reached up and unbuttoned the top two buttons of her blouse and pushed the suitcase onto the passenger floorboards but she saw no one and soon left the village and the street-lights and was out on the road in the summer night.

She was two months past seventeen, determined and terrified.

When she was in her thirteenth summer she'd find herself weepy or defiant often it seemed at the same time. One evening at the town

3

ball field watching the game between Royalton and Moorefield, standing in her dress and pumps and studying the young men of both towns in their wool uniforms, their muscled arms and sleek ankles, the stretch of their legs as they ran or squatted over the bases, men of twenty or twenty-five, older than she could truly comprehend but for the glimmer that manifested in her stomach and punched up into her chest—these were men and she wanted to understand them but did not. That same evening Frank Chapman, also about to enter seventh grade that coming fall, sauntered up to her and asked where her old man was, why he was not on the home team, then said, "But a course he ain't, he's too old and everybody knows he's full a butternuts." Her hand clenched to fist and shot straight forward, the wet crunch of cartilage along with the crack of current up her arm as Frank's head snapped back and forward again as he sank toward and against her, the blood from his nose soaking the front of her dress as his arms clasped around her for a terrible long time before his knees caved and he sank to the ground. The game was still in paltry play but all of the spectators and most of the players had turned to watch this spectacle and only then did she remember her cry, a voice come back to her as an echo just before she punched Frank.

Asshole!

She'd stood trembling, Frank Chapman cast down before her, his nose a broken fountain spilling slowing spurts upon the ground and she'd looked at those around the ball field and turned her head down and kicked him in the crotch and then turned and ran for home. Up Beacon Hill in the hot evening as his blood dried upon her dress and bare legs.

Driving now she turned the radio on but there was only a hectic static until she climbed the height of land through the narrow gulf and found a station out of French Canada but the fiddle music sent an arc of pain through her chest and she twisted the knob again and

4

found a high-wattage station out of Boston, one she occasionally was able to pull in up on Beacon Hill if the night was clear. "In My Life" was playing and there left behind her was one of the five albums she owned and she welled over with tears, driving as if through rain. Then the song was over and without the disc jockey saying a word another song kicked in, one she didn't know but somehow did, as if there was a sudden vast welter of music that rose out of her chest and came back through the air and over the radio. It had been like this for much of the last year. She crimped her eyes tight against the tears and blinked. A distant world was closing upon her. She didn't understand it yet but it made sense to her. Life, she knew, was different from what she'd thought but also different than it ever had been before. She owned it, and she was not alone. What she heard: She was not alone. Everything had changed. And, though she wasn't yet sure how, she was part of that change. As if the world was ten steps ahead and she was at eight or nine. Only awaiting the guide who would whisper in her ear. Because clearly there were guides.

She had a road map she'd swiped from the Esso station in White River a few months earlier, a map of Vermont, New Hampshire and Maine. When she'd unfolded it in her room she'd seen that most of Maine was missing, as if the great upper regions of the state didn't exist. There were roads up there, she was certain, that ran between the chains of lakes and vast swathes of forest but perhaps not roads any customer of Esso would be tempted to explore. Still this lack peeved her. To pretend a place was less than what it was, a decision some person somewhere made, a judgment passed, at least implied. This place was not worthy of being acknowledged. Or of being understood.

Over the winter as she studied the map in stolen delightful moments as if meeting with a lover, as if making plans in secret, she also came to a more prosaic truth: The folds of the map wouldn't have been true and tight to their rectangles if Maine had not been sliced off halfway

5

across Moosehead Lake. Coherency, comprehension sometimes came at the cost of completeness. And she understood that.

Her mother had taken her by the hand and led her to the bathroom and stripped off her bloodied clothes and listened to the choked sobbing tale as she filled the bath and then stood her in it and washed her down with a lathered cloth. When she went silent her mother kept working, wringing the cloth and rinsing slowly, humming an unknown song as she often did, some tune from her mother alone or perhaps some song other mothers hummed in all places where life notched close to their own. This humming had been part of her life ever since she could remember.

Her mother gently wrung the water from her hair and then bound her hair up in a towel and pulled the plug and she stood waiting for the water to drain. She did not leave the tub until the water was gone and another towel dried her head to foot and one at a time the sole of each foot as she stepped from the empty tub.

"You think you did the right thing," her mother had said, "but you did not. Don't ever hit anyone again whatever they say or do. I never have and pride myself for it and that's a thing to take pride in. People hurt each other all kinds of ways but in the end there's not a thing on earth worth striking another person for. It only serves to make you small. That boy didn't know what he was saying, he thought he did but he was wrong. You acted from love and that's well enough but love's no excuse. What a person sees in another person, and who that person truly is, why, they're often not the same thing in the least. Hitting him doesn't change a thing."

Her mother was now toweling her hair. She said, sputtering, again shaking with anger and cold, "He said Daddy was crazy, said he was full of butternuts."

Her mother, squatting on the side of the tub, reached for the hairbrush behind her and began to work it through her wet hair and tipped her head toward the window where the last summer sunlight low through the trees was pooled up, spilling in, casting them both golden, making shadows on the walls pale as ghosts. Her voice modulated down now as she said, "All of us are different, Katherine, you get down to it. Some just hide it better than others. He's a good man, your father, and he loves you. Truly. You hold that and the rest doesn't matter."

Her mother smiled then and said, "Step out now and we'll get a nightgown and a little ice cream. That sound good?"

She said, "I called him an asshole. But I don't care because he is."

Her mother rocked back on her heels and looked off toward the window and the paling green twilight there and then looked back at the girl and said, "Any other day I'd wash your mouth with soap. So, we'll settle. I'll leave the soap and you'll go direct to bed. Are we agreed?"

It was not a question and she did not answer but went to her room and sat upright on her bed as darkness fell and sometime later she saw her father cross the yard from the house to his workshop and let himself in and soon the one small window there lit up and the heat of the day drained to a small cooling breeze and she pushed down under the covers and slept. At breakfast next morning her right hand ached, her knuckles scraped and swollen. Otherwise the room was empty, her parents each disappeared into their days. She ate a bowl of cornflakes with two big spoonfuls of sugar and left the bowl in the sink with the froth of thickened milk, unwashed.

She turned the radio off and cranked her window all the way down. The sadness could quickly turn to anger but there was no fury in her this night. It was late enough so the June air was cool, almost chill and she turned the heater on low, enough to feel it on her ankles which was all she needed. The road came to a T and she doglegged west a few miles and threaded through the backstreets of Barre and out again on another road north, back in the countryside of sleeping

7

houses, yard lights, passing the Rock of Ages quarry entrance where the great vault into the earth was bright with floodlights and a pair of flatbed trucks passed her going south, the beds holding loads, wrapped in dirty canvas, the blocks of great weight. Then onward around a long curve and a roadhouse with a wide gravel parking lot studded with pickups and sedans, some sleek, some beaten down. A green neon sign in the one high long window. The Canadian Club. There was a small group of men in a corner of the lot who formed a ragged ring around a pair of lone figures but none seemed to be moving. If it was a fight it either hadn't started or was mostly over. Back down through a swale of puckerbrush, sumac and chokecherry, the smell of a swamp and the early summer pumping of frogs. Then abruptly she braked as a tangle of legs like skeletal marionettes jerked and slid upon the slick summer-warmed pavement, the tawny bodies rising and falling, a great set of luminous beseeched eyes turned into the headlights as the doe froze and the fawn scrambled to stand quivering beside her and Katey was rolling to a stop even as doe and fawn fled off into the dark again and were gone. She turned the radio back on but low, a murmur of rising and falling cadences and drove. Around another curve she passed a house with a single downstairs window lit a pale flickering blue-gray—someone likely had fallen asleep some hours before while the station was still on the air.

She came into a small village crossroads, a half a dozen houses and a general store, all dark and without streetlights and she pulled off into the gravel lot of the store. She'd never been there before but knew where she was. The bisected road was a highway that ran east and west even if at this place it looked to be little more than another paved two-lane road. She saw the blue line of the map in her head. If she turned west in a few hours she'd go into Canada and then come back into America somewhere in Michigan and, she knew from that same blue line, if she managed to follow the road long enough eventually she'd reach the Pacific Ocean. Or close to it. The school atlas was not clear on that. And it was a great distance. But not the distance she needed to travel. There was a void within her and one that could be filled only by heading east. She turned the radio back to a volume she could hear and eased out of the lot onto the highway. The void had to do with water in an elemental way; the void itself was much larger than water but it was a place to start.

She would stand in the ocean. She never had but all of her life she'd had some sense of oceans, of unfathomable wide waters, ever since Miss Button's first-grade class when she'd seen the pull-down maps of the world with their great expanses of blue separating the multicolored landmasses, but also a storybook of the Pilgrim fathers and mothers landing at Plymouth, the illustrations showing the small ship in the waves of the harbor, the groups clambering from boats upon a rocky shore and far-off clouds scudding along the horizon and there gained a sense of how land met those waters and knew she wanted to stand within the breaking waves. Once at Lake Fairlee, lying on her back in the water with her head immersed so only her face itself was above the surface and she could look backward and see the world as water first and then upside-down trees and finally the sky where she'd felt she knew something of the ocean. Her father had crossed the oceans but she knew not to speak of that to him and so did not speak of her desire to anyone. And the song of oceans within her became a song of her own and with that became a goal. She had not seen the ocean but would, soon. That was the first thing. There were other things to be revealed or resolved and she did not know all of them. But first she would stand in the ocean.

It would be all of the next day and night and afternoon of the day following before she was able to do so but she didn't know that when she put the truck in gear and pulled out of the parking lot of the store and headed east on Route 2. She didn't yet fully understand the scale of maps but dawn found her much further north and just over the New Hampshire line, where she pulled into the first diner she found and ate eggs and toast with coffee as she studied the map and understood the magnitude of this journey that she'd thought so easy to make those nights in her bedroom. And this excited her as she realized that even the small corner of the world she thought she knew was greater than her imagination of it. She mopped the egg yolk with the last crust of toast and tipped sugar and cream into her coffee again and drank it down before setting off again.

Late afternoon she pulled off onto a dirt track just east of Jefferson with Mount Washington behind and south of her, lost in clouds, lightning bursts around the peak, a violent storm up there but on the dirt road found a log-truck pull-off under faded sunshine and she left the windows cracked and stretched out on the bench seat and slept.

She woke to pelting rain and jabs of lightning in a shimmering twilight, her ankles and hair wet from the rain through the windows and a mild panic but the truck cranked and she sloughed her way out through the sticky mud of the track back onto the highway and the storm was gone and she rolled down the windows as the twilight turned golden behind her and then all around as she passed a black-and-white metal sign with the legend MAINE upon it.

The land was more level though she sensed hills in the distance and roadside were stands of big paper birches, now and then an ash or maple but crowded close were towering hemlocks and tamaracks. It was a land new and strange, on a scale of wildness unlike home.

She filled the truck with gas in Bethel and then stopped at a small Red & White store. An older woman sat behind the counter working a crossword puzzle from a rag-paper book of them, the woman in a sleeveless yellow floral print dress with an open white cardigan over it, her hair in a severe bun that seemed to stretch taut her otherwise plump face. Katey got a can of Vienna sausages, a tin of sardines, a box of crackers and asked the woman to cut a piece of cheese from the wheel under a glass dome beside the cash register.

"How much?" the woman asked.

"Bout like this." She held up a thumb and finger an inch apart. The woman cut the wedge and wrapped it in paper and tied brown twine around it. While the woman was doing this she went to a red soda cooler and lifted the lid, reached down into the zinc-lined case and the ice water and lifted out a bottle of Coca-Cola and set it on the counter next to her purchases.

The woman said, "A dime and nineteen and nineteen again, thirty-two cents for the cheese and the crackers is fifteen. Ninety-five cents, the best part of a dollar." She snapped open a small paper bag. "Where you headed?"

Katey pulled a crumpled dollar from her jeans pocket and smoothed it and laid it on the counter. "Right now I'm looking for a cheap place to spend the night."

"Down the road about five miles is Mosley's. They got tourist cabins. Tell em Nita up to the store sent you. This early in the summer even on a Friday night two three cabins at least will be setting there waiting." She cranked open the till, laid a nickel on the counter and took up the bill. "You all right, honey? You in trouble?"

Katey smiled. "I'm fine. I'm just heading down to the coast to see the ocean. I never have and been wanting to. I graduated high school last week and thought this was the time." It was so easy to lie, against everything she'd ever been taught. There was a sense of power, within, of controlling a situation.

Nita nodded and said, "It's something to see."

Katey took her Coke and popped the top off against the opener on the side of the case and the top fell into the box welded to the side there, lifted the bottle and drank off two slow swallows and then said, "You was me, first time? Where would you go?"

The woman nodded again and dipped her head in thought, then looked up and smiled. She was missing a tooth in the front of her mouth. She said, "I was you I'd head to Damariscotta and then down to Pemaquid Point. You'll smell it before you ever see it. You have to park up by the lighthouse and walk down. That's the place. You go there, you'll know why I sent you."

Katey said, "Damariscotta. To Pemaquid. Got it. Thank you." She took up her small sack of groceries and turned toward the dusk of the day beyond the screen door of the store.

The woman called from behind her. "Honey? You got to change roads a bunch of times to get there. You got a map?"

She turned and hooked the sack on a canted hip and said, "I got a map. A good one. Those people, the ones with the cabins? Their name's Mosley?"

The woman nodded. "They'll feed you pie for breakfast."

Katey grinned and turned and walked through the screen door onto the porch where the daylight was falling toward long summer twilight and she turned and called back to the lit inside, "Thank you, Nita."

"It wasn't nothing. Good luck, honey."

She slept that night hard and dreamless and in the morning sat at the kitchen table with the Mosley wife and five little boys and drank coffee from a big white and blue speckled enamel pot and ate pies made from last year's canned blueberries and venison mincemeat studded with raisins, the crusts rich with lard. The Mosley man had left before daylight to drive north most of an hour to work in the woods and the boys peppered her with the questions of boys and she answered with smiles and the least said as she could. She caught the wife studying her, a woman who didn't have to know the secret to know she was hearing one. Katey smiled and left under a robin's-egg sky, a skim of high haze.

She stopped twice to study the map and once had to backtrack near a dozen miles because she'd reversed a number in her head but made Damariscotta an hour after noon. Twice she'd crossed long bridges and thought she was crossing bays or inlets but signs told her she'd crossed first the Sheepscot River and then the Damariscotta

River and the size of them awed her a bit and excited her greatly. In the Sheepscot beneath the bridge there'd been a pair of old wooden ships, still sprouting masts and spars, heavy ropes weathered almost black and she wondered how old they were and why they'd just been left there and then was on up over the arching bridge and there were gulls in flurries all about the bridge, their raucous harsh cries a sweet counterpoint to the dense funk of air. The sky had grown low and leaden, a pounded sheet of rippling metal, and down the rivers she saw large fishing boats making way back upstream as sailboats of all sizes angling with or against the wind, most headed downstream. She turned the radio off and dangerously leaned to crank down the passenger window and a blaring horn allowed her to jerk the truck back into her lane where she waved and smiled at the angry fist of the frightened driver as they passed each other.

She hadn't eaten since breakfast but wouldn't stop now. She made her way through Damariscotta and found the road leading down the peninsula, a road of mixed gravel and packed broken shells and around her the fields gave way to scrubland covered with juniper circles and sprawls of low bushes with dark, almost purple leaves, the houses also grew small, none more than a story and a half and time to time she'd round a curve and the ocean spread before her but from a height, the white foam of waves breaking and stippling the surface of the long reach of water, closing again so only the land and sky were to be seen, then a sudden glimpse downward toward a small harbor with houses and sheds and wharves or a small cove lined with stunted evergreens, a single fishing boat caught there motionless. She passed through Bristol and then New Harbor and both times wanted to stop, to walk about these places, these villages by the sea but drove onward.

As she went the sky grew more dark and it seemed the water did also. The sky so many gray-wool fleeces piled against each other and seeming just overhead yet stretching endless as the sky spread wide and far and she realized she was almost at the end of land. Strange almost, as she was still high upon a ridge, much of the water hidden as the road twisted and turned.

She turned a last curve and the stark white tower of the lighthouse stood before her, topped with a black-painted lantern room. Next to the tower was a small building set with windows, perhaps a storage shed, perhaps the keeper's house. She could not tell. The parking lot was empty but for an older Dodge truck parked alongside the lighthouse. She cut the engine and rolled to a stop. After so long waiting for this, she simply sat in the cab. Listening to the lift and roar of the breaking waves somewhere on the rocks below. That she could not yet see. But the sound rose up through her, gooseflesh broke her skin and she shivered and laughed at the same time. Beyond, at a far distance, great enough so there was a discernible arc, lay the horizon where the sky met the sea. Wiping sudden tears from her eyes she stepped down out of the truck.

She wanted to approach the tower, the possible house, to see if she could find the keeper but was overcome with a deep shyness. Thinking the sort of man who'd have this work would be a solitary man, not wanting to be bothered by stupid questions, questions at least that he'd find stupid. So she circled about and found a path that led onto the ledges below the light.

The ledges were much higher and wider than she'd expected, leading downward in a multitude of choices before leveling out as they narrowed into a long spit of heaved-up rock, the ledges almost pale white here where only rain struck them but further below and out the spit they darkened to charcoal where the tides overran them, where at the edges there were rising slaps of waves breaking white suds, smacking upward before sliding back.

She made her way, a few times easing down with her palms on the stone behind her as she scooted slow and cautious on her bottom along a wider or steeper ledge. And was glad she was alone this day, overcome with an abundance of caution she'd not want witnessed. As

she descended the ledges she also descended toward the booming of
the breaking ocean and the sound was magnificent and with its
rhythmic constancy greater than any thunderstorm she'd ever known,
much greater than ice-out on the river, a power that she began to feel
pulsing as if it would meet and join her heartbeat. The only sound
otherwise came from a pair of gulls that swarmed about her head,
their cries incessant and hungry, their furious wingbeats unheard.

At the bottom of the ledges the base of the spit was still wide, the
way forward an uneven mix of slabs and juts of stone. On both
sides the surf was breaking but still far away and she'd gotten used to
the sudden surges and the spillover and the draining off. She made
her way along and found she was indeed where two worlds met:
The stones held pools of water and, hands on her knees, she studied
the shells and broken claws both dark green and bleached white, the
long gnarled strands of seaweed upon the rocks, here and again small
fish flashing iridescent silver in the pools. Racks of stones the size of
her fist lodged between fissures on the rock, other places streams
of wet gravel of rust-red, black, green, blue, white, all brilliant and
glistening as if refracting light pulled from the depths. Shards of blue
and green bottle-glass worn smooth to a softness at the edges when
she picked them up. A slender long bone lay dried and caught in a
crevice of the higher rocks and she plucked it up and held it. Turning
it about in her fingers. A bone so light it was as if she held nothing at
all, the wingbone of some seabird. She wanted to keep it but also
wanted her hands free and knew it would shatter in the pockets of
her jeans and so glanced once behind her and saw not only was she
alone but was far out from the ledges, the lighthouse still seeming
solid but much smaller than she expected. She turned back and once
again unbuttoned the top of her blouse and eased the bone down
under the mid-strap of her bra, turning it gently so it was caught by
the strap but aligned not up and down but almost sideways against
her own ribs.

She turned back to face the ocean and the spit of land and for a moment remained fully upright, her chin lifted, her spirit high. She was farther out than she'd thought and now the breaking waves flooded lightly both sides close enough so they approached her sneakers. But she could now see the horizon of sky and sea meeting on a flat plane and far out a break in the clouds cast a sheet of lemon light down upon far distant waters and she felt the great joy of being in a place she'd always dreamed and now, here, found it to be as complicated and beautiful as all her life and she thought this was how it should be.

She went forward down the spit. Which was narrowing, the splash of surf higher and closer but she walked upright, no more caution of hands and feet, not striding but feeling her way upon this place of long dreams. One wave boiled high and soaked her feet and ankles and then was gone in a slippery froth of bubbles. Then came another and she was slightly giddy with the notion of the ocean finally meeting her in this way, the seas touching her as if welcoming her home. And yet each footfall forward she looked carefully how she set that foot down, found her weight there, her balance, and then moved up the other foot. She was delighted and cautious. She was in homage.

There came before her a high slab that cut across the spit at an angle, steep-sided and nearly smooth, the rock face dry as water swarmed around it, making a trough one side to the other at the base. Half again as high as she was and knife-edged at the top, as if some ancient giant being had been knapping a flint and grown weary or abandoned the job and left it here as a guard against those enemies who might come from the waters. Fissures ran like woodgrain across the slab and she paused and studied them and knew she could lie flat against it and make her way up to see what she would see upon the other side. She sloshed through the tide-flow before the slab and felt the hard suck of opposing currents against her calves but then was sprawled against the face of the rock, arms outstretched to reach high, her feet lifting one then the other to find purchase. She rose and her hands caught the top and she pulled herself up so she was peering down the other side.

She gulped air and held it, her fingers clenched against the rock. Below her was a dense dark water, lifting as if by a bellows, lungs of some vast kind, the water heaving and falling but slowly sliding against the rock, welling slightly and falling away and welling again. A presence of great fatal danger, lazy within its own power, coiling and uncoiling, coiling again. And though she could not see beneath that viscous surface she felt the unfathomable depth of the water, and most of all, what made the greatest flush of terror through her was knowing if she offered herself to the water as she'd imagined doing all these years, this water would suck her down and kill her while all around her the water continued doing only what the water did. The crash of ocean meeting land. Timeless and eternal and without care for those creatures great or small that might be trapped at this juncture and perish from the earth. She was shaking and very cold and yet could not break her gaze from the waters below, a thrall of terror within her. She clung hard to the slab of rock.

A gull beat down toward her, close above, hovering as if to learn if she was food and she looked up and raised one hand and batted it away. The gull swung and in long elegant glides swept away over the waves off to sea. She kept her eyes on the bird even as she clamped her hand again upon the rock, the slab she lay up against. A great and ancient wall that stood before her and the ocean. She was cold and sweating and turned her head sideways and laid her cheek against the cool rock.

With deliberate caution she made her way halfway back up the ledges and turned to sit, knees drawn up and her arms wrapped around them, her chin on one knee. From the moments against the rock now far away below until now she'd been of a curious mind; not blank so much as a heightened intensity of focus upon her

17

movements that seemed to close out the world around her except for the inescapable pound of the waves upon the rocks.

Off to the southwest the sun had come out, streaming over her shoulder, afternoon light against the water and the dark scud of clouds paling east and north before her, the water vast and fractured by light on inward rolling waves to the horizon. Her back was warm; her feet in her sodden sneakers still cold.

This is it, she thought. How it will go. Whatever I find will be different from what I thought.

Still gazing out at the sea.

And then felt her hunger, the long day since her pie breakfast and with that knew she had to get along. She stood and turned her back on the sea and above her at the top of the ledges there stood a man looking down at her. He wore green khaki trousers and a blue shirt with rolled-up sleeves; a sheaf of white hair tore back and forth across his head in the wind. She walked up toward him and he watched her come. As she grew close she saw his face was weathered and folded in creases but his eyes were of a clear pale blue. He hailed her with a lifted hand before she was within speaking distance and she did the same and went on toward him.

Once before him she found she was still breathless.

He said, "I saw you out there. A wonder, isn't it?"

She could only nod but her brain was whirring, knowing this was the man of the lighthouse.

He nodded back. "It's a odd day. The glass is dropping. That bit a sun is about to be snuffed out. Radio reports a mighty storm off of Hatteras." He shrugged. "Most all it means for us, likely, is a couple days of rain, maybe a bit airy. But then again, could boil on up from there and come upon us a full-blown storm." He looked away from her and looked back. "Name's Fred Jewett. I'm the keeper." He stuck out a hand.

She took it and shook firm as she'd been taught. "I'm Katey Snow. Good to meet you, Mr. Jewett."

He looked off at the sky and fished a pack of Lucky Strikes from his shirt pocket, tapped one free and dug a dented Zippo from his trousers and spun the wheel with his thumb and made fire. He watched the smoke and then said, "Your first time here?"

"I drove a couple days to see the ocean and now I have."

"It's awe-inspiring, isn't it?"

"It is. A little frightening too, up close."

He nodded. "I'm here every day. And it amazes me every day." He paused, then said, "It's like looking at the stars. When you really look. You know?"

"Yeah." She grinned, suddenly shy.

As if he felt it, he said, "I got to get on." And gestured with his head toward the building. "Anything more I can do for you?"

"I appreciate your time," she said. Then she said, "I'm wicked hungry. Is there a good place to eat that won't empty my pockets, Mr. Jewett?"

"It's the coast," he said. "Long as you like fish you'll eat good anywhere. I like Tommy's up New Harbor, myself. There's a sign."

She took his hand again and shook it. "Thank you. It's been a pleasure."

He nodded again, looked off and she knew he was done with her. She stepped around him and crossed toward her truck. The other truck, what she'd assumed was his, was gone. As she pulled open the driver door he called after her.

"Keep an eye on the weather."

She flashed back a grin. "I'll do it."

She drove out to the road and slipped the gearshift into neutral and pulled up the handbrake. Then reached inside her shirt and freed the bird bone. Dull-white and smoothed by water and light as the air it once rode. She set it up on the dash, where it would ride safe. Then let off the brake and dropped into gear.

19

In New Harbor she circled about the village twice, enough that she passed the same older woman twice and so slowed and asked for the restaurant and was sent down to the docks. Tommy's was a long narrow place of weathered wood at the end of one of the docks with a painted signboard and a window to order and pick up food. She parked in the crushed shell lot and walked up onto the dock and stood back, studying the board. Mostly it was food she'd never eaten before. But the smells flooded out and smothered the brackish water and her stomach rumbled.

Except for a couple with a baby at one of the tables she was the only one there. She stepped up to the window and after a moment a boy her age leaned forward toward her, looking down. He wore a white T-shirt with the sleeves rolled up and had a white paper hat tilted on his head, his hair long enough to cover his ears in the ragged way of a boy trying to look cool but not quite sure how.

"Help you?" He smiled as his eyes cut down to her chest and slowly dragged back up. She thought Thinks he's the big deal in New Harbor, even as she noted the roll of muscle where his forearms led to his elbows and the pale hairs along those arms, the cords in his neck and a single dimple more like a crease one side of his mouth. His smile faded under this scrutiny and she knew he was less sure of himself than he wanted her to think.

"I'll have the lobster roll, the medium bucket of clams, fries and slaw. And a chocolate shake."

He whistled and said, "Hungry girl."

She said, "I am."

"You want that regular or malted?"

"Malted. Thank you."

He jotted it up on a green pad and gave her the total and she paid and then turned away, looking out at the long dock, the other docks or wharves, the boats tied up, the stacks of domed slatted lobster traps, the oily slow water pushing back and forth. Gulls on most every upright surface, post or pillar, the sky with high wedges of streaming sunlight with fleet clouds casting shadows passing over the land where she stood, the water about her. As she waited the couple with the baby finished and left and she gained a small pool of dread that once her food was ready the boy would want to talk more with her. And did not know, could not make up her mind if that dread was if he would or wouldn't. But had an answer ready if he tried to.

He called, "Miss? Your food's ready."

She turned from the water and a cloud passed over the sun and she felt the press of a fresh breeze.

He had everything lined up on a dented, wash-polished aluminum tray and was back from the window at a small sink scrubbing something she couldn't see. Under his apron he wore shorts that came to above his knees and the backs of his legs were golden and finely haired. Somewhere between her chest and belly was a hum, a faint and far distant relation of what she'd felt looking down over the rock an hour before.

She pulled napkins from the dispenser and rattled the tray as she pressed them in a wad against her fork and knife and he glanced back from his work and flashed her his ready smile and said, "You all set, now?"

"I believe I am." Her mouth felt as if it twisted around as she spoke.

He nodded and said, "Let me know if there's anything you need." And went back to work.

The tray was heavy as she lifted it and she slid her hands to get balance and said, "Thanks. I will."

She walked the dozen feet to the table farthest away, stepping gingerly, her legs uncertain with her as if the fright she'd felt an hour ago was only now released fully within her, her steps over the wooden planks as cautious as her making way back along the rocks. She had to stand a moment before the table before she dared lean to set the tray down, the world heaving, the water just dockside lifting and falling. She stood looking down at the food and felt a sweat break upon her face, under her arms. She reached down and lifted the tall metal shaker of chocolate malt and drank down a couple of long swallows and felt her throat burn with the pleasure of it, almost a choke of freeze that brought a smart of tears to her eyes. She set the drink down and then eased into the chair as the cold-burn subsided and she studied the food before her.

There were little cups of melted butter and a clear gray broth and she didn't know what to do with them and so she ate the lobster roll first. The lobster meat was delicious, slick and salty with the taste of butter. When that was done she pulled a clam free from its shell and it was good but with a trace of grit and sweet but dry. The next one she dipped in the butter and it was much better but still the grit cracked against her teeth and she paused and thought about it, eating fries and slaw. Then she pulled free another clam and swabbed it in the broth and then the butter and the world was right. Under the table she knocked her knees together, something she'd done since earliest memory when delighted with food. As simple as ice cream could bring this on; also rare times; Thanksgiving, Easter dinner, hot dogs on a summer night cooked on sticks over a wood fire outside. Meals up on West Hill when her grandmother was still alive.

But never anything like this. A couple of times trout fried with bacon, food she understood that had been given to her father and her mother prepared and often as not the two of them ate alone. There was a fish truck came Thursday afternoons late spring throughout the summer to Royalton she'd heard about, knew it came from Maine but the one time she'd asked her mother about it was told it wasn't for the likes of them, that it was for the Catholics mostly, the summer people also, the handful that had bought used-up farms in the hills above the village.

Her mother had been wrong about so much and she'd known that for a long time. She ate the last fry and the rest of the slaw before eating the last clam. By then the broth and butter both were cool but the clam was sweet as the first, sweeter even, for being the last. The past few years Katey felt as if she'd been watching her mother from a tilted distance, as if unsure of what she was a witness to. Only knowing it was a woman living a way she never intended to allow for herself.

She rose filled again with purpose and carried the tray to the counter and the pretty boy was waiting for her.

"Was it good?"

"Of course it was."

"So . . ." he said.

"So?"

She watched him swallow, his Adam's apple bob up and out and down again.

He said, "If you're up for the summer I'd be happy to show you around. And there's movies in Damariscotta. Or we could go out after lobsters, my uncle's got a boat. Or anything. If you'd like."

She nodded. Then said, "Sounds nice. What's your name?"

He grinned again. She knew it was nerves. "I'm Mark," he said. "Mark Crowell." And he stuck a hand through the window.

She reached and slid her fingers along the back of his hand and took them away and said, "Sorry, Mark. I'm only passing through. I was you I'd watch for some other girl to come along."

She turned before he could speak and walked down off the dock toward the truck, playing it cool, almost jittery, a sense of playacting; also the overall drama of the day behind and what lay ahead. She got in the truck and cranked it up. She drove on out of the lot and up through the village.

Going over a height of land, still on the narrow point, in the rearview mirror she saw a dark roll of storm clouds far behind her. She guessed that was about right.

Once again she was on her way. Now headed north. When she could, she'd turn east again.

Two

Ruth

HE WAS THE towhead boy with a gap between his front teeth, skinny limbed but wiry-strong and she'd known him all her life in the way of knowing everyone in a small town but he first impressed her the year they both were seven at the outer edges of the Fourth of July picnic that followed the church service. Each year one or another of the town fathers, including her own twice, read aloud the Declaration of Independence, with the minister leading prayer and the choir singing patriotic songs. The town soprano, an aging widow who favored elaborate hats to counter her rusty black skirts and ancient green sweater even on the hottest days, a homely woman who with age gained a reserved and sublime beauty, stood alone and without accompaniment—a frustration the organist, a woman of her own generation, suffered by folding her hands over her lap and watching the performance with cool and precise admiration that fooled no one in attendance—sang the national anthem with delicate vibrato and hidden but real pride in sustaining easily those difficult high notes, the song ending as a silence fell upon those gathered with no few moist eyes, a silence held long enough so the pigeons in the steeple could be heard by those below before the appointed boy tolled the bell fourteen times, one each for the original colonies to become states in the new union and the final time for the little republic that became the fourteenth state. In which they all resided.

The bell also the signal for the picnic and other festivities to begin.

She was in the shade of the elms along the North Common, away from the hubbub to cool off from the heat within the church as well as the swelling emotion she'd felt this year, a turmoil she didn't fully comprehend but resided within her as a timorous bird's-nest gathered in her breast, wanting only to step away, to take a moment, when a firecracker went off right behind her. She jumped and gasped, then turned, furious at the intrusion and saw Oliver Snow dashing away off among the trunks of the other elms. Glancing back once to witness the aftermath of his effort, grinning at her scowl.

After that, best she could, she paid him no mind. After that she saw him everywhere she turned. He was the boy who would not be ignored.

In the fifth grade he bested her in a spelling bee after she stumbled over "incongruous" and he prevailed with "prognosticator." He was an unlikely victor, a casual scholar although even then he was known to be a reader. As was she. They'd run into each other at the town library. In his glory he was oddly adult, stepping across to where she stood holding back tears and gravely shook her hand and congratulated her, as if she and not he, had been the winner. The prize a certificate for a banana split. At his own father's mercantile, which housed a soda fountain as well as the town's telephone service switchboard. He offered to share the reward with her and she demurred; it would be two years before she realized he was offering her an early attempt at a date. He only tossed up his head and grinned, his hair flipping away from his forehead, hair now the pale yellow of fall birch leaves. In the summer before seventh grade he walked up to her

25

in the library one warm afternoon, flies droning against the windows, the place empty but for the two of them and the librarian who was shelving books, and asked her if she'd care to go to the picture show that Saturday night, when the stage and the painted mural backdrop at the town hall was replaced with a hand-stretched canvas screen to hold the movies stitched through the projector by Doc Durgan who had a feel for such devices, was in fact responsible for bringing this possibility about to save the residents the drive over the three long ridges and valleys to the Playhouse in Randolph. Again she'd said No. She went anyway with a pair of girlfriends as she most always did. And saw him at intermission as she bought a paper sack of popcorn, the brown paper translucent with loops and whorls of butter. He grinned and lifted a finger to his dipped brow. A salute, a greeting, but the smile also asking the question of why not with him, after all. She'd clutched tight her bag of popcorn and turned to speak to her friend Gladys. She didn't have an answer for Oliver Snow.

Even though she lived two miles up West Hill and he lived less than a quarter-mile down Creamery Road they were village children. They attended the two-story academy that schooled the village elementary students on half of the first floor and the high school students from the entire town in the rest of the building; those students who attended neighborhood schools from first to eighth grade up at the crossroads of West Hill, Taplin Brook, Brocklebank, King's Valley, Kipplin Hill; those children of farmers and loggers and trappers and those make-as-best-they-could, which was most of them—those children who came down to attend high school which were not so many after all, making graduating classes of sixteen or nine or twenty-one. Year to year would rise or fall. Girls in flour- or feed-sack dresses bleached or worn so the imprints were faded next to girls in their dresses made from bought bolts of cloth, some few mail-ordered from Montgomery Ward, boys likewise in trousers and shirts and vests as their fathers wore, hard shoes from September to

Before We Sleep

May next to boys in one-strap overhauls with the same boiled collar-less shirt day after day, barefoot until the ground froze, then wearing home-cobbled boots worn thin and resoled many times or needing it, some even in grease-softened and waterproofed handsewn deer-hide moccasins some great-great-grandmother had learned to make and no reason seen yet to quit, together they all came. To learn and advance. As if pulled by something beyond their own ken or reck-oning but there. As her father explained to her.

So she and Oliver were village children and seen so in the eyes of those high-hill hamlet children but both also knew they were different. And she did not care and he did. How blood flows down.

Her father, Nathaniel Hale, was the superintendent of the county schools, including of course those of the town. This bought her no favor—in fact her teachers if anything were more firm and exacting with her as if recognizing her intelligence and demanding she do the same, that she rise to their expectations. He rarely appeared at the village academy, preferring to meet with the school board in the town offices. Otherwise his county office was in the village of Orange and he held his handful of weekly hours there. Mostly he could be found in Montpelier striding the halls of the capitol building, cornering politicians to discuss legislation one hour and the next sitting with them over a meal or cigars or late afternoons a glass of whiskey in one or another locked office. He was a man of large girth, precision-blue eyes, an oiled thatch of squirrel-colored hair. He wore steel-rimmed spectacles that he'd lower with one finger down his nose to meet eye to eye if the occasion called for it—equally for firm-ness or mirth. He was well-liked and well-feared and knew the strength of a quiet voice from his own father. Ruth was the youngest of his three daughters, younger by fourteen and sixteen years, a source of embarrassment to her mother who became pregnant after she'd believed herself to have gone through the change. Ruth thus grew up as an only child and also the baby of the family. Her mother understood this quickly enough as the older girls left home and so became even more firm with her than she'd been with her sisters. Ruth having no way to know this except as a natural state of affairs. The gaiety that occurred when Margaret or Betty were home for holidays with their own growing families she attributed to adulthood, a notion enforced by the affection and special attention those women paid their much younger sister.

The family was unique in other ways and she knew this quietly also. The quietness was part of being a Hale. Her grandfather had been a state legislator until he was felled at the early age of forty-six by a bad oyster or a bad heart, depending upon who was telling the tale. He'd read law with Ephraim Allan himself, against the wishes of his father who wanted one son not headed out to the western prairies for the deep loam and easy riches promised there but Aldridge Hale was determined and so made hay in the summer for his father and boiled sap in the spring to make sugar but otherwise spent his time in Allan's office or in court and quickly proved adept at writing opinions for his mentor and passed the bar at the age of seventeen. He opened a law office in the village and so made his own hay with his townspeople and also aligned himself with a larger firm in the capital and made his mark as a defense attorney, the man to hire if you were in dire trouble and could provide a glimmer of escape. When Aldridge ran for the legislature it took many of his neighbors by surprise; most all thought he'd become a judge or simply continue making good money. His landslide victory over the five-term incumbent was understood as a mandate, not least by himself. He kept the farmhouse on West Hill and the orchard his own grandfather had started but had the house rebuilt in the 1890s on a slightly grander, more genteel scale, sold off the rest of the land to neighboring farmers who were happy to acquire these fine upland fields and pastures. The orchard he studied much as he had the law all those years ago. He hired the best man in the area to prune and tend and oversee harvests but studied his own trees and the other varieties in the area before corresponding with distant university and state nurseries over the years and so to the Baldwins and Seek-No-Furthers and Yellow Transparents added Gravensteins, Wageners and Pippins and took particular delight in corresponding with the breeders at the agricultural experiment station in western New York over trials and errors, much of which they all suffered. Or enjoyed. Both.

Ruth's father kept the orchard up, like his father employing the best man he could find to run the operation in all aspects; depending on that man to replace old trees with the best new stock, to do the work his father had otherwise done. He enjoyed the idea that he was keeping his hand in, that each fall apples went down the hill to the village in slatted crates stamped in block print, Hale Orchards. On then by rail to the Boston markets. He kept to his roots.

So Ruth grew up among the orchards. In spring the trees heavy with white blossoms studded with faint pink hearts. Blown off the trees like a late magic snow. The busy low song of bees at work. Wandering, head down, searching for and finding four-leaf clovers. The heavy red-and-green-speckled fruits in fall and coming home after school to the songs of the apple pickers, the lovely skeletal lace of dark branches against winter twilight.

The ice storm in the late winter of her thirteenth year would take the orchard away except for a single tree that bore Macouns. Her father surveyed the damage and declared he was too old to start again. The tree would serve to provide the household with applesauce, with dried apples for pies through the winter. He could buy cider. In truth he was glad to be done with the larger burden.

Silver hair foxed his temples and he'd pause on the landing going up the stairs. He continued to deliver graduation addresses at every possible school in his district. Those inevitably hot early June afternoons and evenings. His country accent returned and thickened on those occasions, leading off each address by intoning, "Boys and girls, parents, teachers, dignified guests. We are gathered here on this lovely afternoon . . ." And on from there.

She loved him dearly even if he seemed more grandfather than father as the years went by. He kept peppermints or butter-rum Life Savers in his pocket, it seemed just for her. He'd debate her on topics of the day during dinner but listened intently to her raw and juvenile opinions, as if learning some key and new information. He loathed FDR but quietly admired the man for his accomplishments. In later years Ruth understood this seemingly perplexing contradiction prepared her for the twists and turns her own life would take.

Oliver Snow's story was different yet oddly similar as they both knew and would take delight in probing one certain summer. She already knew much, or thought she did.

Oliver had lost his paternal grandfather at a young age. One difference was her grandfather was dead before she was born while Gideon Snow had died when Oliver was four—his most clear memory was of pulling a wooden duck on wheels that rotated brightly painted red and yellow wooden wings on the porch of the house on Creamery Road while the older man, maddeningly not held in memory but just from sight, sat in one of the wooden rockers that lined the porch in deep shade and clapped his approval. Beyond that, Oliver said, was a keen sense of the man, as if always now just out of reach. Ruth also had a memory of him—his funeral was the first such event she'd attended and for her, the sense of loss all those years later was the absence of any sense of Oliver from that somber afternoon. She recalled a yellow jacket lofting slow and lazy above the mourners and her fear whenever it drifted toward her. Shivers through her when between the backs and shoulders of those seated before her she glimpsed the wooden casket, not certain then exactly what it held. She knew death—only weeks before had been jerked alert at breakfast by a crash against her kitchen windows and gone onto her own porch to find a lifeless oriole that had broken its neck smashing into the glass. She'd carried the bird to her mother who lifted it from her hands into the lace handkerchief she always kept tucked into a sleeve, placed the little package on the table and waited while Ruth washed her hands with castile soap at the kitchen sink and then had walked with her daughter out to the far end of the flower garden and dug a small hole with a pointed spade and allowed Ruth to fill the hole, finding first a small slab of white granite shaped like an arrowhead to set upright at one end of the grave. But the mystery of human death still loomed, unconnected in some vital way to the death of a bird.

The most immediate consequence of his grandfather's death for Oliver Snow was within the month, his father, Ed, began teaching the boy how to play the fiddle, producing a three-quarter-sized instrument and every evening through that fall and winter after supper the two of them would retire to the parlor and tune their instruments and then work through the simple lessons, the scales, the first attempts at songs, stabs at bits of jigs, reels. They kept at it, Ed now much more so than Oliver, after that winter and part of the next, until the father realized he was pressing the boy in a way he'd once been pressed and so was content to let his son fall away from the lessons. There was no great insight in this, indeed a smack of selfishness: Neither Oliver nor his father had the talent that Gideon Snow and others before him had possessed. But Ed was determined to make himself the best fiddle player he could be. As homage, as knowing a latent talent had been subsumed someway and was determined to see it out. He became satisfactory and was satisfied with that, and smart enough to know only pleasure those times Oliver took his small fiddle from its case and played his own awkward tunes. The father thinking, Time will tell, as it does, as it would.

The Snows were new to the town by the terms of the place and oddly so, though the truth, as it does, would out soon after their arrival. Not even hidden so much as placed before the town as a silent fact, with the shade of a challenge or a threat or both within it. They'd come not north but south, from Canaan up near the border with Canada. Gideon and his young wife arriving already in possession of the deed to what was then little more than a mercantile of second stripe and enough cash money to buy the rundown house on Creamery Road. But his ambitions and pockets were both deeper than first appeared and before Oliver's father was born the mercantile had been transformed into a drugstore, apothecary, tobacconist, stationer and purveyor of assorted sundries. This against the unmistakable evidence for the move south—Gideon's wife had the thick dark curls worn long, the snapping eyes, the inflected speech and the pedestrian and utterly foreign name of Marie. He'd married a French-Canadian. Gideon Snow told the tale to any who would listen that first year: "Yuh, my Great-Grandsire was among the first settlers up to Ryegate, come over with a bunch of other Scots, you know it was them first settled up there? Anyways, one of em had a fiddle and played the old reels and ballads and—you know, it's a fact he was in the midnight raid on Ticonderoga and the story is when the sun rose and the British flag was down he stood out there in the cold and fiddled all them old Revolution ballads; broadsheet songs made up in Boston or Philadelphia and went singing through the air at the time. 'At Concord Bridge We Stood.' So I'm a fiddler from my blood and my Da went from Ryegate to Canaan when I was a lad and Canaan was filled right up with the Frenchies but I didn't know any better except they played a whole raft a tunes and then I got up into my dancing years and met Marie one night—now you fellers seen her, isn't that so? Well, that was that. I haven't looked back and never will. It's a weak man that would, is how I see it. Say, you tried these Indian Maid cigars? Best Havana wrappers rolled around prime New England leaf, right down to the tobacco sheds along the Connecticut. Two for a nickel, four for a dime. That's how good they are. Gents?"

Before We Sleep

Marie might've been Catholic but she attended the Congregational Church often enough if not every Sunday. Some of the women pursed their lips and narrowed their eyes, hearing her lilting English but the men found her voice sweet as birdsong and not some few admired her slight form through the long dresses and sleeves of the times and their wives knew that in the way women do and Marie for her part never had eyes for any man but Gideon Snow. She worked exquisite lace and could slaughter a hen from the backyard flock neat and swift as any of her neighbors. To church suppers and town meeting she always brought braces of apple tarts, crustless but the apple slices making tight whorls cooked amber with their sugar glaze. She raised three sons, Edward, James, and Merle and buried her only daughter, Mary, from the Spanish Flu. James went off to California with a plan to ranch or build a business and ended up a newspaperman, a journalist in Sacramento. Merle attended Amherst College and developed ideas for educational reform and helped open and close half a dozen schools in a decade around southern New England before taking a job as an English instructor and Latin tutor at Exeter where he eventually gained status as a revered and formidable grand old man. He married late in life and seemed destined to remain childless until he and his wife adopted a young student whose parents had both been killed in an automobile crash—a youth of considerable fortune and only a single maiden great-aunt who was not capable or interested in taking on a rambunctious young boy. When she died the school reaped a windfall and named a set of rooms in the library that held rare collections after not her, but the boy's parents.

Oliver's father, Ed, married Jennie Pease when he was twenty-one and she seventeen, the youngest daughter of a great tribe of Peases from up on Kipplin Hill, a great beauty with white-blonde hair that held throughout her life, like their son's. The Pease family held a large acreage of thin soil, grown-up pastures and ledges, the pastures

33

studded with boulders and rocks where the ledges failed and dotted with low circles of juniper and studded with purple thistle and burdock. Once, almost a century ago, it had been a prosperous sheep farm but was now like other hill farms, stumbling along from pillar to post and paying taxes with bushels of parsnips or a hog or whatever else might be parted with at the time the final dunning of the year arrived. The people in the village thought he'd been lust-struck by her beauty but in fact she was a gentle soul and deeply intelligent. In the first six years of their marriage she buried three stillborn girls and then came a gap of three years, during which rumors of miscarriage passed among the women of the village, before Oliver was born.

At that time Grandmere Marie still kept her bedroom on the first floor, entered into through a short passageway off the kitchen that led nowhere else. In the years after her husband died she'd gone gray and then had lost her sight but sat her days making lace by feel, the patterns woven into the tips of her fingers as a spider makes webs. When she realized her vision was going she'd sat and written out a dozen of her favorite recipes and without explanation handed them to her daughter-in-law. Who studied the onionskin paper, the thin, arching perfect penmanship, the top of each page labeled with a name she recognized and already knew how to make after those years of sharing a kitchen. The rest was French and incomprehensible to her but Jennie neatly folded them, once, and slid them into her recipe box. She waited two days so as not to be seeming to be either accommodating or dismissive and then turned out a perfect pork pie. Served up and the old woman had finished her portion with applesauce and sipped her black coffee and said, "Yes."

One morning in early September when the goldenrod and purple asters were blooming, the first spots of color showing on certain maple trees, Marie disappeared. It was mid-morning before anyone knew she was gone. Her dresser drawers were pulled halfway open and the old cracked-black leather valise was missing from her closet. On her dresser was a note in English. "Goodbye my loves. I have taken the boat for home." The alarm was sounded and neighbors drove the roads, the state police were called in, and packs of volunteers hiked up and down the slender branch of the river that ox-bowed behind the village. Thrashed through the woods, swamps, puckerbrush, up the feeder brooks. Used long poles to probe beaver ponds and cellar holes filled with trash. To no avail. No body, no sign of her was ever found.

The village, township, county and state all weathered the Depression better than many places. Life in most respects was local, food was raised by most all, and if not, their neighbors. A barter economy was a hundred and fifty years strong. For the most part clothing was made, not bought. The harness-maker was a fair cobbler. To make do, to do without, were not signals of poverty but of self-reliance. All families, at one time or another but all in living memory, had suffered setbacks of various sorts. Few banks failed, and those were in Burlington or Bennington, Saint Johnsbury, Rutland. The rest were all local endeavors each to its own town and so avoided runs, panic. If you put your money in the bank it was in the vault, or the safe in smaller banks. The greatest effect was political as not only the newspapers relayed the events of the greater world but also the slowly creeping electric lines and thus radios, a few powered from batteries or small home-jiggered generators run off a small windmill designed to draw water from wells, or older one-lunger gas engines that twenty or thirty years ago had powered milk separators, silage blowers, home-fashioned sawmills. Men would argue Roosevelt's New Deal, though they saw little of it. A CCC camp had been set up down near Sharon and unemployed young men from New York or Boston were brought in to build trails in the newly minted Green Mountain Forest or help with the spring logging. A few men died on those jobs, lacking, all agreed, the common sense a more local boy would have. A handful of native sons returned home from their failed endeavors in the wider world but for the most part simply put shoulder to the wheel of what they'd thought they'd left behind, now rediscovered and savored. A good ham supper on the table end of day.

The radios proliferated and brought not only news but music, humor, drama. Women first and then men altered daily routines to be in the house at certain times. Children as well. And as the decade churned on, the talk among the men and not a few women turned to Germany, to Hitler and Europe and the general consensus was this was a problem for France, for England. More than a few were uncertain where Poland even was but most agreed Uncle Sam had straightened things up twenty years before and this would not be their fight. Everyone admired Lindbergh and most agreed upon America First. Why not? All knew the butcher Abner Heitmann in Royalton, and knew his grandfather had come from Germany to Connecticut and then north to set up shop and not one of them thought he was an agent for the Nazis. He was an American, almost as much as they were. Just a few generations shy.

December 1941 changed all that. The dirty stinking Japs. Before that day less than half the men in the town were even aware of what was happening in Asia and of those that were, most would be hard pressed to point out the Imperial adventures on a schoolroom world map. But of infamy Roosevelt spoke and they knew it to be true.

On the ceiling above Oliver's bed were tacked charts that in black silhouette showed front, side and, most importantly, bottom outlines of the Allied and Axis planes, fighters and bombers, sea- and land-based. Learning them all, matching the shapes with the names and countries of origin seemed at first like a school exercise and then became more similar to walking in the woods and knowing the species of each tree he passed regardless of the time of year—knowing not only the easily identified leaf shapes but also how they budded in spring, the bark surface, the distinctive winter spray of stark branches against the sky, a knowledge he'd acquired without knowing he was doing so at a time in his still-young life he could not pinpoint but that resided within him. At a glance the name and model, the branch of service, the country of origin sprang to his tongue. Then as the first year of the war turned and he became active as a plane-spotter, he gave thought to this array of knowledge and unlike trees on the hills, realized that one single false identification could be disastrous. He lay on his bed and mulled this idea, then mulled where he lived and the globe in his mind and tightened focus. The long-range bombers were key, both American, to recognize what he was most likely to see, and German, for highest alert, highest probability. It seemed unlikely the Japanese could fly to Vermont. He also paid close attention to American fighter planes. If the Nazis could fly bombers across the ocean he concluded there would be a good chance at least a few U.S. fighters would have a chance to chase after them. Most of this done with a taped flashlight and blackout curtains snapped tight to his windows. Downstairs the radio was on, news, the big band music his mother liked, a drama, all indistinct. Most nights also the fainter mournful spray of notes from his father's fiddle, in warm months from the woodshed adjacent to the house, in winter from the cellar. His father no longer played the dance music, the jigs and reels, but a slow beseeching music, tunes that seemed to be trying to find a way home. At least it sounded that way to a boy whose world was on fire.

He'd signed up as a Youth Air Guard. Afternoons when school let out he'd thump down from the high school classrooms with his books and homework and walk through the village, stopping always at his father's store where he'd drink a Coke and eat a handful of oatmeal cookies made fresh each morning by Gertie Harrington against the bills for pain medication for her husband who was dying slow, confined to his bed, coughing terribly as if he could pump the cancer from his lungs and breathe free again but was mere months from smothering to death. Oliver sitting on the stool and drinking the delicious cold drink from the bottle with its lovely curves he comprehended deep inside but did not understand why it gave him such pleasure, eating the cookies that his father had gently asked that he consume rather than anything else because the cookies were always short of butter and sugar and at best studded with a pair of very old raisins, his father leaning close only once to explain, "If I don't have to throw them away I can look her in the eye and tell her how much the children love them. If you have to, take a Mounds and eat it if you're starving up on the hill." Oliver took the candy bar a couple of times but then stopped. The cookies weren't so bad and the Coke made up for them.

He started up Beacon Hill and partway up walked out of the village. Toward the end of the street there was a two-story house with an attached set of sheds that rose and fell in height before ending in a small barn. Not so different from other village houses but for where it was and some other quality he could not name but that he liked the place. An old man lived alone there and time to time he'd come upon Alden Jenks out working in his yard, pruning his apple tree or plucking the fruits, splitting firewood or stacking it neat as a worked puzzle inside one of the sheds, tending his gardens, and he'd pause and chat. Alden Jenks favored layers of sweaters and green wool pants, sturdy boots laced halfway and double-knotted. His hair was white and cut very short all around and his cheeks blushed pink. Always it seemed he was glad to see Oliver turn into his yard but then would stand and look off over the village and say, "You think about it, there's not one ever sees the same thing the same way but two will always swear they do," or "It's always worse than it was, then." Or, if it was raining, "Damp, ain't it?" Crusty old Yankee starch but Oliver liked him. The way he'd sway his eyes just to light upon the boy after speaking, as if sharing the humor of his making such comments. Looking away again.

He went on then uphill and the dirt street turned into a rough track through a belt of young second growth: maples and both silver and paper birch, hemlocks and ash, butternuts, all beset by an understory thicket of blackberry canes, sumac, chokecherry and swales of high ferns. He emerged into a steep climb of short-shorn grass studded with outcrops of ledge, a row of ancient sugar maples marking the crest above, trees scarred by lightning strikes, some half-dead but also half-alive and those halves so much greater than most trees he knew, a stone wall jigging between them, the stones some the size of automobiles or doorframes and in other places a careful buildup of smaller stones that could each be carried in a curled hand and worked into place. Trees and walls the remains of something else altogether gone.

Then past the trees and wall and up on top of the world. A great spread of field atop Beacon Hill. Hayed twice each summer by the Farnsworths who came over from West Hill to do the work worth the trip. Standing there he could see the village below as if a model rendered. The valley extending north and south. The dark swath of the river. Up and outward the far distant ridges to the south, east, and north, extending into five other townships. West obscured by the clump of West Hill. And there beside him, the spotting tower of raw hemlock planks and uprights, the ladder nailed to the side, little more than a platform raised some thirty feet into the air. Enough to gain an even greater vantage. He had a pair of decent Feldglas 08 binoculars someone had brought home from the First War that his father had bought or taken in trade for goods or services during the Depression and while daylight held he'd do his homework, pausing when he thought of it, or the rare times he heard the drone of an airborne engine and scan the skies. After dark he'd study the stars and watch, almost hopefully, for the lights of aircraft. So far he hadn't seen much.

One afternoon in mid-August of 1942 he wasn't there an hour when he looked down and watched her come out from the woods, crossing through the goldenrod and blooming purple heads of milkweed and work her way toward him. Some of the old maples held single branches that were red and orange, the green of the leaves slightly weakened, paling toward autumn.

Here she came in a cream-colored skirt and a short-sleeved peach blouse and saddle shoes, her book bag over one arm and looking up at him as she made the top of the hill and climbed the tower. He stood, leaving the book he was reading facedown on the platform flooring. She paused at the top, looking him frankly up and down before she stepped within. Later he'd wonder if she'd been waiting to be invited in and decided not, that she'd only been catching her breath. The lower hem of her skirt was dotted with the green triangles of beggar lice.

"Hello, Ruth. I thought I'd found a place where I could be alone but count on you to flush me out." His face was hot.

"Stop that." She bent and picked up the library book and looked at it, then closed it properly and set it back down. "*Sister Carrie*. The library had this?"

His face was hotter. "You have to ask for it."

"Tell me when you return it. I'll wait a week or so if that matters to you." She threw up her shoulders in a shrug and then said, "Have you seen anything interesting?"

She was flip and it didn't square with her coming here and he understood she was nervous. Yet here she was. He said, "I've seen more falling stars than I ever thought possible. And one time last summer I saw bands of green light wavering against the sky, the Northern Lights. And I could swear I heard them, also."

"You can't hear them," she said with a scowl. "So you haven't shot down any planes?"

"That's not why I'm here."

"I was making a joke."

Both quiet a long moment then. Abruptly she bent and lifted up the Feldglas 08s and walked to the southern edge of the platform and he watched her go. She lifted the binoculars and steadied herself and then gasped. He stepped behind her as she turned and said, "It all jumps so close. What am I seeing? Is that the Royalton Methodist steeple? Can't be."

He leaned forward so his chin was just above her shoulder and took the glasses and peered out and said, "No. That's the Barnard Congregational. Up high like that."

He reached his left hand around her and brought the glasses back before her face, holding them with both hands and let her lean in. Her back was against his chest and his arms were around her head and he could smell her hair. He was breathing against the back of her ear, a pink whorl of flesh at once delicate and crushingly strange.

"Yes, oh my goodness it is. It's so close."

"How the whole world seems, these days."

"I know." Then, still looking through the glasses, she said, "First week of school in Biology old Phillips is going to break us into pairs to dissect. I know he's going to stick me with Gladys, maybe Annie Gilman which would be the worst. I thought I'd ask you and maybe we could go together to him and say we'd like to team up."

"Why me?"

She turned then and he pulled his arms away, a cautious awkward moment where he almost grazed her shoulder lifting the binoculars away from her, keeping his grip tight on them. She leaned back against the rail and he stepped back but just only. Her face was serious, eyes measured, lips parted as she breathed through them. She said, "Because if I have to do it I want to learn as much as I can from it. Not waste time calming down a girl all worked up over nothing."

He surprised himself by mildly responding. "Okay. Sounds good to me."

Both then quiet a moment. He said, "You walked all the way up here to ask me that?"

She went pink but held his eyes and said, "Friday night of Labor Day weekend there's a dance out to Corinth at the Dreamland Ballroom. They say all the boys who turn eighteen this year will be out there, before school starts. I thought maybe you and I might go. There's a orchestra from Boston and everything."

Now he went pink, hot in the face anyway. He looked off and said, "I've heard about it. Trouble is, I can't drive. I mean, I can drive but I keep missing getting my license. My dad needs his ration tickets for deliveries, getting about."

"I can drive. And my father has plenty of gas rations—his job, you know?"

"Well." He briefly considered just leaping over the railing and dropping to the earth, let it damage him as it would. Sweat pooled under his arms and ran down smarting into his eyes. He said it: "Ruth, truth is I can't dance. All I'd do is bruise your feet and most likely drop you on the floor I tried any of those moves. I'm sorry."

"Oh goodness," she said. "I can't either. It looks so smooth and easy but I just know I'd cross my knees and trip you up. But also. Well. If you were willing . . ."

"What?"

She looked off and back at him and said in a sudden rush, "Last time I was up to Barre and went into Evan's Music I picked up a book on how to swing dance. Some others too. The Lindy Hop, Jitterbug. It's diagrams step-by-step of the moves. His and her feet. It's kind of funny but I was thinking, maybe if we spent a few afternoons working through it . . ."

She paused and stopped.

It was a cool evening with the last of the rain clouds rolling off to the east, bands of high deep blue sky coming from the west, shot through with swathes of angled sunlight. She drove her father's Buick but only until they were up past the hill leading out of the village when she pulled to the shoulder and stepped out, walked around to where he sat and said, "I thought you might want to drive."

He looked at her and then slid partway across the seat and leaned to open the door for her. He then settled behind the wheel and powered up the big car and took them down the road. Windows open and the last of summer blowing across them.

The Dreamland was the last extant building from the Corinth Fair which in the last century had been one of the great fairs in central Vermont but had died off after a fire swept the grandstand during the sulky races in 1898, killing five people, three of them children. It had been a dry summer anyway and the bare wood was old and a pile of sawdust under the seats, kept there to cover wet patches of the track in the event of rain had caught fire, it was never known how although both boys with matches and a dropped cigar were cited as possible causes. After the fire someone had planted a homemade cross as a memorial on the site of the grandstand and others has planted flowers and the following year the fair officials had held off building anew and while the fair sputtered on for a few more years that was mostly the end of it. People went south to Tunbridge and the September fair held there. A fellow from Vershire bought the land on which the Corinth Fair had been held and tore down all the remaining sheds but kept the one large hall, used in its day for everything from vegetable and floral displays and contests to line and square dances at night, and the Dreamland was born. Rose from the ashes. That man's son took it over in the late twenties and strung his own electric line in from Bradford, tacking the line to trees where he had to and erecting his own poles roadside when he could and before the war the Dreamland was a great string of twinkle in the vast bowl of dark valley on summer weekend nights. Lit up also on New Year's Eve and people made the trip if the snow allowed despite the smoking cold of the ballroom, hauling with them old buffalo sleigh-robes pulled from attics, quilts off beds, men and women both in long underwear and woolen trousers, sweaters and scarves and mufflers. Crazy to dance the frigid night to a thaw. Coal braziers set up among the musicians of the orchestra and this night only any and all form of libation were allowed and encouraged. At midnight there was a great show of fireworks up into the night sky, again as if to taunt the winter before the long rides home.

Summer weekend nights were more sedate, at least in the decades before the war. Though it was said by some, with bitterness or fond memories, that to get into the Dreamland a man had to have a bottle of whiskey in one hand and another man's wife in the other. People like to talk and people give each other plenty to talk about. Perhaps the Dreamland Ballroom existed for that purpose, which in the end is reason and purpose enough.

Ruth and Oliver danced. Very badly at first, even worse than their initial attempts to her Victrola and the frequent pauses to study the diagrams. His heart stammered so loudly it overrode the music and her own throat was constricted and her lungs wouldn't draw air. She was certain she could smell her armpits and he was aware of the tumescence that threatened his trousers. Then the music took hold. The orchestra was from Boston, composed of nine white men and four black men, the first Negroes either of them had ever seen save for their own townsfolk done up in burnt-cork blackface for the annual minstrel show put on in the doldrums of February. The music rose and fell in coils and spirals that twisted and turned back upon themselves, sliding along a heaving thick underbelly of bass and horns and drums, the clear tinkle chime of a brush against a snare drum, the slap of traps and cymbals, sounds explosive and contained, controlled at once even as nothing could be anticipated except their bodies had fallen into sway and syncopation and they moved through the steps now forgotten except in central core recesses of their bodies, brought to leaping joyful life as they meshed with the music.

Idiot smiles pasted to their faces. Or a corner of a lip tugged between teeth as one or the other, both, were caught in an eddy of deepest concentration as if nothing ever before in their lives and nothing ever after that moment would be as important as hitting the next step together. And then they did. She slipped her head back and her hair was damp and he felt the moisture on his face and grinned at her as her face turned to a mask of ferocity, the music thrusting her back twirling and bending for his outstretched arms to capture, trusting, knowing that she wouldn't crash to the floor. That he would save her. And he did. Each time.

During the intermission they drank lemonade from pint Mason jars rattled with ice. They stood out in the parking lot under the stars of heaven and she drew out of her handbag a package of Old Gold cigarettes and a Zippo that gleamed in the night and tapped the tight new pack so three cigarettes extended forth and offered it to him.

"I don't smoke," he said.

"I don't either."

They stood in the warm late-summer night and smoked cigarettes each in their own hesitant delicate way and both coughed but faintly and with the other deliberately not noticing, but watching about them in the parking lot as people moved and fell apart, some odd skeleton or shadow of the dancing now paused as flasks were passed, cans of beer were offered. They stood silent watching as a couple walked among the outer ring of parked cars, searching for an empty backseat, both pretending they weren't watching.

He said, "I could use another lemonade. You?"

They danced again and he felt her most acutely when she was gone, twirling out and away or in her pause or when she was returning to him, as if she was a magnetic field that he yearned toward. Once back in his arms she was both strangely foreign and ever-known. The swell of her forearms in his hands, the jut of her hips just below her waist as he lifted and spun her. Her laughter as she turned neatly under his outstretched arm and came in again, her back against his chest, laughter heard over the full throttle of the orchestra as if it drilled through for his ears alone. A message, a sema- phore of sound cutting through the swelter of music, a vital sound meant for him to hear. And the orchestra was closing down the night in a turbulent full cascade. "Sing Sing Sing." "String of Pearls." Then, "Coming in on a Wing and a Prayer," the last chorus suddenly pitched down low and slow, a dirge pinked up by the clarinet to stop it from being fully mournful and the dancers, all of them, collapsed against each other and held on as they staggered together until the final notes tickled away and it was a huge room of exhausted couples clinging tight to the night, to each other; each their own story and many with those stories held tight and close as a folded secret. The drummer crashed the big cymbal one final time and they all stum- bled awake from the dream just ended.

Ruth and Oliver emerged into a world lit by fireflies, a thun- derous vacuum of silence, the lovely giddiness of knowing it was mere hours until sunrise and a new day. That belonged to them. The smell of crushed sweet fern all about them. Flowing through the open car windows with the heater on. They each smoked another cigarette and he watched the spark trail behind as they threw the exhausted butts out the windows. Upon the crest of Brocklebank Hill he slowed the car and pulled to the shoulder, the dashboard dials throwing a faint pool of thin yellow light upon his lap. Ruth looked straight ahead through the windshield but did not question the stop. Her face was reflected in the curve of the glass, a ghost of her face, large eyes and a smudge of cheekbones and nose, her hair a frame that dissolved into the dark of night, her mouth most clear, lips parted as she breathed.

He turned toward her and slung his right arm out across the top of the bench seat and said, "Ruth?" but she also had turned and came across under his arm and her face lifted to his as he lifted his other arm from the wheel and met her coming embrace.

At some point she pulled back a moment and reached to kill the headlights and also punched a button on the Buick's radio and again, as from a great distance but also as if played only for them, music filled the car. When he finally cupped a breast through her rayon blouse she sagged and came up, biting his tongue. She ran her hands through his hair, holding his head, pulling his face tight against hers. He placed his hand on her knee and she lifted it off and said, "I turned in my last silk stockings," and he understood all she was truly saying. After a time he reached and turned the key and killed the engine and went back to her although she'd not left—it was only his moment away.

In the village they stopped again and came to argument. He wanted to drive her home and talk with her father and she knew better. Behind them was a faint pink edge to the hillside, out beyond the village some few stars still burned. Her whole body was sore and ached and was restless, exhausted. She offered to drive him home. The village milk wagon went past in the new fog rising from the river, the clopping of the horse's hooves coming through the pinking air, a reminder if they needed one of the coming day. He stepped from the car, surprising both of them.

"I'll walk. It's just across the Common and up a bit. Save you the trouble."

She stepped out also and spoke to him across the roof. "Oliver. It's no trouble."

The morning deputy sheriff went by on the main road, slowed and Bob Martin peered at them, the cruiser's headlights cones in the fog. Then went on.

She said, "Don't do this. Please. It was such a nice night."

He looked down, back. He said, "I'm not doing anything, Ruth. Not really. But right now I need to go." And turned and walked across the North Common until he was a film in the fog. She watched and waited and as if he could gauge it, just before he was swallowed altogether by the fog he turned and lifted a hand. He stood a solid moment. Then turned again and was gone.

Ruth's mother was a woman who looked as if she could be fifty or sixty-eight. Stout of bosom and sturdy of frame, she kept her hair in a tight bun, wore skirts and dresses, blouses and sweater sets so elegant they appeared plain, much like the handkerchief she kept up her left sleeve, as if from another time, which in most ways she was. As a young woman, the portrait in the hall between dining room and library attested, she possessed a fine slightly arched nose that with age had grown bulbous, almost tuberous. Yet her nose became her still. Her hair was silver and her eyes dark—not black but a density of brown as a deep pool of water glanced by sunlight. She was a Putnam from all the way over at Shelburne near Lake Champlain and in some ways remained so all of her life. She hadn't married beneath her but very nearly so and despite the awkward arrival of her third daughter so late in life, she loved her husband deeply, was aware that he slept with certain women as the fancy took him and forgave him outwardly by never mentioning it but he made himself smaller within her by doing so. Nevertheless she loved to sit by the fire of an evening and have a whiskey with Nate, not merely listening to him but waiting and then with the acerbic wit and insight he so loved, would speak her mind. He listened to her; aware she knew of his ramblings and so even more trusted her judgment as well as her silence. Her given name was Georgette but she went by Jo for those few who did not address her as Mrs. Hale. She did her own cooking but had a woman to clean and launder once a week and now employed the first woman's adult daughter, who was grown and married but was referred to by her maiden name, as if it was her mother who still worked in the house. With the exception of holidays, large gatherings, other rare events, Jo Hale cleaned the house before the cleaning woman arrived. She tended her own flower garden and did so in wide-wale corduroy pants in shades of deep green or brown, with tucked-in blue chambray work shirts above, also a wide straw hat upon her head. Her garden shears and spades always sharp and well-oiled. Throughout the summer and into the fall she kept the house filled with cut flowers. Certain places such as the dining room table, the library, the flowers were arranged in lead-crystal vases but in the kitchen, even the bathroom, she was happy to use old green-glass Mason jars and those old jars, sprouting arrays so carefully chosen they seemed to be simply clumps torn free and tucked in, gained majesty and a purity of form. Light fell through the glass and water, the twined stems.

She was stalwart within the church although privately held to the teachings of Mary Baker Eddy and began each day with tea, toast and a silent reading from that small blue book; was easy and cordial with the women of the village as well as the farm wives who came her way and during the past two years spent Tuesday and Thursday afternoons in the basement of the town hall rolling bandages, bundling wool scraps, writing letters to unknown boys from the lists provided from the USO and once a month helping to weigh and pack barrels with horded bacon grease, lard and tallow. In the fall she paid out pennies to the pound to the poor and often illiterate girls from Kings Valley, the backways of Brocklebank, who hauled to town in wagons or hand-sledges the large old burlap wool-sacks stuffed with milkweed down pulled from the cracked pods, girls, always, each with their wretched clothes and downcast eyes, reddened and split fingers who came down skittish as wild creatures from the swaybacked ruined farms without electricity or telephone, children who'd left school well before the eighth grade to stump along best they could with their families until one way or another they became pregnant and one way or another among their own kind but not kin a husband, a man-child like themselves was found, or maybe an older man who'd buried two or three wives but needed someone to keep house, cook as could be done, warm his old bones in a cold bed. In that wretched season Jo kept a finger lightly upon the scale and a pocketful of peppermint candies to hand out with the payments. She reimbursed those overpayments from her own money.

Some few women of the town thought she believed herself to be a grand lady, in some way better than themselves. She was not unaware of this but understood the error in judgment was their difficulty, not hers. Even if, mildly and without satisfaction, she knew it to be true. She owed no apology for her intellect or birthright.

In October of 1942, Evelyn Chapman, the eighth-grade Home Economics teacher, abruptly left her job to travel one hundred fifty miles east and take a job at the Portsmouth Shipyard, this action still a novelty although other young single and married women would follow in the coming years, to the Yard, and a multitude of other war effort jobs around New England, many never to return, having had a taste of another life. At the time though it was simply an immediate crisis with the school year under way and no obvious candidate for the job. Jo and her husband sat in the library, the radio turned low to Walter Winchell. Ruth was in the kitchen doing geometry homework while surreptitiously reading a recent issue of *Screenland*. Nate Hale was muttering about the Chapman girl as he called the thirty-two-year-old and shivering his jowls with a vivid disappointment over one who could so easily throw over the terms of her admittedly paltry contract. Jo twirled the last of the diluted nightcap in the heavy glass, swallowed and set the glass down a bit harder than intended.

"It's basic cooking and sewing," she announced. "I'll do the job. Pay me half whatever you paid the Chapman girl and that will satisfy any who would question and you may, of course, continue to search for a more qualified candidate."

He looked at her, wondering if she thought he'd been sleeping with the girl—he tended to eschew girls quite so close to home. Still, he reddened a bit and coughed into his stronger drink before saying, "That would be extraordinary. For only the shortest possible time, to fill in, of course. She left us in a lurch. But the sewing part—they do use machines, you know."

Jo stood. "I can learn," she said. "What I don't know, the girls will show me, I expect. There's always at least one clever girl that simply seems to know how to use something new, even if she's never seen it before. Well! I feel as if I'm contributing something real, now. Good night, Mr. Hale." She crossed over and leaned to plant warm lips upon his forehead and he responded, "Good night, pet. I'll be up soon. I'll check Ruth's homework first."

"Oh," she said, as she glided from the room with the faint skim of a smile upon her, as a cat that's figured out the new mouse hole. "Please do."

Being within the school she'd have a cautious but much closer look at Ruth, caught in passing but also the undertow of talk spilled over from classmates, perhaps even her new colleagues—though she recognized those adults would most likely keep her at a distance, uncertain of why she'd been placed among them. Jo was fine with all that but her daughter had grown to be a mystery to her: She knew Ruth was spending time with the Snow boy and this didn't disturb her very much, at least not as much as the times. Everything was accelerated from her own youth, the war did that—too quickly by her lights. Also, dresses and skirts were shorter, just below the knee and lacking pleats so little of the woman's form was left to imagination. The newest rayons were almost sheer, clinging to upper bodies, hair was worn long, parted on one side or another like a man and then falling free to shoulders where it might be curled under. Stockings no longer could be had except on the black market and they were not that sort of people but Jo quivered in guessing her

51

daughter might enjoy the fresh press of air up under those short skirts.

The summer Jo Putnam was seventeen, two years before she met Nathaniel Hale, there occurred a tragedy connected closely to her Shelburne home. Their cook was an Irish woman, Irene Cuddy, with a daughter, Maeve. Jo was aware of the girl in a vague way; Maeve attended the local schools and Jo attended the Academy for Girls at Follett's Bay. If there was a Mr. Cuddy she had no idea, never even wondered but in the callow way of a young person simply assumed there was. She'd seen Maeve time to time over the years and thought her pretty with her black hair and blue eyes but the girl always looked boldly upon Jo before ducking her head down and away, as if she didn't like her. Beyond that she knew little of the girl and held less interest—later she'd examine this part of herself and her life began to change at that point. After the terrible weekend, all of which Jo learned about later, most gained the middle of the following week one evening when she'd left her bedroom and tiptoed down the hall to sit in her nightdress at the top of the stairs and listened to her parents talking out of sight, below.

Irene asked for the weekend off, unheard of but her urgency was clear. Late on Sunday morning came a long distance telephone call— the first such the household had received. They'd only just returned from church. Her father then made a series of hushed calls and left the house. Her mother refused to answer questions or offer any explanation and the two of them sat through a wretched parody of noon-dinner, served cold by the woman who otherwise was the weekday housekeeper. Her mother time to time set down the fork she idled in swift tickings against the china and turned her face, dabbing her eyes with a handkerchief. Then left Jo on her own for the afternoon.

It was late on Monday when her father returned. Mrs. Cuddy had taken her daughter to Montreal to see a doctor, a surgeon, someone recommended to her by a woman of the town who'd claimed to know of such matters. What Jo overheard that weeknight hidden on the stairs was that, once he'd arrived in Montreal, her father had paid sums in fees and bribes to have Maeve's body released and sent home, to have Irene Cuddy released from the Royal constables and allowed to accompany her daughter, further sums also to facilitate whatever paperwork was necessary, which, she gathered, was a considerable amount. The doctor, whatever he was, had vanished. The constabulary did not seem interested in him. Maeve was buried that Monday night after dark in a far corner of the cemetery behind Our Lady of the Snows and her father then had paid Mrs. Cuddy the remainder of her month's wages. She understood, without a word passing between them, that she was to leave town. That he was not part of this unfortunate business. And Jo, upon the stairs, thought But you were. And understood more. Suddenly, midsummer and she was wracked with chills as if it were January and the coal fire in the grate had died. She'd gone then to her room, pulled woolens and feather-stuffed quilts from the chest, spread them upon the bed and lay under them, back up against the pillows, legs twined together to try and draw heat where there was none. Shivering as her understanding of all she'd heard cascaded upon her. The window open and summer moonlight upon the wide lawns and gardens. She thought she'd never be warm again in her life. Then hours later woke from a deathly slumber to a sunlit morning, most of the covers pushed off in some forgotten fever of the night, a single sodden sheet pulled tight around her.

She would keep an eye on Ruth. In a world changed, she would do her best to protect her youngest, a girl dear and almost unknown to her. A girl, she thought, unknown to herself.

The morning after the muted community celebration to welcome in the new year of 1943 she realized, with the welling dread that she was already too late, that her daughter was set on a course of passion lacking all coolheadedness, the least semblance of forethought, of any practical sense. Jo and Nate had left shortly after the bell was rung to welcome the hope and promise of the flip of a calendar page but she was still awake hours later when she heard the door softly shut downstairs, the car coasting away on the packed snow downhill before the engine was fired, the creep of the girl gaining the stairs, the unsteadiness of her cautious tread.

She stayed abed. This talk, she knew, was almost certain to fail but the best hope was mere hours ahead, in the cold light of day.

"No, Mother. We won't wait."

"I don't understand. Why not? Other girls do."

"Other girls? Other girls! Do you know why they wait? Do you?"

Jo was quiet a fatal moment. "They're practical."

"And so am I. Next fall, I'll attend the Lyndon Teacher's Institute. I've made my application already and attached a letter explaining my circumstances, my intentions. You might be surprised to learn they welcomed me. The dean himself wrote a letter applauding me for my sense of duty to my future as well as the man I love. 'These are extraordinary times,' he wrote, 'and they call for extraordinary measures.' That, I say, is practical."

"Hotheaded is what I say. You risk being a widow before you even undertake life."

"That's just it! I want Oliver to go off to war without a doubt of me, knowing I have the ultimate confidence he'll make it through. I have to give him that, I'd not be true if I didn't. I love him, Mother, and he loves me and nothing else in life is promised us, is it? Nothing at all."

Jo said, "Have you spoken with your father about all this?"

Ruth said, "No, I have not." She looked away and back and her mother knew what was coming: "I was wondering if you might? I'm happy to afterward, but I thought you could better explain it to him. You know how he flusters me."

Jo Hale stole that moment to consider all she could not say: Oliver Snow was a fine, bright young man, with a streak of melancholy came down from his father and grandfather. And the strange disappearance of the Canadian grandmother—Oliver Snow was, to her mind, a man unlikely to survive this war, a dreamer and one at best half aware of all that went on about him, with an ethereality he didn't yet recognize but would catch him one fine day. And she could say none of this. She had spent her life wrestling with her own deeply held understandings of who around her fit in which way, and the times she'd been proven wrong. Her gut ached and her arms were goose-fleshed just before noon on the first full day of the year and she wanted a cup of coffee, the one before her gone cold, and more, wanted to pour a bit of port or rye into it. She looked back up at her daughter and said, "I'll talk to your father. But after, you will as well."

Ruth stood and leaned and threaded her arms around her mother's neck and brushed her lips against her ear and said, "Thank you. Thank you so much. Oh, I love you."

Jo rose into her daughter's embrace. Held her shoulders and looked deep and strong into her eyes and said, "I love you too, baby girl."

Ed Snow had packed away his fiddle after his mother disappeared, pushing the scuffed and worn alligator-hide case deep on the top shelf of the closet, behind his polished black funeral shoes fitted with trees. In the years since he'd been called upon many times to play at kitchen parties, tunks and wakes and refused all but two. Saying it was old-time Canuck music and no one wanted to hear it, they wanted the new music and his fiddle wouldn't swing. The way it was. The two exceptions he'd said nothing to his wife beyond promising he'd be back and then drove off and didn't return until late afternoon of the following day. Once he was simply back in the store when Oliver came by after school—the other time he drove in as they were seated to supper and had a sack of dried sausages that he hung in the cellar while whistling an unfamiliar jig before coming back up to eat stewed chicken and baked Hubbard squash with his wife and son. He never offered to share the sausages and in the way of these things Oliver knew not to ask even as time to time over the coming months he'd sit across from his father at breakfast and eat his oatmeal and bacon while his father held the tight leathern sausage in his hand and chewed with concentration directed somewhere far away, groaning now and again. A sound close to one Oliver recently discovered he also owned.

But when, following the wedding and the dinner, and the guests were spread between the library, dining room, and parlor of the Hale place up on West Hill, Ed Snow walked into the room with the old case and lifted the fiddle and tuned it, tucking his chin down low to bring the strings close to his ear, Oliver wasn't surprised. His father, happy with the tuning, lifted his chin and surveyed the room. Seemed half the town and half the county was packed into the house but all fell silent in a moment, a telegraph person-to-person seemingly at work. Ruth stood feet away by the fireplace, the butternut wallboards behind her in a soft late winter afternoon glow, Ruth in a grand white gown, her grandmother's wedding dress dug out from a chest up attic and altered to fit by her mother and a seamstress all the way from Woodsville, Ruth flushed peaches and cream, beautiful as Oliver had ever seen her.

His father spoke in a clear voice, respectful and assured. "If I might," he said with no hint of seeking approval, "I'd play a pair of the older songs. My father played them at my wedding. There were a whole pile of em played that day, but these two, why, they're a pair of tunes for the bride and groom. Songs for luck and long life, and for the strength you need, separate and together." He bowed out a short couple of measures and spoke again, "The groom's song comes first, the bride's after. The way it is."

He tucked the fiddle under his chin, bent at the waist a bit and extended his arms slightly as if not to gather the instrument to himself but himself to the fiddle. He bounced the bow once upon the strings and then played. The groom's song was a jaunty reel with clear fast runs and clever fingers flying to a blur up and down the neck, the bow rising and falling and that arm's elbow as if pulled by wires unseen. Music fleet and nimble as a man must be and flowing with color and joy and glissandos neat and contained. There came a bridge that slowed and stretched, a short low passage dropped in that suggested the long years of work, of shouldering the burdens of life and then the bow danced and quivered again upon the strings: an old man with a pipe in a chair beside the stove, grandchildren rolling on the floor like puppies, old friends around a table playing cards or lifting a glass and telling old thrice-told tales. A short sweet taper then up the neck and trilling off to sudden silence.

Ed Snow tapped his foot four times in that silence and played again. This time without fancy work, finger or bow but a lovely and haunting steady rise and fill, falling off and rising again. Most in the room felt the song register within, as if they should know it and perhaps some few once upon a time at some house party or kitchen tunk had heard the song in a slightly more rousing version, perhaps with the words sung in a quavering voice over the music but played as it was this afternoon none could put a name to it. To many it seemed only a slow lovely piece played for a young woman on her wedding day, a pretty tune, a moment, an indulgence for the groom's father welcoming this young woman. A lovely thing.

Oliver Snow stood listening. He alone, standing next to his bride, knew not only the name of the song but also the words, the name of the ballad. "Lady Franklin's Lament." A sad tale spun over sad music. He felt a blush of anger toward his father and then a wrench of love in his heart for the man, for everyone present in the house on this day. Most of all for his wife.

When the song ended, the polite applause had fallen away, he stepped forward as his father was bending to replace the fiddle in the case.

In a strong clear tone Oliver Snow said, "Dad? Aren't you forgetting something?"

Ed straightened, the fiddle gripped by the neck. "Am I? What would that be, eh?"

"Could you give us a waltz? Just for Ruth and me?"

His father appraised him, nodded and for the shortest of moments studied the big ceiling beams overhead even as he brought the fiddle back against his tucked chin. People understood also and pressed back, making a small opening upon the floorboards before the father of the groom. Oliver turned to Ruth and silently extended a hand. She stepped forward as the first notes sang out. To most all listening the song in tempo and tone was not so different from the lament just played but for the sharps, and dips of color, the full notes one into another rich as polished hardwood lit by flames of some remote fire. Echoing the suddenly clear bright fire in the room, a music crisp and dulcet at once.

As Oliver and Ruth Snow danced their marriage. Waltzed together on a late winter afternoon. Both frightened by what lay ahead. Both together, and each differently, bold and brave.

Three

Katey

THE RAIN CAUGHT up with her hard just outside of Belfast, the wipers black streaks against a sheet of water and the otherwise long June evening slammed down, shutters closing upon the day. She wasn't hungry, her stomach rumbling still with the grease and brine of her shore dinner but she needed to find a place to sleep for the night and was acutely aware that her envelope of money might not be sufficient for her needs. Leaving home she'd thought so but not quite three days out she was understanding how little she truly knew.

All she had were the eight years of Christmas cards, a packet held with a drying and frayed rubber band found in a shoebox at the back of her mother's closet, five-and-dime cards with printed holiday greetings and underneath a swirl of ink sending Christmas Greetings and All Best Wishes for the New Year to Oliver & Ruth but on the envelopes the same swirl but more contained and the return address *Brian Potter 41 Cannon Street, Machias Maine.* She calculated she'd been seven when the last arrived.

The rain and dimming evening so dense she almost struck the woman. Which first glimpsed she thought was a bear, a short thick shambling figure and she hit the brakes hard and felt the back of the truck slip right and she pumped the brakes and turned into the slide and came to a stop beside the woman. The woman carried galvanized tin buckets in each hand. Before Katey had a chance to react the woman popped open the door handle, leaned and set the buckets on the passenger side floor and heaved herself up onto the bench seat and slammed shut the door, leaving Katey only enough time to bend and pull her own suitcase up on the seat next to her.

"Hoo!" the woman said. She wore heavy sodden skits above green rubber boots, at least two pairs of sweaters the color of wet cowhide, with a blue-and-white-striped railroad hat atop her head, her hair down her back in a thick braid, twined a dark color from the rain but with silver and white threaded through the braid. She turned, her face bright with color and cold. Her cheeks were plump and lined, red with chill and early summer sun, her skin creased and wrinkles stretched from each eye out to her temples as if some fey bird had clawed her. Water beaded on her nose, thick and wrinkled. A powerful scent like a wet dog rolled in mud and dipped in woodsmoke roiled the cab.

The buckets were filled with the tightly furled spiral heads of new ferns.

"Thanks for stopping," the woman said. She was missing two front teeth, an upper and a lower but offset and the rest of her teeth were the color of old parsnips. Her eyes luminous as if they too had been rained on. She stuck a hand out, fingers with scabs and scars along the backs and said, "Name's Molly Ivey Lucerne. Where ya headed?"

"Machias." Katey was still stopped, the wipers slashing mostly useless against the rain, the headlights dull cones thrown forward to smacking wet pavement.

"Tonight?" Not incredulous so much as dismissive.

"However far I get."

"Hoo! Well, drive on. Wicked rain, ain't it? Caught me by surprise. I'm just up the road, outside of Stockton Springs up Muskrat Road." Kept her eyes on Katey. Then said, "You carry me home I'd not forget it. What'd you say your name is?"

"I'm Katey."

"Could you stand to crank that heat, Katey? I got a chill with the rain."

Katey shifted down to first, then let the clutch out and they rolled forward and she geared up. It was slow going. After a short bit she said, "I can carry you to Stockton Springs. You show me where to let you out. I got to get on far as I can this night."

"Whatever you say. But this storm is going to blow out of here by midnight. Stop early, up early, you can be in Machias sometime early afternoon. However you want."

Katey wondered if there was an invitation extended but couldn't and wouldn't ask. So they went on in silence. Just the slap of the wipers, din of rain, suck of tires on wet pavement, the engine a low steady and comforting rumble. Warm from the heater and Katey cracked her window an inch and felt the cool air strike the side of her face.

Molly Ivey Lucerne said, "I never been to Vermont."

Katey looked at her.

"Saw your plates."

Katey said, "I never been to Maine."

"Why'd you want to?"

"To see the ocean."

"Found it yet?"

"I did."

"What'd you think?"

"It scared me."

"That's good. Good to be feared of something so big and don't care less. Can drag you down."

They rode silent.

Katey said, "Most things can, you let them."

"Some things can, let them or not."

"I guess that's true."

"Hoo, yes! So you seen the ocean but on to Machias?"

"It's family business."

"I'm sorry."

Katey glanced over. "Sorry?"

"Family. Who we're stuck with and mostly a mess, what I learned. Until you can learn to do without em."

"Is that what you do? Do without?"

Molly Ivey Lucerne said, "Now and again one or another shows up on my doorstep—I can deal with that. Real trouble is, they're still all crawled up in my mind. You can't ever get rid of that."

A quarter-mile on Katey said, "That's an interesting way to see it. True, I guess."

"True is what's true to me. Might be true to you, might not. You get on in years, you see most people do their best. Might not amount to much but it's the striving that counts."

Katey chewed on that and drove on. They came into Stockton Springs, not more than a dab of houses and a store, the neon of a bar, the gloom of rain beating down.

"Where do I let you out?"

"Muskrat Road's a mile up. To the left. I went right I'd end up in water. But you should carry me home."

Katey said, "What you doing with all those fiddleheads?"

"I'll fry some up for supper, the rest I'll carry down the morning to the store—they sell em there to those won't gather their own."

"What store? We could stop now."

"Hoo! The owner isn't there of a evening. Has a girl ringing the register instead. He's the one buys."

"I was only trying to save you a trip."

Before We Sleep

"Listen." Molly Ivey Lucerne turned her upper bulk sideways. "I told you—you stop now, be in Machias in the afternoon. What you plan? Waste money in some No-tell Mo-tel? I'd feed you supper and it's a warm bed, dry too. And not charge you a red cent."

She glanced at Katey and made a smile, as if knowing her unease and said, "I give up trying to roast little girls in my oven a long time ago. Some think I'm not the brightest flame on the birthday cake but if there's ten candles I'm sharper than the other nine, all put together. You out chasing what you don't know, well girl, you need to learn when to trust, when to cut and run. Up to you. There's a blue painted mailbox the side of the road coming up, just beyond that is Muskrat—turn or stop, it's your choice."

Katey pumped the brakes, downshifted and looked over at the woman. Who was studying the rain and wipers on the windshield. She looked back and saw a big pale blue RFD box glinting in the rain and thought She's odd but I've seen worse. Odd but kind.

Katey said, "You need to check the box?"

"Whyever?" Molly Ivey said. "It's not mine—Joe Rangely's. Now there's a odd soul. Not bad, just odd."

Katey clicked up the turn signal and they both heard the snap of the electricity within the cab. She drove into the turn and said, "What do I look for?"

The house was back from the road through a swale of scrub brush and young trees, once a pasture. Once a farm or a go at one. The house was wood-shingled and the wet glistening roof as well. Behind, in the twilight, a caved-in barn and behind that a wall of cedars and hemlocks. The rain pelting down, a liquid screen over all she saw. Nigh upon dark but a slow dark, one that could pour back down into the earth fast if the rain quit and sky cleared. Late golden blades of light slashing through the trees, lighting up a side of the house, casting long shadows. If the rain quit. Which there was no sign of happening.

She left her suitcase and offered to take one of the buckets but Molly Ivey Lucerne was striding along through the puddles and plash. Through a woodshed ell and then through an unlocked door and they were in the kitchen.

Along one wall was a white enamel sink-and-counter unit, a white electric range and next to that a refrigerator humming along. Wide pine floorboards scrubbed to a soft glow, a simple table and pair of chairs. A fish-cannery calendar on the wall of flocked wallpaper, the calendar showing May, the page not yet turned. There was a circular fluorescent fixture in the ceiling above the sink and another over the table and they glowed and hummed and brightened. The faintest smell of Pine-Sol. Beyond the table stood a door into a dim room, the kitchen lights enough to show a couch and set of padded easy chairs. A television on spraddled legs with rabbit-ear antennas on top, augmented with twists of aluminum foil.

Molly Ivey set a colander into the sink and dropped a double-handful of fiddleheads into it, turned on the tap and carried the two buckets through a door to the cool pantry and returned. She'd taken off the railroad cap and left it in the pantry. She shut the tap and placed the colander on the drainboard and turned to Katey.

"You particular about what you eat?"

She wanted to say she'd just eaten but of a sudden it seemed that was hours ago and she guessed it was. She said, "Not terribly."

"You should be. Most all those things you get off a store shelf, those supermarkets, it's not a thing you should eat. Cans of stew or soups, potato chips, hot dogs, all doctored up to make em taste like something good but they're not. Most of em just imitations of food. And what's a imitation but one thing fake standing in for another real. A hot dog looks like something else, a honest sausage. All loaded up with chemicals and God knows what to make em taste like something you want to eat but the good parts is stretched thin—how they make em so cheap. Now, you can take it too far the other way, also: Father ate bacon breakfast and supper often as he could, honest bacon made right but anything too much isn't good for you. Keeled over dead of a heart attack when he weren't but a year younger than I stand now. It's got so it's hard to trust a thing, you didn't grow it yourself or known the person who did. But just last winter there opened what they call a health food store down to Portland. Milk & Honey; that's the name a the place. Folks a bit strange but they mean well. What they sell is in bins or sacks; you can dig your hand in it and feel it's real. So when I can, that's where I go. What I'll feed you for supper. Them fiddleheads and a pot of stick-to-your-ribs rice and a couple brook trout Joe Rangely brung by this morning before I set off. All right?"

Katey sat back and down in the chair. She said, "Sure. Sounds good." Caught where she was. A snatched thought, she said, "You thumb a ride to Portland? When you need to? And back. Those folks happy to carry what you bought?"

"Hoo, lord no! I only thumb round-about. I got a car. Bought it new off the lot a year ago. I'm not poor, just live light. It's one a those pony cars—"

"Pony cars?"

"A Mustang. Dark blue with light blue interior and a convertible top. Snazzy, is what it is."

"I guess! A boy I sort of know, a couple towns over, he had one. Fire-engine red. He liked to run it fast up the valley roads, wouldn't take it off onto the dirt roads. Is what I hear. I saw him go through a couple of times. I guess it's parked now."

"What happened to him?"

"He signed up. Last I heard he was a Green Beret. What the word is, anyhow."

Molly Ivey had started rice and again rinsed the fiddleheads. She put a pair of cast-iron skillets on the stove burners and was letting them heat. Had taken a plate from the refrigerator that held a pair of trout, gutted but otherwise intact.

She turned and, shaking her head, said, "I watch Cronkite most nights but I can't say I understand that business. I don't want the Ruskies in my backyard any more than the next person but for the life of me can't figure out how they'd get there to here. But folks thought the same of the Nazis, the Japs. I don't know. Let me fix this food. I'm tuckered—maybe I'm too old to be climbing down river-banks to the beds of ostrich ferns. I don't know—somethin will kill me and I can't choose what it'll be."

On a shelf above the stove there was a black-and-gold radio the size of a child's shoebox and Molly Ivey turned it on, and for moments an unfamiliar guitar sang sweetly high and fast before she spun the dial with her right index finger and hit upon a swap-and-shop call-in show and left it there as she worked over the fish and the fiddleheads, making supper. Katey sat silent, smelling butter and bacon grease and then the trout skin browning which brought to mind those suppers she'd had as a young girl—the gifts of trout given to her father. She was tired and her spirits were low, wondering why in the world she was upon this chase and then recalled the conversation from March that had set her off and knew she was doing what had to be done, what she had no choice but to do or hold regret and questions all of her life. Then came to her an image of Molly Ivey Lucerne squeezing down into the driver's seat of a Mustang and almost laughed but then watching the woman work over her stove, the sturdy heft of her thighs and backside, the spread of her back under the sweaters, she thought This wasn't an accident, meeting her. Suddenly sleepy, warm, the smell of food, Katey smiled, thinking I ended up like this, it wouldn't be so bad.

They ate. It wasn't how her mother cooked but she had the comfort-sense that she was home. The rice was dusky brown and sticky and she followed Molly Ivey's lead and melted a gobbet of butter into it and added salt and it was good—reminding her of the oatmeal her mother made but without the sweetness. The trout flaked off the fine thin bones and the fiddleheads were the best she'd ever had—crispy on the outside and sweetly slippery as she chewed them. When they were done Molly Ivey set her fork on her plate and said, "Most people give thanks before they eat and I understand that—holding off on satisfying your appetite. But I like to do so after—to me it feels more complete that way." And without pause she folded her hands before her and kept her eyes open and someways off from Katey and said, "Thank you Lord for the gift of this day and for this food and for my company tonight, for all good things. Thank you for gifting us all with eyes to see and ears to hear and help us keep those all wide open as can be. And bless the traveler upon the road, wherever they may be, whatever joys or travails they may face." She looked at Katey. "There," she said.

They were up at first light and drank strong coffee and ate toast from a dark dense loaf studded with sunflower seeds. Katey offered to drive Molly Ivey and her buckets of fiddleheads to the store in Stockton Springs but she declined. "He don't open till seven today and you'll be an hour onward by then. I won't sit outside waiting, like I'm anxious to sell. I may be different but I'm not poor. I'll take the pony car. It confuses em."

An hour later Katey was driving along Route 1, dropping and lifting the visor against the rising sun as the land rose and fell about her, the road dipping south then up a rise of land and east again. And all the time the sense of water, deep, endless, close upon her. She passed over many bridges and did not know if the waters below were rivers emptying seaward or bays reaching inland; inlets, outlets. Now and again she rose high enough to see the broad expanse stretching to a distant meld of water and sky, the water this morning only a lesser darker blue than the sky vaulting upward. The sun now high enough to heat the clear thin air and soon the cab was hot and she rolled down her window and then leaned to roll down the side window and air passed through, over and against her, cooling her and whipping her hair against her face. She turned the radio on and worked through the dial but passed over song after song—there was nothing to fit her mood because her mood was leaping and bouncing, refusing to stay in any one place.

She came to Ellsworth and rolled slow through the town and passed three different churches with full lots and only then realized it was Sunday morning. She slowed even more and came to a stop in a gravel parking lot of a general store with a set of Texaco pumps out front. She thought How could I have missed that it was Sunday? And then thought Couldn't be a better day, time I hit Machias he'll be home and fed and napping on the couch. He wouldn't be at work, anyway. Most likely. And she teared up, not knowing anything, anything at all. Except she wasn't so far from the place she'd had in her mind these months. And then thought of Molly Ivey Lucerne and decided how that woman presented herself, how she took on the world at her own pace and by her own figuring, was a gift bestowed along the way. Thought also of her own mother and the small tidy cramped world she'd made of her life and ground her teeth and promised not for the first time that she'd never live that way, herself, ever.

She rolled the truck forward to the pumps and filled up with gas and went inside and bought a Coca-Cola and a Hershey bar with almonds, paid the clerk who was reading the Sunday Portland newspaper and who set the paper on the counter and continued reading as he took her three dollars and made change and handed it back to her. She couldn't see what it was that absorbed him so but never in her life thus far had she been so happy to be ignored. She went back to the truck and stuck the bottle between her legs and drove out of the lot back onto the road, tearing the wrapper off the chocolate with her teeth and ate it down before the warmth of the day could smear her fingers. Then drank the cold Coke and felt ready all over again. Even, perhaps, more so than ever.

The day was still clear and growing hot but as she passed into Machias she felt herself grow cool, slightly remote, calculating. As if what lay ahead would be happening only to some unknown version of herself. She drove through the town, peering at street signs and doubled back and stopped at an ice cream stand and asked the girl directions to Cannon Street and made her repeat them and got back in the truck and turned back once again. She went two blocks and pulled a right and went two more blocks and turned left and glided along, the radio now on but the music low, a thrum in the background.

Cannon Street was only a few blocks long and dead-ended at a low fence beyond which stretched the ball fields of a school, the long low two-story pale brick building of the school out ahead in the heat-haze, a school recently built. She sat parked for a moment trying to take it all in. The houses just passed were mostly familiar to her, old two-over-four houses that had been expanded over the years, most white with green or black trim and shutters, a couple painted yellow with cream trim. But there stood a difference between these houses and those from home and it came to her: it was the expanse of sky, the lack of hills. She was upon a tableland, close to the ocean. She wiped sweat from her brow and reversed in a three-point tight turn and went back down the street. Now peering close, seeking numbers on doors, above doors, some houses lacking them altogether or hidden from her sight. Where she could spot them. Then saw 64 on the left-hand side and changed her focus to the other side and slid along a block easily and then slowed and nudged the truck almost against the curb, peering into the shade of the trees, the halos of sunlight. She passed a man out mowing his lawn in green workpants and a white T-shirt and behind him saw the oval plaque that read 47.

She drifted along and counted and stopped and looked. A white house, green trim. A garage that once had been a small barn. A blacktop driveway. The lawn recently mowed, modest flower beds. A pair of yellow birch between the street and the house and a larger silver maple just back from where the driveway met the street. The garage door was swung open and she saw the tail end of a station wagon and thought That's what I guessed. He's got a wife and family. She sucked in a corner of her lower lip and bit it and thought Or he lives alone but raises golden retrievers and needs a big car to get them around. Nodding her head in time to a music that was not playing anywhere except within her. And she let out the clutch before she let herself think again and spun the wheel easily and pulled up into the drive and came to a stop. She reached and killed the engine.

For a moment silence swelled over her, silence and heat of day. She ran both hands curled to fists down the tops of her thighs and considered the packet of letters in the glove box and knew this was not the time for them, wondered if there ever would be such a time and stopped herself. Ran her fingers through her wind-tossed hair and opened the door and stepped down onto the driveway. His driveway. And felt the heat of her jeans sticking to the backs of her thighs and wondered if she hadn't better have worn a dress and then wondered why. Out loud but just audible to herself she said, "Stop being such a chickenshit." Then walked up to the house.

No one she knew used the front door so she went into the garage and beyond the station wagon saw the three steps up into the back entry but also, there against the back wall sat a man at a workbench. A pair of bare lightbulbs were suspended over the bench, the back wall fitted with pegboards that held tools and brackets for tools and spread out on an old oil-stained towel were the disassembled pieces of some small mechanical device. The man wore a green checked short-sleeved shirt and old khaki trousers and he was twisted around on his metal stool, peering at her. A pair of metal rimmed glasses well down his nose, he looked at her above the lenses. His face showed weather, lines and creases, the red-burn of a man used to being outside year-round and his hair was combed over but neat and gray. White. He looked at her a beat, then turned and carefully placed a pair of needle-nose pliers down on the towel, depositing some small part. Then he turned back.

"Can I help you?"

She was flustered. "I think I might have the wrong place."

"Could be." He kept his eyes upon her, waiting.

"I had this address. I just drove in—"

He leaned and looked beyond her and then back and said, "That your truck?"

This was clearly not who she was looking for but it was an unsettling question. And he was looking at her as if he was seeing something he wasn't sure of. She said, "That's an odd question. Of course it's my truck. Why do you ask?"

He said, "Not many girls favor a truck. Specially an older one. What is that? A '56?"

"Look, I have this address. I'm looking for a man named Brian Potter."

He studied her another long moment, then said, "Why?"

"It's kind of a long story."

He waited again, then reached under his bench and pulled out a three-step stepladder, snapped it open and set it a couple of feet away from him. He said, "Why don't you set there on that ladder and tell me your kinda long story. I got time."

Upon her was a remembrance of the afternoon out on the rocks in the ocean and the unsettling pull of the ocean and her own upwelling fear, the two twined. She swallowed and swallowed again and said, "I think I got the wrong place."

He'd tilted his head and after she spoke he shot one wiry white eyebrow up and then nodded toward the stepladder. "Could be. But

71

I'm Thornton Potter, Brian's father. Why don't you set and tell me what you're after. What'd you say your name was?"

She sat upon the stepladder, her feet up on the bottom rung so her knees jutted up and she held them together, let her arms swing loose at her sides. She said, "My name's Katey Snow. My dad's Oliver Snow, of Moorefield, Vermont."

He took up a thrice-folded leather pouch and opened it and took out a briar pipe with a charred bowl, then took fingerfuls of tobacco from the pouch and filled the pipe. He did this slowly and with deliberation, as if he was thinking or meditating through his actions. He reached and took a kitchen match from a box on the workbench and struck fire from the thumbnail that cupped the pipe and shot jets of smoke until he was satisfied, then took another long draw and let the smoke dribble from his mouth and float upward, the pipe cupped in his hand. Throughout he'd not looked at her and now he did. He said, "In the war. Spring of '45 in Germany. Your father saved my boy's life. You know the story?"

"I don't."

"Your father never told you?"

She took a breath. Then said, "He doesn't talk about the war. Any of it."

Thornton Potter nodded. "How old are you? Eighteen?"

"I'm seventeen."

He said, "Most men don't. Talk about it."

She nodded. "I know."

"Brian didn't. Much."

"He came to see my dad. Before I was born. He came to thank him."

"I know he did." Thornton smoked a bit and then said, "From the first he got home, he wanted to. But he went to work and was trying to get his life back on track, figuring out what to do next. As did many. But it was on his mind—he lived here with Mother and me a

72

good many years. It was the summer of 1949 that he was able to make that trip. It seemed he just couldn't buckle down until he had that behind him. I never been in that place, so I can't judge but I can imagine it's a powerful pull for a young man. To see and thank the man saved his life. He'd been working up north through the winter with the paper company but out in the woods, cruising timber. And they cut him loose come spring. He drove back in that summer, had a old Chevrolet rumble seat that got him around. And some money saved. Well, Brian always had some money saved—I taught him a thing or two along the way. And he told us it was time for him to go and see your dad. And he did. Was gone a few weeks, although I got the sense when he returned that he'd done a bit more than just visit with your dad. I could see that—a young man still, with some money in his pocket and the feeling of having time to kill. He never said where all he'd been when he rolled back in. September it was."

He paused to fire his pipe again and said, "What is it you're after?"

"Is he here?"

He looked about the garage as if he might discover his son hidden someplace and looked back and said, "No." And nothing more.

"Could you tell me where he is?"

Again he said, "What is it you're after?"

She put her elbows on her knees and lowered her face to cup with her hands, the long swath of hair a further veil between them. She'd come prepared to lie to whoever she had to lie to but hadn't truly expected she'd have to—she'd come expecting Brian Potter. And thought of her father and not for the first time silently asked him to forgive her and then lifted her head and reached to push back her hair.

Her voice steady as if held in a glass she said, "I'm not sure. My dad's not well. He hasn't been, maybe your son told you, but he's gotten worse. I don't know. I guess I was thinking because of their history, maybe he'd come see Dad again. Maybe that'd help. And maybe Brian could tell me things that could help me understand my dad. I just don't know. I'm sorry. I just thought—I heard that story about Brian coming to see Dad, and why, and I seized on it and well, I guess it's stupid but here I am."

Thornton Potter smoked and set his pipe down on the bench, leaning it against a set of fused metal tubes so it wouldn't tip and said, "There, then, Katey Snow. Hold on, hold on. What we need I think, what we need, is Mother. You wait right here a moment. I'll be right back and with the best help a person could ask for."

Spry, he popped up from his stool and went up the stairs and out of sight through the woodshed entry. She heard a door open but not shut and then heard him calling low, "Louise? Louise! Get down here." Then, muffled, she heard steady slow steps descending a staircase and then from within she heard the murmur of muted voices, indistinct. Only slightly louder she heard Thornton say, "All right then. But you see for yourself." He walked back through the shed and she was standing when he reached the outer door, where he stopped at the top of the stairs.

"She said to have you come in. She won't come talk to you in the garage as if you were some boy or stranger that just washed up here. Tell me, have you had dinner?"

"I had a late breakfast," she lied. "I don't want to be a bother."

"You're here. Perhaps that's a bother, perhaps not. You came after something and Mother would know what that is. And she's only warming leftovers—we ate a hour or more ago. I'd say, looking at you, there's not much extra meat on those bones. Come along." He stepped back and held open the door and waited.

She went up the steps and into the entry, onward toward the kitchen. He fell into step behind her.

The kitchen was small and yellow, the windows throwing light dimmed by curtains tied back with ruffled edges, the stove and refrigerator both pale green, the table and chairs deeply polished honey-toned wood, chunky colonial reproductions. The walls held photographs and also framed floral needlepoints, two of the frames encrusted with small white seashells and on one wall there hung a cuckoo clock of darker wood, with wooden oak leaves and acorns, two brass pinecones suspended as weights on chains beneath the clock. She could hear it marking time.

The woman turned from the stove. She was slight and trim with a mass of chestnut hair curled tight in waves above her forehead, layered down over the ears so only the lobes showed, those filled with elegant round pearl earrings. She reminded her of Lady Bird Johnson in an everyday dress. But she was prettier, her features more delicate, her mouth a neat bow of deep pink lipstick.

Thornton introduced Katey.

Louise extended a hand and shook neatly, once. Her eyes in some appraisal, she said, "Oliver Snow. It's been years since I heard that name but then a mother never forgets such a thing, how important it was, he was, to our son. And now you're looking for Brian? It's not much but last winter's chowder out of the deep freeze, warmed up, a tossed salad and some Parker House rolls baked this morning. Why don't you sit? There's milk or water. I don't have soda."

While speaking she'd ladled chowder into a bowl and placed it on the table, alongside another bowl with chopped dressed lettuce, a plate of rolls. She turned to the refrigerator and lifted out a carton of milk and poured a glass and set it on the table.

Katey felt she was on a rolling deck but she sat at the table. She said, "I'm really not hungry."

"Of course you are."

The bowl before her was steaming curls down into her stomach and she lifted her spoon and turned it over in the chowder, a stew of cream thick with fish and cubes of potato, translucent shreds of onion all in the steam rising. She could also smell the yeast rolls. She was ravenous and off-kilter and knew it. She paused and said, "Thank you."

75

"Tell me then. What it is you need from Brian?"

Katey had buttered a roll and she chewed it slowly, taking time, assessing. She then took a long swallow of milk, thinking Lie but stay as close to the truth as possible.

"Now that I'm here," she said, looking at her, "I'm not so sure. My dad, he's not been right since he came home from the war. From before I was born. Lately it seems he's worse. Tell the truth, I thought maybe Brian might visit him, help him somehow. Now I'm here that doesn't make sense. Maybe, I was thinking Brian could tell me the story of what happened, that changed my father so. No one else can, really."

She looked at the two watching waiting faces and ate a spoonful of the chowder, then another. "Mother won't tell me, if she even knows. He's a quiet man, my dad. Messes with fiddles and people come to see him about them but he's in his shop most of the time. So I thought,"—she shook her head—"I don't know what I was thinking. Except maybe Brian Potter might help, one way or another. Going to visit my dad was the idea I set out with but maybe he could just explain things to me. Enough so I could go home. Understand my dad a little better."

Louise looked at her husband. Thornton Potter knew she was looking but only nodded, his eyes on Katey. Who returned his gaze and hoped she was convincing enough.

Louise said, "You eat up, dear."

Katey said, "I've been driving a couple of days and not eating right. Candy bars and Cokes and that's about all. I hadn't realized how hungry I was."

Thornton said, "Louise? Let this girl eat. Why don't we walk out to the garage and speak to each other?"

The woman looked back at Katey. Who'd buttered another roll and now lifted her salad fork and held it above that bowl. Louise answered her husband but looked at Katey. "All right. We can talk."

Then they were gone. Footsteps out through the old woodshed and then the soft shutting of the door into the garage. After that, silence. Thinking They don't buy it. The way the woman looked at her. What she'd overheard the man say to his wife before he summoned her inside. "See for yourself." She could only guess what he'd meant but thought Whatever they walk back in here with, this food needs to be gone. I need to be right where they expect me to be.

She ate. The food was good and some other way balanced just right for this day. Sitting in the kitchen of the house he'd grown up in, eating food he'd also eaten, made by hands that loved him. Hands that would either send her on to him or not. And how could they not? Accuse her of who she was? They might wonder, might think it but how could they give voice to that question? She ate the last roll and scraped the last of the chowder from the bowl. They could not. She was certain of that. But also this: Surely they'd call their son and alert him that the daughter of his old friend was coming to see him. But there are two in that game, she thought, and his knowing could work in my favor.

She stabbed the last shreds of lettuce as the door opened and they walked back through into their own house and stood, arrayed side by side across the table.

She said, "I feel I'm a huge bother to you. I'm sorry. It wasn't what I intended."

Thornton glanced at his wife, standing with his elbows slightly out, his thumbs tucked into his trouser waistband by his hips, fingers spread below.

Louise said, "I'm sorry about your father. But Brian had his own difficult time. I think it best that you not see him. But Father's not sure. He'll walk you out to your car. I have a migraine coming on. If you'll excuse me I'm going up to lie down."

Katey pushed back from her chair and speaking as she stood, said, "I'm sorry—"

The woman had turned and was already out of the room.

Katey looked at Thornton Potter and finished her sentence in a diminished voice.

"—if I upset you someway. But thank you for the food."

Both stood looking at each other as they listened to the footsteps steady and even, so precise as to be a struggle to be so, going up the stairs.

She waited and he crossed to her and extended an elbow and, his voice oddly and sweetly tentative said, "It's not easy for her but she'll be all right. Shall we go?"

Katey slipped her hand into his elbow and made there a moment of pressure, acquiescence, complicity. So joined they turned together and walked out through the woodshed, down to the garage and continued on outside, up to her truck.

Blinding sunlight hit both, now apart, blinking. She opened the door of the truck and sat on the edge of the seat with her feet down on the running board, shaded now and this allowed Thornton Potter to move forward enough to also be out of the sun.

Without preamble he said, "That fall after he got back visiting your father, he saw a man killed working in the woods. A sawyer dropping a tree and the butt end of the log kicked back and up and took the lower half of the man's face off. Brian quit that day—hadn't been back at work two-three weeks. I told him, You got the G.I. Bill, go over to Orono and talk to the people at the University and he said he'd think about it. But instead he went down to Bucksport, to the tavern down there and came home with a job, tending bar. This did not please his mother but he told her it was too late that year to get in the University and it was just a job, that he could make decent money. And he'd be better set for college the next year. That was the beginning of a long piece of time for us. We didn't see him much. He'd sleep till early afternoon and leave at four and be gone most nights about twelve hours. Most times when he came in he was quiet and we only knew he was home when we saw that old doodlebug parked in the drive when we got up in the morning. A time or two he woke us, stumbling up the stairs. It bothered Mother but I figured, all he's been through, he needs to cut loose. Then sometime late winter or early spring he ran into Deedee Springer. Debra, her name was but all called her Deedee. She'd been a year behind him in high school and left town for Rhode Island to work there and was all those years before she returned home.

"She was a slip of a girl with dirty blonde hair and a face shaped like a heart, always looked younger than she was. Mother was none too pleased—she grew up out on the Falls Road in a rough house and her father worked, when he did, as a carpenter, but one people seldom called on twice for a job, if you get my drift. But there's not one of us chooses our parents, best I know. And Brian was lit up with her and I knew that was a good thing. You, you're young. Let me tell you something about being a parent because, God willing, you'll be one, one day: You do your best all the way but a part of that is understanding from the beginning that when they try to walk, they're going to fall down. That never stops. So when you think they're falling down you still have to cheer them on. Or as they get older keep your mouth shut. And Deedee was a girl with a big heart. Sometimes that counts for more than anything else a person carries in this world. I saw it in her and she knew I did. I liked her."

In his long pause Katey said, "What happened?"

He nodded. "What happened was this: They were together two years. Almost two years. Then on April 8, 1953, about three in the morning—it was his night off and they'd gone to a house party up toward Northfield and they were driving home. It was raining and certainly there was fog in the low spots of the road. Later he told me he was most likely driving faster than he should've been but they were in high spirits, laughing and singing along to the radio. Running fast all the sudden his car slipped off the right-side shoulder.

He tried to get it back on the road but that shoulder just sucked them along, was slowing them down and he gave her the gas, trying to get the power up to pull back onto the blacktop and the bridge over the arm of Middle Lake loomed up and they slammed hard into the abutment. There it was."

He paused, wiped his brow with the back of his hand and squinted as he looked down upon her. She saw it as if a movie reel but said, "Tell me."

"Brian came to his senses and opened his door and stepped out. The headlights had quit but there was a moon and, he told me, it was as if he could see through bright daylight. The passenger side of that car was crumpled in like a beat-up accordion. Deedee, she never felt a thing."

"Oh, no," she said.

He took a step back, looked up at the sky. Then he came forward again and crouched to look up at her. "Yes," he said. "We thought it was hard until then. The worst part for Brian was how he stepped out of the car and was fine. He walked away. And she did not."

Katey's throat was tight, her eyes wet. "I'm sorry," she said.

He blinked himself but said, "Like Mother, I think you should leave him alone. But that's your choice. You only need to know how he got where he is, is all. What you do with it is up to you. When you leave here, I mean."

"That's fair."

"There is no fair to it. He quit drinking and went to Orono and got himself into the University and studied forestry—he had plans to work in timber management or something like that. But it was also out of his own loves, from boyhood, that he now returned to. He'd left all that after the war but when Deedee died it was as if he was trying to find some other part of him he'd lost. All spring and summer he was out in the woods, along the rivers and streams, the beaver ponds, fishing for trout. And his second year of college he took up bird hunting again. Partridge and woodcock. That was a bit of a surprise because when he first got home from the war he left his rods on their racks but packed away his shotguns. But he never again went to deer camp with the other fellows. He was cleaning a brace of woodcock one afternoon and I asked him, I said, You can shoot the birds but you won't go after good honest venison anymore? He only looked at me and told me, That's right. As if I should understand and I guess I do. Something about size and scale—who knows, maybe even more than that. I would not describe him as happy then but more a man who'd reached down in and found the last truths he could still hold to.

"The summer before his senior year he was down fishing the bogs along Englishman River and he walked out with a full creel and drove a mile up the road and there was a woman with a flat tire. Judith Trask. Summer people they are, all the way from Virginia. Comfortable I guess but not so much as some—they own a little island in Larrabee Cove. A great-grandmother came from up here but went south and married into the Trask family. She was a Larrabee and the island come with the marriage. It's not a grand thing—you can row out there in a dinghy but the house is nice enough. Well, he fixed her tire and they got to talking and she took him home for lunch and that was that. She brought him back to life, listened to his stories I'd guess but herself there across from him made simple evidence. That life is relentless, demands of us to take up the reins of life and drive the wagon. And she was, is, an interesting wagon, herself. They spent the summer together and then she and hers went back south and he went on for his last year of school. But that fall he took the train to see her, visit her family, all those he hadn't met that summer. He came back and I asked him how it was and he told me it was the best he'd ever seen. I already knew he was gone, and was glad of it, you can imagine. But I asked him what he meant and he told me, The fishing isn't much; they're big on bass and

81

bream, catfish which are ugly things but the birds. It's hundreds of acres of farmland filled up with quail like hells-a-popping. Grinning as he said that. I said I meant how was it with Judith and her people, and he grinned again and said, Didn't I tell you? We're getting married next summer.

"That's where he is, you want to find him. I'd echo Mother: I don't think he'd be of any help to your dad. Or you. And it's a long drive. Even for a '56 Ford. That's a good truck. I think you should go home. All you need to help your dad is to be kind and to get on with your own life. That's truly what a father, any father, wants."

She nodded. "I guess so. I guess you're right."

He nodded also. "I am." He stood then, a slow lifting as if his knees ached. Other parts also. He said, "Still, I'm pleased to meet you, Katey Snow. And Mother would say the same, she was able. You drive careful now." And he turned, began to turn.

"Wait," she said. "Wait a moment."

He turned back and stood. An old man, worn and strong. Waiting.

"You never said where he was. The town."

He sighed and said, "It's not more than a crossroads. Outside of South Hill. A place called Cranston. It's almost in North Carolina, a long ways from here."

"Thank you," she said. "I just wanted to know. I can't imagine going there."

Four

Ruth

FOLLOWING THE DIRECTIONS of his telegram she rose early on that March morning and made coffee, quietly to not wake her mother. Then last thing called and woke the school principal at home to inform him she was sick and could not be in that day. She did not cough or make any false gestures; the natural distress in her voice was enough. Let herself out of the house and started the Buick and drove off down the hill toward the village. Her father dead nine months, dropping like a sun-struck man two weeks after V-J Day, as the first detailed accounts of the atomic bombs began to come in, both on radio and in the newspapers. He'd been pacing the lawn, awaiting supper, the still-bright light of midsummer softened, tasting autumn. He held a celebratory tumbler of whiskey but when it fell from his hand it was untouched, his face screwed with a frown of caution, concern, worry. Not so many years later she'd realize he was the first person she knew that saw the future in those otherwise heady days.

The snow had rotted away on south-facing fields and pastures and the roadside ditches were full of rushing water, the river also once

83

she came into and then left the village. The eastern sky was pink and to the south was dark and snow squalls passed around her; she passed through them. For a short time she was in a full swirling storm of snow and ten minutes later she'd turned at the bridge to Royalton and headed east along the river, toward White River Junction and the train station there and the sky broke and a dense bar of sun pooled against her windshield and threw the chopped ice floes on the river into jagged relief of white and dark, light and shadow.

He could've taken the bus to Randolph. Or the train on to Royalton. But he'd asked her to meet him at the station in White River at 7:15 in the morning. Alone. It was six months earlier than she expected. Best she knew he didn't have the points for so early a discharge. But then he hadn't been forthcoming in his few letters to her. Last she'd heard he'd been in Stuttgart, Germany. But now, driving, she reflected that he hadn't told her what he was doing there. Once the war ended in Europe his letters had been much as before, short, somewhat abstract as if the censors had still been at work but without those blacked-out sentences. As if he'd grown used to writing that way. More truly she'd grown used to reading this code of non-code.

After following the rising sun for most of an hour she parked at the station in White River and was again in a snowstorm. Heavy wet spring snow. A weekday morning, the lot held only a handful of cars. Trucks backed up to the freight platforms. The world of the war, the rhythms and routines of daily life were still overlapping in all ways. No one knew what normal was. Housewives still hoarded bacon grease. Magazine advertisements promised many fine things to come, soon. Young women were suddenly out of work, replaced by the men returning. No one knew yet what to make of this peace. Except the swelling understanding that the world they'd been fighting to save was going to hold a bold new face—one hidden still, as a young girl who'd turn from her ardent man, tuck her chin to her shoulder and show him the back of her head. As if saying Read your future in the strands of my hair. A world aquiver.

He was the last one off the train. So much so she almost thought she'd gotten the time wrong. But then there he was. In a pinstriped suit she'd never seen before, coming toward her across the wet floor of the station. He was very thin and the suit draped upon him. He'd paused a moment and glanced twice around before his eyes lit upon her. Dense and flickering in his sockets. He walked up to her and stopped a foot away but raised his hands and held her shoulders. His hands trembled. She felt a tremor throughout her. He said her name. Then leaned and pressed dry chapped lips upon her forehead.

"Oh, Oliver." She'd imagined this moment over and again. She hadn't expected him to sweep her back in a welter of passionate embrace but something more than this. His very eyes seemed to tremble.

"Could you," he said. "Could you take me home?"

"Of course. Do you have luggage?"

Now a faint wisp of smile came and went. "That's not a word I've heard in a while."

They collected his duffel and a battered trunk on the platform and shared an awkward moment as they looked down upon it—clearly more than he could manage. She turned and found a porter with a hand truck and palmed him a quarter and ten minutes later the luggage was stowed in the trunk of the Buick and they stood together at the back of the car. The snowstorm was gone at least for the moment and through pale skies above the station was the round disk of the sun, colorless, almost a full moon behind clouds. She held out the keys in the palm of her hand. He looked at them, looked at her, then took the keys and got in the car.

He'd leaned across and opened her door for her.

They drove up the valley along the river. There was some traffic now, a weekday morning with people coming down out of the hills and headed to work in White River or Lebanon, Windsor. School buses making cautious way. His hands slipped loose and easy upon the wheel but she saw his eyes so very busy, flitting not just at intersections or where a side road entered, the clumps of children huddled waiting for their bus but constant, in a motion of awareness upon every rock outcropping, every thicket of trees, down toward the river where an undercut drew close upon the road. And a tang rose from him, a smell she couldn't place but metallic or acid, raising an unformed memory of chemistry all those years ago.

He reached and turned on the radio. The morning call-in of shop and swap, country voices not always clear punctuated by breaks from the station reporting on the weather, high school sports scores, an advertisement for Victory Bonds, reminded all that the war might be over but great challenges, great costs lay before them all. The occupation forces in Japan, in Germany, needed support. He lifted a hand from the wheel and dove his index finger down upon the radio dial and shut it off.

"How's your mother?"

"Shaken but stalwart. She'll live to be a hundred. Your letter meant much to her."

"I wrote . . . yes. And my parents? When did you last see them?"

"At church, Sunday. And I had dinner after, as I always do."

A small flick of glance toward her. "You still go?"

"To Sunday dinner? Of course."

"I meant, to church?"

"Why wouldn't I?"

It was snowing again and he drove the best part of a mile before he said, "No reason. It's good you do."

"Oliver?"

The snow was a sudden squall and he drove with all attention ahead but he answered her. "I need to go see them. This morning. You can drop me off and go on to school."

"I took the day off."

He glanced at her. "I appreciate that. I do. But I need to see my mother, just now."

Then why didn't you call her to pick you up? She said, "Of course you do. Oh, sweetheart, I'm so glad you're back!"

The sun was streaming from behind them, the car filled with sharp golden glow. He tapped a finger atop the wheel and said, "Me too." After a moment he said, "When I'm done there, shouldn't be too long, a couple hours at most, where do I find you?"

She took a ChapStick from her bag and rolled it over her lips, looking straight ahead. The camphor fumes rose to her eyes and she blinked back the water there. She turned to him and thrust the stick out toward him.

"Here." Her voice a rough rasp. "You need this."

He slipped his eyes over hers and back to the road. "I guess maybe I do. Thanks. I'm out of practice, for most all good things." He held the ChapStick but didn't use it. After a moment he said, "So, Ruth. Where do I find you?"

"I guess I'll be at home."

"Home," he said. It wasn't a question but almost, a tilt toward lift in his voice. Then he rolled the balm over his dry cracked lips. Made the turn north out of Royalton onto the valley road. And sighed. A small ease of pleasure, there. Then he handed it back to her and said, "Well. We'll see, won't we?"

She was furious and ferociously calm. Ed Snow came out onto the porch and stood peering at the car as if to determine what all this meant, as Oliver hovered over the open back, tugging at his duffel atop the old trunk and Ruth stood back only a moment, then said, "Oh for God's sake," and elbowed her husband aside and heaved first the bag and then the trunk out onto the curb. Ed called, "Jesus Christ! Oliver? Is that you?" Behind him Ruth saw the door open and Jennie Pease Snow was pushing past her husband. But Ruth was already in the car, the engine whining as tires slipped in the slush and then caught. She went on without stopping but making her turns and twice oncoming cars blared horns at her as she cut before them and then on up West Hill and finally home. Where she sat in the car with her forehead down upon the wheel, crying. After a time her mother came out wearing one of her father's old overcoats and bent to look upon her through the car window. Ruth waved her away, her forehead aching from pressing against the steering wheel, her hair loosened and down about her face, her eyes swollen. Jo rapped knuckles against the glass and then jerked the door open and reached in to switch off the engine. After a moment all the world held was the huff of her mother breathing and the drip of water off the eaves. Jo said, "Whatever it is, it's nothing so bad a cup of tea won't help."

Ruth blew out of the car and made for the house, quickly upstairs to her bedroom. She paced back and forth. After a bit she realized no one—not even her mother—was following her up. She was chilled and some way she couldn't name, felt unclean. She undressed and wrapped in a threadbare robe and went down the hall on bare feet and ran a bath until it was full and steaming, poured in a handful of soap flakes and watched the bubbles rise.

And standing there thought I am no kind of bride. She reached in and pulled the plug and went to her room and dressed again for the day. She leaned close to the mirror and drew her eyebrows, deftly turned red her lips. She leaned close and looked and saw her puffed eyes and pulled back and looked again and thought I am what I'm stuck with.

She went down the backstairs to the kitchen and fried an egg and made toast and ate standing up. She gained a bit, not much but some, enough to know she was possible. She took the cozy from the teapot and poured a cup of tea and, steam swirling up, carried it through to the library where her mother sat beside the fire and took a chair, sinking back and took a sip of the tea. Gazing at the leaping and twinkle of flames, reflecting. Not wanting to look anywhere else. But only to wait what the day would bring.

Her mother said, "He's home?"

"He's down to his parents' house."

"That's understandable." Jo's voice was kind. She said, "I expect he'll be along shortly."

When Ruth did not respond, Jo asked, "Is the tea hot? I could warm it."

Ruth looked from the fire to her mother and said, "You know it's hot."

Jo nodded. "Yes," she said. "I do."

Her mother had drifted off into the kitchen sometime before she heard the truck coming up the hill and Ruth had stood and gone to the window to watch Ed Snow's old International pickup truck pull into the yard, the truck outfitted with a homemade wood flatbed and atop that a peaked-roof enclosure in order to make deliveries of any sort called for. Oliver stepped down from the truck and reared back and surveyed the house. He was wearing old dungarees belted tight, a worn red flannel shirt and over that a red-and-black-checked Johnson wool coat. Old rubber boots planted in the mud. The clothes all hung upon him as if there was less of him all ways. He was bareheaded and there was color in his cheeks, spotty blooms that didn't suggest health so much as the blush of fever. Then he spotted her through the glass and waved. She lifted a hand and waved back and went out to meet him, feeling she was overdressed and off-kilter and so as she passed through the mudroom entryway she pulled from the hook the canvas overcoat her mother had been wearing a little more than an hour before. Stained and several different shades of brown but blanket-lined and smelling, if not of her father, at least of home. Draped over her shoulders, she went into the day.

He held open the passenger door of the truck and said, "I'd like to show you something."

"All right." She stepped into the truck and smoothed her skirt beneath her as she settled. "Oliver—"

"Please wait, Ruth." And he leaned and pressed his lips to her cheek. She smelled the ChapStick and felt the softening of his mouth and, oddly or not, this was enough to still her.

He drove down West Hill and into the village and he drove with only the slightest hesitation as he looked at her and away and back again. The snow had stopped and the sky had broken into high great swathes of blue with, one side or the other, ranks of dark clouds so the village and the hills were spread with golden sunlight or banks of shadow. As if the day was split in halves. Where the sun struck the hills there were fans of red halos about some of the trees, the sudden swelling of maple buds. The long dead grasses so swiftly exposed seemed yellow, showing still the compression of the swiftly melted snow and within those open fields were dark trickles of snowmelt flowing down. She could smell woodsmoke but also wet earth, a scent almost forgotten after the months of winter. In the village, across the sparse open ground of the North Common, a band of robins flittered, relit, worked the open grass with their beaks and then flitted on again.

She had a moment: He's come back in spring, like all good things.

He turned up Beacon Hill. He said, "Do you remember Alden Jenks?"

"He died."

"I know. Mother wrote me. I always liked this place." He turned into the driveway just before Beacon Hill went from paved to dirt and off into the woods above. He shut the truck down and said, "Can I show you?"

The house stood behind heaps of rotting snow, a path carved through the banks to the back door. The house once was white but now was the color of the old snow. Peeling green paint on the shutters and trim. She saw smoke rising thin from the ell chimney. It was an old house, over a hundred years, two-over-four around a center chimney and then the added ell for a summer kitchen that became the full kitchen over time. Attached to a woodshed and then beyond that, a free standing small barn. Like most, now a garage; once upon a time not only a carriage barn for a horse and buggy but likely also a milk cow, a flock of hens, even perhaps swine. She realized she was holding her breath. She let it out and in as neutral a voice as she could find she said, "You bought it?"

He came around the truck and waited before her. He said, "I had some money saved. Mother and Dad put some up and I understand Moorefield Savings owns a bit of it too, but I can set that right in a bit—I've got some more money coming to me. Now, let me show you around."

He held out his hand and she took it and stepped down. He said, "I came up earlier and got a fire going in the range." And then led her through to the ell door and went in to the chill woodshed and then through the back door into the kitchen. The house was very empty, just an old white-enameled range and an icebox. The walls were beadboard painted white, once, and the floorboards were old wide pine painted gray. Oliver dropped her hand and squatted by the range, opened the firebox and pokered the fire and added split sticks from the scuffed woodbox. He shut the firebox and stood and turned.

"Mother and two of the village girls cleaned this place out and scrubbed it down best they could. It wants paint and, well, just about everything. But it's solid. There's a good Sam Daniels furnace in the basement to warm the whole place. Come summer we can paint any way you want. And Alden had some electric installed and also a telephone, fact is the phone is still here, which is a small miracle considering how short the country is of spare phones. And the home appliance fellow in Barre told Dad what he hears is by fall, maybe even summer, we could be in line for one of the new electric ranges and a Frigidaire, also. Wouldn't that be grand? Brand spanking new. And the rest, the rest, well, we can make it yours any way you like. Here Ruth, let me show you around."

They went through the house. Entering each room he paused and she did so beside him. She could smell the ChapStick, also a hint of peppermint on his breath, mothballs from the Johnson coat. In three of the four downstairs rooms the fireplaces from the central chimney had been bricked over although the hearths and mantelpieces were intact. Each of these rooms was badly papered, the wallpaper gone yellow from years of pipe smoke, loose edges pulled free. The room closest to the kitchen was the largest and she guessed it had been Alden Jenks's bedroom, scuffmarks on the floor where the feet of a bedstead had scraped gently over the years. A row of pegs along one wall. Single naked lightbulbs hung from the center of each room, long strings with metal cones dangling at the ends. In each room also rectangular metal registers were set into the floor, through to the cellar for the furnace heat to rise. The rooms smelled of mouse droppings, old wallpaper paste and the more recent sharp scent of hard soap. Upstairs the rooms had sloped roofs, single windows set into the end gables. The walls here were plaster, cracked in places but otherwise solid. Round cast-iron registers were set into the floor. The window shades were pulled down, yellow with age. The same scent of soap, the unpainted pine floorboards clean and worn with over a hundred years of footfalls.

Ruth walked through all of this with her husband. It was nothing she'd expected. Oliver remained quiet and she didn't know if he was reading her thoughts or his own hesitation, his own worries. What had he done? What he had done! He—somehow—while off at the war, with the help of his mother, had made a home for the two of them. It was not the house she'd expected to live in but even as she thought this, she realized how unlikely it was that they'd have lived on with her mother. In her shock and grief after her father died, with the uncertainty never voiced if Oliver would even survive the war,

Ruth had clung tightly to the idea of her childhood home, of she and her husband, when he did return, remaining there. Now she was brought up short by the audacity of her thoughts—that he'd be willing to do such a thing, that her mother might be willing to be partner to such a plan.

Back down in the kitchen he left her to tend the stove and she stood at the old deep soapstone sink and looked out the window set over the sink. In the backyard there were heaps of old snow, a thicket of twisted ancient lilacs, a handful of apple trees, the swollen buds visible in the stronger light of morning. She thought Underneath that snow are flower beds, a garden space, other things to be discovered. They were high enough so she saw a broad pie slice of the village and valley below. The Academy, an expanse of the South Common, the church steeple, the courthouse roof and a handful of houses. It wasn't the house on West Hill, where she'd always imagined herself to be living. But there standing at the sink she thought This was possible, even a good thing, a very good thing. Their own home. And he'd provided it, had made it happen.

And turned to look at her husband. He was at the other window, one hand splayed against the glass as if it held him up. There was a sag about him and she realized this sag was the most salient feature of him she'd seen this day. Home from the war. She had no idea of what his war had been and she had a tremor that she might never really know. But knew he'd talk to her. As the months went on. Because this man shared himself with her. He always had. She reminded herself that he knew her also.

She said, "I think this could work."

He studied her. "Do you?"

"I do."

"That's good, then."

She went to him and wrapped herself around him. The room was warm and she was moist and brought herself against him. You're home, you're home, she breathed to him and he bent closer as she kissed him. All the while thinking she was kissing a hemlock tree bowed over with winter snow, how pliant but stiff his back was, his kisses hungry against her lips, her tongue. His hands upon her back, almost as if they didn't yet trust they were upon her.

She reared back, still held, still holding. She looked at him and said, "I knew it. I knew you'd come home."

After a moment he said, "I know you did. Perhaps that's why I'm here."

Sparkling, she teased, "Did you doubt it? Truly?"

He appraised her. Later she'd realize he was appraising himself. He said, "Doubts? Oh, I had terrible doubts."

She reached and ran a finger from his forehead down between his eyes, along the length of his nose and settled against his mouth.

"Shh," she said. "There's time for all that later. Just now, the question is, How do we make this a home? Between now and nightfall?" And ran all hot.

A dark swarm of confusion passed across his face and he frowned in concentration. Then said, "We don't need so much. Do we?"

Ed Snow found a couple of cans of paint, a soft yellow like good butter and the three of them spent a Saturday in early May painting the kitchen. The house was furnished, sparsely but well. A cherry sleigh bed in their bedroom, a sturdy table and chairs with delicate strong arched backs in the kitchen. The smaller of her father's desks also moved into the kitchen at a side window looking onto the yard where she'd sit evenings and correct papers, draw up lesson plans. An older but working Philco radio. A shutter-front hutch filled with china and glassware. Odds and ends but a start. How it felt to her. And she'd grown comfortable with the idea of putting things in place slowly, of building a home rather than trying to do it all in a hurry. At the end of that very first day, when Ruth and Oliver had used his father's truck to bring down the bed from West Hill, her clothes, a chest of drawers, oddments also, sitting by the range in the kitchen to warm themselves, Oliver shrunken with fatigue and flushed with either fever or life, Ruth unsure how to ask which, herself also drained, his mother had knocked and let herself in with a hamper holding a Dutch oven of chicken and dumplings, a mincemeat pie freshly baked, a quart jar of pickles and a pint jar of cider the color of amber. Also a percolator and a half-pound of ground coffee for the morning, and she'd laid all this out, the chicken atop the range, the pie in the warming oven, the rest on the small table and kissed her son on his forehead and turned to Ruth and said, "Best advice my own mother ever gave me when I married Ed and moved down off the hill to town. Live in your house a year before you change much. See how it's set for the seasons. What looks like a good idea in June, come January you might well regret."

Two months later they were painting the kitchen yellow. Mid-morning Oliver set his brush down and walked outside. Ruth and her father-in-law worked on. The color was delicious and she was delighted to see the transformation, sprung to other possibilities that lay ahead. Ed Snow was up on a stepladder and softly whistling a slow air, a lovely thing, she felt, that filled the room in just the way it needed to be filled. Then without looking at her, without missing a stroke of his brush he said, "There he is. Out in the garden kicking around. Looking for rhubarb or whatever might be popping up. You two? You all right?"

She was quick. "Of course we are. Settling in." Then she said, "It takes time, is all. I understand how it must be for him."

He glanced down at her and then worked on. After a time he said, "What I understand is you and me, we're painting. And he's not."

A few minutes later he resumed whistling.

Oliver was a tender considerate lover. Rarely did he fail to kiss her and thank her for a meal, hold her hand as the spring evenings lengthened and into the long summer twilights as they walked up Beacon

Hill and through the woods to the height of land, the freshening grass there emerald green in the late sunlight. Sometimes one or the other thought to bring his old binoculars and they'd climb the tower there and spy out over the land, shoulder to shoulder. In the bed he was also tender, a bit cautious as if he feared hurting her. Often as not, after the kissing, nuzzling, stroking flanks and sides, she would be the one to press him back and mount him, leaning forward to graze his lips with the tips of her breasts until his tongue stroked and then his lips closed upon a nipple. And she would rock her hips against him until she felt her breath catching and then leaned close again and waited for him. Afterward they'd lie side by side and he'd cup her chin and turn it to him and he'd kiss her and speak her name.

All lovely and fine. And yet she couldn't help but recall those few short weeks three years before after their marriage but before he left on the train for his basic training and eventual deployment, sleeping together in her childhood bedroom in her parents' house and how he would hold her head with both his hands, running them over her with urgent hungry strength, turning her, part by part, limb by limb, as fit his mood and how this felt so right to her, surrendered to him was the word ringing throughout her then, surrendered because he was her husband and wordless he required much of her, most of which she'd had no idea existed or was possible until his panted commands. Free of harshness but for the pulse of him, the need of him, for her. Those nights and not a few stolen afternoons, mornings upon waking, she felt bruised and sore and delightfully so. As if in becoming a bride she'd become a woman. He'd hold her head between both of his hands and run those hands over her as if discovering what he'd always known and at the same moment informing her of his strength, his power over her, and how that power was only possible because she allowed it, invited and welcomed it, from him. His bride.

Which she was. Perhaps more so than ever. Her job, one of her jobs, was to bridge those three years, to understand he was the same man but also a different man. A changed man. The man she loved and she did not doubt that. Her husband. Who turned to her after she made love with him and stroked her chin and spoke her name and kissed her.

He had night sweats. Shuddering in sleep as the sheets grew soaked through, clammy and hot and she'd slip from the bed and fetch a wrung washcloth with cool water and bend over him, still sleeping, and press it to his brow. He muttered some few times and she'd lean close to his ear and whisper What? What did you say? Words enough to shut him down. Sometimes she woke from deep sleep and knew, even before she was awake that she was alone. The first few times she'd rushed down through the house calling his name in a half-whispered voice. But, moonlight or starlight, the house was dark and sometimes she found him sitting in the rocker beside the range and some other times she stood at the sink window and watched him standing alone out in the garden. Twice she went to him and led him back to bed and while he followed meek as a child she felt she was interrupting some-thing and he was indulging her by coming to bed and after that, though she didn't stop seeking him, once she found him she left him be and some time later always woke as he slipped back into bed beside her. Silent as he could. As if he didn't want her to know he'd been gone. But most times, once under the covers and settled, he'd reach a hand and touch her, fingers running down her back, his hand laid upon her upthrust hip. A few short strokes to her hair.

She waited, but he did not speak about the war. A couple of times, late at night after lovemaking when he was attentive, she'd said, "If there's anything you want to tell me?" and the first time he told her he loved her and the second time he'd said, "No. There's nothing." After that she did not ask.

In June, as Ruth was finishing her school year, Oliver went to work in his father's store, Snow's Mercantile. Even with the enforced stasis of

97

the war years the place had grown from when Oliver's grandfather Gideon had purchased the rundown general store. It wasn't only the apothecary, which had been the original mainstay beyond the few shelves of canned goods and a small counter to one side devoted to cigars, pipes and bulk tins of various tobaccos, the racks of packaged cigarettes. Or the small back room that held the local telephone switchboard. Originally a two-story building, with an empty upper floor but the first floor had been expanded over the years to the very edge of the lot it stood upon and the larger rooms divided to form a warren of connected rooms and the upper floor now held a set of offices as well as a room devoted to footwear and shelves of work clothes. Downstairs there were rooms filled with gardening tools and hand tools and grindstones, axes, scythes and cases of pocket knives. Packets of vegetable seeds and a rack of drawer-bins that held seed in loose bulk. Other rooms held kitchen goods; pots and pans, iron skillets and spiders and Dutch ovens, salt cellars and pepper grinders, tablecloths, food mills, apple peelers. Or board games and children's toys; teddy bears, Flexible Flyers, packages of jacks and playing cards, a handful of china dolls in a glass case, yo-yos, slingshots, baseballs and a selection of ash-wood bats made up in Newport. A corner held a handful of musical instruments; guitars and mandolins, fiddles, tambourines, a pair of button accordions, a cornet, a clarinet, a tuba almost green with age, a rack of harmonicas, strings and reeds and valves. A stand of sheet music. Another room held the sparely available hunting rifles and shotguns, boxes of ammunition, also traps and scent-baits, fishing rods and lines—in spring and summer cartons of nightcrawlers. Tubbs snowshoes in all designs; bearpaws and cross-country, mountaineers. And the main rooms with their shelves of food in tin cans, also local canned goods, racks of candy bars and huge jars filled with penny candy; horehound and lemon drops, peppermint wheels, caramels, licorice twists. Shelves with bolts of cloth, spools of thread, pins and needles, even a display Singer sewing machine. Racks of magazines. On the wide front counter beside the brass National cash register there was a twenty-pound round of sharp cheddar. All in all a vast and sprawling business and with the war ended the bare spots on the shelves were slowly filling in. One front window held a display of various items on sale within, the other was papered over with advertisements promising goods on their way.

Oliver went to work on a Monday morning. The evening before Ed and Jennie invited Ruth and Oliver for Sunday dinner. Oliver shaved twice beforehand and so had dabs of tissue stuck to his throat and right cheek. Wearing the pinstriped suit he'd arrived home in but filling it out a bit more. Ruth wore a yellow summer dress with short sleeves she'd owned since before she was married but had saved, best she could. They ate a bleeding-raw rib roast with new asparagus, mashed potatoes and a salad of black-seeded Simpson lettuce drizzled with cider vinegar, a rhubarb fool with sweet clotted cream for dessert. Over the rhubarb fool and coffee, not seeming to notice that her son had sweated through his shirt, Jennie reached an index finger to dab up the last of the cream from her bowl and said, "We're thinking, it works out, we'll change the name. Drop the mercantile altogether. Just E & O Snow's. Sounds good."

"Well, now," Ed said. "Don't get ahead of yourself, Mother." He turned to his son. "It's a nice suit. But tomorrow wear plain trousers and a shirt. If you want to wear a necktie that's fine. But if you do, roll up the sleeves of your shirt. People come in because they feel comfortable and we want to keep it that way."

Ruth stood. "Let me clear. No, Jennie, please. More coffee, anyone?"

He left the house each morning at ten minutes before eight and returned at quarter after six. War Time had ended the fall before but it was June, after all, and the days were long. The walk home longer because of the hill. He ate a sandwich at noon that his mother had made, identical for her husband as she'd been doing for years. Ruth prepared an evening meal. He'd come in and kiss her and then go draw a bath and emerge half an hour later and sit to eat, his wet hair grown out enough to show the raked tracks of the comb. He wore his old clothes then, shirts and trousers from before the war and she sat across from him and saw how he filled those clothes a bit more, even as his cuffs—shirts and pants—rode a bit high. The first evening she'd been waiting at the road, watching him climb toward her, and when he drew close enough she ran the dozen steps and circled his head with her arms and said, "How'd it go?"

"I don't know," he'd said. "About how I expected."

She almost asked what that was, then caught a quick look at his pale hardened face gazing past her and was quiet. She ran her hands up and down his back and said, "It's bound to feel strange, your first day. Are you hungry?"

He'd looked at her and smiled. He reached and touched her face and said, "I am."

At the end of the week he brought his pay envelope home and placed it on the table, before her. "There's that," he said. "Monday morning take it to the bank, put what you can against the house and some in savings and hold out what you need for the week, otherwise."

"I'm off for the summer but I get my salary straight through, every two weeks. Had you forgotten that?"

"No." He paused and looked off toward the range. She had a skillet supper of rice and canned corn, topped with slices of Treet, pressed out of the can and fried in bacon grease, a spoonful of chili sauce stirred into the rice. And a salad from the garden, strawberries and whipped cream for dessert.

He said, "I'd think it best if you put your salary against the house."

"I was thinking to save for a new electric range, also a Frigidaire, once they're available. The paper says it could be early as this fall."

He took a deep breath, let it out slow, then said, "I said put what you can in savings. But Dad knows the dealer in Barre. We'll get what you want quick as we can. But I want to pay the house off. We own it, no one can ever take it away from us. Everything else we can do as we go."

"All right," she said. "I'll do that." She rose and went to the range. The kitchen was very hot though she'd made the least fire possible in the firebox. She heard his chair scrape back as he sat at the table. She served the food onto two plates, arranging it to give him more but make the portions look the same. Her back to him she said, "Bob Martin is back. Gladys stopped by this morning."

"I saw him. He was in buying cigarettes and beer."

"Well, he had a tough time, with his knee all busted up and that burn the side of his face. Anyway, Gladys wanted to know if we might like to go the Playhouse tomorrow night? The four of us?" She turned and placed the plates on the table, stepped to the tap and opened the spring line and filled two tall glasses that clouded fast with the cold, brought them to the table and sat. He'd diced the meat and mashed it in with the rest and was eating. She made a small noise, not quite a clearing of her throat. He looked up.

"No. I'm sorry but no. You can go if you want."

"Oliver."

He finished his food and drank off half his water and looked at her. He said, "There's windowsills gone punky on the south side where that cedar tree blocks the light. I aim to replace them tomorrow. Get started at it, anyhow."

"All right. But you're not going to do that all night long."

He paused then. After a moment he said, "Aw, Ruth." Then: "Ruthie." He'd never called her that but would again. "All Bob's going to do is drink more than he should and want to talk about things I don't want to talk about. He's not a bad fella, not a bit. But honey? It's hard enough standing at the counter of the store and

101

smiling and going on with folks about what they need and helping them and all the time feeling like I don't fit. Not here. Not anywhere. Not in this life." He paused again and said, "It's terrible is what it is. And worse, because I ask you to understand what you can't understand."

She placed her hands flat on the table and looked across, seeking his eyes that came and went. She said, "I'd like to understand, Oliver. And I bet one day I will. But there's no hurry. I love you, is all you need to know."

He stood. Tears pouring down his contorted face. He said, "People."

After a long moment he sucked air and said, "I'm going for a walk up the hill. I need to be alone."

She wanted to hurl from her chair and drag him to the ground and whatever way she needed to, break him from this awful moment and knew she couldn't do so and so only nodded and said, "I love you, Oliver." Crying now herself, hating that she was crying.

Shaking, he said, "I love you too, Ruthie. I'm just not sure what that means, anymore. But it means something, doesn't it? It has to. Oh, what sense is there in any of it?"

Then he was out the door and gone. She stood where she was, all of her in tremble. Slowly then she folded down to the floor. A glass broke free from her hand and rolled across the floorboards, throwing out a slop of water and then chiming hollow against a foot of the old range.

The summer did not progress so much as lurch forward. Twice in the coming weeks Ed drove Oliver up the hill early, unexpectedly, to drop him off. Both times Oliver entered alone, his face pale, a sheen of sweat, not speaking as he went through and drew a bath, the door shut with a clear and decisive click. Not wanting her. Both times his eyes red and swollen. When he'd emerge later he'd be dressed in old clothes and go to puttering about the place, inside or out—whatever project was under way. She left him alone, although her own day was fractured and his presence was a heavy pressing shadow upon her. She'd fix supper and wait for him. Both times he appeared and sat to eat and spoke with her then about what he was working on, as if nothing untoward had occurred earlier. She felt she was almost breathless to catch up in a race set to terms that had never been made clear, rules hidden from her. He was pleasant and kind, solicitous of her. Other evenings he'd arrive home with a smile and often as not a fresh cut of meat wrapped in bloody brown paper, a small household gadget that they lacked or was new to the market or both. Most evenings after supper they sat on old chairs in the garden and watched the summer day fade from the valley below up to the hills above, not silent but in easy small talk, with easy silences in-between. Smacking black flies. Until they'd go in to bed. Or sitting up listening to the radio. He'd kneel before it, twisting the knob, not interested in the regular programming but seeking the outer reaches of the dial, wanting music. Any music at all but most happy when he'd come across a broadcast of a symphony. He'd turn that as loud as the static would allow and they'd sit within the shroud of tonality. There were a handful of radio dramas that she liked but she was happy to sit with him, if he was happy. And nights he couldn't find those broadcasts he was kind and would dial back to the programs he knew she enjoyed. Sometimes but not always sitting through them with her. She was comfortable with that: her own father had disdained those radio plays and so, mostly, she felt it was something about men. It didn't escape her that most of the sponsors and advertisements for the radio plays were directed toward products that women would use. She was also free of embarrassment.

More troubling was her stack of summer reading. Teaching tenth-grade history had proved to be wonderful, challenging and utterly exhausting; even before Oliver arrived back in March it routinely kept her up to midnight, working through student papers, preparing lesson plans, reading the assigned works ahead of her students. And so her own reading, the reading she did not only for pleasure but also to associate with the larger world, to feel herself as more than a lone drumbeat, heartbeat in the world, the pleasures and joys of books, all those had been put aside for the school year. The librarian, a spinster half again her age that she'd known since she was a girl just old enough to hold her own library card. Ginger Dana had suddenly become closer to her in age it seemed and also, once Ruth was teaching, would inform Ruth of new books that came in that Ruth would be interested in and quietly agreed to hold those books to be available for her, come summer. Mostly these were not recently published works, since the library didn't have the budget for such acquisitions, but donated books or books larger libraries were discarding. Still, they were new to Ruth.

For new fiction she read the *Saturday Evening Post*, purchased for years at her in-laws' business. Other articles also. She loved *Life* for the photography that, starting during the war, had made the world smaller, brought faraway events and places close. And put faces and landscapes to the news broadcasts on the radio. She still had a passion for *Screenland* although after Oliver returned it was several months before she found the nerve to buy a copy and bring it home. And every few weeks her mother would pass along several recent issues of the *New Yorker*. Improbably, her father had come across the magazine somewhere in the late '30s and taken a shine to it. As a young teenager Ruth had mostly only cared for the advertisements and about half the cartoons, others she didn't see as funny or was puzzled by the intent. But now, this summer, she was able to read again, and widely.

It was as if Oliver had never read. He ignored the stack of books on her desk, on the night table her side of the bed, the magazines that she ordered neatly as her mother had, on a low table before the old sofa in what Ruth grandly or hopefully called the parlor. She kept another pile of magazines in an old wooden sap bucket in the bathroom and if he ever so much as glanced at them she couldn't know it—their order never changed except when she moved them about or added new issues.

She thought perhaps he'd lost the habit, although she knew there had been a great and wide effort to bring reading matter, books and periodicals, to the men in the service. She thought it as likely that his distress, his obvious if quiet struggle to adjust to life after the war, had some way severed him from his old passion, one, after all, that they'd shared. Perhaps he'd forgotten the joy, the solace that could be found within pages, within the intellectual exercise of struggling to understand how and why people did what they did and how it made life more bearable. For this she knew—he was a man for whom life was a fraught trial.

She was twenty-one years old. And so was he. As with so much else, she believed time would return him to himself.

And there were times she believed that to be happening. One Thursday he laid an advertisement torn from the weekly paper before her on the kitchen table. Saturday there was to be an auction high up out on the Williamstown road. The last surviving of three spinster sisters who ran their family's farm had died, with the contents to be sold. She knew the place, barely. The last sister had kept a cow and bees to the end and made occasional trips to town in spring and fall to sell honey in quart jars, ginseng root by the bundle, crates of preserves and also real mincemeat—beef and venison cooked with suet and raisins. She wore clothing a hundred years old and drove a single horse hitched to a buggy with a tattered canopy. The horse in blinders and with a beribboned straw hat with ear-holes tied to its head. She was not the only one so, but notable nonetheless. And now gone.

105

Oliver said, "Dad says we can use the truck. I think we ought to go. No telling what we'll find."

Ruth said, "I don't know. There feels something tawdry about it. Grave-chasing."

Oliver said, "Well, Ruthie, she's the end of the line. That family has been there since 1800 and froze to death, maybe twenty years before that. A long time. We can at least go look." He glanced about, said, "We're still a mite short of furnishings. If we don't get it, someone else will."

Saturday, as promised, they took the truck and walked through before the bidding started. It was much as Ruth expected: a broad array of old stuff no one used anymore. Then Oliver motioned to her and took her aside and waited until they were alone and knelt to pull a blanket from a desk with bowed legs and a perfect surface with a small rise at the back that held three drawers, all fashioned from bird's-eye maple. Dovetail joints fine as babies' teeth held it together, with draw pulls of ancient brass the color of moss. "When it comes up," he said, "we aren't interested. At first."

"It's lovely," she said.

"What we do, is find some other things, interesting but ordinary, that we buy first. So no one catches on."

"What do you have in mind?"

"It doesn't really matter. Box lots. Whatever catches your eye. But buy a couple of them, not quick. Put some space in between."

They were crouched down next to a slew of cardboard cartons and old milk crates. She was reaching box to box, fumbling around. One held old ten- and twelve-stick tin candle molds, another empty glass and clay inkwells, empty stoppered jars of ink, a third heaps of sap spigots.

She said, "The inkwells. They could be interesting in school. Different from what the kids use, but they would understand them. And, well, I like them myself. The clay ones particularly."

"Good. Buy em. But find something else. Maybe that old apple-corer. Those old ones work well. But only if it doesn't come up too soon after I buy the table."

She looked at him. "What is it? What else did you see?"

He sniffed the air. "Someone's cooking hamburgers. Let's go get one."

They walked out of the house into the yard where a tent was set up and chairs arrayed. The auctioneer was testing his microphone and speaker powered off a car battery. Beyond the tent was a hardwood fire burned down to coals and a metal grate laid atop it, hamburg patties and hot dogs cooking on the grill. A washtub of ice with bottles of soda to one end. He bought them both burgers and bottles of orange soda and together they strolled away from the crowd out into the reaches of the yard. Old maples lined the drive and an elm towered over the yard and they stood in its shade and ate. She wiped her mouth and said, "All right. Tell me."

He glanced around, then said, "There's six real old dining room chairs. Not all clumped together and some missing back-spokes and some missing a foot support or two. But nothing that can't be fixed. Could be the best of what's here. My guess is they'll come up as a lot—that auctioneer ain't a fool but they look rough. So I aim to go after em. If they come up first, we got to forget about the table—people will be on to us. But it works like I hope, we might just hit a ringer, today."

She drank the last of her soda and dropped the bottle in the grass. She said, "However it goes, you want me to keep bidding on the inkwells, the apple-corer?"

"Unless I wave you down."

"How do you plan to do that?"

"Any lot we've talked about, if I pass on it and jam my hands in my pockets, we're through."

"All right. I think I got it."

107

The auctioneer hie-de-hoed. People milled back to the tent and they both turned. As they were going in, she caught his arm. He stopped and bent back, talking to her ear as many others also were doing. He said, "What?"

"Oliver? Is there anything else you're wanting today?"

He was quick but she saw the dart of his eyes. Then back and he said, "No, ma'am. Let's see how far we get, as it is."

Then he drifted, leaving her, plunging into the crowd.

And she wondered what he'd seen that he'd not spoken of.

Some days, some moments, seem charmed. As if a measure of grace swept down and along, throughout the entire day. Time they drove off, late afternoon, they had not only the desk and the chairs, the box of inkwells, roped down in the bed of the truck, but also a trio of matched coal-oil lamps with brass fittings and frosted glass globes about the chimneys with snowflake patterns cut through the frost, for, he said, when the power goes out; and also, his pride in hiding them from her until he'd bought them, a glow over him as if he held the sunset of the summer day within his cheeks and forehead: two crates of books. Complete late-nineteenth-century sets of Dickens and of Hardy. Calf bindings and onionskin pages laid in over the engraved illustrations, the spine titles in gilt relief. He showed them to her only as he was loading them and she lifted one out and held it in her hands as they drove home. *Martin Chuzzlewit*. The cover soft and elegant as a glove from another time, calling her to pull it on, to take it in.

He pulled a cigarette from the pack on the dash and smoked, intent on his driving. Then he looked at her and grinned and said, "That was a pretty good haul, wouldn't you say?"

"Oh my gosh! Oliver."

He said, "Well, we're not done yet. I was thinking, we get home, unload this stuff and then drive over to Onion Flats and grab a bite and roll on into Randolph and go to the movies. Make a night of it. Whaddaya say, Ruthie?"

She was her mother's daughter: Along with slowly working on the interior of the house, she took on the yard. Perhaps once there had been order there but it had long passed. She took a saw and cut deadwood from the lilacs, pruned back the spirea, dug up by the roots goldenrod and wild grapevine, thinned the weeds from a patch of lily-of-the-valley, trimmed back the high tangled canes of red, yellow and white roses. She wore dungarees and checked summer shirts with the sleeves rolled up and the tails also, knotted over her midriff. When she could she'd make her way to the house on West Hill and return with boxes of transplants: bleeding hearts, daylilies, dahlias, bee balm, a carefully dug shoot from the smokebush; hostas and clumps of periwinkle and pachysandra for the shaded spots. As she worked she also, inevitably, pulled stones and rocks from the soil, the mostly flat stones in irregular shapes but only a few inches thick and, inspired by a photograph essay in *Life* about the islands of northern Scotland, built carefully balanced cairns, mostly where piles of stone accumulated, because nothing else was growing there. Something took her about this process, to the point where walking in the woods above the house she kept her eye tipped for rocks that would serve her and carried them home. And soon she was shifting soil and plants again, studying the lay of her garden and creating terraces, building walls of layered stone to mark and hold them.

Her father-in-law came by one afternoon, unexpected, and found her working on one. Stood waiting until she sensed his presence and looked up, sweat beading and dropping from her nose.

Ed Snow said, "You want me to ask Walter Payne if he wants a helper?"

She stood and ran a grimy hand across her face and knew immediately she'd left mud tracks there. She grinned and said, "I think I've got all the rock I can handle, right here."

He nodded and said, "Yup. I guess I shoulda told Oliver but somehow I wanted to try and surprise you both. There's an electric range in the back of the truck and Tuck Braman is in the cab, to help wheel it in and also with his tools, to wire it up. You'll be cooking cool by suppertime."

"You what?" she said.

"The thing I been thinking is, we don't just haul the wood range off and scrap it. But work it into the side parlor with the bricked-up fireplace, knock a hole through to the chimney six feet up and hook it up there. A backup, you might say. Or a warm spot come winter. Or both."

"Goodness," she said. "I'm a mess."

He grinned again. "Nothing like you will be a couple hours from now." Then he stepped close and winked and said, "Don't say nothing to him but the word I got is sometime August, I'll be able to get a new Frigidaire, also. Think a that."

She scrubbed her palms against the fronts of her dungarees. More smears. Then said, "We don't want anything other people can't get."

Ed nodded. "It's a trickle now but a flood soon. And he earned it. You worry what people think, remember this—they don't know a damned thing."

She'd read *A Tale of Two Cities* in high school and liked it well enough but Thomas Hardy was new to her and she ran her finger along the row of books and settled on *Jude the Obscure*. She liked the title and she quickly warmed to Hardy's world that seemed close to the one about her. It took longer for her to fully understand the story. Years.

The summer went along. Oliver spent most evenings and weekends working on the place and took on the project of reglazing the windows and also the storms, which stood in dusty ranks at the back of the barn, in the low ell that once held animals, and in the process began construction of a simple workbench and area, with basic tools. He was pensive and silent much of the time but was quick with a joke or to compliment her on a meal. He noticed the work she did and spoke of it. And there were nights she'd wake alone and stand at the bedroom window to see him in the yard, slightly hunched, one arm wrapped around his chest as if cradling a wound he'd never revealed to her, the other hand passing up and down, the small flare as he smoked. Sometimes she'd wake only as he settled back into bed, the smell of tobacco strong about him. She came to love the smell, understanding that something of his smoking drew him both away to a place he needed to revisit but also knowing it was some portal home. Other times he came to the bed and nuzzled her, a seeking probe of cautious lips upon her shoulder or arm until she turned to meet him. She'd almost forgotten the man, the boy, who in his eagerness and urgency had gently bruised her, had twisted and turned her as if she was his own thing, had grown used to and welcomed now the man who was tentative, who silently asked for her to accommodate him. His hands a swimming glide upon her hips, his tongue a hot swift probe to her nipples above him. Brushing his face.

He took to walking up the hill to have lunch with her. Carrying a paper of thick-sliced bologna and a loaf of bread. Or hard salami. A jar of mustard if they were out. A couple of candy bars and twin bottles of root or birch beer in his trouser pockets. She'd told him she could warm up leftovers of which there were plenty or make lunch for him if he'd only tell her what he wanted in the morning but he'd said he liked it this way. Showing up, with most everything they needed. He liked to slice cheese and place it upon a mustard-slathered slice of bread, then fry the bologna in grease and set it sizzling atop the cheese and slap the other slice of bread on top, letting the heat melt the cheese. Four days of this passed before he could convince

111

her to try it and she was shocked to discover how delicious it tasted. He peeled and sliced apples and ate them with peanut butter. Slouched back in his chair, the radio turned loud if he found a program to his liking. Then rising and kissing her and walking back down to work. She'd wash the dishes and often as not eat the candy bar, leaf through the new magazine he'd brought, see her afternoon rising, slowly, before her. Languorous, almost as if they'd made love. The way he walked off, downhill, not quite sauntering but with a relaxed comfort in his stride. He was coming home, more so all the time, was what she thought. And she was meeting him, understanding how slow such meetings can be and all the better for taking time.

He'd barely had time to walk down to the store the morning mid-August when his mother pulled in, got out of the truck and walked toward the house. Ruth was washing dishes and had a kettle of chokecherries simmering on the stove behind her, ready to make jelly as she watched Jennie Pease Snow come on. And felt it like a stone in the pit of her stomach.

"I'll not mince words," Jennie said after accepting a cup of coffee, settled across the table from Ruth. "Ed's not happy I'm here, but for that matter I'm not happy, either."

"He seems to be settling in," Ruth offered.

"We'd hoped." Jennie's eyes were off just over Ruth's shoulder and she was blinking a slow but steady bat and Ruth realized her mother-in-law was holding back tears. "But truth is best said straight: Ollie's not good in the store. Oh! He can be. Johnny-on-the-spot. But then he'll disappear and we'll find him out back, sent after something or another but nowhere near where it is. Gone to cut a screen for a window and we'll find him up among the boots and overhauls, cross-legged on the floor. Or out the back smoking, rubbing the toe of a shoe in the dust. Times he'll be at the counter and be asked for something and him setting on the stool with his knee over the other and he'll peer about and then send the customer off to seek what they're after, themselves. Now that's not such a hard thing, the way it sounds, but it's not the way Ed does business; it's not what people are used to when they walk in the door. They ask; we get it for them. Most, after all, know where to find things. But now the store is filling up again and with items people've been waiting for. New and old, you see what I'm saying? It's all wonderful, thank the Lord, but people are confused by all of it. And there he sits behind the counter with a cigarette the corner of his mouth and a far-off look in his eye. I told Ed, and he didn't want to hear it but I told him anyway: We can't have it."

Ruth sipped the now cool coffee and said, "What can I do?"

"What can any of us do? He's my boy and to see him like this? It's a terrible thing, for me. If I had a answer I'd speak my mind about it. I don't think it's you; hell, honey, I don't think it's any of us. Ways, I know it's not even him. Not a choice he made. But that's one thing and time can work on it, is how I see it. He's a good man, we both know that."

And Ruth was cool herself. "He is indeed. If you're telling me you're letting him go, you should be telling him. I've got a good job, myself. We'll be fine." And not saying, because she didn't need to, that she had greater resources to draw upon as well. Ruth said, "Of course, I appreciate all you and Ed have done."

The older woman reared back slightly, tossed her head. That white-blonde hair thick as a mare's tail, snapping blue eyes. Jennie Pease Snow said, "I remember how it was to be young and feel you had to be ready to do battle with the world. No, we're not letting him go. Comes the day, it'll be his business and don't you forget that. But the time being, Ed and I agreed it'd be best if Oliver worked afternoons, driving deliveries as they need to be made, and then a few hours at night, stocking the shelves and cleaning up. Taking inventory. Mostly alone you see. And we already told him. And he agreed.

Liked the idea, I could see he did." She paused and said, "In a sense he'll be learning the guts of the business in a way he'd not, otherwise. There's a purpose to all things."

She stood and said, "Best for him and best for us and in the end it comes to the same thing. You want pint jars for chokecherry jelly, I'll send some if you need em. Strain it three times to make it clear and hold the sugar to keep it tart, my mother told me. I never made it myself, never had the time. But it's some good on toast, isn't it?"

He took it in stride. She didn't ask how he felt about it but it was clear soon enough that he liked the arrangement. Many days he was about the house and he took on more projects, and his father found more paint for them. One day Oliver left early and drove up midmorning with a load of planks in the back of the truck and soon enough was tearing up a section of the front entryway, wood punked and rotten—something she hadn't the faintest idea of—and then went to work replacing it. Evenings he was out of the house from nine to midnight and she missed him but his time about the place during the day made up for it. And she was not altogether unhappy having those evening hours alone. She tuned the radio as she pleased, she read, she worked on lesson plans for the coming school year. And when he'd come in he often woke her and they'd sit talking or loving, or loving and then talking. So she'd wake some mornings late, hearing him whistling as he worked down below. She'd rise and go down to the kitchen to find the percolator of hot coffee, bacon cooked and waiting for her.

One afternoon she was on the small lawn, reading in the shade and lifted her eyes to watch an unfamiliar car climb the hill, then turn into their driveway and pull to a stop. Oliver stepped out and walked over, grinning, twirling a keychain around an upraised index finger.

"What've you done? Did you buy yourself a car? Or steal it?" she teased.

"C'mon. Come take a look," reaching his other hand down and she took it and was lifted up. Despite herself, she was intrigued. From her father she gained a love of automobiles that most of the other young women she knew did not have: Father and his Buick, his devotion to the sleek lines of the car, the long swept hood holding the powerful engine, the narrow elegant grille on the front, the lovely interior. And before that, of her youngest memory, was the Packard, with the fold-down roof, headlamps like bulging eyes, and again, long sweeping lines, a lovely vision of a memory being curled against him as he powered the big car through a snowstorm at night; she had no idea what they were doing out in that storm, where they were going or returning from, guessing he'd taken her to a school-board meeting or something like that, just the two of them, her mother waiting at home but the vivid memory of the warmth of the car, the warmth of his body against hers, his brushed woolen overcoat against her cheek, a smell, also, his bay-rum aftershave and then the world outside, the two cones of light converging and a splattering constant barrage of snowflakes against the windshield, the darkness above from where the fast flakes came, the sense of a small warm place moving through a dense dark night.

The car before her was nothing like those but she liked it none-theless even if she'd seen dozens of them in the past years: a two-door coupe from before the war with small round windows behind the bench seat and the spare tire centered against the trunk, the car almost saucy somehow. Painted a gun-metal gray, and, as she walked toward it, she took it in all over again and liked what she saw. Less modest than first glance; jaunty, indeed.

She looked at her husband. "What's this, Oliver?"

He tossed the keys toward her, a gentle underhand. Still, she missed them after a quick swipe but rose up fast with the keys in hand. He said, "Why don't you take it for a spin?"

115

Something in his grin. She said, "Come with me."

"Why should I? It's your car."

"I don't need a car." The keys hot in her hand.

"You're going to walk down and back to work? I don't think so. Not my wife. Now, go on. Take a drive."

Time to time the thought came to her that theirs was not a normal life. But then, quickly, what did she know of a normal life? What, exactly, was normal? If sometimes he was distinctly absent, not gone somewhere else so much as not fully there, she wondered what to expect, anyway. It was not as if he'd been away on a long pleasure cruise. And other things, bits of knowledge, came her way. Bob Merton was said to be drinking too much, in a not-always-quiet way. Other stories. Articles about men home from the war, trying to adjust to this new world. One in which no one quite seemed to clearly see that path forward—as if victory had diminished meaning and purpose. And other things uncertain: the Soviets, those great allies, were of a sudden a menace in Europe. And the atomic bombs— the photo essays were disturbing as well as the lesser disturbance of a photo essay of a college football team from somewhere in the Midwest—Nebraska, Kansas, she couldn't recall now, but a coed cheerleader holding aloft a placard begging to give the rival team A Tomic Ache. And the newsreels out of Germany, the death camps, something she did not yet understand but for the clear thrum of a deadly menace. A stain great and dark lay over the world and she realized victory had not obliterated the stain but only made it more clear, brought it to light.

She lay on her side watching her husband sleep. Wondering what those fluttering lids had seen, what his ears had heard. What his own hands had done. She forgave him all of it, whatever it was. Wondered if she'd ever know. And recalled what his mother had said about time. And her own mother, a lifetime ago, it seemed, about patience.

She thought perhaps a baby might pull both of them forward, not away from the past so much as toward the future. She also felt a hint of caution spring within herself: Her own employment was steady and certain, if barely undertaken; approaching her third year. A baby could thrust Oliver onward into life. But she was not yet certain of that. Thoughts at three in the morning.

Summer ended; the school year began. The long days of early September allowed summer to close down slowly. Most days held no threat of rain and she often walked down to the Academy in the morning and back up again in golden glowing afternoons and she'd work outside until dusk and still have time to read papers, mark margins, review the plans for the days ahead. Her first year of teaching she'd felt thrown into a wringer washer; but the second she had a better sense of how to proceed and so she kept the work-load light until the third week of September, the actual end of summer. This was not a fluke of discovery but a thought, an observation dredged from memory: She'd been in sixth or seventh grade and one night at the dinner table her father was holding forth. She had no memory of what had caused his fulmination but ever after, the essence. "Look at those children off the hill farms— the ones who don't start school until the harvest is done. They come in fresh and clear and ready to learn. No—it's not the escape from the labor, that labor is their lives. It's the closing down of days, the march toward winter, for what is winter but the interior season? Interior not only of being more house-bound, barn-bound, but also the interiority of the mind. Most literally, time to think, minds with the space and openness, the freshness if you will, to tackle new ideas, fresh concepts, minds, damn it all, ready to learn, hungry to learn. I tell you, Jo, there's something to this. If I could convince the powers in Montpelier, a ridiculous thought, but if I could, to give me five years where the school year started mid-October and ended mid-May but school ran from seven in the morning to five in the afternoon, why, I think those children would learn more, absorb more, in those hours than our present system. And it's not just those farm children, not at all, but all children. They need their childhoods, they need to be outside and running about as children need to do, be it helping on the farm or splashing in brooks, fishing, getting up ball games—whatever it is, but *on their own*. Exhausting themselves but tackling life full-on. I swear, we'd see a great difference. If they'd only let me try it."

Her mother had pointed out the other seasonal absences that would disturb his plan—deer season, sugaring in March, times when older children were out of school for days, sometimes weeks. Plus the daily chores, mornings and afternoons these children were depended upon to help perform. But her father had replied, "They would make do! The parents would make do. For it is a lesser season. And if they had their children for the longer length of the year . . ."

He'd never won that argument even in his own home but his daughter remembered it and so in her second year teaching trimmed back her expectations for those first weeks, the last also. Made it possible for children to miss school if needed at home without, well, truly missing school. For the others, the near majority who were there almost every day, she saw her silent, never-mentioned plan as simply a way to allow them to engage. To reenter free of panic or turbulence. Three weeks of easy reading, simple assignments, minimal papers due. Token tests. Enough so none of her colleagues caught on, leave alone the bullheaded administrators; enough though so she saw the truth in her father's words. And felt distinct pleasure that in such a way, small as it was, his idea might be vindicated.

And there was pleasure also in easing back into her third year of teaching. By fall she could barely remember the last months of the previous year after Oliver returned. How she'd worked through the rest of that year. So she, too, was beginning again. But, as she thought of herself, as more so.

One afternoon she'd driven to school under a sullen sky with a steady drizzle and drove home to a breaking sky with high shafts of sunlight bold and strong, flooding light down upon the village, and the streets and roads dry, pulled in and found mounds of cordwood dumped in the yard. A splitting block surrounded by piles of firewood ready to be moved into the shed for the old range, most down the bulkhead to feed the great furnace for the winter. Oliver at work with his shirt off, his upper body still slender but she saw then that he'd gained strength through the summer, slowly, working about the place. He'd heard her coming and wiped sweat from his brow and grinned as she stepped from the car parked just short of the woodpile. He said, "Why don't you change out of those fancy duds and let's move some wood. I got an hour before I have to be down to the store."

"I could do that," she said. A little irritated. She'd wanted to make a cup of tea and relax and then take on the handful of papers. They might be meager but the closer she looked the better idea she'd have of what to expect in the months to come.

"While you're at it," he said, "could you bring me out a cold beer?"

Suddenly short she stopped and said, "Last I looked the icebox was empty of beer. Ice, too, pretty much." Then turned and went on, feeling like a snipe.

And he was right behind her. So she threw back the screen door and entered the house and stopped. A brand-new Frigidaire sat where the icebox had been, gently humming. The icebox moved to the side, compartment doors ajar. She stopped and something small tore within her and she turned and said, "Damn it, Oliver. I wish your dad would let us get things as we can. I know he means well but, but . . ." And then she sank to the floor and was crying. She didn't even know why she was crying but she was.

And he stood over her. So it seemed. He said, "Ruthie. I earn it."

She looked up. "Do you? Do you, Oliver? Is that how it is or are your parents betting on a future they pray will come? Are they? Because I'm not seeing it, Oliver. I wish I was and I hate myself telling you this but I'm just not. They can't even have you in the store regular hours. What do you do, Oliver? What do you do?"

He stood looking down at her. Then lifted his eyes and his chin and stepped over her and opened the refrigerator and lifted out a bottle of Narragansett and turned and walked out of the house.

Half an hour later when she went to look for him, he was gone. The bottle of beer sat opened but untouched, upon the chopping block. She lifted the beer and considered it but she didn't care for beer. There was a bottle of rye in the house, those rare occasions when she wanted a nightcap, always when alone, always silently toasting her father's memory first, then thinking of her mother, who best she let on, best Ruth knew, was happy rambling about the big empty house up on West Hill. Perhaps not so empty—filled as it must be with a lifetime, a good chunk of which Ruth had no memory or even knowledge of. Ruth sank down on the round of raw, freshly sawn wood, the sweet scent of autumn rising from it, and considered her day. Which had been grand until an hour ago but that hour was enough to sour everything. And she was to blame. All he'd been doing was making sure they'd be warm in the winter; proud of the new appliance, which, she could admit now, she also was happy to have in the house; and wanting to share that moment with her. And now he was gone.

Her first thought was to go looking for him. Enough so that she walked to the Chevy and sat behind the wheel. There, she didn't calm so much as slowly realize that he'd left because he didn't want to be there and she was responsible for that. She leaned and rested her forehead against the wheel with the weight of her fault.

After a while she went in the house and changed to jeans and a workshirt and moved all of the split wood to the cellar, trundling down the rough stairs through the bulkhead and up again. Even with her small loads the work was finished soon enough. She took up the axe and set it down again—she'd never split wood and knew this wasn't the time to try and learn. Dusk was pooling from the shadows as the sun sank and she was suddenly cool, the sweat drying against her as the day died. She thought again of driving about the village but knew she wouldn't find him.

She returned to the house and stood before her desk, turned the light on and off again. There would be no work done this evening. Finally she went to the new Frigidaire and stood before it, listening to the hum. She reached and tugged the handle and nothing happened, paused, and slid her hand to the other end and the door swung open. Bright and clean, a small fog of cool air rose about her. A truly wonderful thing. And she saw it was partly stocked—some few items from the icebox but a grocer's box worth of new items; jars of condiments, fresh eggs, a wedge of cheese in paper, a couple of other butcher-paper-wrapped bundles that she knew held bologna and hard salami and on top a larger package with the black grease pencil scrawl *T-bone*. A treat clearly intended for their supper. And a second bottle of Narragansett.

She opened the small freezer compartment. A cave lined with frost. Empty but for two metal trays with a lever along the top. New ice cubes in the making. A novelty for her. And she saw it then—the meal planned and the two beers for Oliver and the new ice for her own celebratory drink. This late in the fall the ice for the icebox was furred in sawdust and the ice pick largely retired—the ice only for keeping food fresh or worked over hard to free clean ice for special occasions.

She walked to her desk and stood looking at the telephone. Snow's Mercantile closed at seven but he might be there; where else would he have gone? On foot? Truth was, just about anywhere. Including his parents' house. But it was more that stopped her—the telephone switchboard was still in a side room of the Mercantile, one with its own entrance and otherwise apart from the store. But she couldn't bring herself to ring through and ask Doris Chapman to connect her to the store—Doris would know not only who it was, and if he was there or not, her calling would be noted. Especially if he was not there or did not answer. So wherever he was, he was beyond her.

She went and drew a bath, leaving the bathroom door open so a small shaft of light came through from the hall. She stripped out of her jeans and workshirt and again the smell of wood and her own sweat flooded her and she almost cried again. Then poured soap flakes from a box as the water thundered in and watched the small lather of bubbles rise. Lavender replaced wood and sweat. She tied up her hair and stepped in and sank down slowly until she was immersed, the nape of her neck resting against the lip of the tub, the soap bubbles swathing over her. Gently she scrubbed herself and then remained, lying in the tub with her kneecaps rising and gleaming in the light, staying until the water grew cool.

She pulled the plug with her toes and when the water had drained stood and toweled herself off. Reached up and untied her hair and shook it free, feeling damp cool ends flagging her shoulders. She left her clothes on the floor, kicking them into a corner, and padded down the hall and into the full dark of their bedroom, resisting the urge to turn on a light. She felt she deserved to be in the dark, a senseless penance but what she had. From the hook on the outside of the closet door she lifted down her summer nightgown and pulled it over her head. This night in September, she knew, would be cool enough so by morning she'd want flannel but was unwilling to rummage in the chest or closet or drawers—she had no idea where that nightgown might be. And, without Oliver, perhaps she deserved to be cold.

She was atremble throughout her and had the sudden urge for a cigarette, knowing even as she did that she was struggling to find, to make some connection with her abruptly absent husband. She was the one he could trust, the one who took him as he was, and she'd let him down. Her mind cast wide: Though he smoked he was occasional more than regular with the habit and wasn't like some men who kept cigarettes about the house. A pack in his pocket, was Oliver. Then had a memory of a week ago, perhaps more, when they'd been driving back from her mother's, back from a dinner where he'd been funny and charming and attentive and after the three hours he'd tossed the keys to her car to her and sat in the passenger seat while she drove home. But along that drive he'd pulled a crumpled pack from his trouser pocket and lighted a smoke and then opened the glove box and dropped the remainder of the pack within. Perhaps it had been empty, perhaps a bent cigarette or two remained.

She went down through the mostly dark house, pausing in the kitchen to find a book of matches in a drawer and went out into the night. On bare feet into early autumn dew, then the gravel of the drive, the car ahead a lump in the night. When she heard the sound.

A low keening. Muffled and distant and indistinct but a sound of pain. An animal caught or injured, possibly a human crying a terrible strangled register. She stepped back off the drive and into the dark, toward the bulkhead. And from there saw a wobbling light issuing from the single window of the workshop the back of the barn. There was no electricity in the barn and she walked on ginger toes along the side and the sound grew both more and less clear.

She rounded that back corner and stopped before she reached the window. The light was from an old kerosene lantern within. She tiptoed forward and peered through the glass.

There, seated on an old upturned apple crate was her husband. The lamp burned on the workbench he'd built that summer. His eyes were closed, his head bent down as he worked a bow against an old small fiddle.

She backed away from the window and stood fully on her bare feet in the cold grass. After a bit she went around to the woodpile and slowly and cautiously carried the smallest round her scrabbling fingers could find back around again to the back of the shed. She set it upright in the grass, out of the thrown rectangle of wobbling light and perched upon it, listening to her husband play the fiddle.

It was a simple piece he was playing, a jig or reel or lament—she had no idea, but the sort of song a child would learn. A single verse followed by a chorus, both of no more than a half-dozen notes, repeated over and over. There was a bit in the chorus where the tempo increased and he labored over that, slowing down in fact to find the notes and get them right. And in both chorus and verse he hit wrong notes and would pause and the bow would bounce and scrape and then he'd find his way again. Times he'd get it right all the way through and times that would happen over and again and he'd pick up the tempo a bit, seeking the time of the tune he heard in his mind against what he was playing. Then again he'd miss and scrape and halt and slowly find his way again into the song.

She sat a long time, listening. The log was small but large enough so she was able to lift her feet from the cold ground and tuck her heels atop the wood and hold her knees with her arms and rest her head on one shoulder. At one point she stole off the log and again glanced through the window, the least slice of vision into the room.

His head was lifted and his eyes were closed, his face lit by the glow of the lantern and a good bit more. The bow gliding and his fingers upon the neck of the fiddle moving as if the music was flowing through them down upon and out of the strings, the body of the little fiddle. She watched, long as she could. She'd never seen him so peaceful.

He was still playing when she went in to bed. When she woke in the morning he was beside her, his slumber deep. She slipped from bed and went down, the night almost as a dream, but knowing something had changed.

Something good, she hoped.

Five

Katey

She spent the night in Portland in a cheap motel on the edge of town. The windows didn't open and it was stuffy and warm, the sheets on the bed seemed to have been scraped with a dull razor and the mattress was lumpy. There was a television but it was connected to a device to feed quarters into and she wasn't about to spend money that way. She wished there was a radio but was also half-glad there wasn't. Music had not been kind, this day. She'd thought she wouldn't be able to sleep but moments after she turned off the light and heaved back and forth punching the pillow, she paused, then slept hard.

What happened was half an hour or so after leaving Machias she fell apart. All she'd been doing was driving south, backtracking her day, the road toward Ellsworth, tumbling gently all that she'd just left, small tentative probes from her mind about the people she'd met, who they were, how they'd looked upon her, what they'd said, the impossibility of it all and yet a sense of determination was gritting along within and then "Homeward Bound" came on the radio and she broke down. Pulled off in a sandy turnout past a crossroad hamlet that had no name, or not one she'd seen. She was weeping with her forehead against the wheel.

Home, homeward. She wanted to go home—the house on Beacon Hill, her bedroom, the living room, kitchen. She'd left town without telling anyone. She wanted her mother, her father, his kind placid somewhat quizzical eyes, the moments of tentativeness she caught out on him since she'd been told the truth, and her heart felt to be a raw swollen thing cramping inside her. The money in the envelope—she guessed she'd lost her job now but there remained the letter from the University welcoming her to the class of 1970. There was money enough, she knew. From her grandmother dead these five years. She wanted to call home but couldn't, what would she say? They knew, she was certain, what she was up to. Many things, but her mother was no fool and would've discovered the missing Christmas cards if she even needed to look—again, how much did they know before she'd even undertaken this trip, how much guessed at what she'd do? Her father, certainly. The one who watched her. Her mother, less so. Pinned down into her dry dutiful life, grinding on, living through her work, a loveless marriage.

What she endured. Her mother. What she endured to walk each day about the halls of the school, to maintain herself in the village, the town. Her sense of self. Arch and removed. Brittle. Yet proud also, her chin high, mouth set firm. It was as if, Katey thought, there were two Ruth Hale Snows: the daughter of her parents, and the wife of her husband. And there also, as if on a cushion of air, she floated through both identities within the town, the village, her work at school, for the simple and extraordinary reason that the town saw both of these Ruths, understood, accepted and even embraced both.

Or tolerated because they had no choice. And who among them would give voice to that toleration?

She wanted to call home and could not. Whoever answered, whoever accepted the charges, she couldn't speak to. Neither of them on an early summer Sunday afternoon.

But Virginia seemed impossible. The *idea* of Virginia seemed impossible. Not only the considerable distance but following through on this impulse. Not so simple an impulse she reminded herself but then had no idea what it was. Some emptiness wanted filling.

Her nose and chin dripped snot and her eyes were sore. She sat up, using both hands to push upright from the wheel and heard and felt the smacking suck as her forehead pulled free.

Outside, beyond the windshield, the afternoon lay before her. Lovely and long. And it came to her then: I don't have to decide anything right now. I'm on my own. And like a small distant bell ringing clear up a valley on a Sunday morning she recalled Molly Ivey talking about the health food store in Portland. And thought Maybe, this day, that's enough, to stay close but see something I never seen before. To take a bit of time, to allow her mind to settle. To allow the day a chance to settle. And out of that some direction might well arise.

She still hadn't figured out distance. Midafternoon and even on Route 1 South it seemed she jigged and jagged north or west along or around the inlets and bays as much or more than headed south. South-southwest was what it was. When she finally got into Portland she drove the angled streets of the rundown downtown and stopped twice on bold whims to stop passersby and ask where Milk & Honey was. The first knew nothing, almost alarmed by her or the question. Circled three more blocks and saw a kid, a teenage boy kicked back against a lamppost, smoking a cigarette tucked into the corner of his mouth. Maybe fifteen. He listened, then swept her up and down with lust-addled eyes he failed to hide with a curl of scorn in his voice as he told her.

Walking distance. So she fed a nickel into a meter and locked the truck and walked.

Still warm but with a rosy-tint westward, lengthening pale shadows, shafts of golden light pooling down cross-streets. The store was small, the one wide window a spatter of mimeographs, ads, small broadsides; above that on the glass puffy letters in a rainbow of colors naming the store, the two words curled around each other, the letters distorted to make a circle. It took a moment to parse but whenever she glanced back she wondered how it could've confused her—so clear it seemed. Another sign with the hours, closed for the night. She leaned close to the glass and cupped her hands against the glare and peered inside. Best she could see it held a jumble of bins and large jars, hanging utensils and cooking equipment she didn't recognize. And more crazy-quilt paint upon the walls. But also up front and center in that window was an old hand-pushed wheeled garden cultivator, a close replica of the one her dad used. And this glimpse of the familiar was enough to hold her overnight. To find a motel and return in the morning. A welter of curiosity, she was. And, unaccountable, a tremble of delicious excitement. The first articulate glimmer that her own mission was far more than what she'd laid out for herself. Not only chasing the past but some tendrils snaking toward her. Of what to come, was already coming. A new world from that of her parents. Hers.

She drove around the block twice and had the location set in her mind and then eased out of the old city and found the motel. Then walked down a couple of blocks and found a diner open and mostly empty on a Sunday night. She ordered a grilled cheese sandwich and a bowl of tomato soup, broke oyster crackers into the soup and ate. Drank a root beer and paid up and tipped a dime to the older waitress and went out and in the falling warm twilight walked back up to her motel and let herself in. And slept. In the morning she was parked outside Milk & Honey when it opened at ten. As she pressed through the door a set of small brass chimes tinkled, a pleasant welcoming sound. It seemed she was alone in the store although a small turn-table was set up on one shelf and speakers attached high in the corners, the music the sweet ache of love, or solace—recordings her mother owned—Bach's cello suites recorded by Pablo Casals. She wandered. Along with the bins and crocks of dried grains and beans, flour and meal, there were also big jars of nuts and seeds. All with handwritten labels in an ornate script. Most of the varieties were ones she didn't recognize—some few names she knew but had either never seen or seen in their raw state. There was a rack of gallon Mason jars filled with dried herbs, again all labeled, again only a handful she knew. And some of those few she had never thought of as herbs. These held labels with more description—what the herbs could be used for, in tonics, teas, infusions.

She wandered on. There was no cash register but the counter near the front was clear enough. Upon it, among many other things, was a small brass ringed dish with a cone of incense burning. A rich and soothing curl of scent throughout the store. She'd heard about incense but never seen any and so leaned close and inhaled and her nose tickled and she reared back, wondering if this was something like pot. Or pot hidden by another name. Then saw a smaller shelf that held packages of different sizes, most labeled in a strange script she'd never seen before—some few in rough block-print English. She picked up two or three at random and smelled—each was different, each was lovely. A vague sense of peace and ease came over her. She wandered on.

Past food mills and mortar-and-pestle sets (which she recognized from Chemistry) though these were in marble or other stone, others in the same worked brass of the incense burners. Tea strainers made from metal, also bamboo. Distinct designs but their function was clear. Short knives with wide blades and grooves in the blades for a purpose she couldn't discern. Pottery teapots glazed in colors and designs she'd never guessed might exist, but did. A rack of soaps and lotions; again nothing she'd ever seen but there was a comfortable feel to the smells of the raw bar soaps, reading the labels of the other products—Dr. Bronner's Castile Soap—We Are All One and on down in small print endless or at least she didn't get through it all—again she felt like she was stumbling toward a home she'd known was waiting her to join but even this moment, she wasn't sure where she was, what this place, however comfortable, intriguing, confusing, what exactly it was. For her.

The side of the album came to an end and the needle rested, popping a slow twitch of amplified sound. Then behind her she heard a swish and turned to see a panel of raw burlap lifted as a man pushed through. He walked around behind the counter and, eyes on her, placed the arm back in the cradle and flipped the album with his fingertips and set the needle back in the first groove. And said, "Good morning, young lady. What may I do to assist you?"

He had an accent she had no means of placing, although in a vague sense he sounded like Groucho. But he was short and gently rounded, with a thick mustache and wispy flyaway thin hair almost down to his shoulders; his face reminded her of Albert Einstein. He was not what she'd expected, though she couldn't quite say who she'd expected except someone younger, much younger. A few years older than herself. Perhaps in a paisley Nehru jacket or striped bell-bottoms or both. She flushed, feeling her ignorance, ideas born from television and magazines; only the music she heard, the album covers and liner notes she pored over, felt as if that world existed.

She said, "Yesterday up past Belfast I met a woman who told me about this place. She fed me some bread she'd made; it wasn't anything like I'd eaten before but it was real good. And I was driving back down today and thought I'd stop in." His eyes were a watery blue, the whites rimmed a bit red as he held them on her as if expecting more and so she nigh blurted, "Casals. Cello suites. Aren't they sublime?"

He said, "Pablo Casals discovered them, you know. They were not played. Practice, maybe. He found old sheet music and played them for years and years, knowing from the first, I think, that he had found something no one else had. Perhaps that is what makes genius. Seeing what is before us in a new way and then digging, digging, deeper and deeper—for that is what it was to practice those suites for so many years—"

"How many years?"

"I don't know—a dozen, twenty? A long time. Because he was reaching for something he heard in his mind, that he heard from the page, maybe pieces from his instrument, for a very long time, before his cello matched what his mind heard from the page. That is something to ponder, yes?" He gave an almost sly smile and before she could respond he went on: "This woman is Molly Ivey Lucerne. She is an interesting woman. Smart. Smarter than perhaps she knows. But she understands the food. Food. Now wait."

He came past the counter and went to one of the shelves, took down a jar, then walked down an aisle for a round package in bright colors with a label she could not read. He came back around the counter and said, "It's mostly the young people. Which is a good thing, because the young will carry it forward, will bring the world back into balance, if such is possible. Perhaps," and he looked up and smiled at her. "Perhaps possible is the best we can hope for. But wait again. We don't know each other—another problem. So much, people today, they go to the supermarket, the clothing store, wherever, and make business with strangers. Is this good? I don't think so. We need to know one another. The world is big but small, yes? We must know each other or the danger is great. The world only grows larger, out and out and out and soon it does not matter, soon we expect only to deal with strangers. So, I am Ernst Behr. You are?"

"I'm Katey Snow."

He made a small bow of his head and extended a hand and she took his hand. He did not shake it the way she was used to but held it within his and he said, "It is a blessing to meet you, Miss Katey

132

Snow." Then lifted both their hands and pressed dry lips to the back of her hand and released it, gentle as freeing a small bird.

She had no idea how to respond, to thank him, to offer a blessing in return, or just wait and see what happened next. So she did.

He was already at work, there on the counter. He opened the jar and lifted a mug from a rack overhead and poured a dense juice, lighter than cider but full and thick and then tore open the package and pulled free a thick round of dry bubbly cracker and broke it into pieces and arrayed the pieces next to the mug.

"There," he said. "This is organic pear juice from California. You know pear juice? Delicious. Drink this, you drink autumn. The bread is a dry bread made to last most of forever. Originally from Armenia. Made here by Armenians, old family. Old food. This same bread has been made three thousand years. Think of that. Now, try."

"It's good." The juice was sweet upon her tongue but also she felt as well as tasted the fruit. As if she was drinking a pear. And the bread, the thick cracker, was salty and slightly sweet and then, as she chewed, both bread and juice seemed to transform within her mouth and become some other food altogether.

"Yes," he said, his eyes still upon her. As if he saw the transformation. He smiled then and said, "What else can I help you with this morning?"

"Who are you? Where did you come from? Why are you here?"

His smile was gone. "Good questions, Katey Snow." He paused and looked away and then back. "I am the man who is where he is, because it's where I must be. Such is life. The juice is a gift. And you want the bread—I'll sell you a new package. And, and, your journey: As Steiner said, 'That which secures life from exhaustion lies in the unseen world, deep at the roots of things.'"

Then he went again across the room and plucked up two folded-down and taped brown paper bags from separate shelves and set them on the counter. He said, "These you want, also. Dried apricots without sulfur, and almonds. All together, food complete. Yes?"

133

"What do you mean? Apricots without sulfur?"

He cocked an eyebrow and said, "You have eaten dried apricots?"

"At Christmas my mother gets them as a treat. Dates, also."

"Dates are good, yes. But the apricots. What color are they?"

"Orange? Maybe bright yellow?"

"Have you ever eaten a fresh apricot? In summer?"

"No. They don't grow in Vermont."

"Or Maine. But they are that color. Orange-yellow. So people expect apricots to be orange, always. But when fruit is dried, the color changes. As with raisins, yes? You understand?"

"Yes."

"Now, raisins, they are not called dried grapes. Like prunes; dried plums."

"Because they have different names . . ."

"Exactly."

"What does this have to do with sulfur?"

"Any fruit can be dried. Always this has been the case. But we have fallen away from that knowledge. A dried grape is a raisin, a dried plum is a prune. But what is a dried apricot?"

"A dried apricot?"

"Yes. But then. The problem." He tore the tape and unfolded the top of the bag and held a round brown oval, wrinkled and ridged, out to her. "You see? This does not look like fruit. Maybe a dried ear. Another story. But so the scientists, the food scientists, they discover by spraying these dried apricots with sulfur, they stay bright orange. They look, what. More like an apricot. Which is good, yes?"

"I guess."

"Exactly." He leaned toward her. "Except it's not. Now, every-thing on earth comes from the earth. Sulfur is not bad for us. As it is, small amounts, in water, food. But to make apricots look different? That is not good. Why must a dried apricot look like anything but a dried apricot? There is no reason. To be able to do a thing, that is not enough reason to do something. Believe me. I know."

She thought about all of this, all that had been said. And came back to her question of who he was and his vague answer and something of that morning, something else of those past months rang clear within her and she returned to what he'd said when she asked who he was, where he was from. His vagueness but also his willingness to share.

She said, "What you said, about the unseen world, the root of things that saves us, something like that? Where did that come from?"

He studied her a moment. Then said, "Wait." He turned and walked back through the store, through the burlap curtain and was gone. She fiddled with the paper bags, curious about the apricots. Aware also that there came from Ernst Behr a comfort, a sense of a man who held a weight upon him, within him, but also a man who offered no threat. Who seemed to hold an understanding that he wished only to pass along. And so was patient, curious. She was a little enthralled, knowing she was meeting someone whom she'd only vaguely sensed, perhaps only dreamed about.

He returned carrying before his chest in both hands a slender book with worn blue cloth bindings. He went again behind the counter as if to keep this space between them was in some formal way important to him. Wordless, he handed the book to her. It was about the size of *The Catcher in the Rye* but thinner, less than half a deck of cards. Centered on the front was flecked and faded gilt lettering. *On Anthroposophy.*

She wanted to open it, scan the pages but did not. She knew, from books her mother and her grandmother had owned that the pages were of thin paper and the type was fine—that the book held more than it appeared it might. She held it and waited.

Ernst Behr also waited, watching how she held the book. Finally he said, "That is a collection taken from various writings; a book made from other books, if you will. From the writings of Rudolf Steiner. Who I quoted earlier. It is a book you can read from first page to last but also a book you may open wherever and touch upon a thought, a wisdom, that will help explain whatever question life might bring before you." Then he smiled and lifted his shoulders in a great shrug. "Or not. At that moment. Perhaps it will be later. Some things work that way."

"I'm learning that's true."

He smiled and then his smile faded and he was silent a long moment, his eyes cast down, his face serious and she watched him and felt the sadness emanate from him. She waited. Perhaps he felt her waiting, perhaps he only needed the moment but he looked back at her and his features were calm, at ease within himself again as he had been.

He said, "You asked who I am, where I came from. Those are very important and difficult questions to answer in the usual understanding. But let me say this: When I was your age, even ten years after that, I thought I knew all of what life wanted of me, all of who I was. And then greater events, larger forces took control. Terrible times, times no person should have to endure and times that some way or another it seems most people have to endure. All places, even the ones that think it has not happened to them and so it will not happen. But those terrible times happen over and over, all places. Perhaps not to you. Or not yet. But to others, less distant than you think. But me—what helped me survive those times of my own, beyond a great amount of fortune, luck, were the ideas I held dear and true to me. That I knew were true however much the world around me insisted upon proving they were not true. Because what beats strongest in the human heart is not what is, but what may be. And this leads us, and, also leaves us, with the philosophers, the visionaries—those who think and can articulate that thinking, in ways the rest of us can grasp. And hold on to. Because we know there is truth there. It is almost like religion but with a small but very important difference: We understand we hold the power of change within us. Even if the world does not seem so at the time. We know it is mankind that can make change. Sound simple? No, it's very hard. But true. And knowing that, for myself, made possible to survive what couldn't otherwise be survived."

Katey placed the book upon the counter next to the food and studied it, ran her fingertips up and down, the fabric so worn she could feel the threads, the small indentations where the gilt was stamped through. Took a breath and looked up and said, "Ernst Behr."

"Yes."

"You're German. You were in the war."

"I am. I was."

She held a breath, thinking. Remembering the afternoon before. And did not so much take a chance as say what had to be said.

"My dad was also in the war."

He said, "American. The good guys."

"Well, they were! The British couldn't have done it alone. And the Russians, well, we know how that worked out."

"Ach, yes. It was all very complicated. Not so much for America but for the Continent, East and West, very complicated. Nothing was as it seemed except for this: There were only bad ideas and worse ideas and all of it was like a very bad rainstorm, where all you got was more mud, long days growing even longer, roofs leaking, cellars flooding. All upside down one day and even more upside down the next. But you go on the best you can, doing what you have to do, what you are told to do. Very much doing your best at all times to at least appear you are doing all you are told to do—also simply hoping to survive—nothing lasts forever although there are things you almost wish not to survive and there are times when it seems the worst might indeed last forever. And then you begin to see that it

137

won't. In ways those were the best and most horrible of times. There was hope, held hidden deep inside again. And fear. Desperation pushes out the deep ugliness in many men, especially men with any power at all. And . . . Well, Katey Snow. I am here. So I survived. I see the question in you—No, I was not a Nazi. I never joined the party. That made it more difficult to survive the early years except for the strength within my spirit. Which can be squashed like a bug—I saw this many times. But I also knew others. I was not alone. Even the times it felt that way, deep down, always, I knew I was not alone. Even if I did not survive I knew I was not alone."

And he reached then and, much like she had, ran his fingers over the book. Then he looked up at her and said, "So. I am here in Maine. Selling food and other good things. How a life turns out."

Then he turned away. But not before she saw the welling in his eyes. He walked the two steps to the turntable and lifted the needle from where it was softly popping and only then did she realize the music was gone. He didn't flip the record again but only placed the arm in its cradle and dialed the power knob down to off and there came a final pop through the speaker.

While he was still turned away in a small voice she said, "My father won't talk about the war."

He swung slowly to her and said, "Most men don't."

"Some do. Several kids I know, their dads were all in the service. And those men, they've told stories. They go to the VFW—that's the—"

"I know what it is. And they sit and drink beer and talk, tell stories. Where they were, what they did, how it was. Yes?"

"My dad goes. On Thursday nights. But he doesn't talk."

"Neither do I. Talk about the war. I don't mean your VFW." And he made a small smile. "I doubt I would be welcome there, even if I was inclined. But I'm not. Those men, they talk of things that might be true, might not be true. What they might wish was true. Or even, what they say is not what happened but what they wished had happened. Instead of what did. Do you understand?"

"No. Maybe."

"What is inside those men, all men, what they did or saw, for each it's different. It's memory. Memory is like dreams. Parts feel as if you can reach out and touch—other parts are gone. Just, gone. You make sense best you can. Each and every person differently. Sometimes this is because of what you, this person, actually did or saw, witnessed. Other times it's what you failed to do. And even more times, strangest maybe but like dreams, it's a collision, better word maybe, collapse, of memory and dream. So you don't know what is real, what the mind allows us to know. So. How to cope with this? Some men talk, truth or hope of truth. Some stay quiet. Again, truth or hope. And, then, this also, plenty of men know very well what they saw or did and this also makes them talk to try and change, or remain silent—if they deny memory a voice then it does not have one. Yes? You see, I am saying there are as many reasons for how a man responds to war, such terrible war, after, as there are men. How it is."

She wanted to tell him that her father didn't talk to most people about almost anything at all. But she didn't know how to explain this, to explain all of him to this wondrous stranger. So she said, "What he does, my father, is he fixes fiddles. He repairs them, I mean. From accidents or sometimes just age."

"Fiddles? You mean to say violins?"

"That's right. Just, most of those who he works for, they play fiddle tunes, old tunes come down within families. Dance music, mostly. But they're violins. I don't think a one of them has ever been used to play anything but those old dances; jigs and reels and old ballads."

"No. You misunderstand. He plays? He also plays these violins?"

"Of course. His dad and grandfather did, too. That's how it got started."

139

Ernst Behr nodded. "So music. A man does not wish to talk but he makes music. You do not understand?"

"Music." She paused, uncertain. Deeply not wanting to be wrong but suddenly seeing the direct line between what her music meant to her and what his might for her father.

Behr was flushed, lit with his understanding. He said, "Always. Forever. As long as it's been. Music, the making of music, allows a person to express what they feel but that which words cannot hold. Where language fails. Music, making that, allows the soul to express itself. To release joy, yes, but anguish also. What can't be said in words can be said in music—No. Can be released in music. Arising from within the battered soul, flowing out, measures of peace found, released. But, also like those stories other men tell, never complete. So is done again and again. Is this the man you're speaking of?"

"I think so."

"If you think, so it is. So, you see—he has been telling his stories of the war. His war. Perhaps now you can listen?"

Again she said, "I think so." And then trembling throughout but not knowing she was until she spoke again she said, "Thank you."

"You're welcome, Katey Snow. Now, shall we settle?" He spread his hand, palm down and fingers open over the food on the counter.

At the same time came the light jingle of the brass chimes over the door. His eyes went up and she turned, wanting to see who had broken the conversation; also, who had entered this rare space.

The girl was wearing overalls smeared with dirt and trails of fine sawdust, a pumpkin-orange T-shirt likewise dirty and with dried sweat stains under her armpits, L. L. Bean hunting boots with the rubber bottoms and leather uppers, the boots laced tight around her ankles with the tops spread open and the overalls tucked down within. Her hair was long and blonde, parted roughly in the middle and falling about her face. On her back she had an Army surplus rucksack of green canvas and leather straps. Filled but not bulging. In one hand she held a round leather case, as if for maps. She looked left, right, peering as if seeking something, then her eyes slowly settled upon the two at the counter.

Ernst Behr said, "Good morning, young lady. And how may I assist you?"

So close to the way he'd greeted Katey if not the exact words; she could not remember now. And felt a pang of jealousy or something like that; the intimacy of what he'd just shared with her, how he'd known and responded to her tentative queries suddenly seemed open to whoever walked through the door. And the girl was someone walked off the pages of *Life* or *Newsweek*, out of the television news. A creature strange, unknown. And who now lifted one arm to unsling the rucksack and dropped it to the floor, then rested the leather tube across it, gently.

She straightened and spoke, eyes sweeping Katey quickly and then settling on Behr. "Can I get a little honey and tahini? And some pita? I missed breakfast to catch a ride up from Harpswell with Jean to 1 and thumbed down here. Got dumped at a diner and just standing outside the air reeked of rancid grease so I kept coming. I'm about starved, man. Ah, hold on. I'm so burned I'm not thinking. Steven told me to stop here if I could. Feels like a thousand years ago. But I got a list."

She slid down on her knees and began to dig through her rucksack. "Hold on, hold on, I know it's somewhere."

"Steven? You are from Franconia?" Behr said. "You're hitchhiking, how will you mange? Steven buys bulk lots."

The girl was cross-legged and held a composition book, leafing through pages. With one hand she kept pushing hair behind one ear only to have it fall free again. She looked up. "Here it is. Yeah. Hundred pounds of whole wheat, forty of lentils, another—well, here, I'll just tear it out and leave it with you. Steven or one of us'll drive over next week to pick it up." She grinned. "If that works. I'm Phoebe."

141

She pushed up off the floor and walked over. She had a loose-limbed stride, both easy and sensual, as if she worked outside and also knew her body well, all ways.

Ernst Behr said, "So, Harpswell? You've been to the Readings'?"

"We're having some problems with building. Well, not problems so much as things we wanted to make sure we got right. And since I was the one who drew them, it seemed best for me to take the plans and come see how it should look when it's done. And ask a few questions. I liked Lawrence well enough but Jean's a little uptight. You'd've thought the whole idea came from Lawrence, the way she acted."

"I haven't been there but saw photographs in the paper. The big dome's impressive. A grand thing. And the article said they're building a second one. Is that right?"

"Oh, it's more than that! The second one is set up like a workshop—part office and part hands-on school—where people can come see how it's done. But what was really groovy is the third dome they've got going—made to be a greenhouse to grow food year-round. It's almost done so this summer they can test out the soil and the irrigation and get the vents working to release heat when it's too hot and then by fall they'll have a good idea how it works, practice, not theory, and then see how much they need to fire up the wood heaters and how much the sun and natural condensation works. It's real gone, man. On the coast of frickin Maine."

"Ambitious? Yes. But then, the world is full of new ideas, always. Some good, some bad. Exciting when they are good. Did you get the answers to your questions, there at Harpswell?"

"Mostly. I think. The inherent tension capacity of the triangle wasn't really in question—but we've been having problems with the curve ratio as we go up. And I think I got that answered. But also, I think we might have some issues with the base platform, we mighta got that wrong and if that's what it is, well, there's not any of us going to be happy. But better now than later, is how I see it."

Behr nodded. "All things are such. More rare to see it so, Phoebe. Let me see the list, now. You say a week, maybe two?" He took the paper and leaned over it, frowning as he ticked an index finger down.

"What's the problem, man?"

"Oh, there is no problem. I have all of this. But it's much inventory to hold, not sure when it will be sold. You understand? My suppliers, they're once a month by truck. What happens, I hold all of this and run out for the people who walk in the door?"

"No, no. I can pay you, I got the bread. It's no problem."

"Yes, that is good. But still, these two weeks? I am a small space. This is—" He glanced back at the list, then to Phoebe. "This is five, six hundred pounds of food. Paid for but I'm storing it. Precious room to store what I must buy, for, say, people who walk in and want five pounds of lentils. What do I tell them—the lentils I have are sold so come back a week, maybe two and I will have more?"

"I think that's your problem, man."

"And I say Steven may come purchase what he wishes and take it away." He spread his arms wide. "Look. I am a small space. And that, I like. But my storage is in the basement below—even smaller than this space."

Katey had been listening, off to the side, ignored, and feeling as if the two were speaking a language she did not know. French she knew better than this exchange. But for a single word—also the vague sense of a door. A possibility.

She said, "Franconia? New Hampshire?"

Phoebe turned and gave Katey a long appraisal up and down that lasted seconds. Phoebe was maybe twenty—Katey's guess—but also clearly light-years away, and both recognized that. Katey flushed hot and sucked in the smallest bit of lip between her teeth, to remind herself of herself, to not be overwhelmed by this girl. Whose eyes pegged her as the country-mouse that she was. Still, Katey knew she might hold a trump card and so waited in silence. Something she'd learned from her mother. Or, it came to her, perhaps her father as well. Or more so.

"Yeah," Phoebe said. "Franconia College." Her voice still larded with doubt.

"Over 302, right?"

Phoebe paused again, reconsidering many things, Katey guessed. And was suddenly nervous herself, for other reasons than before. Phoebe said, "You headed that way?"

I can be, Katey thought. Unsure if she should be but also intrigued. Her mind held the map still and knew it wasn't more than a three- or four-hour drive. It wasn't as if she had a plan, a clear plan. She said, "Yup."

Phoebe took a breath, let it out. Katey got it—remembering when she was a freshman, how the senior girls ignored, or cut glances, remarks. Until they needed something. Phoebe said, "You heard. It's almost four hundred pounds of food. What you're driving, can it handle that? You're not driving a Beetle, are you?"

And Ernst Behr spoke up. "If she is, it wouldn't matter. An honest hardworking automobile. Load the backseat—it's no more weight than a couple of good-sized ladies, yes?"

Katey said, "I'm parked right out front. The Dodge pickup truck. Under the hood is a flathead 6. Pile whatever you want in the bed— all it'll do is make the truck drive better. You need help with that?"

Phoebe had hooded her eyes. Ernst Behr flicked a smile upon Katey, then returned to the list. Katey rolled back on the heels of her sneakers and popped her thumbs through the belt loops of her jeans and waited. Phoebe looked up and said, "Getting this stuff there today would be cool. Bread for gas?"

Katey considered the unknown, then said, "Let's see how it goes."

Phoebe's arms were brown and wiry-strong but Katey kept right up with her as they loaded the factory-sized sacks of flours, beans, grains, the ten-pound tub of honey, another of peanut butter. Several cardboard cases of tinned goods, jarred goods. Then finally a regular paper grocery sack of lesser items Phoebe had purchased for herself. And Katey's crackers, jar of pear juice, almonds and dried apricots in their own sack. And the book.

Ernst Behr paused her within the store, his hand on her elbow, Phoebe already in the truck, waiting. He said, "They are young, full of ideas, ideals, also. Good people but young. Not as young as you perhaps but perhaps not as old, either. Trust yourself, is what I mean to tell you. And Steven Christensen, he has wisdom but not as much as he thinks. Or what the others think. Remember that. And also, this: On your journey, Katey Snow, remember me. What we talked about, I have talked about with few others. There now, go in peace, keep eyes open wide."

He was pressing her hand again between both of his and she said, "I will," and swiftly leaned and kissed his cheek.

She followed the signs for 302 out of town and then once again was traveling through the countryside, aware she was headed west, vaguely toward home and so all that lay behind her seemed also to now be in front of her. And also was vigilant for the road signs as they passed through towns and other roads intersected—for all obvious reasons she didn't want to make the first wrong turn with this older girl beside her, the cargo in the back. She was filled with questions but wanted to ask the right one. And she didn't know what that was. So she drove and dug in the paper sack and lifted out the almonds and apricots and set them on the bench seat and then took out the jar of juice and tucked it between her legs. She twisted off the cap and set it upside down on the dashboard. Driving. Aware Phoebe was watching her.

She said, "You came in saying you were hungry. So am I. We can share, or eat your own, I'm happy either way. But can I ask a question?"

"You like tahini?"

"I don't know what it is."

"It's ground-up sesame seeds. Like peanut butter, only better."

"That sounds good."

"I'll make sandwiches. What's your question?"

It was a pretty June day. A few ragged high white clouds against a blue sky. Both cab windows down and the air through them pleasant, neutral, sweeping through the truck. Rolling over gentle hills, past farms, houses, through small villages. Monday morning. People at work. The road empty. Phoebe had a Swiss army knife and also an old mess kit dug from her backpack resting on the floor at her feet. She twisted off the lid of the tahini jar and used a metal folding spoon to stir the separated oil back into the thicker paste. Between her legs she had an unopened jar of dark wildflower honey and had opened the bag of pita and torn two in half. She paused and glanced at Katey.

Katey said, "I guess it's two questions."

"I can handle that." And grinned. And suddenly she seemed more at ease, relaxed, no longer the older girl but a fellow traveler.

"So, where was it you were coming from? I mean, what were you doing? I didn't understand most of what you and Mr. Behr were talking about. And, where are we going? I mean, I know where Franconia is, generally. But I never heard of Franconia College and I just spent the last year looking up what I thought was every college in Vermont and New Hampshire plus a few others."

"Aw, man, where'd you learn to count? I'm kidding. I'm just kind of toasted. Ready to get home. Let's start there. Franconia College is a different sort of school. Best seen, not described. Which in a couple hours you'll have the chance to do. Might be your bag, maybe not. But for me, it's home. At least for now. It's brothers and sisters. You'll see.

"And I just spent a week down on the coast with some old folks who were hip to it all a long time ago. They got cool shit going down but they're old. Like the dude back there with the store—he's got a good trip happening but thinks he's in 1935 or something. You know? Okay, the Readings, Lawrence and Jean? They been there on the coast of Maine growing organic and living with only what they can make or trade for years and years—he was an old socialist or Wobbly. He's written books, ya know? And he got the dome thing early on and met Bucky a long time ago and so they tore down the house they had there and built a dome and that worked so they built another. Which was why I was there. A crew of us are building one beside the beaver pond at Franconia. And like most things, you get deep enough in and questions come up. So I went over there to talk to the Readings. Larry, what he asked me to call him, he was helpful, looked over our plans and listened to the issues we're dealing with and then walked me around and pointed out where they'd run into the same problems, or close enough, and how they solved them. Not answers—every moment, every problem, every question in life has a different answer. But good clues; he's a smart old goat. So I got a pretty good idea what to do once I got home but was helping out, a way to pay for what I'd been given and so spent a couple days working in their gardens, the big ones outside—aw chick, soil smelled so good you could almost eat it, but it was long days and yesterday evening before supper I walked down the spit to one of the tidal pools and there was nobody else there so I stripped down and was being washed clean by the churning water, so sweet that was, I felt like a grandmother was rocking me in her arms and then I finally stepped out—I didn't want to miss supper, there was only the one chance—and grabbed my clothes and was dancing about to dry off and just feeling the sun at the end of a lovely day and looked up and there was Jean, on the rocks above me. I stood waiting while she walked down and she asked me was I waiting for Lawrence and I told her No and she asked me if he'd told me to come down here and I told her No and she looked me up and down and I looked her straight back, a wizened old woman trying to protect what she couldn't if he decided not to let her and I knew that and so did she. Then she told me she'd drive me up to 1 first thing in the morning and I told her I was down with that, all I could learn from him I already had, and there wasn't anything from her I wanted or cared to learn that I hadn't already.

"And then, silent but side by side, we walked up to the guest dome and she had soup and bread waiting for me and she left me there. It was just me, most of the time they have a bunch of freaks there, working for free and basking at the knees of Jean and Larry. So later I rolled one and walked out and sat up high on a rock where I could look down on the starlight dancing on the water and it all felt good. Ya know? I'd gotten what I needed. And Jean didn't piss me off anymore. Because she couldn't."

Throughout this Phoebe had been a brisk efficiency, smearing torn pita with tahini and honey and passing them over to Katey and eating while talking while also grubbing through the sacks for almonds and the dried apricots and offering them to Katey while eating also and there was something in this, along with the spill of words that gave Katey comfort; as if the girl beside her was a strange creature never before seen but glimpsed somehow, deeply familiar. So comfortable in who she was and what she was doing, where she'd just come from but also where she was going. And, it seemed, where Katey also was going. A dual stab of curiosity and anxiety about that. She told herself that once she got there she could unload and go on. Or maybe stay for the afternoon. How Phoebe had talked about the college; home. Of a different sort than any Katey had known.

She said, "These apricots, you gotta chew em. But they taste awful good. I like the rest of it, too."

Phoebe looked over and grinned. Then reached a finger and dabbed it against Katey's cheek and took it away and rubbed the spot of tahini onto her overalls. She said, "It's almost like they set out to hide the world from us, you know?"

148

"Yeah. I think so."

Phoebe pulled a pack of rolling papers from the bib of her overalls and then a small paper sack and Katey had a small panic but it was only a sack of Bugler tobacco and Phoebe made a cigarette. She held it between her fingers and made no move to light it. She said, "You know this one?"

"Which one?"

Phoebe sang, barely, "There's something happening here . . ."

She waited and then Katey sang, "What it is ain't exactly clear . . ."

And both together sang mostly through the rest, both garbling parts but both also rising up hard and clear on the chorus, louder and stronger and the more they sang the more the song came to them and they sang the final verse and chorus three times around without stopping, whooping it through the cab and out the windows and when they finally trailed off Phoebe lifted a clenched fist and pumped it three times and in the silence ringing turned and said, "Yeah. That's what it's all about."

Then they were out of North Conway up toward Glen and saw a sign for Santa's Workshop and one for Story Land and beyond that Jackson but followed the curve in the road, dropping into the eastern end of Crawford Notch. Phoebe lit her cigarette and pushed down in her seat, lifted her arms to cross behind her head. She said, "It's a couple hours to Bethlehem. I'm gonna crash for a bit. As you mighta guessed, it was a weird weekend and I'm fried. But wake me up in Bethlehem, okay?"

"So I don't miss the turn?"

Phoebe grinned and said, "How'd you get so smart?"

"Just lucky I guess."

"Or local. But yeah, wake me up."

"You mind if I play the radio?"

"Anything good, turn it up loud. You heard Hendrix yet? Joplin?"

"I don't know. Maybe."

"You'd know if you had."

She'd forgotten. As the truck rolled down into the depths of Notch the memory came back, a flitting but soothing thing. Years and years ago, perhaps ten or twelve she'd ridden over here, coming the other way, with her dad to deliver a fiddle to a man up somewhere beyond Jackson. She'd been six or seven. She recalled it was an early fall day, waking in the morning—it must've been a Saturday because neither her mother or she was up early for school, waking in her bedroom that was above the living room just off the kitchen and through the open grate in her floor she could hear her parents and her dad talking in that soft easy and determined voice of his, only determined if you knew him, how soft his voice was, and she stirred from sleep to those voices from below and so woke knowing the day before her was going to be an adventure. Her mother was not protesting but in the way she had was trying to make sure this was what her father really wanted, that it was no whim and Katey was wide awake by then. Hearing her dad say, "Now she's started school, I don't see as much of her as I like. It would be nice for both of us." Her mother had said, "Because she's started school doesn't mean you have to spend less time with her," and after that was a silence and she couldn't hear it from her bedroom but knew her dad was sighing, which is what he did when he felt he'd explained himself and had no more words, the way he did. She hadn't heard what he wanted but only it was a thing that involved her, so she scrambled from bed in her pajamas and flew down the stairs into the kitchen and had said, "I want to do it. Whatever it is. I want to go."

And her dad had ducked his head toward his coffee and her mother had stood and said, "Well, not before you eat a good breakfast and get washed up and in decent clothes. I'm not sending you off looking like a ragamuffin."

Her dad said, "Ruth. It's a long drive."

"Then you should've thought earlier about taking her along."

And Katey said, "Where are we going? There's cornflakes. And I can be ready in two flicks of a mare's tail. You'll see!" And dashed from the room and up the stairs. Her parents both of a sudden chuckling, her mother saying, "I don't know where she gets half of what she says."

And her dad saying, "She soaks it all up like a sponge. Do we have cornflakes?"

Then she was out of earshot and pulling on clothes.

She remembered that. But not the drive over. Maybe climbing into the truck, not this truck but an earlier one, maybe climbing into that and driving out of town. The sense of adventure pounding high. What she remembered was sitting in the cab hours later with the windows rolled up most all the way because there were dogs on chains in a scrubbed-bare dirt yard before a one-story house sided with slab wood over tar paper and watching her dad and a man talking on the tilted porch that ran across the front of the house. She knew these sorts of houses from up on Brocklebank, or Kibbling Hill where some of her schoolmates came from, knew they were poor, knew something of what that meant, and the man there on the porch with her dad had a wild beard like Chaddy the hermit and he was yelling at her dad, holding the fiddle tight but yelling and her dad stood there, with one knee cocked, studying his extended shoe as if to find something there, on his shoe or the boards of the porch, looking down and nodding. The dogs on the chains couldn't reach the truck and had quit trying, were just lying in the smooth worn troughs of dirt they were used to. She smelled woodsmoke from the house and thought it was awful early to have a fire going, then guessed that like Chaddy all the man had was a wood range to cook on. There was also a smell in the yard, sort of a stronger smell but like when she pooped but before she

151

flushed. And the man was yelling at her dad and he just stood, nodding. She was almost frightened but not—no one ever hurt her dad and she could see he wasn't frightened but just being patient which she knew was how he accepted the storms other people felt within themselves but he didn't. Then another dog came around the corner of the house, this one not on a chain. It was an old dog with a sharp-pointed nose and long white and brown and black hair. There were patches almost to bare skin on the dog but its nose was up and it came wandering toward the truck as if it smelled her and as it came closer the dog began a slow tired swish back and forth of its tail and she could see that the dog had clouds over its eyes. But it walked right up and paused beside the truck and she could hear it pulling air through its nose as it moved its head side to side and she knew it was smelling her and then it squatted back on its haunches and with a great effort heaved upward so its front feet landed on the running board and its nose was close to the small gap in her window. And the dog began to lick the glass, great broad swipes and Katey knew all the dog wanted was to say hello. So she rolled the window down a couple more inches and reached out and stroked the dog's head. And the dog made a low sound that was not a growl but a sound of pleasure. And the man on the porch had stopped yelling but was walking back and forth with the fiddle tucked under his chin but without a bow. As if he was listening to sounds only he could hear.

"I'm sorry you had to hear all that," her dad said, when he got back in the truck. Driving away from the house. "For some reason he thought I fix these things for free. This time, it was easier to do it for free than not. But he's the one drank too much beer and tipped over and cracked the back like he did. So, maybe it wasn't as free as he thought. Anyway, Katey-did. We have the rest of the day and let's see what we can make of it."

But when they passed Story Land and she begged to stop he shook his head and said, "Junk." A few minutes later though he pulled off and they went in the diner and had hot roast beef on toast with mashed potatoes all slathered with gravy, and root beer floats. And then they drove back through the Notch. The steep sides were in beautiful color and coming below the steep narrow head of the Notch he pulled off again and parked. He led her along a path that went into the woods, crossing a stream on an old wooden bridge with no sides, the bridge made of logs split in two with the flat sides up, dark old wood, and then on through the young growth of maples with their leaves showing splotches of red and paper birches with some few golden leaves and if she asked where they were going she didn't remember but guessed if she had, he'd only said he wanted to show her something. And knew there was as good a chance that she simply walked along with him silent because she was used to him doing this sort of thing, trusting him always and absolutely. And then, it seemed in memory it was not so far but might've been—the day was warm and pleasant but not hot and there were no bugs, no blackflies or deerflies or any of the stinging pestilences of spring or summer in the woods—they came slowly and then all at once into a different place. The trees were almost all evergreens—later she'd think most likely hemlocks and white pines—but they were immense. The biggest trees she'd ever seen. They were so big that the old maples up on the top of Beacon Hill seemed like small things, young trees. Most of them were free of branches a long ways up. She could only see scraps of sky above the thickly woven high tops. And the trail was now only a narrow path that wound between rocks and boulders all covered with moss. The forest floor was free of young trees, brambles, almost everything she thought of growing in the woods. There were no stumps but here and there pieces of huge decaying trees whose butt ends rose above the ground several feet before the tops sank into the earth. And over everything grew mosses and ferns; most all unlike anything she'd seen. The ferns were high up above her waist in patches or low barely rising above her ankles and of all possible sorts, with strange leaves and fronds—some she only knew as ferns because they couldn't be anything else. Likewise the moss: not only the pale or dark green low furze but also rising six or more inches in patches of passing strangeness, in shapes and forms she'd never before seen. Again, she knew they were moss only because they couldn't be anything else. Some few pale gray and rising on thin stalks but in clumps, with rolled small perfect balls at the tops of the stalks. Other strange forms resembling pale green antlers, as if some strange deer had passed through and shed their horns. And along the sides of the decaying logs were lichens and mushrooms, spatters of yellow and orange spots, bulbous growths spouting. It was very quiet but far above the faint swish of the high tops of boughs weaving patient and strong in a breeze unfelt there below.

They settled on a boulder side by side, the rock the right height and with a slabbed top that made for a good seat. Once settled her dad looked down and pointed. She followed his finger and saw slender white forms rising a few inches before curling downward and turning outward as to make a small bell. A flower, surely, but without color. A ghost of a flower. She said, "What's that?"

"Those are called Indian Pipes."

"Did Indians smoke them?"

"No. I imagine the Indians had a different name for them. Sometimes names are nothing more than what remind us of something else."

He never laughed at her questions.

She said, "What is this place? It's almost scary but peaceful too."

"It's a very old piece of woods. Somehow, for good reasons I guess, it was never cut down once us white people came here. So, when the Pilgrims landed, these trees were already old. Or at least pretty good-sized. There's not many places like this anymore. I wanted to show it to you."

She looked about. She said, "It looks like a good place for fairies to live. Don't you think?"

He said, "Yes, I do. Fairies and gnomes and who knows what else like that."

"Trolls?"

He paused a moment and then said, "If there's any trolls they wouldn't be like the ones you think of. They'd be, might well be, say, under that footbridge we walked in on. But not to terrify us or anything like that. Only maybe to protect the fairies and gnomes from folks intent on doing them harm. Or that don't understand."

"That's good. I wish I could see one—I'd tell em I wasn't up to mischief. Or see a fairy for that matter."

"Why can't you?"

"Because they're magic."

"That's right. But here, now, you can feel that magic all around. Right? And see it too. Even if you can't see the fairies or gnomes. Or trolls, thank goodness."

She looked all around again. She felt the least shiver but it was split between fear and delight. Mostly delight. And high overhead a few narrow beams of light struck through and hit against the upper levels of the trees and turned them golden and soft and the day fell soft and sweet about her.

And her dad, the way he did, sang to her. His voice was low and sweet also, as if he held the song in the back of his throat and only just allowed it through. Only enough for her, because it was only for her. Although as she listened she guessed any nearby fairies would like the song and know she and her dad were good visitors.

Shady grove, my little love
Shady grove, I'd show you
Shady grove, I'll take you there
And shady grove will know you

"Hey. You okay?" Phoebe had reached and patted her forearm upon the wheel.

Katey had been crying. She dipped her chin and snuffed in snot and said, "I'm good. An old memory is all. I've been here before."

Phoebe dropped her hand from Katey's arm to her thigh and rubbed there gently, then took her hand away. "Old memories," she said. "They can damn near kill you."

They rode silent through the rest of the Notch where it was still late spring—pale green leaves, pockets of swirling cool air, the smell of brook water. And then climbed up out of that rare and strange place to where the land again leveled and they were back in early summer.

Katey sat in the field in the dusk, at the outer reach of the fire. She was exhausted, exhilarated, a little sore, and full. Closer to the fire Phoebe sat back to back with the girl Susan who was playing a nylon-stringed guitar, a simple pretty melody that Katey didn't recognize and if there were words Susan wasn't singing them but rather crooning a sweet *Oo loo la lah, la lah loo, loo oo loo la lah* . . . Sparks drifted upward into the clear green light spilling through the trees surrounding the small field. Across from them, Luna sat cross-legged with Chuck stretched out on his back in the grass, his head in her lap. Beyond them was the burble of the thin brook as it flowed over the dam of the beaver pond and beyond that the half-raised structure of the dome upon its platform, a series of triangular ribs rising to a jagged unfinished top against the sky. Night was coming down. The flare of a white gas lantern moved about within the skeleton of the dome and threw shadows and flares to compete with the fire—Steven up there poking along and studying the results of the afternoon of work, work informed by the notes and thoughts Phoebe had returned with.

Katey rested easy. No one had even asked who she was, beyond Phoebe's brief introduction as they commenced unloading the truck hours before, and no one had asked where she was from or wondered about her willingness to stay. It seemed enough that she showed up with Phoebe.

She still had little idea of where she was—she'd briefly glimpsed a massive five-story white building when she'd turned off the road to follow this rough track to the site of the dome and had passed a long low workshop and two small cabins, one of logs and one an older small farmhouse. But quickly she'd figured out that this project was part of but also separate from the college—that it was taking place in summer seemed answer enough. At least joined with the easy ebb and flow of the group. Clearly they held a vision undertaken but also she—daughter, granddaughter, great-granddaughter of school-teachers and administrators—understood this vision had been sanctioned and approved by whatever powers needed to do so here. Beyond that, there was little that corresponded with her vision, already old, perhaps waiting to be old, of college life.

What they'd done was worked. Katey had helped the others unload the truck and carry the food into the cook tent which was an old canvas fly stretched over a framework of poles to make a lean-to with a long table that held a pair of propane camp stoves, plus stacked milk crates that held pots and pans, iron skillets, an assemblage of chipped and mismatched crockery and jars, tins and sacks of provisions. Meanwhile Phoebe and Steven were up on the platform with the unrolled plans, measuring tapes, a plumb bob and a bubble level. Time to time she and the others would hear one of them raise their voice. The girl Luna had begun to work a mass of bread dough on a board on the table while Chuck got the fire burning again and began raking coals into what Katey figured out was a portable reflecting oven, set outside the tent, to take heat from the sun as well as the coals underneath, to bake the bread when it was ready.

They all turned when they heard the screech of nails resisting a pry-bar and watched as one section of the dome wall was taken down. Then Steven spoke to them.

As she'd been told, he was older—into his early twenties. He wore overalls with no shirt and steel-toed work boots. He was tall and moved with the confidence of a man inhabiting his own space. His beard was full and black and his hair was curly and reached his shoulders, tied back from his forehead with a rolled red bandanna. He said, "I knew it when I saw it which is why Phoebe did her thing. We got carried away and so that part got off-plumb. It's not easy, we're talking shaving edges to get true joints. All joints look true—it's the problem of seeing in your mind what will be, before it is. But we're doing what's never been done before: All of Fuller's domes have been built by people who knew everything about them and most of them were overseen by Bucky himself and no one knows more than he does. So we're out here—you dig it? On our own. Making it from the ground up. It's good, we're good. It's just this one section and that's fucking *increments* right? So we go slow and measure once, measure twice, measure one more time and then we make the least shave with a plane. Maybe two, but Phoebe and me, we're over your shoulders all the time. Do you hear me, people? We got this *so close.* That's what you have to groove on. We got it so close, and we knew enough to stop and look again. Everybody down? I thought so. Let's get to work."

Now he stepped out of the dome, through the opening where one day a door would be and as he did he shut down the lantern. He came to the fire and set the lantern in the grass and swung to the woodpile and with careful deliberation placed three chunks upon the fire. Then he stood waiting, looking about.

Katey sat in the grass at her remove and watched as one by one all of them looked up at him. Susan dribbled a last few notes from her guitar and set it aside, away from the fire but in the grass where the dew was coming down. Katey thought *At least put it up somewhere, on the table. You're only asking for trouble.* Her dad's voice.

Steven spoke low but certain, doubtless. "It's dip time, my sisters and brothers. Well, brother. Chuck. Time to wash clean. They used to call it baptism to make it special. So people would do it. But we're old time. Older time. Get the sweat and dust and dirt off us so we'll wake ready to go. Dig?" He swept his gaze again and missed Katey altogether this time. He said, "Hey, Phoebe, let me get a hit of that?"

She lifted up the cigarette she'd been passing back and forth and Steven smoked deeply and let loose plumes that came across the field to where Katey sat and she smelled something like balsam needles. He did it again and then handed it down to Chuck. Then he turned and stepped away twice and lifted his feet from his boots, stepped again and reached and undid the straps of his overalls and let them drop. And Katey watched his legs and back but mostly his butt as he walked away. Then the others were rising and pulling off clothes and she watched them also, not moving herself, amazed by how ordinary and clumsy and beautiful these naked people were. She'd never seen anything like this. Then she heard the soft swoosh of water as Steven dived into the beaver pond. Out of sight from her but she saw it in her mind's eye. Enough so she barely saw the others walk from sight around the dome.

But she heard them. Laughing, gasping. Splashing each other. Long moments of silence where she wondered what exactly they were doing and then again would come a splash, a laughed-up splash. Voices. The strokes of arms through water. Swimming. All they were doing was swimming. On a lovely summer night after a long day.

He came walking into the firelight. He stopped there and looked out toward her. Drops of water beaded in his hair, his beard, upon the crotch of his thick pubic hair. He bent and lifted his overalls and shook them free of the fine sawdust, stepped into them and then walked toward her, hoisting his straps as he came.

He knelt before her on one haunch, his other knee up and said, "You're Cathy."

159

The way he said it, with a curl of a question, made her realize he knew that wasn't her name. That he chose this false error in an attempt to unsettle her. His very presence unsettled her although she wasn't sure why but also guessed he knew and intended that as well.

"No, I'm Katey," she said, her voice flat. She almost said Katey Snow and last moment decided to keep that to herself.

"Katey." He reached and took her hand and squeezed it gently, tenderly, but when she didn't respond he let go. She composed her hands together in her lap as he flashed a smile, white teeth in his dark face. "I almost got it right, didn't I? When you rolled in with Phoebe I was so excited to find out if she'd learned a thing from those people, so glad to see her back, knowing she'd done her job and that we'd be back on track here, I heard her when she said your name but the moment was all about her. You dig that?"

"Sure."

"This is a whole new scene for you, isn't it?"

She shrugged but couldn't help herself. "I think it's pretty cool."

"It's very cool. Now, I say that but I also think it's only the way things should be. We're working not to make things right but to do things right. Like for a little while, maybe a hundred years, maybe more, maybe less, we—humans—have got way off-track and now we're nudging our way back to how things should be. Or maybe I'm wrong, maybe it is a whole new way. I studied history and a few other things at Berkeley before I heard about this place and headed east. I heard the name and it rang like a bell in me. But let me get back—so, history—once there was a time when the village all worked the same land and all people worked together and so life— come hard, come easy—was good. Right? And those villages were all built around a church. Or a monastery or even a cathedral. And that was where the power lay and the people believed, because they were told to believe this, that all things came from adherence to the church. Because the church spoke the language of God and God was either happy with his people or unhappy but only the priests could talk to God or listen to God. So the people depended upon the church to know if they stood right with God. But I thought If you take God out of the village and just let the village be the people, then maybe the people will find that God is not far away but right there, within them, within the fields and forests, within the magic of the earth. Which is what gives us life, dig? And then I heard about this place and thought There's something else happening there. I wanted to check it out. So I headed east and took a bus up from Boston and walked around and haven't looked back. This is sacred, what's going on here."

No one had ever talked with her quite this way and she felt as if words were out in the air that didn't belong only to him but to her also. As if her thoughts had been given breath, voice. But she said, "Yeah, I guess so." All she could manage, all she trusted herself with. Because she had other questions. And hadn't known she did until she agreed with him.

"Wait," he said. "You're thinking there are bigger things, that it's not as simple as I say. That the world is filled with great wrongs, terrible threats and fears. Of course it is. Where do we start? The war? Okay. Stop the war. Civil Rights? I was in California when the Watts riots went down. I've never been south, never went down there to join hands and try to help our black brothers and sisters safely to the polls. Never had my head bashed in or been shot and tossed in a river. No, I have not. Should I? Wait. How about the Bomb? Which is not a bomb but hundreds, maybe thousands, of warheads. On each side. MAD. Mutually Assured Destruction. Got that right, didn't they? What about the poisons that fill our rivers, our air? Not just the places you hear about which is bad enough but what worries me is the places you haven't heard about. Yet. And some of those same companies are the ones that made so much money during World War Two and then had products that they needed to figure out a new use for. And they did. And now they're at it again. Napalm? Man, what the fuck are they going to use napalm for once this shit in Vietnam runs out of steam. Even if we win and I'm wondering what that would look like? China and the Soviets just sitting back and saying, That's cool, you got Japan, you got half of Korea, just nuzzle up a little more to us. No fucking way. And then, and then, you have to wonder, where else are we—the U.S. I mean, where else are we poking our nose in other countries' business? You think we're done with Cuba? Yup, got out asses kicked in Piggy Bay and Khrushchev blinked on the nukes, best we know. But Fidel is standing strong and proud, and Che's out there somewhere, down south, way down south, south of Cuba, ya got that, spreading the word. And I bet you anything right behind him is a CIA spook or somebody like that, waiting for a chance. So, aw shit, sister, it just goes on and on. The machine. Orwell. Big Brother—is that the Soviets or is it LBJ and Hoover? Or both. You get thinking like this and it's dominoes or endless chains that wrap around each other and twist and turn and it makes your head hurt and your heart want to explode in your chest, the more you see, the more you know. You dig that?"

The others were back around the fire, dressed and the fire burning higher and she was tired and wondered where she'd sleep and it came to her she could always sleep in the truck but wasn't ready to make that decision, wanted to see what else the night held, what it would be like to move in to around the fire and sit and listen or maybe sing with the others. Curious about the burning balsam scent again floating through the night, soft pillows of smoke here and then gone.

She said, "But you have to take a stand. Right? What you're saying is it's all hopeless and so all we can do is hope it all falls down. Because we can't do it all? But if you think that way, we can't do anything? Right?"

Suddenly clear and strong and a little angry.

He looked at her and then reached and placed a hand on her knee, left it there. He smiled and said, "No. We tear it all fucking down. But we start from a strong place. Which is this. Not talking about it but showing the world a new way to live. Maybe that old one, some way like it, but really a new way. And it's not just us—others are doing it too. So, enough of us do that and we have a base, right? Maybe a place to retreat to if things don't work out as fast as we'd like? But also a base, a model to inspire others. I'm talking about a core, you dig that concept? A core is where we came from and where we return to and it never changes, never crumbles, never falters. Because it's so deep within us that nothing can fuck with it. We get that core, others get that core and what we have is a huge net, solid and also invisible, that spreads all over the earth. Big parts are already there and always have been—think about it—how they live in Nepal, Afghanistan, India. What's going on in France, right now. But others also: The Amish, Quakers, the Tinkers, gypsies, all those people who've been living quiet mostly on the outside because they won't live on the inside, most have been doing so for centuries. There's a reason. Same way we have a reason. For being up on this mountain building a dome. Let me tell you something about domes, why we're building one? Buckminster Fuller, the guy who thought them up, did so a while ago. And the Army got interested because Bucky saw them as a way to build cheap but strong housing and after World War Two there was a great need for that in Europe, hell, everywhere. Around the world. And they did some prototype towns. Kansas, I think. Maybe also the Netherlands or maybe Germany. And it worked. Worked real well. Cheap to build, cheap to heat and cool, comfortable, friendly. And they'd last forever. And somebody, meaning some big defense contractor, got wind of it and probably took a look and shut the whole deal down. Why?"

"I don't know."

He grinned at her. And shook his head. "Because there wasn't enough money to be made from it, that's why. It was too good for people. Think about that—a way to live, a house, a neighborhood, a town, a city, all made from buildings that were so good for people that someone with the power, the big defense companies, the military, the government, some combination of all—likely not just ours—Ha—a joke there but what I mean is other countries joined in, is my guess. And they shut that whole idea down. An idea that worked and they saw it worked and it scared the hell out of them. So, Katey: You wonder if I'm bogarting somehow being up here on this mountain in New Hampshire? Instead of down in the trenches? But this is a trench, right here. You bet it is. A new way to live needs a new way to live. Big ideas need smaller ones to help hold them up. This idea got stolen once but we're the housing outlaws. Sneaking it back in. And there's others like us. Bucky's still out there—he knows about us. And also, to go way back where we almost started: One day I will come down from the mountain. When the time is right, I'll know."

He reached a palm flat to the earth and pushed upright. For a moment his shadow obscured the fire and loomed over her. Then he said, "I'm going. You come, too?" He turned then and was gone, a shambling form in and out of the firelight.

She hadn't understood half of what he'd said. Or maybe she'd understood half of half. Not a quarter, not demarcated so easily, but rather large parts of some larger part. She wasn't sure she liked him although much of what he'd said she found interesting, even compelling, and she understood that she came from quiet people, not only her father and mother with their own particular silences but from a community that spoke little, letting unsaid but commonly understood words fill the gaps. And of that, a world complete. But a small world. And Steven Christensen spoke, perhaps wildly,

Before We Sleep

perhaps not, from a sense of tribes, from a wider and wilder world. As if he not only saw fault lines but had assembled a vision for how those lines would split, and be split, for the new world. So it was less not-liking him than being uncomfortable with his certainty, also his grasp of the present, as if he held an understanding that was still beyond her, and perhaps it was this—that intentionally or not, he'd in the course of what—twenty minutes, half an hour?—allowed her to understand how ignorant she was. How much there was to learn. And how much had been hidden from her in the intentionally or not but mutually agreed-upon small community she sprang from. And knew now, knew again, she was leaving behind.

She sat, watching them all about the fire, their ease, repose, the end-of-day fatigue but also of knowing one another, of fellowship. Of a small tribe fully and quietly aware they were part of a larger tribe. And Katey still felt on her own. But closer. She was also aware that now and then one or another, mostly Steven and Phoebe, also Luna, seemed to glance out toward where she sat.

She wondered if Phoebe was Steven's girlfriend. And flushed with the question and flushed again over wondering why she'd asked herself such a thing. And guessed it was true. Then shivered in the falling high mountain air and steeled herself; she rose up fluid and walked in toward the fire. Just as Susan tossed a big chunk of wood on and sparks dazzled upward. Luna watched her come and stood. She was a tiny birdlike woman with long hair the color of honey and she seemed to sway with the pulse of the flames and she held out a sweater and said, "It gets cold fast at night, here. Why we have the fire. Why don't you put this on? Are you okay? We weirding you out a little?"

Katey took the sweater and pulled it on, the heat of the fire warming her also. She said, "No. I'm good. I really am."

"Cool. You want to get stoned? Smoke with us?"

Katey settled down on the pressed dry grass around the stones of the fire ring. She said, "I don't know."

"That means you do."

"I guess you're right."

Much later she sat upright in the borrowed sleeping bag on the floor of the dome, her knees pulled up, the bag a wrong cocoon around her. Overhead the stars held and flickered, chill and distant. He'd come some unknown time earlier, waking her as he unzipped the top part of her bag and slid in on top of her. When she woke his hand was already over her mouth. His other hand stripping down her jeans. He was naked. Her lips spoke Don't against the press of his hand. As a wedge his joined knees cleaved her thighs and spread her. He whispered You want this. Then he hurt her, a red pulse pumping inside her, far too long—so brief. When he was done he sagged against her and she thought he would smother her. He tried to kiss her and she turned her head away, closed her eyes. Then he was gone.

The drizzle of water over the beaver dam was a song in the night. Constant flowing, downhill and gone.

She reassembled her clothes. Then quiet as a thief and feeling somehow a thief, she pulled herself out of the sodden ugly bag and made her way across the starlit dome and down out, her knees shaking, her brain a red tumor, murderous and wanting to cry but slipping silent as a thin blade toward the shadow of nighttime trees and the snout of the truck. There she sprawled against the hood, her legs weak and shaking. Then turned as she felt her gorge rise and vomited into the grass. Over and again. Sour chunks and then a hot bile that burned the inside of her mouth, her throat. Every time she thought she was done she smelled herself and choked and the bile rose again. Her stomach ached, her thighs were shaking and sore, her mouth foul. She pulled off the borrowed sweater and scrubbed her face and lips with it, breathing in the woodsmoke, sweat, odors of someone else. She vomited again, then balled the sweater and threw it down into her vomit. She wondered that none of the others had heard what had happened, or none heard what was happening now. The stream of water over the dam was all she could hear. She turned back to the truck, opened the door and stood, her hands up holding the top of the doorframe. Her knees week, thighs trembling like trout pulled from a river, barely able to stand.

A hand touched her shoulder and she almost collapsed. The hand was joined by a second and held her under her arms and then circled her and held her upright and the girl's voice was in her ear. Even as Katey realized the girl was smaller and struggling to hold her. Luna was saying, "Oh, God, I'm sorry. I heard, I mean I heard but didn't know what I was hearing really until you left. Are you okay? No, shit, of course you're not okay. Oh, I'm sorry, I'm sorry."

Katey felt stronger—not alone. But was plunged with shame at being witnessed and grateful to not be alone. She pressed herself to stand upright and firm and turned in the dark—Luna a small shape riven out of darkness before her. But as she turned Luna stepped closer and wrapped her arms around her again and hugged her close and Katey was crying again.

"Listen: He tried to do the same thing to me," Luna said. Then she said, "He almost did the same thing to me. But it was different. Oh, I'm sorry, I'm so sorry."

Luna was speaking low, just above a whisper. For herself, Katey had no voice. She wanted to thank Luna for coming out, for not leaving her alone but she had no voice. But she was able to move her arms about the smaller woman and slowly the rest of her followed, her wounded body up against another body, and they stood rocking together in the dark.

Then Luna said, "Are you leaving now?"

Katey had words back. "I am." A rasp emitted.

"Can you take me with you?"

In her pause she felt the distress of the older girl. But was doubtful; cautious. In her mind she saw herself in the truck driving off into the night. To be alone with herself and then knew she didn't truly want to be alone with herself. She also felt an urgency to leave, some distant alarm within her wondering if Luna had come or been sent to slow her, to contain her.

She said, "Where?"

"It doesn't matter right now. Just not here."

"You don't have to get your stuff? Just drive away?"

"Isn't that what you need? It's what I need. I can get my shit later this summer. If I come back. Or when I come back."

"You serious?"

Luna stepped back but reached and ran her hands down along Katey's face. A caress, no mistaking. Luna said, "If you doubt me I'll walk out to the road down the hill and you can pick me up there."

Katey said, "I'm going now. You want to slide in?"

Once inside the cab Katey could feel Luna shivering and only then knew she was also. Her teeth clattering. She started the truck and rolled on down the starlit path of road past the bulk of the dome, dark. As they came into the wider opening she could see the pale ghost of the large building, also the bulk of the mountains east and south and above those dense dark cutouts the crazy starfield, an immense spread. She'd always loved the night sky but this one felt cold and remote; careless of the life far below it. They came to the edge of the path, ready to turn onto the road and she eased in the clutch and pulled the knob for the headlights and the world grew close, pinned down in the meeting cones of the twin beams. In pause. She was uncertain where to go, which way to turn. She turned the heat on.

Luna said, "What is it you want, now?" A kind voice.

"I should go to the police." Then, she named it. "He raped me."

"I know. I'm sorry." Then Luna was quiet. A long quiet.

Katey said, "And I could use a cup of coffee."

Luna said, "There's nothing open in Franconia this time of night. Littleton either. The closest place is a diner in Saint J. That's a hour."

Katey heard the omission. She said, "What about a cop?"

Luna said, "There's a cop. One. There's state police in Twin Mountain but that's north and east from here. A hour also. And . . ."

"And what? What about the local cop?"

Luna was quiet, then said, "Why don't we drive to Saint J and I'll buy us breakfast there and we can talk along the way?"

Katey killed the lights except for the dash and said, "Why are you here? Really?"

"To get out. Like you but for different reasons. Listen, how old are you?"

"Seventeen."

"Okay. Short version: The cop will love your story but only because he hates this place. You're of legal age—so it's a question of consent, right? And Steven will swear you invited him, wanted him. And the cop won't care because he's not after Steven, he's after all of us. Including you. You'll turn into just another hippie girl and what happened won't matter. They'll turn it into something else. Maybe you got jealous, maybe you were high, maybe all those things and more. Do you understand? They hate this place and will use you however they can and they can do it well. So, so, shit, I'm trying to tell you this is a heavy situation: Those fuckers will use whatever they can to shut this place down and you, you'll end up being raped all over again but in ways you can't imagine—in the papers, on TV, in court—you and me, we stopped at the town cop's house tonight and woke him up, even if we drove to the troopers in Twin Mountain, either place, even if I tossed the little bag of grass I got before we were there—between talking to us and taking the next step, like waking up a judge for a warrant, somehow there'd be a bag of weed found on each of us. And it would go down like that. Do you understand?"

"So I suck it up and drive? That's what you're saying?"

Luna sighed. She said, "Okay, listen: Wherever you live, you go out on a date with the coolest guy in school, the one you always liked and trusted and everyone thought was an outstanding guy, right? You know what I mean. And after the date he drives out somewhere where you're not sure where you are and he tells you you're going to fuck him or he'll leave you there. Or he just fucks you. Rapes you. And then he takes you home. You don't say anything because you don't know what to say and he doesn't say anything because in his mind it either wasn't rape or he's already done with you. Or both. And you both know it. He drops you off at your house and drives off. And you slip in and hope your mother is asleep and maybe she is or maybe she isn't but if she's waiting you don't tell her anything except you're tired and want to go to sleep. Because, really, you want to be alone. Because you already figured out that no one is going to believe you and he's going to deny it or most likely say you wanted it and all the sudden everyone is going to think you're a slut. Because that's what they do. Does that make sense? You understand what I'm telling you?"

Katey turned the heat down. The cab was hot and she ached all over, her thighs were sore and twitching still and she felt a slick wet smear in her underwear. Finally she said, "Yeah."

Luna said, "I know it sucks."

"Yeah."

They were both quiet then. Luna reached over and placed her hand over Katey's hand upon the wheel. She didn't squeeze but gently worked her hand atop Katey's as Katey realized she was gripping the wheel so very hard. And slowly her hand relaxed and as it did so did the rest of her. Not much but enough.

170

Finally Luna spoke again. "Tell you what? Let's drive on to Saint J and I'll buy us breakfast and we can talk some more along the way. And when we get there if you decide you want to ditch me—go to the cops, go on alone, whatever, I'm down with that. But meanwhile I'm hungry for bacon and I'm guessing the ride would do us both good."

Katey again turned on the lights and eased out to the road, paused and said, "Which way?"

"Down the hill into the village is fastest. After that I'll point out the way."

Katey said, "You mind if we try the radio for a bit?"

"Down with that. I could use some tunes."

The radio delivered and so once truly out on the road, they sang along, Luna as promised pointing out turns along the way. But both belting out, filling in for each other when they dropped the lyrics— Katey more often than Luna but it didn't matter. Both released.

Then the radio dissolved into static and they rode in silence a little while and after a bit Katey said, "Was that you?"

"What?" But she knew what, the treble in her voice.

"The girl in high school."

Luna was quiet a bit and then said, "Yeah. But that's not important. Well, it's real heavy, it's not going away anytime soon. Maybe never. But what's important is that you understand rape is not sex, it's not making love. It's—fuck, I don't know what it is except wrong and nasty and makes you feel like shit—dirty. But it's not making love. That's what's important—that you know that. Because some day you're going to meet a guy, a great guy and you're going to be nervous and anxious but you're going to want to do it with him. And when you do: Oh, baby, it's the best thing in the world. Like you can't believe."

171

"I always thought so. But right now I can't ever imagine feeling that way."

"Yeah, I can dig that. What can I say? You meet the right guy and all that will change? Sure. But also, most guys follow their dicks, ya know what I'm saying? If there's a chance, they take it. Not all but most is my bet. So. What does that mean? Is one chick's nightmare another one's dream? I don't know. It's mighty fucked up is all I know. But you gotta hold hope. Because the good guy, he comes. He really does. I want so bad for you to know that—not just because of tonight. But because it's true. I know."

Finally in Saint Johnsbury they got a little lost, then saw the diner but that side of the street was filled with cars and so they circled the block three times, each time spying and then missing the closest parking space. By the time they finally parked the truck and walked uphill to the diner they were both giddy, entering the only packed place in the small city at three in the morning. Yet for a moment the place went quiet, all eyes on these strange women. Then to a booth and alone with menus, hidden and soon forgotten by the crowd. A woman with a collapsing beehive of silver hair and bright red lipstick came and took their order, then brought them coffee and soon after, platters of food.

Lightened moods, both, Luna waved a strip of bacon at Katey and said, "So, you. How'd you end up at Franconia, anyway?"

Katey drank orange juice and then said, "It's a long story. But I'm trying to find a man who was with my dad in the war. And I think I found him, but he's somewhere way down south. I'm not sure I can handle that trip. But I sure don't want to go home, right now. What about you? Where are you from?"

Luna laughed. "I'm from all over. Most recently what most people call home is San Diego. My dad's an anchor-cranker. I'm a Navy brat. Grew up all over the world—well, Hawaii, the Philippines,

Japan, mostly. And my mom stayed stateside for a while to raise me and my brother and two sisters in what she thought was a good place. But I dunno. I never fit in, anywhere. Inside my own family even, mostly." She shrugged and ate a triangle of toast smeared with grape jelly from a little plastic tub. "How it works, sometimes."

"How'd you end up here? At Franconia College?"

"I read an article about it. A weekly newspaper the library in San Diego had called the *National Observer*. And I thought, That's the place for me. Of course, my parents didn't know a thing about it—they think it's just a northeastern private college that gave me a pretty good scholarship and that was enough. Oh, I guess maybe a part was they were almost as happy to see Little Miss Trouble go as I was to get out. Oh, and yeah, my oldest sister, Laurie, and her husband and their kid live in Massachusetts and so they felt she'd be close and keep an eye on me. Or be able to do so. You know, the stories people tell themselves to let happen what they want to have happen anyway. Funny thing is, they don't have a clue about her. They did, they'd never have sent me east."

And she paused a moment and brightened and said, "I'm not trying to bum a ride. But that's what you should do. Come down there with me. Think about it: You don't want to go home, not right now. Not tomorrow morning. And you might want to explore that southern guy thing for your dad. But most of all, Kevin and Laurie are cool—not hippies but good hearts—he's a graduate student in Amherst and they're both antiwar, all that shit. And if you want to talk about what happened I can't imagine a better person, either one of them. Or not say a word the whole time you're there, and they'd be down with that too." "After all," Luna said, "you got me."

Katey had eaten her bacon and toast. Her home fries. On her plate remained the two eggs, yolks cut open some time ago, the whites with black speckles of pepper, cold.

173

And she leaned over peering down upon her plate, studying it, and then began to cry. Small huffs and tears sliding down her cheeks, dropping onto the plate.

She lifted her head and looked at Luna, still crying. She nodded. After a bit she choked out, "That sounds okay, maybe."

Wondering if her mother had been raped.

Six

Ruth

On a Friday in the first week of December there was an early snowfall, several inches of wet heavy snow. She made it back up the hill after school, the short day already shutting down to an ethereal dusk, the bare trees, branches and trunks limned with snow, spatters of sleet on her windshield. Oliver would be leaving for work after supper, although a couple of months into the school year Ruth had talked with Jennie and an arrangement had been worked out. Saturday nights he'd have off, even if it was the busiest day of the week—there was another clerk who, before the job became Oliver's, had been the night stockboy and also took inventory and so, weekly for that one night, was reinstated to his old position. If the man objected, Ruth never heard of it although she recognized within this silence the great power that Jennie, through Ed, exerted over the employees. Work was work and the man should be glad of it. And it meant that Ruth and Oliver had Saturday nights together. Ruth was also quick to figure that Jennie's benevolence had a smack of self-interest. She wanted a grandchild and this might help. Perhaps also, perhaps, Jennie recognized that beneath all of these efforts to accommodate her son and his father and her daughter-in-law, ran a very real strain. Not that she'd ever speak of it. Not that any of them ever spoke of it.

When she stepped from the car she felt the impact of the sleet on the wet snow, the snow was less, packed down by the not-quite rain. The wind had stopped and behind a thick gauze of cloud she could see a halo of moon overhead and she felt the cold, as the temperature was dropping with nightfall. So would come a freeze and soon, a glaze of ice crust over the snow. She was without care—Ed Snow's truck sat in the drive with chains already mounted on the tires, a job Oliver had done sometime while she was gone and so he could safely crunch in low gear down to the store and back up again later. It wouldn't matter how strong the freeze, the layer of snow and sleet below would make good traction. She went into the house to make supper, to turn on the radio, to stoke the furnace and parlor range, whatever needed to be done. For that matter, clumping along in the galoshes pulled over her shoes, she might well open the door and find Oliver had done all those things and was seated at the table or fussing over the stove. Times, he liked to do so—the electric range still a force of wonder for both. But she didn't expect it and this day collapsing so rapidly into night with slight partition between the two, was no exception. The house was empty, although it was warm—he'd filled the stove and, as she set her bag of papers and texts and books waiting the weekend down, she felt the warm sweep of a draft across the floor and realized for the first time this season he'd also set a fire in the basement furnace. He was taking care.

She smiled. She felt life was creeping back in, not only with them but with everyone they knew. The war had changed things, certainly, and just as certainly all were rising out of it. She wasn't sure but guessed it had been Jennie who had told her she needed to be patient last summer when she felt she was failing him somehow. Perhaps it had been her mother. It didn't matter.

She set to making supper. Like almost everyone else she shopped on Saturday. Some mornings she'd wake to discover Oliver had brought home a handful of goods after his night shift—most often things he liked. Once back in the summer he'd offered to take a list with him and so relieve her of the Saturday morning chore but he'd mislaid the list and brought home four grocery boxes of oddments, redundant condiments, cans of soups or vegetables they had no need for and three packages of steaks he'd cut himself. The steaks were thick and delicious although three meals of beefsteak in one week was a bit much—not that both didn't crave the meat—it was an indulgence of expense. And she'd still had to go down to buy the laundry powder, the paper goods, all of the other items he seemed to be oblivious of; as if such things came with the house and never needed replenishing. A man, was what she thought.

So that Friday evening was leftovers and odds and ends. There was the end of a tuna casserole and a bowl of pickled beets. She hard-boiled two eggs and then chopped them over the beets while the casserole warmed in the oven. A large heel of a loaf of bread that she sliced while butter melted in an iron skillet, then dredged the bread on both sides in the butter, arrayed on a cookie sheet and shaved cheddar atop to melt in the oven. There was no dessert, and then she found a scrape of cottage cheese in a wax carton in the back of the fridge, studied that and found a can of pineapple rings in the pantry. She fried the rings in the leftover butter until they were brown on both sides, laid them in a pie pan and used a butter knife to dab the remnant cottage cheese atop the buttery caramelized pineapple and slid that also into the oven. Turned down the knob for heat and had supper waiting for the table.

The door pushed open and he stood there a moment, cold air flooding in as she turned toward him and she cried, "What happened?" He was struggling for breath and the knee of his right trouser was torn, a dark egg was building above his left eye and his face was wild, his eyes scattered and jittering. His lungs sucked air. Cradled in both hands was his fiddle. Blood seeped from a cut on his right hand. He looked at her and was silent but stepped in further. She moved toward him and a guttural gurgle passed his lips as he moved around her. And she thought He's only wanting to get to the parlor, where the case for the fiddle rested, open. He wouldn't leave it in the unheated shed behind the barn overnight. She knew the reasons why and then knew this was different. She shut the door and turned to watch his back, waiting.

He didn't pass through to the parlor but set the fiddle on the table. Put both hands down either side of it and leaned upon his hands. Looking down upon it. His breathing still heaving.

She came up behind him and placed a hand on his shoulder. Let it rest there, a quiet moment. Then she said, "What happened?"

He didn't look at her but said, "I slipped on the ice."

"You're bleeding. Let me get the Mercurochrome."

Now he turned. He said, "No. I'm fine." Then his eyes blinked. Blinked again. He turned away from her and leaned again over the table. "But I broke my fiddle. Oh, Jesus, my feet went out from under me and I went down with it held against my chest and I did everything to stop myself but still I heard it popping like twigs snapped."

Then he said, "Oh dear."

"How bad is it," she asked. "Is it ruined?"

"I'd think, how if felt." A long moment. "I don't know."

"Well, look and see." Her hand rubbing the cords of his neck as he peered down at the table, at the fiddle.

After a moment his hands came free of the table edge and he lifted the fiddle, then turned it over, studied it, then a soft suck of air from him as he again set it carefully as a newborn upon the table.

She waited, kneading him.

He said, "Well, it's bad. The bridge is snapped off. And the back is cracked. A hairline but a crack is a crack. And likely the body is

178

separated from the sides—you can't tell just by looking. The neck is the same way—damage you can't see."

She said, "Who can tell you, better?"

"I don't know. My dad, maybe. Or just me, looking at it longer."

She took a long pause and then said, "What I think? Is you can fix it. If it's not smashed to flinders, which it's not, I think you can fix it."

He turned then. Faced her. He said, "I don't know the first thing about such things."

"Maybe not," she said. "But I think you do. I think you just haven't wrapped your mind around it yet."

He was silent again. Then turned back to the table and lifted the little fiddle up and with his careful hands turned it about, peering close. Took his time. Then set it down again and turned and said, "I don't know."

"That's all right," she said. "I'm filled with *I don't know* more of the time than I care to admit. Why don't you sleep on the idea? No telling what your mind will churn up. Meanwhile, is there the least chance you're hungry for supper?"

She woke in the night, spooned tight against him. From beyond the windows she heard a scrape of wind, now and again a splinter as small limbs from the trees gave way with their coat of ice, a sharp snap. She knew he was awake also, could feel the tension in his back, the careful slowed flow of his breathing. He didn't want to talk. She guessed the ice-snapped twigs, branches, might echo in his ear the sound of the crack of the fiddle as he wounded himself trying to save it. She didn't know—it could be other things kept him awake. She didn't know him, so many ways. But knew him better than she ever had before. There lived a question in this contradiction but she wasn't sure what it was except that some part of her feared it. Feared both the question and the possible answers. She pressed forward a bit, the length of her against the length of him and nuzzled his neck briefly, barely, as if she were sleeping. And then she was.

When she woke again it was to an empty bed and an empty house. The storm had passed and pale sunlight struck though the one east-facing window; a day already well under way. There was a pocket of warmth about her under the covers and she held there a bit, savoring the warmth and unsure of her day. Then an idea came to her and she flushed with it and pushed out of the bed and danced on the cold floor as she shucked her nightgown and dressed quick as she could and went down the stairs, already feeling the heat rising. Downstairs was warm with the furnace and parlor range filled and the percolator sat upon a ring of the electric stove, curls of coffee steam from the spout.

Otherwise the house was empty. She walked into the parlor and the fiddle case was gone. And she recalled her words of the night before but also the thought came to her the middle of the night. She drank a cup of coffee and stepped out into a new day. Every tree was outlined in thick white frost, not just around the yard but spreading down into the village, outlining the bends of the river and rising up the hill beyond where the crown of the hill was a shimmering halo of trees clearly defined, clumps of intricate dazzling lace, backlit by the sun and the dense blue sky above. A morning to take your breath away. The truck was gone, the chain-marks biting hard through the shimmering ice. Down the hill but where else would he have gone?

Midmorning there was still no sign of him and she'd finished her Saturday cleaning. She sat at the table and drank another cup of coffee as she wrote out her list, then dressed and went out. The sun had done its work; the ice retreating into slush and the air was warm—a moment she almost felt springlike. She got in her car and easily drove down the hill.

She was distracted in her shopping, checking her list and returning to aisles just gone through to retrieve this or that forgotten item, when she realized she'd somehow expected to find Oliver here. And was grinding a pound of coffee, anxious of a sudden to finish up and return home when she felt a hand on her shoulder and his father's voice: "Ah, my lovely daughter-in-law. Such a pleasure, always my eyes. A vision. And here, this morning, gracing my premises. To what is owed this honor?"

She took the bag from the snout of the grinder, folded down the top and set the coffee in her basket before turning. She said, "Morning, Ed. I'm doing my shopping, much like half the town. Saturday morning."

"Of course." He grinned but his eyes were serious. They'd never talked about it but she was certain that, while Jennie might feel Oliver was simply taking time to renew himself, to come fully home, Ed might suspect, as Ruth herself did, that a more fundamental change had occurred—that the lighthearted boy was gone for good and whatever version had replaced him might temper in time but would never become the lighthearted easygoing near-duplicate of his father in the family business.

And out of her own worry and uncertainty, without having thought she would, she now asked, "Say, Ed? Oliver hasn't been by this morning, has he? Early?"

"Not that I've seen. Why would he?"

Backtracking, she said, "No reason. Just curious."

"Are things all right? You got a problem?"

"No," she said. "We're fine."

"So where is he, then? You come asking me."

She paused, knowing, though Oliver had never said as much, that his fiddle playing was a secret from his father. For his own reasons, perhaps reasons from both of them. Or maybe it was a secret best not held, especially given the accident the night before. Her words to Oliver about finding a way to repair the fiddle now struck her as bold nighttime talk that withered in the hard bright light of day. And she had a vision of Oliver driving the truck around the backroads, up amongst the hills, holding yet another skim of grief or sorrow upon the well of it all within him—a small grief she thought but one that could loom large for him. And an idea bloomed.

She said, "Ed? I want to buy a fiddle. You have any back there with the instruments?" As, keeping her face turned toward him she made her way down the aisle, toward the end that would connect into the room where the musical instruments as well as the children's games and toys were displayed.

He followed, studying her. Then reached and placed a hand on her shoulder. She almost shivered under his touch but stopped and turned again as he asked, "What do you want a fiddle for? We got violins for the kids, not sure one of em could truly be called a fiddle."

Quickly, as if her teeth might clamp her tongue she said, "He's been playing the fiddle. The small one you gave him a long time ago. He's been doing that six, seven months. I do believe it gives him solace. Eases something inside of him. I don't know but I know he's been doing it regular."

Ed interrupted. "Not surprised. He's got it in the blood. Letting a music come out is good for any man. Why you looking for a fiddle— I know that one you're talking bout—it's small, made for a boy, but it's good. No need to buy some cheap ill-made thing. I never said that—I don't sell that sort of stuff. But . . . what? You looking for a Christmas present, is that it?"

And then she told him of what happened the night before. Holding back only her suggestion that Oliver might repair it himself but otherwise repainting the scene at the table, the wounds he'd gained on the ice, his litany of the damages he understood had occurred upon the little fiddle. As she did so, she felt a greater understanding of her husband's pain and sorrow, also how terribly glib her suggestions had been. And remembered his hidden wakefulness in the night, a condemnation now of her thoughtlessness. Some inner part of her writhed and she wanted only to be home. She knew her father-in-law was looking at her but she studied the shelf before her—reached out and ran a finger across the label of a jar of jam.

"You," Ed said. "You wait right here. No, finish your shopping— I'll be a few minutes. Maybe ten. You get done and I'm not by the register you can sit in your car, you'd rather. But I'll be quick as I can. I got just the thing for him."

Wicked can be December—not a full winter month, but also only a paring of fall. The late morning was warm, eaves dripping but on north sides making icicles, heaps of snow disintegrating into gray slush, then water, flowing away to meet other small braided channels of water, downstreet, all flowing down. Downhill. Toward the suddenly roaring river, open and free of ice and so taking in this flow of melt. She sat and smoked with the car door open and her galoshes propped up on the small running board. Waiting and again unsure of what she'd done. People, mostly women, most whom she knew, flowing in and out of the store, passing her, waving and calling H'lo, Good Day, the like. Responding in kind but brief as she could, letting them pass by and no too few of them, she was sure, passing by happily, others the curious sideways glance, and those also waving and calling with good cheer. She knew what each one thought and intended and she knew nothing at all.

Ed came out on the stoop of the mercantile and peered about. Cradled against his side was an instrument case. He spotted her and came over and handed it to her. She turned to place it on the seat beside her as he said, "There. I put new strings on it. Take that to him." Then he was gone. As if he knew she needed him to do this, in this way.

She drove up the hill and carried the groceries in and put them away. Then she returned and lifted out the case and stood in the warm sun and turned it over in her hands. It was old, the alligator hide chipped and fungal. But it seemed a good weight in her hands. She carried it in and placed it on the kitchen table. She looked at it a moment, then carried it into the parlor and set it on the side table, where the small fiddle's case had always been.

She waited until it was an hour past noon and couldn't wait any longer so she opened a can of soup and warmed it and ate it with a peanut butter sandwich. She had a fresh chicken to roast for supper— what they ate every Saturday night, so most Sundays she made a chicken pie with the leftovers. Then she made a pot of tea and sat with a cup and saucer at her desk and began to correct papers. She struggled to concentrate for a bit and then was well lost in her work.

But heard the truck when it pulled up outside. She started, glanced at the clock and saw if was almost half past three. Her first thought was That chicken should already be in the oven but she was up and moving toward the door, then fell back and stepped to the side of the kitchen window that looked upon the yard. He was out of the truck, lifting a wooden chest from the bed of the truck, glancing toward the house. She pulled back, feeling she was spying, then eased forward and lifted the edge of the curtain to watch as he carried the chest around the back of the barn to his workshop. He came back and did this again, a different chest, longer, narrow. Again he cast an eye toward the house, but briefly. She watched then how he walked; the least bit of a stride, and knew whatever this all was, he felt it to be a good thing. The third time he pulled out a pair of old milk crates packed to the brim and again headed to the barn. And she had a flurry.

Too late to roast the chicken, no idea if he'd had lunch, no idea what he was up to. So she put the kettle on and poured out the cool tea and rinsed the pot and waited for the water to boil. She'd have tea ready and that was the best she could do. She took a package of sugar wafers from the cupboard and spread them on a small plate. The kettle whistled and she filled the teapot and behind her the door opened. She turned slow but easy, no false smile spread but her face piled up with curiosity and concern. And he saw that, as he'd likely expected and gave her a small grin. He was carrying the case of the busted fiddle and he set it on the table. Then he stepped and held her elbows in his hands and kissed her forehead, nose, lips.

"My Lord," he said. "What a day I had."

The kiss upon her lips sparkled through her. How could I not love this man rippled her brain, and then the shock of idea that she might not love him. Never before thought.

"Where'd you go?" she asked, a fair and neutral question.

"Canaan," he replied. "To try and find a man called Archille Descoteaux." He paused and said, "What you told me yesterday? About letting my mind rest and seeing what might churn up? It worked."

She couldn't recall that particular statement but nodded.

"And I finally went to sleep last night—this morning, knowing there was something and I woke early and the name was right there, front of my mind. So I let you sleep and made coffee and thought about that name. And I knew he was from Canaan and I knew he made fiddles. I don't know if maybe my dad told me about him when I was a little boy or maybe my grandfather—my grandmother for that matter. And I thought about going to ask Dad, guessing he'd already be at the store but then I thought, I do that he's going to ask questions maybe I don't want to answer but more than that—he finds out I'm headed to Canaan he's going to turn up other names; great-aunts or -uncles, second cousins, people he'd want me to look up. Which was not my idea for the day. So I just drove on up there. I should've left you a note—now that I think, I should've—but at the moment it was important I just go. As if I could be talked out of it so easy. A harebrained notion, it felt a tad bit.

"It's a fair drive but I left early and it was early still when I got there and I just went into the store and asked if old Archille was still alive and where could I find him. The fellow said, 'What you want him for?' and I said, 'I got a broken fiddle I'd like him to look at,' and he said, 'He don't do that sort of work anymore,' and I said, 'I'm looking to see if I can learn to do it myself.' And remembered then to buy some cheese and dried sausage and a couple cans of food to take as a gift, the way those things used to be done, and the storekeep told me where to find him.

"I drove out and found the house easy enough, right where he'd said it would be. One of those old houses with a shingle roof and clapboards once painted yellow and trim once was blue, all peeling, and no car in the drive but the porch stacked high with wood, upstairs windows patched with cardboard or tin hammered flat. An old daybed out on the porch, the stuffing sprung. So I stepped out of the truck and carried my little fiddle and walked up and knocked. And he opened the door and spoke French and I excused myself in French and he nodded and told me to come in. Gave me a chair and poured tea thick as pitch for both of us, asking me who I was and I did my best to tell him and that got things going. Ruthie, I don't know how this whole business will work out but if I get a reason to go up again, I'd take you, I would, if you'd come—"

"Of course I would."

"—Because, because, well, it was interesting. To see something of where I came from. To hear him, to see him but also—no wait: He had on those old black wool pants with faint white stripes in them and a hand-knit sweater that looked to be about two inches thick and maybe once years ago he stood five feet tall. A mustache like a paintbrush but fresh-shaven otherwise and a tousle of hair still mostly black. With eyebrows to match and a goodly spurt of hair from both ears. A grand old man, is what I'm saying. And all the time we're sitting drinking tea his eyes were jerking to the fiddle case I'd laid on the table but he kept on talking about family, and I have to tell you mostly I couldn't tell if it was mine or his or the ways both met up and linked one way or another. Likely some of all."

Oliver paused then, looked off from her, ate a sugar cookie and swallowed the last of his tea. She waited because she knew he wanted her to and then he said, "What you have to understand is Archille Descoteaux is famous. His brother Hermenegil, also. And their father, Arthur. And going back from them, I'm sure, but those were the ones came down from the Townships and made fiddles. Beautiful fiddles. Likely, some one or more of Descoteauxs have made fiddles three hundred years or longer. Not violins, they'd never known what a violin was, but *fiddles*. From log to lacquer and every step in between. Well, I'm boring you, aren't I?"

"Not one whit. Go on, tell me more."

"Long and short he was in the middle of a story about Alice Evangeline, who was either his grandmother or a girl he'd loved long ago or maybe even was a song—he kept going from English back to French—it didn't matter because I knew he'd taken me in, you know what I mean? That I was home, as far as he was concerned. Almost as if he'd been waiting for me. Then he ended his story or maybe stopped it midstream and reached and tapped the case of my fiddle and asked me what I had there, what I wanted from him. I told him how it came to me and then what happened—that I found it again after so many years and then slipped on the ice and busted it.

"He opened the case and lifted it out and held it up, turned it, around in his old hands, back and forth, up and down, brought it close to his face—Ruthie, I swear he smelled it. Then, his hands still running over it he looked at me and said, 'Yup I made this one. I remember her. Ain't forgot a one of em. But I can't help you—my eyes are gone, my hands shake, can't barely slice cheese without making blood, let alone shave a splinter clean or lay a bead of glue. I was to rummage I might find a bridge could work or be sanded

187

down to size. But I ain't it, no more, yes?' He reached up and tapped his temple and said, 'A old song. The mind knows what the hands can't do. A sadness, is all it is.' Then he ended, 'Imagine that.'

"I sat there a moment. Then I told him I wanted to try and fix it myself. That I believed I could. That all I wanted was what he still had—what he could tell me of what I should do. Now, he reared back in his chair and looked hard at me. I sat there under his gaze. I thought he was about to send me on my way. Then he was up out of his chair and told me he could tell me what to do just fine but I'd still lack the tools and goods to have it work for me. And he waved at me and I rose up and followed him about, into the next room as he boxed up things and then pointed at a pair of tool chests and said I'd need those, also. All the time telling me how to fix all the things he'd seen when he looked at my fiddle, some I had no idea about being broken or might be. But as we walked about and he loaded me down with all of this stuff, what he was telling me made a sudden sense in my mind. As if the things he was telling me that I didn't know, I already knew. And the tools, it was the same—I knew once I got them home I'd understand them. I'll make mistakes. I know that. But those mistakes will get me closer rather than farther away. Does that make a lick of sense, to you?"

"I saw you carrying those tools. Back behind the barn."

"I saw you peering out."

"You can do anything you decide to do, is what I think." Then she stood quickly and walked into the parlor and brought out the fiddle in its case and placed it before him. But she reached down and snapped open the clasps and let him see what she had.

She said, "I'm sorry. I told him little as I could but I got this this morning from your father. I wanted to please you and I wasn't sure how to do that. So this is what happened."

He'd already reached down and lifted up the fiddle and turned it, studying it. Then he smiled at her and set it back in the case. He said,

"Some days are good days. Did Dad tell you this was my grandmere's fiddle? It was. And Arthur Descoteaux built it."

He closed the case and went around the table and leaned and kissed her again. He said, "One day I'll play it. That will be a happy day. But, meanwhile, I have a fiddle to repair."

She said, "I never got the chicken in the oven."

He glanced at the clock above the calendar on the wall, back to her. "Well, it's late isn't it? Maybe we should go down to the Dot and eat a hamburger and milkshake? A piece of pie?"

"I could do that." Then she said, "I love you, Oliver Snow."

His eyes cast about and landed away from her. He said, "I love you too, Ruthie."

Four months later, early April, the snow rotting, mostly gone, he drove north again on a fine day, the sky fleet with clouds, flocks of robins swarming here and then gone again, roadside ditches sudden snowmelt brooks, crows winging over fields of old grass still pressed flat with the weight of snow, here and there in south-facing spots up against foundations yellow and white crocuses bloomed. A day both warm and chill as the clouds fought the quickening sun, heat on in the truck to keep the fiddles—he carried both with him—as even-tempered as possible but also the scent of the earth flooding in after long months where the best scent hoped for was a crushed balsam branch, the peeling bark, small rotted spots on firewood, otherwise scent and smell was of humans and their doings; sweat, pies or bread baking in the oven, Ruth fresh from a hot bath, the shampoo she used, the lather he built with his brush and mug to shave each morning. Also the fine sawdust he planed or sanded in his little shop with the old potbellied stove sparking warmth, stovepiped through the shed roof, rosins and pitch and glue, lacquer, waxes. Those scents also.

He went alone but was not breaking a promise so much as she was busy with early rehearsals for the annual spring theatrical performance, and he was ready to go. He offered to wait until the weekend but she'd looked at him and told him to go along—he was ready and she was not.

Much like the first time, she was home from school long before he drove in, although it was still light out. This time she didn't realize he was home until the door opened and closed behind him. She looked up from her desk, him standing just inside the door, his jacket off and his shirtsleeves rolled up, his face flushed as if he'd spent the day outside in the sun and wind. But his hands were empty and there was a peculiar glaze, almost a puzzlement to his eyes.

She knew he'd worked and worked on the small fiddle. More than once undone what he'd spent weeks on, only to try again. And knew that when he'd set out this day, it was only because he'd been certain he'd gotten every last bit right, finally. That he was more than happy, that he was satisfied with his work. And there he stood, empty-handed, a confusion swarming his face.

She stood as she also said, "Oliver? Are you all right?" Moving toward him. Thinking he'd failed in some essential way, worried that this was true. "What happened?"

He blinked and looked at her, a focus pulling tight. "I'm fine, I guess." Then he said, "Ruthie, it was the damnedest thing. I handed that little fiddle over to him and he peered and sniffed like he did before and then took up a bow and played a jig like sweet fire out of nothing I ever heard before. Then I got out the other fiddle and we played for a long time. There wasn't any talking except we were talking back and forth through the fiddles. It was . . . there's no words, is what it was. It was a grand thing."

She paused herself and then said, "I don't understand. You did a good job, right?"

"Seems so."

"So where's your fiddle?" She corrected herself. "Fiddles?"

190

He nodded and said, "That's it. They're out in the truck. Along with four others he gave me. Four fiddles beat-up or broken or somehow not right that people have dropped off with him the last few years. Hoping he would fix them."

"He gave them to you?"

"He can't do it anymore," Oliver said. Then he said, "He thinks I can."

She nodded slow and advanced a step and said, "And you? What do you think about that?"

He said, "I wouldn't have them in the truck if I didn't think I stood a decent chance."

"Good," she said, as she stepped again toward him and suddenly, swiftly, he came to her, their arms entwining.

That summer Ruth, without consulting Oliver, agreed that the two of them would meet Pete and Noelle Sutton for dinner. When she explained to Oliver she said, "She's an old friend I haven't seen forever and I just couldn't say no. Pete's a claims adjuster for Farmers & Merchants in Barre, she says he's grand at it and is moving on up, soon, in the company. I get the sense she's lonely up there. What's the harm, Oliver?"

He'd paused and then said, "None, I guess."

She drove; Oliver happy in the passenger seat, smoking, the windows down, the summer early evening unrolling beyond the car. The farmers were making hay and the scent of it passed through as they journeyed through the end of a long day of labor for those people, then up through the Williamstown Gulf with its narrow wedge of sky and pressing sides, the road winding hard and tight, big balsams and tamaracks either side of the road, beaver bogs and swamps wherever the land would open up. The air sweet with tannin, open water studded with blooming lily pads, the coming twilight seeming to rise from this place, the booming calls of

191

bullfrogs, a ripple upon still water of a rising trout. Then up on the high land along the ridgetop with the Green Mountains to the west, the far distant peaks of the Whites to the east. Again in full flooded sunlight. Again, open land about them and the smell of new-mown hay. The Andrews Sisters' "Toolie Oolie Doolie" coming through the radio. A silly song but it fit her mood. And Oliver, who didn't care for the song, happy also, one finger tapping time along the edge of the door while he smoked.

They threaded through the east side of Barre and north again a mile or so until the Canadian Club appeared, a long and wide low-slung building in the middle of a large parking area; this Friday night, early as it was, filled with cars. He cupped her elbow as they made their way to the door, her new heels leaving her slightly off-balance in the gravel. Pete and Noelle were already there, had a table and Noelle had a glass of beer, Pete one of ginger ale but soon enough they learned he also had a bottle of rye in a paper sack not so artfully disguised in his jacket pocket. Noelle rose and hugged Ruth, and Oliver stood beside the table and shook Pete's hand, then all sat again. Ruth glanced at Oliver and he nodded and then asked the waitress for a bottle of Ballantine's and two glasses. They sipped the beer and ordered iceberg salads and then steaks and baked potatoes. Pete queried Oliver about his insurance coverage and when Oliver allowed that he thought he was all right, Pete assured him he was probably wrong. He said, "We seen the worst it can get, buddy. Now, no man wants to end up like that and none of us will but you got to be thinking ahead. You got your car insurance a course but what about fire? What about your house? There's a world of problems a man can have with a house. Or, say, you're up on a ladder painting that house and you fall off and ruin yourself for work—that's your disability— it's not only you, you know, but this pretty lady. And your kids. You two got kids yet? Noelle?—" He turned to his wife who shook her head. He said, "We're waiting a bit, also. Not for lack of trying. My dad told me, half the fun of kids is in the trying, in't that so? But seriously, buddy, you got to think about exigencies—what goes wrong you don't expect, can't foresee. That's what insurance is all about—those old-timers, they thought it was a waste, a scam but these are modern times and no man knows how things will work out, in't that the truth? Now, damn, that looks like a steak. A steak and a half, I'd say. Thank you darlin." He addressed the woman serving their food. "You got any horseradish?" Then he looked back at Oliver and said, "I'm not gonna bother you about insurance any more tonight—since that's what you think I'm doing. But do yourself a favor and tuck the idear away. And anytime you want. Give me a call or come by the office. Now, then, bless the taters, bless the meat, bless the Lord, let's eat."

The paper bag rolled down, scrunched around the neck of the bottle he reached it toward his glass and dribbled rye on the table as he filled his glass. Took a neat hard swallow and sawed a chunk of steak and chewed it. The waitress brought a paper cup of creamed horseradish and he sawed another chunk and dipped it, and chewed. While he was doing this Oliver reached out and snagged the cup and tipped a bit of the horseradish onto his plate, had the paper cup back before Pete knew it was gone.

Throughout this Noelle was talking to Ruth and Ruth was doing her best to be in two conversations at the same time—not so hard for an English teacher but not what she'd expected from this night out.

And then Pete began to talk about the war.

This night, at least, it seemed his war had been a war of women. The English girls were an odd lot, some okey-doke, the others aloof. But the French girls had been so welcoming, so grateful. So delightful and happy to welcome their liberators. He'd looked at Oliver and said, "You know what I mean, buddy? How they was."

Only then did he realize no one else was speaking. That their table was shrouded in silence. He looked down upon his ruined plate, then reached a wavering hand and refilled his glass and drank off half of it and smacked it down. He said, to the still-silent table, "How bout dessert? I hear they make a wicked bread pudding."

Oliver spoke, a throaty rasp. "I saw plenty of people do horrible things. Some to survive. Some because they could." Then he looked around, as if surprised to find himself standing. He said, "I never cared for bread pudding."

Ruth drove. Partway home Oliver spoke. The windows were down, the night warm. Still the passing trails of curing hay. There remained an improbable smear of light in the western sky. He lit a cigarette and, wordless, passed it to her and she took it, thankful. He lit another and dragged deep and watched the smoke skim out into the deep dusk. Then he said, "Please? Don't ask me to do that again."

She nodded, a gesture she thought might be invisible to him. So she said, "I won't."

She drove on, silent. A round of questions circled her mind. He smoked and watched the falling dark beyond his open window, his face turned from her. The questions rattled her mind and she drove as they sifted down and finally she settled on one. Very simple but seemed most essential this night. She said, "I thought you liked bread pudding."

He said, "You know I do."

She'd heard stories. Mostly from other women. But a couple so terrible they were featured in the newspaper, over the radio: a man in Island Pond had run a garden hose from the exhaust pipe of his car in through a window one night and was found in the morning by his two-year-old son. A farmer in northern New York, while milking one afternoon had upended a handcart with three cans of milk and after an argument or altercation with his father in the barn had bludgeoned the older man with a peavey handle, then walked to the house where he drove the point of the tool through his mother's breastbone before walking back to the barn loft and hanging himself with a length of hemp rope. The story told by tracks in the mud of a rainstorm already passed.

But there were those closer to home, these whispered mouth to ear, spoken of in hushed tones while preparing church suppers, chance meetings in the village; less gruesome, less newsworthy, little known and thus mostly hidden. But cumulative and frightening. Butch Harrington woke from nightmares up out of the bed, swinging wildly against attackers unseen, and had broken furniture, pictures, windows to the point where his knuckles were bleeding, as if awake, he was still snared by the nightmare, and his wife Evelyn had taken to sleeping on the parlor daybed; Orville Maxham worked his farm up on West Hill dawn to dusk and sober as a post and each night after dinner strapped his three children for misdeeds he'd counted throughout the day; Jared Moore was at work each morning at the gas station in Tunbridge where he could fix any problem that drove or rolled in with a smile and a toss of his head but after work picked up two six-packs of Black Label beer and sat in his car on the North Common, smoking and listening to the radio until just before the Double Dot closed at nine, when he'd roll in and sit at the counter, eating a cheeseburger and a piece of pie before lurching out and driving the three blocks to his parents' house where he'd walk in and brush awkwardly past either that tried to speak to him, crash his way up the stairs and collapse on his bed, fully dressed; Burt Rogers who played ball with the Royalton team, single and handsome in a chiseled Clark Gable way but was observed and then was regularly noted for the interest he showed between innings to the prettiest of the ten- or twelve-year-old girls.

They went along and Ruth concluded things weren't so bad—not what she'd expected but Oliver was kind, tender and absorbed in

195

what he was doing. And he kept steady with his night work for his father. He was also distracted and, times, distant, but she recalled her own father and it came to her one evening that this was partly the way of men, at least of some men. And perhaps not a bad thing—she herself had periods of time when she wanted quiet, wanted to lose herself in a book or her work or even simple dull and necessary routine. As that year rolled over into the next she felt her mother-in-law's frustration with this seeming stasis that had overtaken her son but it was Ed who showed up one morning the spring of 1949 to talk to her about it. In his usual way, his arrival predicted nothing of import—a Tuesday morning of Spring Vacation, Oliver in his shop and Ed arriving to deliver an Easter leg of lamb he'd taken in trade against paying off a debt from a family up on Kibble Hill: winter foodstuffs and Christmas gifts for the young ones.

He sat at the table and took the cup of coffee she offered, thick with cream and sugar the way he liked, then said of the lamb: "I got eight of the Jeasly things—a bumper year for them and thankful for it. But it's not all will eat lamb—I passed em out as Easter gifts to those about the store would take them. I know you like it—and Mother'll bake a ham so I guess there'll be leftovers aplenty. Figured you'd do best with the lamb."

"I appreciate it, Ed. What we don't eat I'll send home with my mother, when we're all said and done come Sunday."

"How is she?"

"Feisty and fine. Feisty when I ask and Fine is what she says."

He laughed. Then said, "Is that how you see it?"

"Best I can tell."

"You see otherwise, anything I can do, you let me know."

"You know I would. But thanks for saying it."

They sat quiet a bit and Ed drank the rest of his coffee and Ruth knew he was after something more and waited. Finally, with nothing else to do, he set his cup down and stood and sucked his teeth through closed lips, then spoke.

"Mother—Jennie that is—is worried about Oliver. Thinks he won't come round and do his part at the store—all this fiddle-making and hiding out from people. I just want you to know I see it another way. First, those fiddles, they're in the blood. I'm happy as can be he's set himself upon that. Somehow it never took between him and me and I gave myself to the business and don't have regrets, there, you understand? But don't think I don't hear what people say. He's good. And that's a grand thing. Second, now, look at me: I'm a young man, see? I know you don't think so but I am—"

"I know you're young."

"No. How old are you? Twenty-four?"

"I'm twenty-three, Ed."

"Yup. And I've not forgot how it is. I'm forty-seven and to a young woman like you I look old. But I'm not. God willing, I got another thirty, maybe more, years to me. I do. So me, I'm patient. If it takes Oliver ten, fifteen years to find himself back at the store the way I run it—well, that's good. I'm not going nowhere. You understand?"

She waited a good long pause and quietly said, "Thank you."

"Don't thank me. Thank him. He's a good man. Doing what he needs to do. And damned glad he's doing it."

He brushed one hand against an eye and then turned and walked in his sock feet to the door where he pushed his feet into his unlaced boots, small puddles on the floor. Took down his wool jacket and shrugged into it and turned.

"See you Sunday?"

"Church and then dinner all of us. I'll have the lamb and a pie and Mother's got an endless supply of apple-mint preserve. We'll be there."

"Yup. Good day, then."

197

"Ed?"

He turned back. "What is it?"

"Do you really think it'll work out as you say?"

He took a moment. "All I know is most things work out. But how I say? Only time answers that question." Then he asked, not for the first time, "The two of you? You all right?"

She flushed brightly warm. Her face right down to her shoes. She said, "We're good. Like you said, most things work out."

"And take time."

"I'm learning that."

He waited the least beat. "Gonna take all my life, is my guess. Yours too, likely."

"That's a terrible thought."

"You think so? Me, I wouldn't have it any other way. Keeps you thinking, right up to the end."

Then gone.

Spring creeps in, back and forth, a season unsure of itself. Then around Memorial Day and school graduation, often the same weekend, summer arrives. Apple blossoms throw brilliant canopies about the trees, then rust and blow away. The lilacs bloom, the gardens are sprouting and gaining fast, the leaves one week are pale green crowns against the sky, the next are dense and dark and throwing full blankets of shade upon lawns freshly mowed, road-sides, carpeting woodsfloors. Might come a few cool days of showers mid-month that only prompts higher the grass, the hayfields, the spill and gurgle of brooks. By the end of the month winter and snowbanks and ice are a flickering memory. Summer in full riot— the songbirds back and some already fledging young, swarming the fields and woods, over every yard and corner, the smell wafting of first-cutting hay, the sun rising before most people are out of bed and long evenings, the day extending itself with a lazy lengthened twilight toward ten o'clock, as if reluctant to give itself to nightfall. Another world of a sudden from the long cold dark now forgotten.

She'd had a wondrous lazy morning. Oliver had come home in the early hours after his work at the store, woke her and kissed her and left her again. She woke to hot coffee and an empty house. He'd gone up toward Derby, answering a call that came in over the telephone about a fiddle a child had dropped on granite flagstones the day before and that the caller—the mother in this case, needed for the coming Fourth of July and a kitchen tunk that evening. Whatever the damage, it was unlikely the instrument could be repaired so quickly but Oliver was on his way to do the best he could and, Ruth knew, taking along his grandmere's fiddle, to loan for the event. The first time he'd offered such service and Ruth wondered if it was because the player was a woman, then pressed the thought from her mind. Oliver worked within his own code, and the code was about music and nothing else. She knew that.

She made toast and drank coffee as she sat and read the paper. After a while she went out to the garden and harvested the last of the peas. Then she took a book outside and sat in the shade of the apple trees and read.

She heard the car coming up the hill and startled. It was no car she knew, and she knew everyone that had reason to drive the hill. When it turned into the drive she was not surprised. Where else might a stranger be going? Still, she only closed the book on her thumb and held it on her lap, not wanting to leave the story, not yet willing to cede even this small portion of her day to a stranger seeking her husband. The rumbling engine shut off and then nothing. No slam of a car door, no one calling out. She sighed and stood, left the book on the chair as if a promise to herself she'd return soon and walked around the house to do whatever she could for whomever it was.

Not a surprise, the car was a ruin of a thing, a jalopy pieced together from other ruined cars. A couple of the older high school boys, a couple of younger men in the area drove such rigs. She tried and failed to suppress judgment—it was a certain sort of young man who chose such a vehicle. And had a ripple of doubt—if the driver was looking for Oliver what sort of disaster of a fiddle might he have? And the means to pay for repair? Then caught herself as a blush of recognition came over her—she was making an assumption once again about someone most probably of French Canadian descent. Had she learned nothing? Then saw the plate on the front of the car. Come all the way from Maine. A signifier of serious intent. And still the occupant had made no effort to step out of the car and in the same moment she understood she was being watched. Appraised as she stood also, waiting.

She walked up to the car, stopping a few feet from the door, the open window. A man, indistinct, sat behind the wheel. Smoking—she could smell it, his head turned away as if he was studying the village below.

"Hello," she called. "Can I help you?"

He turned and leaned an elbow out the window and pushed forward to rest his chin upon his elbow and looked up at her. "I hope so," he said. "I'm looking for Oliver Snow."

He was the best-looking man she'd ever seen. Mouth, nose, eyes, chin, the certain jut of his ears, his dark brown hair grown out from his head like the pelt of some water-living creature but for the cowlick turned up and the curling down upon his forehead. She disliked him immediately.

"He's not here," she said.

"But what they told me down the village? I'm at the right place?"

"He's not here," she repeated. "But if you have a fiddle to be repaired you can leave it and he'll get in touch with you."

He opened the door and stood out of the car. He was a man made right, all his parts aligned as if pulled from a mold. He was wearing khaki trousers over scuffed work boots and a white shirt with the sleeves rolled above his elbows, his face and arms stained dark from hours under the sun. This early in summer even farmers she knew were more burned than dark like this. He was holding out a hand to shake and she took it and felt the softness there in his hand, also the rough edges of old callouses. He was speaking but she was not yet hearing—thinking he worked the woods, this winter, That's how he looks like he does.

He was talking throughout this.

"I don't know the first thing about fiddles. But I am looking for Oliver Snow."

She interrupted him without knowing she was going to. "Who are you?"

"I'm Brian Potter." He paused just long enough for her to realize perhaps he expected she might recognize his name. Then he reached a hand and said, "You're Ruth?"

She felt something was being established between them, with no idea what that might be. She ignored his hand and kept her own clasped before her. She said, "Oliver's not here. What do you want with him?"

He dropped his outstretched hand and snagged both thumbs in his waistband, his hands loose, harmless. He said, "I was in the war with him."

"He's never mentioned anyone named Brian Potter. What do you want with him?"

"I'm not surprised. But see, he saved my life. Which is why I'm here. To thank him for that." He shrugged. "I guess it was a small thing, for him. A moment. But it wasn't for me."

She looked at him again as if seeing him for the first time. She said, "I'm sorry, I don't know what came over me. Yes, I'm Ruth Snow, Oliver's wife. Why don't you come in the house? I'll fix some tea. Or do you prefer coffee?"

"No," he said. "I won't intrude. I'll come another time."

201

"Nonsense," she said. "I won't have it. You've come a long way and Oliver will be back soon enough." Even as she said this knowing it was not true.

"Well, truth is, I could use a cup a joe."

Quickly she said, "You got it."

Before he could protest she poured the cold coffee down the sink, rinsed out the pot and basket and set up a new pot to percolate. As she worked she watched him: sitting on a chair pulled away from the table, his hands easy on his spread knees as he baldly and easily surveyed the room, what else he could see of the house. If there was judgment in him it didn't show and she was proud of her home. She was also curious about him, partly for what he'd said, why he was there, but mostly because she sensed a portal, the possibility of a door into whatever had happened. Oliver's war. And then she halted that thought. As if her mother spoke in her ear, perhaps her father. Oliver held himself close and this frustrated her but it was a choice he'd made and she'd silently agreed to live with it. And she needed to honor that silent agreement. Or she'd be making a betrayal of her husband. A small one perhaps. Perhaps not so small. Digging behind silence—what was that but betrayal?

And she knew nothing of this man seated in her kitchen. He'd tapped out a Lucky and spun the Zippo wheel, pulled the ashtray close and appeared to be absorbed in studying the rings of smoke he lofted toward the ceiling.

The coffee was done and she took the cream pitcher from the fridge and set it next to the sugar bowl on the table, poured out two cups and settled one before him and took the other and sat across the table from him. She waited but he was already turned toward her, his cup lifted from its saucer, his lips pursed as he blew the surface. He drank his coffee black. Sipped and set the cup back in the saucer. He hadn't said a word since coming in and she wondered what this silence was all about—perhaps his own, it occurred to her. Very well probably his own.

"Thank you," he said. "You needn't have gone to the trouble."

"It was hours old, and cold."

Now she felt she wanted him gone—thinking again about Oliver—it could be late afternoon, even dusk, before he returned from Derby. A long trip. But nothing like the trip this man had made. She felt off-kilter, at sixes and sevens as her father would've said. What to do with this man, what to say? Whatever he knew of Oliver at war, whatever had happened, she would not listen to. That alone was Oliver's to tell her and so far he had not.

Brian Potter said, "As I said, it was a small thing for him. What one did if they saw the chance. But for me—well I wouldn't be sitting here, if your husband hadn't seen that chance and acted. Could be he doesn't even recall it—or it was only one small thing in a long day of things large and small. That's how it was. The war, I mean. And also this—you wonder, now I mean, you wonder how many of those small chances did I miss? How many men don't have what I have? The opportunity to try and thank a man? And this, too: How many times did it shave close to me, death, I mean, and I never knew it? Well, plenty, I can say with certainty. Probably freeze my spine forever if I knew the actual number, if there was an accounting laid out for me. But this is what I know for sure and once it was over, that moment, I mean, I made a solemn vow that if ever I could I'd find this man and shake his hand. All I want."

She said, "Oliver does not talk about the war. To me, to anyone that I know of. I don't want to hear your story—that's between the two of you. If he'll listen. I can't say that he will. But he might. The thing is, I misled you. He left early this morning to go up almost to Canada and it will be late in the day before he comes back. He's not here, is what I'm saying. And I'd ask you to stay and wait for him but I have my own work to do and—"

He interrupted. "You don't want me hanging around all day." He smiled.

She said, "That's not exactly what I meant." Considered and then said, "I want you to be able to see him. Clearly you need to and who knows, it might be good for him."

"Good enough." He stood. "But you think late in the day he'll be back around?"

"I know he will be."

He stretched his arms over his head and raised up on his toes. She heard his spine crack as he turned his head side to side. He said, "I'll come back by early evening—if he's not home maybe we can figure out the next step then. Meanwhile, I drove along a pair of rivers—a big one and then up this valley, a smaller one. I've got fishing rods in the trunk of my car—that old wreck. So I'll go chase trout for the day and be happy doing so. Maybe find some feeder brooks and go up those. And don't you worry—I'll be happy as can be doing that."

She felt a panic, as if she'd failed somehow. She said, "You need worms, down to the village is Snow's Mercantile. They sell cartons of worms."

He grinned and said, "Thanks. But I fish with flies. I tie em myself. You know what I'm talking about?"

She said, "A long time ago, when he was a young man, my father did that."

"It's a grand thing. Thanks, Ruth. I'll see you later."

She sat again outside and returned to her book. But the pages made little sense and she wondered if she'd been reading or simply skimming. She'd never cared for historical fiction although Kenneth Roberts wrote of her own place, in the widest of terms—northern New England. But *Lydia Bailey* was of Haiti, and the slave revolt and worse, she couldn't make sense of the plot, or the woman that seemed a sort of dream behind the plot. She thumbed back a dozen pages from where she'd left off and failed to find the momentum, was, in fact, even more lost. Almost one hundred and fifty pages in and she slowly put in place her bookmark and stood, carrying the book to the house.

What troubled her most was she was certain she'd been deeply engaged for most of those pages. And now it seemed, not.

Ruth changed and then drove down to the village and up West Hill to her mother's house. She walked in without knocking as everyone did and surveyed the jars lined up on the kitchen counter. Deep ruby red. Fresh strawberry preserves. There were still a half-dozen quarts of strawberries on the other side of the sink and Ruth guessed she'd be taking home some berries, thought ahead and figured to find some cream in the village, make biscuits that afternoon and have shortcake for dessert that night. All this while passing through the kitchen and dining room and into the library where she found her mother.

Jo was working needlepoint. The house, while not as old as others, was old enough so after sixty or so winters no longer sat quite plumb. Doors between rooms would not always stay open or closed. In her younger years Jo had re-covered a nursing rocker, one free of arms, with a new back, several other seats of chairs as well. But these last years her needlepoint had been a bit less fine, though tight and clean. She was intent upon covering bricks with a single cool color, with her monogram worked upon the top. To be used as doorstops, holding doors open or closed as needed. Understated, hidden unless one looked. Utilitarian.

Ruth sprawled back with a sigh in one of the leather wingbacks across from her mother.

"What is it, dear?"

"Oh. Kenneth Roberts exasperates me."

Jo glanced up, went back to her work. She wore steel spectacles perched far down upon her nose. She said, "I've given up reading fiction. Most of it doesn't make sense to me anymore. Biographies and history hold my interest. Boswell on Johnson remains interesting, if infuriating, often. Gibbon. And the poets; Wordsworth, Keats, Shelley, some of Coleridge. He was a mess of a man but could write, I have to say. And this new man, Frost? You've heard of him?"

"He's hardly new, Mother."

"Perhaps to you. And I've not settled my mind on him—he writes of people I might well know, probably do. How much art is in that, I ask."

"A good bit, is what I think."

Jo only then lifted her eyes and settled them upon Ruth. "Perhaps so. It's all in how it's told. Now then, what brings you here this fine summer morning?"

Ruth paused, took a breath and said, "There's a man come. After Oliver."

"What do you mean? What for?" Jo's tone was arch: a lioness roused to potential danger for a cub and it was nothing more than Ruth expected and still surprised her. Not until this moment sure of how much her mother loved her husband.

"He was in the war with Oliver, he says. He's from Maine. He claims Oliver saved his life."

Jo nodded. "And?"

"And nothing. He wants to talk with him, is all. And Oliver's up to Derby over a fiddle today. The fellow went off fishing and will come back later. I don't know. I guess I hope Oliver makes it home before the man shows back up."

Jo said, "I don't think it's so unusual. Men who met during the war, met in hard ways or strange times, which clearly the war produced an abundance of, I don't think it's strange for one to seek another out. Perhaps if nothing else to gain assurance that whatever that strangeness was, truly did occur. We see it all about us, if you only look: How the war and now life after, are so at odds with one another and yet exist within the same person. Your own husband, I'd say. And Oliver saved this man's life?"

"It's what he said."

"Well, goodness sake. Why wouldn't he come, Ruth?"

"It's not that so much. It's—I don't know."

Jo stood and crossed the library to the walnut stand that held decanters and bottles, racks of glasses and tumblers. As she worked she spoke: "Not even noon but I'm having a neat rye. There's no ice. I'll fix you one as well. There we go. I see your dilemma and have a clear answer for you."

She brought the tumbler with the splash of rye, held on to her own. Ruth took the glass and cupped her hands around it. Jo looked down upon her a moment, then retreated to her chair, sipped and set the glass on the cork coaster on the side table.

She said, "A man has entered your life that might provide you with some answers to what has afflicted your husband. And you might have the opportunity to speak with him, to draw him out, to hear his tale, and in doing so learn things about Oliver that Oliver has not been willing or perhaps able to share with you. Is that it?"

Jo sipped again. Ruth rolled her glass and resisted. Answering her mother, she said, "Of course. If it was you, wouldn't you think that way?"

"I might think that way. But I wouldn't do it. And beyond that, you're making an assumption."

Ruth lifted the glass and sipped. Raw as she was this was gasoline down her throat and it roiled in her stomach and then paced out her arms and flared behind her eyes. She said, "How so?"

"That Oliver will talk to this man."

"Oh, you're right."

"But even if he does, especially if he does, you must wait for Oliver to discuss this visit with you. And if he chooses not to, you must accept that and allow it. What those two might talk about is not necessarily any of your business. Just because they do, does not make it yours. Unless, of course, they choose to include you. That would change everything. Myself, I don't see that happening, but it might. My best guess, my hope, is that after this man has his talk with Oliver and leaves, perhaps, and it might be some weeks or even longer, Oliver will start to talk with you about these things. But you must wait for him. Because . . . Oh my dear. Because if he could, he already would have done so."

"I know."

"So then. You have nothing to lose and everything to gain by your silence. Even if nothing changes. Do you see?"

"It's so hard, is all."

"Of course it is. Men make the work of this world and we women are left to complete the messes they create. So it is, so it has always been."

Ruth lifted her glass and finished the last swallow. "That's a grim outlook."

"No less true, my girl. There's some strawberries in the kitchen you should carry home."

"I saw them. Thank you."

"This man? This visitor? Where is he now?"

"Like I said, he's gone fishing for the day. Oh, like Father used to do, like you told me he did as a young man. With a bamboo rod and flies fashioned from feathers and yarn. He said he made them himself."

Jo looked at her then, lifted her glass for the last least drop of rye and said, "So. He's that sort of man."

Ruth stopped in the village and bought cream, considered the evening meal and weighed against making elaborate plans, leaving it to Oliver to handle this arrival as he would. She bought a wedge of cheddar and a box of elbows. She had the fresh peas and could make a salad from the garden and that, she decided, along with the short-cakes, would provide a comfortable meal. She paused a moment and ran her mind's eye through her pantry and was unsure of baking powder for the biscuits and so added a new can.

Up at the house she mashed the berries with sugar and stuck them in the fridge and set up the mac and cheese to slide into the oven later in the afternoon. Everything else she waited on. It was then noon and she fried an egg and toasted bread and ate that sandwich for her lunch. Then she found *Lydia Bailey* and set it in the basket she used for her trips to the library. Went into her own parlor and ran her fingers along the shelves there and took down *A Further Range* and thumbed pages but she was not in a mood for poetry and slipped it back onto the shelf.

She spent the afternoon cleaning the house. She put the casserole into the oven and went up to take a bath and then dressed in a simple summer skirt and sleeveless yellow blouse that showed off her arms well, then took her measure and left the blouse on but switched the skirt for a pair of old and comfortably worn jeans. Brushed out her hair and tied it up in a bandanna. Down in the kitchen she turned the oven on low and left the mac and cheese to finish slowly. She beat together the biscuit dough and left it on the counter, the bowl covered with a damp cloth—she could bake them while they ate the main meal. The same way she could gather the salad makings from the garden.

It was almost six of the summer evening. She considered again and then made herself a gin and tonic that was mostly tonic and carried that with the most recent *Life* out to the garden and the chair where she'd been interrupted all those hours ago. The sunlight was pleasant, freckled through the old apples, pooled about her, the air clear, free of blackflies or mosquitoes. A line of lumpy clouds floated above the east side of the valley, bellies dark, sides delineated by curves of blue and rose light.

Oliver arrived first and she walked around to meet him. He was, as expected, carrying a fiddle, this one without a case and so cradled in the crook of his arm.

"I'm back, Ruthie," he said. "And boy, do I have a mess on my hands."

"Can you fix it?"

He slipped her his shy grin. "I hope so. But it'll take some time." He was moving around her, to walk back to his shop. He said, "I'm about starved. They wanted me to stay but I wanted to get back. Is there supper? We could go to the Dot. Just let me lay this out on my bench."

"Oliver?"

He heard her and turned. "What is it?"

"There's a man came to see you."

"What man? A fiddle? Ruth, just let me set this down."

She said, "He was in the war with you." But her voice was low, not quite trusting the news she had, not wanting, she realized after, to deliver this to him.

He said again, louder, "Let me set this down. I'll be right back." He ducked his lovely white head, turned and went behind the barn to his shop. She watched him go but also had stopped in some other way. For she heard the rattletrap car coming up the hill.

She stood there in the drive in the paling light as Brian drove in. He hit an old Klaxon horn at the sight of her and pulled up short, feet from where she stood. He stood out of the car swiftly, grinning at her, then bent and lifted out a wicker creel. He looked at the truck, then advanced toward her and opened the lid of the creel.

"He's home, isn't he? That's great. And look." He held the creel before her, a grand mess of trout atop a bed of ferns. "I brought dinner. Does it get better than that?"

She wanted to say she couldn't say when they both heard the door slam shut behind the barn and so both stood mute, watching as

Oliver came around the side of the barn and stopped. His eyes moving back and forth one to the other.

"Potter? Is that you?"

"Oh boy, Ollie." Brian set the creel down and slowly walked forward, his arms spreading wide. "It sure is me. I been waiting years for this. Down to the moment. When I lifted my face from the mud and watched you walking away and knew I was almost dead."

Ruth stood and watched Brian Potter's arms encircle her husband and lift him off the ground. And saw Oliver looking at her over the man's shoulder, his face a stricken confusion, a certain pleading.

Then Brian spun in a circle and she could see nothing until both men were down back on the ground, a couple of feet apart. Each with their hands on the other's shoulders.

She leaned and lifted the creel, carried it inside and rinsed the already gutted fish in the sink and laid them in a bowl head to tail and set that bowl in the fridge. She took out the biscuit dough and worked gently. Then turned the oven back up and removed the perfect mac and cheese, set it on the stovetop and began to turn out biscuits. Doing what she could as she waited what came next.

Oliver popped open the door and stuck his head in and said, "Ruthie? I'm sorry but this guy and I are going down to the Dot and get a burger and catch up. He brought some trout, huh? We can eat it tomorrow, okay?"

Then he was gone. She stood in the kitchen, thinking, I never saw such a panic.

There then began the span of three strange days, as she counted it. Two, she imagined Oliver counted them, if he counted at all. She ate supper finally and went to bed well after ten with no sign of them, even though she knew the Double Dot closed at nine. She left the kitchen light on and the biscuits out, the berries and cream in the fridge. She left a note beside the plate with the stack of biscuits. It was after midnight when she heard the car come up the hill and then some time passed and she heard voices low and hushed through the open window. Twice the beam of a flashlight raked against the sky, the side of the house. The screen door opened and slapped to and she heard water run in the bathroom. Then Oliver came up the stairs with uneven steps and she lay in the dark pretending to sleep as he sagged down on his side of the bed to undress sitting down, some fumbling and a small hitch sideways that he caught with an outstretched hand, a pause as he righted himself and then finished his undressing. She could smell beer and cigarette smoke. She thought Why not? But still she lay as if sleeping and he pulled himself under the summer covers of a sheet and thin blanket, turning away from her to face his side of the bed. It seemed but moments before she heard his breath drag out into gentle snoring. Some time later she also slept.

In the morning as she waited for the coffee to perk she stepped out into the yard and saw a small canvas tent set up in the grass beside the garden, under the apple trees. There was a sag to it and one corner did not seemed pegged tight but it was not a bad job done by men in the dark. Even with flashlights. She walked out and paused by Brian Potter's jalopy, seeing the litter of empty beer cans strewn in the backseat. She'd guessed they'd be there before she saw them. She opened the truck and found a pack of Luckies and a book of matches and sat on the running board away from the house and smoked, considering all of this. And what to do next. Or simply, what to do. And recalled what her mother had told her about leaving them be.

She also knew a thing or two about men the morning after drinking and didn't even have to go inside to check what she had. Instead took the truck out of gear, then pushed it out of the drive as she reached to twist the wheel and got the truck headed down Beacon Hill, jumped in and twisting the wheel and turned the key, held the clutch down as she put it in gear and gained speed. Popped the clutch and drove into the village. She bought a dozen eggs and a pound of bacon sliced thick and went back up the hill, killing the engine to roll in quiet. No one was about although as she passed through the yard to the house she heard deep, nigh-drowning snores from the tent.

She had two big iron skillets and in one she cooked the pound of bacon, stirring it round and round. Too much to cook in flat strips. She lifted pieces out as they cooked and also cracked eggs into a bowl. She left the grease in the pan and got out the trout and cut off the heads and rolled the fish in flour with salt and pepper. Then she fried the trout in the bacon grease and soft-scrambled eggs in the other pan. She worked with deliberation, half hoping one or another of them would arrive and see her preparations. She drank a couple more cups of coffee as she did this work. When it was all done she was still alone. She stepped outside and retrieved another cigarette and smoked that and waited.

The day was fine, clear skies, warming sunlight cast upon her, orioles among the apple trees, hummingbirds working the bee balm in their stammer of flight. Heard feet coming downstairs. She ground out the cigarette and went back inside.

Oliver was in the clothes he'd worn the day before as he poured himself a cup of coffee with the hidden caution of a man atremble. His hair was wet and she knew he'd held his head under the bathroom spigot. The rakes of the comb harrow-marks. He glanced at her, looked away, then turned to her. He lifted the coffee and blew, sipped and then set down the too-hot cup. The saucer rattled.

"Ruth," he said. Then stretched a hand to indicate the food. "This is grand." His eyes were red and filming and she thought he might cry.

She wanted to ask if Oliver and Brian had achieved what they'd intended the night before. But was afraid how it might sound. A condemnation. She was not sure if that was what he would hear or

213

what she might hold. The man sleeping in the tent would leave or not—that was all she knew for sure. And did not want to be part of that decision.

She said, "Are you all right, Oliver?"

He tried out a smile. Said, "Well, my head feels like it got caught between a hammer and a anvil, if that's what you mean."

In the same kind tone she said, "Is it a good thing that he's here?"

Now he got some coffee, his eyes away from her. Then back. "It's terrible, is what it is. But it's what he needs. If that makes a lick."

She nodded. And then said, "Today?"

He ate a curled strip of bacon. Then poured more coffee and held the fresh cup with his hand wrapped around it and said, "We're not done, yet."

She nodded and said, "I didn't think so." Then she said, "What I'm going to do is make myself scarce. You two do what you need to do. And however long it takes, it doesn't matter. He's welcome, is what I'm saying."

"You don't have to go anywhere, Ruthie."

"I think I do. But that's about me, not you. I just want you to spend as much time with him as you want. As much as he needs. Perhaps what you need also, some way. And I'll be about. So, if he gets to be too much, all you have to do is tell me. All right?"

After a time he nodded. Then he said, "The trout. He'll be upset, they get cold."

She said, "It's June. And a warm day. They won't get cold. But go wake him if you want. Because I'm heading out. Mother needs some help, though she won't say as much. You know."

He said, "I love you, Ruthie. I really do."

"I love you too, Oliver." And pulled together every frayed nerve she had, scared as she'd ever been, but walked around him, not stopping to give him the hug she wanted to give. And left the house. Leaving him within it. Knowing he was not alone and the man outside in the tent was but a small bit of what had joined her husband in their house.

She didn't want to see her mother. She didn't want to see anyone at all. She drove to the village and parked behind the school and used her key to let herself in. She thought she'd do a final tidy or do some work preparatory for the start of school almost three months away. But there was nothing to do. She sat at her desk and faced the ranks of empty student desks. A single fly buzzed about the room, striking window after window seeking escape. After a bit she stood and opened two of the windows a scant foot each, then walked behind her desk and pulled down the world map and studied it—it was almost new and so showed the new boundaries, the new world. The world the war had replaced or remade. How vast it all was. How small. No cities were shown on the map, only the zones of occupation. As if Germany had been obliterated and replaced by blank spaces that had no room for people or cities, towns, states. Only overlords. She didn't feel this was a bad thing but rather something earned, the product of war, the spoil of war, a rightful end. And yet there was no way to comprehend anything of what role her husband had in that destruction. Not that if she'd seen a city name or anything more precise, she'd have had any knowledge to tag upon it. But still she felt there should be. Even if those were simply more unknowns.

She sat again behind her desk, looking out upon the empty room. Recalling how filled it had been, seeing those faces. Then thought about what she'd soon be seeing. Those children coming up. She knew them. The din and clatter in the hallways, those certain faces turned toward her, expectant. And thought how much older they'd appear, come fall.

At noon she drove up Beacon Hill. The jalopy was parked in the drive, the truck gone. For a moment she worried about Oliver driving, then thought this might be a good thing. Then thought of men and knew she had no idea who was driving.

Inside, the kitchen was clean, the skillets clean and dry on the stovetop; the bowls and plates and coffee cups washed and upside down in the strainer. As if to let her know they were paying attention. Or what men did when there was no woman there. She had no idea. The heat was turned low under the percolator.

She ate cold mac and cheese. Then poured a cup of coffee and drank that bitter scorched brew. And sitting at the table, surprised herself by speaking out loud. "If I sit here waiting I'm going to lose my mind." Her thoughts had been a muddle; speaking, she held sudden clarity. She'd seen the same thing happen with a student laboring over a draft of an essay, pages long: Five minutes of talk with her and their thesis came clear.

She went up to her bedroom and pulled off her jeans and blouse and put on her one-piece bathing suit and then her jeans and blouse over that. She rolled a towel and carried it downstairs, nested the three empty quart berry baskets, then opened her purse and tucked her driver's license in one back pocket and a five dollar bill in a front pocket. And was out the door.

She drove down the valley on a hot summer afternoon. Some few clouds. The recently harvested hayfields gaining the brighter green of new growth. Cornfields along the winding branch of the river. Knee high by the Fourth of July and it would be, pale stalks against the dark alluvial soil. She crossed the bridge over the White River in Royalton and drove north along the bigger river, the broader valley, the hills farther back and oddly stepped by the glaciers—hills here running west to east and she was driving west. The eastern hips of the hills were low, then rose on an even plane going west until a sudden knob, an upward thrust of hard stone, then a declivity and the slow beginning of another hill. But not broken by valleys, more a series of steps climbing toward the spine of the Green

Mountains some thirty miles west, that ran north and south the length of the state.

Along this road, the River Road, were turnouts, all riverside. Clumps of cars in each one. A summer afternoon. She knew the one she wanted and pulled in and carrying her towel walked down a path to the river. A bend here formed a deep pool but there were also jutting tongues of granite out into the river, beaches of pebbles but mostly larger slabs of stone layered one against another. Riverside elms and maples threw dappled shade and from one big limb a heavy rope hung, knotted three times toward the end, dangling over one of the high slabs to be ridden out over the deep pool and then the sudden drop.

But even this pool was not so swift or deep as others—why she'd chosen this place. There were fewer young men there, only a handful of older teenagers. A gaggle of preteen boys and girls mingled and kept apart. A couple of older teen couples on blankets as remote as possible which was not much. Mothers and young children. She'd wanted peace, away from the world of men and so had found it. Upstream from the bend one older man stood thigh deep in the water casting flies in long deliberate arcs, his clamped pipe emitting blue jets of smoke.

She lay out on her towel, spread on the hot ledge, on her back, her eyes closed against the sun. Voices came and fled over her, high shrieks from the younger children as they thrilled to the sudden chill of the water. The splash from someone plunging from the rope swing. And above and around all of that the heavy slow rush of the water, a constant sound rising and falling in braided rhythms, as if carrying the day away.

When she grew too hot she rose and walked down on tender feet to one of the pebble beaches within the shelter of the curve and made her way out into the river. The ripples of cold up her thighs and slapping at her belly. Then she let herself down in and hung

217

there in the wash of the current before pushing out into the deeper water. It was very cold down around her toes, feet, ankles, then cold all around her. She turned so her feet faced the current and lay back in the river, her toes rising above the surface as she floated down around the bend, then along a smooth stretch of the river until the current nudged her toward the gravel shore above the next bend.

She climbed out and squatted on the stones, holding the delicious cool as the sun warmed her back. Then she walked back up along the twined and braided paths until she was back beside her spread towel. She was calm and satiated and nowhere except exactly where she was. She stretched out again upon her towel, wanting nothing, needing nothing, beyond the bake of the sun and then the return to the river. Already, all tension drained from her muscles. What a summer day could do.

Over the best part of the afternoon she repeated this process two more times. The last time returning to her towel languid, almost stumbling, water- and sun-drunk. Then upon the towel she spent even longer, turning time to time to let her suit fully dry against her. At one point toward the end sitting up cross-legged to run her fingers through her knotted hair. Down below her she watched a young woman she did not know help a little boy of four or five in and out of a pool small for anyone else but large for him. His wild cries as he sank down to sit in the cold water, then bursting up, his skin pimpled with cold, his face a gorgeous scream of pure delight. And all throughout this the woman kept one hand free toward the boy while with the other she held back a toddler girl with ropy blonde curls, wearing only a diaper, red-faced angry because she was denied the water. Finally the woman, with great effort, guided the boy out of the water and up onto the ledge above her, after which she walked into the pool to her knees, the girl cradled against one hip, where then the woman let free the boy and lifted the girl high in the air with both hands, brought her down to kiss her and then lowered her into the water. The girl was silent as her face turned from sunstruck delight to slow comprehension, delight for a moment, then shock and outrage as she felt the cold. And her mother swept her back up from the water. Holding her tight.

Ruth pulled on her clothes over her mostly dry suit and left, her day, her afternoon, not done. She made her way out to her car and turned about and drove back down the River Road, through Royalton and on to the Ellis farm. At the stand she got a wooden flat and nested in the empty quart baskets after turning her own empties in and walked out down the long rows to the section the woman at the stand had indicated for her, crouched on the hay mulch with the flat before her and began to pick strawberries. It was the same place her mother had come, although she'd bought berries already picked. It was the same place many years ago where Ruth and Jo had picked berries and Jo had to keep telling Ruth to put them in the baskets, not in her mouth. The field was long and broad, ran along the river but was belted by trees and here and there thin needles of shade ran out over her. Still hot. Summer. She ate the biggest berry she'd yet found. And smiled. But come winter she'd have jars of preserves for toast or perhaps a pie. She had rhubarb canned as well.

And then there in the field came back the memory just gained and left behind of the mother and her children. A clamp or clench in her stomach. She sat back on her heels and looked at the sky. Not a cloud in sight, the vault of blue near to black as afternoon turned so slow to evening. She wanted. She wasn't jealous, was grateful for all she had. Truly she was. She wanted and hoped. The woman was younger than she was but not so much. And she was young. And Oliver was young. Time lay ahead. And if she'd learned nothing these past three years she'd learned what you get comes different than how you'd thought. Almost always.

Or perhaps always. And that was how it should be. For how else does life reveal itself to be what it is? How could it?

Meanwhile, she had berries to pick. Which she did. The job at hand.

The house was empty when she returned. She wasn't surprised, although it could've gone either way, all she knew. It was still only the truck that was gone—they were off somewhere. She made no effort over dinner but instead cooked down the strawberries and canned them, listening to the radio. When she had the two dozen jars cooling from their bath, lined up on the counter so she could check the lids in the morning, it was after ten o'clock. She ate cold mac and cheese and then a big bowl of broken biscuits covered with crushed strawberries and a mighty heap of whipped cream. It was all wonderful; she was ravenous and exhausted.

She went up to bed. Sliding her heat-burned skin under the covers she thought she'd wait up for a bit but there wasn't a book beside the bed. She turned off the switch, bringing darkness down. Next thing she knew there were birds singing in a fog-paled dawn beyond the windows and it was a new day.

And nothing had woke her during the night. She was in a house alone.

Midafternoon she heard the truck drive in. She was cleaning the pantry shelves, wearing old slacks and a worn-out workshirt of Oliver's, her hair tied up under a bandanna knotted in the front. The pantry had shelving on all three sides that rose from her knees to the ceiling. There were bins for flour or potatoes, dry goods, built in under the shelves. The pantry had missed spring cleaning, intentionally. With summer and the garden and other fresh foods, the pantry stock diminished and so there were fewer cans and jars and tins to move about, to reorganize. There was also a thick coat of dust on all the shelves, the higher she went, the more there was. So her hands and face were grimed and moist with the effort on a hot afternoon, trousers and shirt as well. A basin of dirty soapy water stood atop the step stool, a rag twisted brown draped on the side of the basin. She had a flash of irritation, then calmed—she'd known when she'd started the job they might arrive back. Perhaps she even wanted them to arrive then, to see her in hard earnest labor while they were, well . . . up to whatever they'd been up to. Then felt a little small because of this thinking and went into the kitchen and washed her hands, splashed water on her face.

She heard one of the truck doors slam. Only one. And thought What has come now? She stood at the sink, drying her hands well past need on an old hand towel, facing the wall, waiting.

He rapped gently on the screen door and she turned and faced him. "I was cleaning the pantry," she told him. "Come in. Where's Oliver?"

She stepped away from the sink but only just as Brian Potter opened the screen door. Once through he stopped and let it shut behind him. His clothes were wrinkled but somehow still neat, his face ashen, his eyes darkly pouched. She held her alarm and waited.

"He's wicked sick."

"What? How? Should we take him to the doctor? Where have you two been?"

He shook his head. "If there was a time to take him to a doctor that time's passed. I think all he needs is to go to bed and finish the sleep he started a couple three hours ago. Which allowed me to get him back here. I'm sorry, that's not very clear. I thought I'd help you get him in and up to bed and then I'd be obliged to explain, the best I can."

His odd formality struck her as a deeply fatigued honesty. She replied, simply, "All right."

Still, he held a moment. She sensed he was gathering courage. Then he asked, "Is he a drinker?"

Ever more alarmed she started forward, then stopped. Brian Potter held a bruised and tested authority about him. She said, "He'll have the odd beer, time to time. But not the way I think you mean."

221

Brian smiled. Said, "Good. I don't think you have anything to worry about there. If he had a taste for it I suspect that's pretty much gone now. Let's bring him in."

She followed him out to the truck. Oliver was slumped in the passenger side, the window rolled down only enough to let air flow over him, the side of his face mashed against the glass, his mouth open and a smear of drool pooled down. Brian opened the door and at the same moment caught Oliver and held him. Together they worked him out of the truck and Brian took Oliver up in his arms as if lifting a sack of flour, a heavy weight dragged by its own inertia but a weight the man was equal to. She quickly stepped and held Oliver's head up, taking some of the weight from his torso into her arms.

She could smell him; a swirl of sweat, bile and the harsh reek of alcohol emitted from his pores, his sweat, his mouth and nostrils. His clothes askew, as if they'd been removed and replaced not exactly right, splotched with stains that could've been anything from dried blood to food to that same food or other food vomited up from him. She looked up at Brian as he said, "You got him, now? Let's go in. Let me hold the most of him."

Which he already was. She said, "Let's go. It's up the stairs and down the hall—"

"I know."

He stepped off gently and she held her husband's shoulders, his head against her breast, and they made it up the steps and through the kitchen to the hall and up the stairs and down to the bedroom, a couple of times missing the pace and having to pause, to regain and move on. But they made it and ever so gently they placed him upon the bed. And stood side by side looking down, catching breath.

Brian said, "I can help get him undressed and whatever else you need. It's not anything I haven't done before."

"No," she said. "You go downstairs. I'll settle him and be down when I'm done."

It took her less time than she thought; less time than she wanted. Worked his clothes off of him and partway through he began to snore, deeply and slowly. Once he was naked she got a wet washcloth and wiped clean his face and then stopped, looking down at him. Whatever else she did now wouldn't matter—when he woke from this fever, this whatever-it-was, that was when he'd want and need to bathe. She rolled him to one side and got him under the sheet and left the blanket off, for now. The room was afternoon-warm and the least breeze played through the window screens. What he needed, she thought.

Downstairs Brian Potter sat at the table with a quart Mason jar filled with ice cubes and water. Only now did she realize how shaky she was and so got a glass herself, and cubes from the tray and filled it. A simple thing that calmed her. She turned around her desk chair and sat and said, "What happened to my husband?"

He waited, then pushed a wry smile briefly upon his face. As if he knew what she was truly asking and had guessed it would be his job to tell her—a realization come to only in the past hours. She saw this.

He said, "The first night we ate cheeseburgers and then went to the VFW and drank beer and he listened to me talk. What I was here for. After a bit I realized that was what he wanted—for me to talk. He was reluctant to have me there but, seeing how I was, he left it to me to speak. As if he'd been ahead of me figuring out how best to deal with me, how best to let me relive what I needed and to keep himself at a remove from it. Which was what he wanted. I don't think I figured that out until sometime last night. Because, see, I was overcome with facing him again, with doing what I'd promised myself I'd do. To thank him, you see."

"You said he saved your life."

"He did."

"Will you tell me about that?"

He pulled cigarettes and a lighter from his shirt pocket and offered them and when she declined he lighted one. He smoked and crossed one leg over the other knee and when the ash grew long he leaned and tipped the ash into the cuff of his pants. She almost rose for an ashtray but knew he was working things out and so let it be.

"I might." He concluded after thinking. "He's not talked to you about the war?"

"I think you know the answer to that."

A pause again. Then he said, "So I have that, also."

She thought again of what her mother had told her and said, "No. Not if you don't want to."

"I can just leave? And you'll be content to have him back and let him recover and leave him be? Not bother him about this weekend, how he returned, the shape he was in? And go on as the two of you have been?"

"It's not been so bad!"

"I can see that." Then was quiet a long pause, looked down at the floor and studied as if he'd cipher some answer there. He looked up again and stood and said her name.

"What?"

"If I give you what you want, it will never be the same. Do you understand that?"

"I have to know. How can I not?"

He stood looking at her and then turned and said, "God damn it." He walked to the screen door and out onto the porch and she leaned and watched him as he smoked again. She waited. And knew then, there, all was about to change and she wanted whatever was made of that change, however her life turned she knew she'd turn with it and knew the man upon her porch had come or been sent to enact that change. And he clearly hadn't known that coming in but he certainly did now—likely had known for hours, longer.

Then watched him turn and come back into the house. His tired face set, his lips asnarl, an arch of anger, distemper. Upon himself, upon her, she did not know. But would soon.

"He saw her last night. Or thought he did, it amounts to the same thing. The blonde girl; did he ever tell you about her?"

"No." Her voice small and uncertain.

If he heard her fear he paid it no mind but filled his jar again at the sink and sat across from her. His face was no longer angry but his eyes distant, red, darkly pouched. She thought This was how he'd looked during the war, the part they were speaking of. Finally, he settled those tired eyes upon her and said, "I don't think a person can understand how it was unless they were there, and if you don't know that, how can you understand the rest? So I'll do my best to first tell that. How it was.

"In May of '45 when we crossed the Rhine it was terribly exciting and simply terrible. Made worse because we'd been sitting, waiting, most of April. We knew the war was almost over, none of us though knew how soon or what we faced. What lay ahead. But the first thing to understand was how enormously different it felt to be inside Germany—all those months since the invasion of France, fighting across France, there was much to be frightened about, and the land itself, the villages and towns, what was left of them, was terrible to see, to be there—none of us knew day to day what would come next. But it was *France*. And then, after some weeks waiting, we went across the bridges made by the engineers and were in *Germany*. Do you understand?"

She remained quiet. He went on.

"Every man among us knew we were winning the war. We were a conquering army. But we didn't know how soon or how long it would take for the Germans to surrender. I guess the generals and high command had a pretty good idea but we didn't. And so we didn't know what we'd face. Or how quickly it all would happen. What we knew was we were there. What that does, in a man's head, is a strange thing. We fully expected to encounter some huge force, the army the Germans had held back for just this event—why would we not expect that? If nothing else during those years we'd learned not to underestimate the Germans. There was talk among the men about new weapons, new bombs the Nazis had developed, for just such an event. More immediately, there was talk not only of hidden divisions but an understanding that every man in the country, the young women and older kids, also had been instructed and trained to fight. So we had no idea. And we crossed that river, that border, and then were within the place itself. All around us. How that works on a man's mind. You're all jacked up and it never quits. But not like it was across France. It was almost as if your mind and the land had come to some agreement: Nothing will make sense and the further you go and whatever happens, nothing makes sense even more.

"How it was. Listen: Those first days, there were no divisions waiting for us. But that didn't mean they weren't there, waiting five miles away, ten miles away. You got more nerved up the further you went. It was slow going. Every bridge, regardless of how small the road, had been blown by the Germans. So the engineers had to work with what they had and rebuild. There were tanks with us, which was good, but made the going slow also. My company, the second day was working across a ruined land but it was country and so here and there were farms, the remains of farms. And on the second day—I saw this—a bunch of us had just passed an old stone barn with the roof burned off some time ago when it blew up. A huge explosion that sent rocks the size of, well, slabs, that had built the barn a couple hundred years ago, flying through the air. I don't know how many men were killed, how many wounded, from that. And only moments before it had just been a barn. That's how it was. It seemed like there were no people, no German people, anywhere. Then you'd see someone dart off into the woods or down a ravine. Doughs chased and often as not came back empty-handed but a couple times I saw them return with someone. An old man with half a leg using a crutch and that leg had been gone a long time. Or an old woman looking at us like we were spawn out of hell. Once it was a kid, a boy not more than seven or eight and he was twisting and fighting to get away, spitting at the men who held him. Someone knocked him over the head with a rifle butt and they carried him away. And there were dead horses on the road we had to make our way around and carts full of household goods and clothing lying there as the people abandoned that stuff and took to the woods or fields or maybe went down into a roadside ditch and whoever had a weapon killed them all and then themselves. And those few people we did see, women, mostly old, men, all old, and kids, there was no joy in our arrival. Contempt and hatred. The weeks before we invaded *Stars and Stripes* had a couple articles about how all Germans were not Nazis, how many had to go along to get along, and I'm sure that was true. But we sure didn't see any welcome then. Some later, after the war was over, but not then. You see? We walked through all that.

"Our division, some of it, we'd been sent across country, not the main roads but small lanes and roadways, so that was what we encountered, what we saw. Stuff like that. Then we came to the Neckar River, and across that the town of Heilbronn. And that was where Oliver saved my life. As we got close the Kraut artillery up in the hills around the town opened up on us and we'd finally found what we'd expected. And the city was burning, from their shells, from ours. Later we learned the whole place had been firebombed back in December but the Air Corps guys were back, doing their job. And our own big guns. We crossed the river at night in amphibious assault boats under a cloud of smoke from the bombing, from the burning. But the Krauts knew that's what we were doing. The sky was red and orange from the fires in the town and obscured by floating oily smoke. And the buildings, it seemed the buildings were all ruins—a wall, a part of a wall, some few standing but with empty windows, burnt out from firebombing, then reinhabited since, best they could. There were snipers up in some of those and we were going forward in the dark, building to building, trying to hold enough of them to shelter for the night. We could tell some of these had been factories or warehouses, those along the river and some blocks in. It was all a mess—we had no idea how many German infantry there were, or where. Except clearly there were a bunch, along with their big guns in the hills.

"And this also—gangs of kids. They knew that ruined town better than anyone, certainly at night. And time to time two or three would pop out, ahead but most often behind and hurl bricks or cobblestones at us. Winged and took down more than a few but they were so fast they were gone before we could do much—and they knew all the ways the interiors of those buildings connected, and how they didn't. We kept learning that over and over the next couple of days.

"We were crossing railroad tracks, five or six lines altogether, the railyard was what it was. And there was a wooden building burning alongside, somehow spared from all the other fires that winter but it lit the place up like daylight and in some other buildings there were snipers, or maybe just one or two—that was how it was. Nothing could be known for sure. Then one of our tanks rolled up and took down the building with the snipers in it and so we started to cross more easily. I was up at one end of my platoon and where we were crossing was just below where the tracks came around a curve. And at the edge of the light from the burning building. I was holding cover for those ahead of me, and once they were across I started out. Not fast or slow but moving and still watching those ruins, my guys piled up against one wall and waiting to start advancing again.

"Just like that someone jumped me from behind and, arms wrapped around me, took me forward fast and then down and we rolled together into the cinders and gravel down into the ditch of embankment the far side of the tracks. As a single old boxcar slammed on past, came out of the dark up around the curve and then into the light of the fire and one of the tanks put an .88 into it and it burst into flame and collapsed off the tracks. Oliver was already up, reaching down to help me stand. Because he alone saw it coming. And I was right there, my back to it, no idea at all. So there, now. That's how he saved my life.

"There's uncountable ways to die in war—I know I saw more than I want to remember, let alone count. I could tell stories about that but won't and I doubt any man will. But all I know, all I can say is, I was nearly run over by a boxcar. It was about a sure thing. It was probably some of those kids that released the brake and got that thing rolling. And over the next few days, now and then when I had the chance, I scanned those tracks and I swear there wasn't another piece of rolling stock in those yards, anywhere. Which makes sense— the Germans had been moving troops east, what few they could. By then we'd all heard about the camps and the Air Corps had been targeting rail-lines, anyway, ever since they got over German airspace. So I was nearly crushed by maybe the last unused piece of rolling stock in all of Germany. But Oliver saw it coming and ran across those tracks and both of us were lucky. Do you see? But he wasn't a hero—I've heard about men and read about situations where someone was called a hero. But there aren't any heroes. There's just men who see what has to be done and do their best to do it. Some succeed. Many don't. But, and I'm maybe getting ahead of the story here or perhaps not, once I got home, once the war was done, I knew there were countless ways I could've died. But there was only that one time when I knew I would've except for another man seeing what was about to kill me and doing what was needed. And what was left of the war didn't kill me but that night stayed with me. So once I got home I knew one day I had to look him up and thank him. If it's one man you know for certain kept you alive, how could you not do that? So here I am."

He took a slow drink from his water and she watched his throat working. His eyes had gone away from her and when he set the jar down he pulled out again his lighter and the pack of smokes and she watched him, the tremble in his fingers as he labored to extract a smoke from the pack and then his struggle with the lighter and once he finally got fire to the tobacco and jetted plumes, she watched him pull himself to his feet, as if there was a great pressure in the room holding him to his chair. Once up, wordlessly he offered the pack to her and she shook her head. He leaned, with great uncertain care, to place the pack and lighter on the table, an offering if she wished to change her mind.

"Yes," she said. "Here you are."

"I think," he said and stopped. Then said, "I think I should leave now."

She breathed. With great calm of voice as if speaking to a frightened horse about to bolt, some creature, she said, "But you haven't told me about her. The girl."

"Oh. No, you're right. I have not." His eyes swaying everywhere about the room except upon her.

"Can you?"

The sorrow of him, his sag, his look upon her finally. "But I have to, don't I?"

"I think you do." She stood and said, "Why don't you step out on the porch and finish your smoke, first? And I'm going to check on Oliver."

He took a long wavering beat and then said, "That would be good."

Oliver was sweating, snoring, oblivious. She wet the washcloth with cool water and mopped his face and went back downstairs. And she paused then, thinking, I can just send him away. I don't have to hear this story. And wished she was strong enough to do so. And wondered if she was strong enough to hear it. She went down the stairs.

She had been gone long enough so he'd clearly used the downstairs bathroom—his face and hair were wet, his hair slicked back with a comb but the unruly cowlick already peaking up wet. He didn't look tired, as if the muscles of his face had tautened while waiting for her. His eyes bright. This vigor surprised her and reminded her also.

"I never thought," she said. "Fried eggs or a sandwich?"

"No, I'm fine. There was plenty of that and more." His voice was relaxed and she then understood his strain had increased. He said, "I'm still not sure about this."

"I am."

He nodded. "I thought so. Let's sit again, I refilled our waters."

And he had. He didn't wait but went again to the table and sat. Beside his cigarettes and lighter, beside his Mason jar, he'd also found the cut-glass ashtray from the sideboard and placed it there. She made her way to her chair, her own water, but he was already talking as she settled.

"It was toward the end of the second day. Things had improved but we didn't know that, yet. We were still in the streets, clearing building by building. Ruins of buildings. Heaps of rubble. The town had been firebombed back in December. Most of what we saw, what we found, were ruins from that time and the winter now over and how people had lived. And still were. And like I said, there were snipers. That's all there were, as far as regular German Army. Snipers left behind. But we didn't know that—we still expected any moment to turn a corner where there would be entire platoons waiting for us. And even though we didn't, it was hard going. Not a square foot of trust all around us. Snipers, you have to understand—those guys are not only really good at what they do, but also this: They'd been left

231

behind, had *chosen* to stay behind, knowing it was the end of the game for them. They knew the war was lost. That they were only alive as long as they could stay alive. Which, except for the few who surrendered, meant killing as many of us as they could, then fading back into the next building. Which I guess they knew as well as the kids I talked about—maybe, likely even, some of those kids were guides. See, there? I'm not painting much of a picture, am I? Except we were figuring it out, that day. Once, I'm remembering this now, we made it around a corner and saw a woman in the street and then she darted toward one of the buildings and disappeared. Except there wasn't a building, just a pile of rubble. And a group of us went up slow and all jacked up and poked around and saw there was a hole in the collapsed bricks and charred timbers and inched in and saw the hole went down. Twisting down. So down we went and came to a door, a thrown-together door of metal roofing and old timbers and we banged on that, hanging back, all of us packed against the sides of the entryway and our rifles ready and grenades to lob, like that. And finally the door opened a crack and a woman stuck her face out and, in German, said, 'No guns here, nobody to shoot,' and we knew what that meant and we could smell them also. It was a basement filled with people, very old or very young and they'd been in there for weeks, maybe months. Living there. And hidden some days, a week or more, waiting for us and terrified and starving and cold and sick and some dying. That was one thing I remember. We got them out of there and sent them back down the line to the medics and the guys taking charge of prisoners. Because, this is key here, every single person was a prisoner at that time. And for weeks, months afterward. Another story, though, that one. But to give you a sense of how skewed everything was those few days."

He paused and lighted a cigarette and studied her. She looked back at him and waited a moment and nodded, as if giving permission. He answered with his own nod, ground out his smoke and said,

"Everybody was exhausted. The spring sun had lifted out of the town and only the hills held light. There were fruit trees blooming. On the hills in orchards and also here and there along the streets. Pale pretty things that seemed to have no place there. Or didn't care what we were up to. I was right behind him. We'd passed a quiet corner, an old brick house with no roof or second floor and most of the first broke open and there wasn't anybody there. Then he heard something and swung about so fast a couple doughs almost fell over him. But he was stepping around them and there she was, a girl rushing toward us as if she'd come out of the air and she was holding out a round metal thing in her hands, thrusting it toward him and saying something in a high queer voice that only later I realized was fright but the thing is, she wasn't supposed to be there—we thought the building was empty and there she was with some sort of bomb in her hands and he opened up and she was blown back against a pile of dirt and burned bricks, the bomb clanking down dead also, and then she was just a girl maybe ten years old in a dirty white skirt and a red-splotched seeping blouse and long blonde hair done up in braids. He yelled for a medic, like you do and she was watching him. He dropped his rifle and knelt down and dug out a gauze pack and pressed it to her chest. Guys were coming up around them, including me and he jerked his head around and again yelled for a Medic and then turned back to her and she was sputtering, trying to breathe and then in that clipped English some Germans had she said, 'I am alone.' And then she died. Eyes open to the sky."

He knocked out another cigarette and smoked and then said, "It wasn't a bomb at all. It was some sort of copper hot water bottle. She was trying to make a gift of it. An offering of some sort. It was likely a family treasure she'd held on to. All she had left. Because over the next few days Oliver asked around, as things settled, and he learned that she and her mother were the only ones of her family that survived the December bombing. Her father had been sent to the

Eastern Front in '43 and not heard from since. She'd had two younger brothers who died in the December raid and their house had been destroyed. But she and her mother had held on. Living with others like them. Then a month before we arrived her mother got very sick, a fever, who knows—most everyone in the town was sick or ill from the winter, from the entire war, from bad food or no food. And her mother died and she was alone. That's what Oliver learned. Her name was Brigitte."

He looked down at the floor then. Spread his knees and leaned his elbows upon them and studied those old floorboards.

Her heart was thumping hard in her chest. Almost a panic with this news, this story. She said, a gulp of words, "But it was an accident."

He looked up but was quiet a long time before he answered her. He said, "Sure, it was. But war is a strange and terrible business. There she was, lived through all of it. And just weeks to go before it was done. Truth is, for her, it would've been that very day. And Oliver knew all that. How it struck him. That, but for him, she'd be alive today. And, I don't know, but I'd say killing her was a cumulative of everything else he'd been through." He was quiet a moment and then said, "She was the moment it became too much, for him."

She stood and took one of his cigarettes and smoked and walked about the kitchen and he watched her do this. She stubbed the smoke out in the ashtray and said, "So. You show up and three days later my husband is lying in bed struck sick from drinking. Is that because you came? Can you tell me that?"

But she waited no answer and went to the sideboard and poured a finger of gin into a glass and then crossed to the fridge and cracked ice cubes and filled the glass with quinine tonic. She offered him nothing but took her seat again and waited, her eyes bright and liquid upon him.

He said, "I think all he wanted was to show me a good time, to keep me here another day and I can't say why except maybe to show me how he was. We drove a couple hours north to a fiftieth wedding anniversary party—the kind the old-time Canucks have. There was a tent set out in a field from the house and forty or so cars and trucks parked around. In the tent there were tables of food and tubs of iced soda and beer, one with watermelons in it—some *Mon Onc* had driven to Boston for those. And the old couple were holding court under the tent, in armchairs carried down from the house. It was a couple hundred people, maybe more. And people playing music all over the place—fiddlers teamed up and fiddlers playing with men or women playing accordions, a pair of guys with guitars playing cowboy songs. A grand old party, it was. And loads and loads of kids—well fifty years married—how many grandkids would there be, and great-grands also? He and I were both wandering around talking to people the way you do and drinking a beer or two—at least I was. And then I saw it all, clear as day. There was a girl cut through the crowd and she walked right up to Oliver and was talking to him and she was the spit image of that girl from Heilbronn. I saw it, even from the distance I was. How do you explain something like that? Chance? Of course there's people in the world look like one another. But there she was. She even had her hair braided up on the sides of her head. And in one hand a fiddle, a smaller one like a child uses. And I saw him lean and talk and then sway back. She stepped closer and tugged at his shirt and he looked around, his face wild as could be and then he was gone. Ran right out of the tent. It took me a while to find him. But, a party like that, there's always a place a few men find, away from the others. Wasn't the house or anything like that. But I got far enough away, out to the edge of all the parked cars and I heard a single fiddle playing and followed that and the old empty chicken shed where a half-dozen men crouched in the dust, smoking and passing some clear liquor back and around; one old guy sitting on an upturned crate playing those old slow sad songs. Oliver wouldn't talk to me but was intent on the drink and I let him be, although I didn't leave. I took a couple sips offered by another fella and it seared my throat. So I sat out in a chicken coop most of the night. At one point I left him and walked back to the tent and ate and kept my eye out for the girl—I wanted to see her again, but I never did. Then when I got back to the coop Oliver seemed sober as a judge and was angry with me. Said it was time to go. And just then another man stepped up with another fiddle and handed it to him and challenged him to play reels and airs and whoever quit a song first got to call the next one. And used his teeth to pull the cork on a new bottle of that liquor and Oliver stood a moment and his knees sagged and I thought There, I can get us home now. Then he tucked the fiddle to his chin and scraped the bow and they began to play. And drink. And play. This went on a long time and the sun came up and after a while I trailed off with a couple other men up to the tent where there was a breakfast spread out and I ate and had coffee and after a while I went back down to the chicken coop and it was empty but for Oliver and the other fiddler, both sunk down in the old hay, both near passed out but both still scratching out songs. Sort of. It was then I was able to get him up and pretty much carried him to his truck and found my way back here. I guess I could've done better but at the time I didn't see how."

There came a silence then that stretched out. Ruth finished her drink and leaned to set the glass on the floor and remained bent over, pressed down. They could hear the Seth Thomas clock ticking the seconds in the next room. Faintly came the sounds of slow labored snoring from upstairs. Incongruously, a flittering rise and fall of birdsong came through the screens. Ruth whispered, "Oliver. Oliver."

Brian finally, softly, said, "You never know. Maybe this was what he needed. To have me come, to have someone with him who'd been there. Sometimes a secret loses its power when it's no longer a secret."

236

Then she looked up. Slowly she shook her head and said, "I'd like to think so. But you don't know Oliver. Sorry to say that, but it's true." Her eyes were filmed, either distance summoned or she was holding tears: both.

"All right," he said. "A man you know in war is not the whole man. Some would argue otherwise but they would not have been to war."

Then he paused again and she felt the weight of him in the room and wanted him to leave and didn't want him to go, not yet. Unsure of how to place this new sense of her husband against all she'd ever known of him; even the silent man since his return.

Brian stood and said, "You see, something like that happens to all of us."

"What do you mean?"

"Say, I'd take that drink now. If the offer's still open."

"Of course. But . . ."

"Why? I guess I have my own story to tell."

She was quiet a moment, then stood. She said, "I don't know how much more I can stand but let me make us both drinks, and I'll do my best. Gin and tonic?"

"I'll do it."

"No," she said. "You won't." And took her glass to the sink and went to the sideboard in the other room and poured out two drinks, this time almost even amounts of gin and tonic, carried them back to the kitchen and cracked out the last ice cubes and floated them into the glasses where they crackled. She left the drinks on the counter and refilled the trays and placed them carefully back in the freezer. Willing the tremble out of her hands. But thinking there was a very good chance ice would be wanted later this afternoon. Or evening.

She handed a glass to him. He was slouched back now in his chair, a leg crossed over the other knee. Again smoking. She wanted one of his cigarettes but didn't ask, only returned to her chair and sat with her knees together and took a swallow of the drink and then held the sweating glass between both hands. She met his eyes and thought again they'd changed, receded someway, even as they seemed ever more fresh.

She said, "All right. But this has to be the last story." She paused as a rill of laughter filled her throat. She said, "I don't think I can take much more."

He looked away and stubbed out his smoke and took a swallow, easily, but glanced at her. Then he said, "I'll do my best to keep it short. This was the fall of '45. We were the conquering army. Brings out the best and worst of men, is what I saw. But during that time, the entire population was under our control. I saw officers almost on a whim it seemed send whole groups of male prisoners off to the new camps, the Allied prisoner of war camps. Schoolteachers, scared old mayors, certainly there were bad men, Nazis trying to hide out, among them. Which was what was supposed to happen. Other times an officer would interview a group of the same sort of men and make a choice, tell them to just go home and get things right best they could. But mostly, nothing was sorted out yet. And our job was to help sort them out, one by one. Until the next stage of the plan was determined. So, well, there was a share of abuse that went on. Or maybe just payback. It's so hard to say, even now. Although, and this is my story, a thing I witnessed, there were plenty of times it was clear, even while it was happening. But there is no judge, no jury. Except how a man feels."

"I'm not a man," she said. "But I'm a fair judge, I think."

"I don't need you to judge. I'm only telling what I saw. The people, they still had nothing. There was some rebuilding but not much. Makeshift schools were opening for the kids. But there was nothing even close to normal life—maybe it was even less normal than how people had lived during the war. Because we ran everything, the Americans and the Brits and also, east of there, the

Russians—now we heard stories about them and maybe that made us feel better about how we were dealing with it all. Or maybe that was just hindsight, or maybe just bullshit at the time. Pardon my French. But the local people, they were still living very hard. And there were plenty among us happy to see them that way. For obvious reasons.

"But here's my story. One afternoon a convoy of trucks pulled up—this was a regular thing by then, the roads repaired and that was how we all got our supplies. And one of those trucks was loaded with tins of gasoline, to fuel all the other vehicles, the jeeps and like that. Well, one of those tins had a leak, a slow drip, and one of the boys of the town had discovered it and he'd got a bottle from somewhere and was knelt down under the truck, hiding best he could as he filled the bottle. Fuel of any kind was precious—meaning almost none existed in the town. Even wood from the countryside was scarce. People had no way to cook except what we allotted. Which was little. That was all part of keeping control. I know, seems like if we'd been more generous it would've showed them how wrong they'd been but that was not the way it worked, those early days.

"That boy was caught. With his bottle of stolen gasoline. They hauled him up to the building being used as a holding area and I was there, inside. I was filling out some papers that were overdue. Anyway, that's where it started for me. These three doughs, I knew them but not well, hauled him in and set the bottle of gas on the desk and they had him terrified already. He wasn't maybe ten or twelve. It was hard to tell—the children were all small for their age. Anyway, they put him nose to the wall and the one guy, Decker was his name, he took charge, and told the boy to keep his nose against that wall but otherwise not to touch it. While they figured out what to do with him. Then they talked and talked. How he was a thief and also how he must've been planning a bomb or something like that. To make from the bottle of gas. And how they should just shoot him and be done with him. All the while the kid stood there, nose to the wall. He didn't have any shoes and his trousers were too big for him and hitched up by a belt also too big for him and his shirt was old. A shirt that had many owners before it came to him. And he kept saying over and over how he just wanted some fuel for his mother to cook with and how sorry he was and every time he spoke Decker would step in and swat the back of his head and ask if they'd asked him to talk. Which they had and it confused the boy even more, although his English wasn't bad—by then most of the kids about town had a fair grasp of English. And Decker would tell him to get his nose back against the wall. And talk to his buddies about should they just shoot the kid now.

"I was done with my paperwork and watching all this and I believed, I truly believed, those guys were just scaring the kid and, maybe also thinking he needed scaring. Because while there was less of it, there was still strange things happening, a guy killed here or there—that sort of thing. None of us had forgotten the stories we'd heard about how the kids had been trained to keep the fight going, after the surrender. So maybe I thought the kid was learning something. I don't know. But I didn't say or do anything. Because I didn't see what was coming—I don't think any of us did.

"Then Decker stepped forward and grabbed the kid by the back of the neck and hauled him out into the street. His buddies followed and I did too. Decker was blown right up in the kid's face, telling him he should make a run for it, that was his best chance. If he could make it to the woods, they'd let him go. The woods were just a ditch and some birch and evergreens beyond but we all knew what he was saying. And the kid had sweated right through the back of his shirt, moving foot to foot, then trying to stand still. Trying to figure out what Decker really wanted him to do. Which I don't think, to this day, any one of us, at that moment knew. Then Decker told him You gotta run boy. You gotta run. And the kid pooped his pants. Stood there hunched over and crying and holding himself while the back of his pants stained and we all smelled it and Decker backed off a step and said Screw this and reached out and slapped the back of the boy's head. Then he, Decker, turned and walked away. And the kid heard those footsteps sucking in the mud and he took off running. But it was a bad and ragged run, as if it would be a miracle if he could even make the ditch, let alone those puny woods. And I watched him go and thought There was none of that had to happen, when one of the other guys lifted his rifle and shot the kid. Just like that. And the guy, the shooter, looked at the boy lying there in the mud and lit up a smoke and looked over at us and said, What? One less bad rabbit to breed, is what I see. So. My story. I could tell more but won't."

Sometime during this telling he'd looked down again at the floor and when he was done he looked up and saw her across from him. Her face ruined and wet with silent tears, eyes wide upon him, her hands clutching her drink red and white as if she'd shatter the glass if she but could.

"Oh, Jeezum," he said and stood. He walked over to her and said, "It just happened, Ruth. I didn't mean to make you cry."

He reached down and cupped her face, his hands running over her wet cheeks. Then he lifted out an index finger and began to wipe away her tears and she slowly rose out of the chair and came against him. Her body shuddering.

Seven

Katey

THE SUN ROSE beyond her left shoulder like a blood blister through the morning fog as she drove to the sister's house outside Amherst near Shutesbury. Her eyes seemed filled with grit. Luna had advised that her real name was Harriet. Her brother-in-law, Kevin, was on a dig in Colorado so it was just Laurie and the little boy, Scott. Katey listened to all of this and wondered how quickly she could get away and then where she would actually go. She was sore and cramped and very tired. Some time since she'd ceased wanting to cry and had turned up the radio as Luna had slept hunched against the door while Katey watched the white center lines of the interstate lane flip past in a metronomic daze.

She stumbled through greetings and ate a bowl of cereal. The little boy sat across from her, watching her until she glanced at him and then he'd look away. And again. Even so young, there was a lupine quality to his features, his jaw and eyes. The sisters were talking in the minor code of sorority, of family, of people and places common to both of them. She was too tired to care. There was a faint smell of sour milk and Luna's sister wore white-and-blue-striped bell-bottoms and a peasant blouse with bright embroidery along the yoke, her breasts swinging free against the fabric.

She slept in a twin bed in a small room lined with makeshift bookcases, with an old desk pushed up against the single window that had an old-fashioned storm window fitted on the outside and the space between the two windows was filled with spiderwebs and dead flies, the glass smudged and streaked with years of weather. The room smelled faintly of damp, of old books, of mouse droppings. She woke sticky in sweat, the blanket pushed back, the sheet twisted about her, a moment of panic not knowing where she was. She'd had this happen before but only until her familiar room resolved around her—this time the panic was longer and only receded enough to propel her from the bed and back into her jeans.

It was late afternoon and she was alone in the house. Her truck was in the drive and the yellow Volvo station wagon that had been there that morning was gone. She walked out to the truck and carried in her suitcase and then showered, the first time since the motel in Portland, standing in the hot steam; lathered for the second time, she stood in mute shock as she realized Portland had only been the night before last. It seemed this could not possibly be right. Her skin felt as if it had been pulled off of her and badly put back on. She was still sore and her thighs ached. She dressed and went outside, around behind the house.

There was a weedy lawn with the flush of new growth and then an old barbwire fence and a hillside pasture grown up with bull thistles and circular clumps of lowbush junipers. Up the hillside was a stand of large trees. She worked her way through the fence, snagging the back of her T-shirt, and then climbed the hill in a slow measured pace, watching to see if there were cattle or some other livestock but saw only songbirds flitting away from her and out of the grove of trees three crows swooped, dipping and crying at her as she came close.

The trees were oaks, which she knew from their lobed leaves. No oaks grew where she was from, being above the northern limit of their range. These were big trees, the bark rough and thickly ribbed, the trees as large as some sugar maples, great crowns high overhead, swaying with the breeze that cooled her shirt against her. She lay down in the thin grass under the trees, on her back, watching the treetops and sky above.

When she'd showered she'd washed dried blood from her pubis and inner thighs. Her underwear was clotted and she'd balled it into the bottom of her suitcase. She lay watching the treetops sway and her ribcage clenched about her heart and she was heaving, trying to draw air into her lungs and she thought she should sit up but couldn't move, as if she was struck against the earth. And she thought He did that to me. It wasn't anything she wanted and realized some part of her had been thinking all night and throughout her sleeping that perhaps it had been her fault, that she'd looked at him when he stood naked across the campfire and there must've been some openness to her looking, some curiosity that could have been seen as desire or intent, that some way he'd felt she'd wanted him to come to her but now, under the arch of the trees, the fluttering and gentle soft rasping of the leaves against one another, she knew this wasn't true. For all the times she'd imagined that moment, that eventuality, all the times her body had contrived with her mind to approximate that event, there had never been the least sense that she would seek or want or desire this sort of breakage of her. And knowing this she understood she was indeed broken. Had been broken and in some awful dreadful way knew then also that she always would be broken. And she rolled over then and spread her arms wide and dug her fingers through the grass stems and into the earth, the roots of grass, the crumbly soil, the old sharp husks of acorns that scraped her fingertips, the minute scamper of ants along her hands; all these things so familiar and yet so distant and strange, more breakage, and she began to cry. Not a whimper of tears but a heaving sobbing upon the body of the earth. Some clear part of her wanting the earth to take her in. To absorb and absolve her. And the earth, it seemed, refused her.

The three crows were back, overhead, circling. Barking against her intrusion. She grew quiet, listening to them. They wouldn't stop and she grew curious. Perhaps there was a hawk drifting on high thermals that the crows were deviling. Or, likely this time of year, protecting nests. After a bit she rolled over and tried to see the crows through the swollen mass of leaves and limbs and then did—only a pair now, high up but perched across from each other. They seemed to be intent upon her. Slowly she drew herself to a cross-legged position, her head tilted back to watch and as she did both crows flapped off, angling down toward her and then abruptly away, out over the hillside. The sharp hard whips of their wingbeats.

When the yellow car pulled into the yard below she started, wishing to be left alone. And then saw the crows fleeing over the yard, almost on a plane with her and she wanted to walk down and see the women and the little boy and felt tugged back into life and as she stood, the crows again veered off and away across the valley and it came to her that the earth hadn't refused her after all. That the crows had beckoned her back.

She walked down the hill, to see what she would see.

She sat with Laurie in ancient webbed lawn chairs around the fire pit as the night came down around them, watching the coals of the fire. Luna was with Scott, bathing him and then putting him to bed. Reading him a story until he fell asleep. Katey had felt an odd jolt when they left, as if she wanted the job herself. He'd been a monster of energy as the women worked easy, a bit wary perhaps, making and cooking hamburgers, toasting the buns on the old oven rack that served as a grill, the boy loping out around the yard with an imaginary six-shooter to hand, killing God knew what all and she'd watched him as she drank a can of Narragansett and twisted the lid off a jar of pickle relish, opened the large bag of potato chips. The boy seemed feral and dangerous, half-formed. At one point he'd darted near and said, "I've got a pecker" and pointed his finger at her and then yelled, "Bang! You're dead!" before racing off toward the corner of the house and she realized he'd said pistol, not pecker. After eating, he'd started it all up again until suddenly he was collapsed against his aunt, a rag doll of a child, dreamy and softened. The back of his neck in the firelight, where he rested his cheek on Luna's knee, curved and vulnerable. Katey wanted to reach and touch his neck. Then Luna eased him up, his arms around her shoulders, his legs around her waist and off they went.

Laurie stretched down her arm to the torn-open cardboard carton, extracted two of the three remaining cans of beer, lifted one to her lap and reached the other to Katey and then passed over the church key on its leather lanyard. Katey punched a pair of triangles in the rim of the can, across from each other, handed back the opener and lifted the can and drank. This was exactly her second beer ever, the first an hour ago. Seeing and understanding their poverty, she'd nibbled her hamburger and eaten a handful of the chips, as Luna and Laurie also did, leaving the boy the fifth hamburger and most of the chips. He'd gulped down a can of orange soda and then eaten a package of peanut butter cups. So the beer worked in her, and she was grateful for it, the easing of her mind, the slight and pleasant dislocation from her outraged body.

Sparks drifted upward, summer stars began to pierce beyond the fireglow.

Her voice almost drifting in the night, Laurie said, "Do you want to talk about it?"

"No," Katey said. Caught herself and said, "But thanks."

They were quiet a bit.

Then Katey said, "Scott's a really cute kid."

"Men can be real pigs. I know. But they're also wonderful, all that energy and certainty and forcefulness in what they believe, how intent they are to make the world be what they want it to be. And they all start out as little boys—you can see them."

Katey lifted her beer, reminded herself to go slow, all ways, sipped and said, "I guess. I don't really know."

"You will. Kevin's a great guy. And he's—we're worried about the draft, the new bill they're writing this summer. A bunch of deferments will be changed. But, also, next year he turns twenty-six and it looks like that won't change. So if we can make it until then he might be safe. My dad thinks he's a pussy, thinks he ought to sign up. Like *he* did. Thinks this is the same war he fought."

"My dad was in the war, also."

"Sure. What's he think about Vietnam?"

"I don't know."

Laurie looked at her. "No brothers?"

"Nope. Just me."

Laurie nodded. Then she said, "You can crash as long as you want. I mean that."

"I might stay another day. I'm awful tired." Thinking she'd drive out in the morning and buy some groceries, not much but enough. Maybe take Luna along and try to figure out what would be a nice treat. Cautiously. Ice cream, for certain.

Then Laurie said, "Harriet's staying on through the summer. She'll go back to New Hampshire when the fall semester starts, but not until then. She got a job today. There's a bookstore in South Hadley. She always was a reader."

They sat silent then, that message out between them. Katey was feeling a bit fuzzy, pleasantly so, but unsure of what words to offer.

Laurie stood and said, "I'm going in. He often falls asleep easy and then pops back up in about ten minutes and when he does that it can take a while to get him down again. But once he's really down, he's

247

lights out until dawn. I've got some weed, Jamaican. We can all smoke a jay, listen to some records, just hang out."

Katey looked at her. She said, "I smoked some last night. So maybe I'll just sit with you two, if you don't mind. I may go to bed soon. I'm still kind of worn out."

"Sure. That's cool. It's a good thing except when it isn't." She pointed down and said, "Bring that last beer, if you want it. Or not. That's cool, too. Whatever you want."

"Thanks. I think I will."

Laurie said, "Solid." And turned toward the house and then turned back. She said, "Katey?"

"What?"

"Harriet? What is it she calls herself, these days?"

"Uh . . . Luna? I think?" Wondering if she was someway betraying. But Laurie only said, "Luna. The moon sister. That figures."

And turned and walked to the house.

She made it halfway through the last beer and was abruptly, absolutely done. She was slung down in a beanbag chair where she pondered how she might stand out of it without falling out, or down upon the floor. Music was playing low, but entered through her nonetheless, a stabbing soaring electric guitar and deep bass, shimmering cymbals, a voice unlike anything she'd ever heard, a man that stabbed again it seemed directly to her groin. The pot smoke was thickly aromatic, smelling a bit of skunk, a bit of spruce needles. Laurie and Luna huddled close on the couch. Smoking and talking low, laughing. Katey felt forgotten and again the waves of exhaustion overcame her and she recalled the fright upon the rocks above the ocean in Maine. The bottomless, unfathomable dark, roiling heedless for her. Then she was up, legs liquid from thighs to knees and she spoke but her tongue was thickened to fill her mouth and Luna uncoiled quickly from the couch and embraced her, then guided

248

her to the office with the twin bed. Or perhaps she imagined that. But certainly when she woke some countless hours later she was back within the bed, the covers pulled tight over her, in her underwear and the same T-shirt she'd worn that afternoon. And her heart was beating against her ribcage as if it would burrow free of her. As if it would leave a fouled home. She pushed up and back into the corner where the head of the bed met the wall, gasping, again sorting out where she was. In panic so acute she didn't understand it was panic—a state of being, a doorway not walked but pitched through.

The room was dark but for a faint bar of light at the bottom of the door. She settled her eyes on that narrow low rectangle of light. Pictured the room beyond and then knew for certain where she was. Doing this, the booming of her pulse in her ears also did not subside but she now understood what it was. What? Her heartbeats had overtaken her, attacking, forcing her to hear them: This is you stupid girl. The sound of the pump that keeps you living. And for what?

Rape. The very sound of the word not spoken but felt, like a chainsaw. Within her. The apple tree that died two years ago was felled for firewood and then the stump left—her father used a chainsaw to whittle it away, a great spewing of chunks and splinters and a boil of sawdust behind the saw as he moved around the dwindling trunk as it disappeared under the high whine of the saw. Then gone. The year before that at the river end of summer with Charlie Hebard, the school year coming, the two of them alone in their bathing suits and sitting on the hot rocks, then kissing and swimming again and then out, prickled skin and kissing again and she wanted, wanted. She did not know, unsure and sucking her breathing in as she tasted his delicious tongue and he'd told her he wanted her and she told him to rape her because she didn't have words for what she did want and neither did he. And they stopped. But not before he slipped a finger under the edge of her suit and touched her pubic hair and her breath caught. A snap between loins and chest, a thick swelling in her throat, then gone. But they stopped.

Perhaps it was the word. Likely that neither knew how to proceed. But the word, out between them. She'd said it because she'd read it and it seemed the thing she wanted, until she said it. Not that other word she couldn't imagine saying although she'd soon enough be whispering it to herself, certain times. Because it was ugly, was what she knew. Rape just seemed what happened. Until she said it.

Sometimes you know what you do not know you do.

She stood from the bed, her heart still a ratchet, and fumbled on the floor for the lump of her jeans and got into them, roughly swerving to sit on the bed again and work them up her legs and hitching up to pull them over her waist. She stood again and eased open the door. Luna was in a sleeping bag on the couch. The light came from a small fluorescent tube over the sink. Katey padded across and ran water, found a jelly jar in the dish drain and drank a glass quickly, then two more slowly. The water had a taste to it—not chemical but slightly smudgy. Not the water she was used to that tasted like nothing but fresh and cold. But water, still.

She was awake and calmer and miles from sleep. The clock face on the stove showed 2:20 in the morning. On the table was an open pack of Parliament cigarettes and she slid one out and made way gently over the linoleum and eased through the door, down into the yard. The sky held a light cloud cover, some few stars. Barefoot, she went to the truck and cracked open the door and let herself in. Sat behind the wheel and dug along the top of the dash and found the book of matches there, tore one out and scraped and the interior lit up orange and she drew smoke and blew out the match, rolled down the window and sat, smoking. Her bare feet in the skim of grit on the floorboards. When she inhaled there was just enough flare to see a reflection of herself in the windshield.

Again, she wanted to go home. Again, she couldn't go home. She smoked and in a quiet voice said aloud, "God damn. I guess I'm going to Virginia." She felt the wriggle of excitement married atop fear. She threw the butt out the window and again, as she had the night before, wondered if her mother had been raped. It seemed so possible. She knew nothing about how she'd come to be, beyond the ugly night in February. It seemed possible. It seemed unlikely. Or very likely—her mother was a woman who could not resist such an event. But then, neither, it appeared, was she. And she then thought I will know when I meet him. I'll see it in his face. Even bland and smooth, it was clear to her, a thing impossible to hide. There would be a twitch, a sudden sideways glance. A moment. And she'd be watching for that, knowing to be looking.

Again, the writhe of excitement. Not even sure for what beyond forward motion. On her way. A catapult from that March night, her trajectory. Inevitable. As if she'd been born to do this, to make this journey. As it seemed, she had.

It hadn't snowed for a week and afternoons walking home from school the sun was high enough so the roadside had trickles of water, just starting to refreeze as the temperatures fell toward night. She was heavy, tired and bloated and had Calculus homework that she didn't want to do. And the laundry basket of contention was full, in her room. And because it was an alternating Tuesday and her mother had a faculty meeting, she was expected to start dinner. Which, because it was Tuesday, faculty meeting or not, meant browning a pound of ground beef in one pan while cooking an onion and a green pepper in another, then mixing them together and adding a quart jar of tomato sauce canned from last summer's garden, a can of tomato paste, a packet of seasoning spices from her grandparents' store while also boiling water for noodles and tearing apart a head of iceberg lettuce from the same store, into a bowl. Setting out the bottle of

Italian salad dressing and the tin of grated Parmesan cheese. And setting the table. To eat spaghetti and salad for supper.

Oh, joy.

Her father was in his workshop. She could've talked to him but all he would've said was Do what your mother tells you. Likely pausing to rub her shoulders a moment, perhaps lift her chin with his large calloused finger and admonishing her to cheer up, that it wasn't as bad as she thought. So she bypassed that possibility. And once in the house skipped all the rest of it, also. She turned the radio loud and lay on the couch and listened to rock and roll for a while and then the news came on and that just pissed her off even more. She took the key off the hook and went out and climbed in his truck and headed down to the village, passing her mother on the way. At the Dot she stepped in the back door into the kitchen and waited until the night cook, Denny, a long tall stooped drink of a man with a purple birthmark across the side of his face looked up from where he'd been grilling a heap of onions on the flattop and asked her what she wanted and when she told him supper for her family he responded he had liver and onions or shepherd's pie made fresh that afternoon or anything off the regular menu and she asked if there was bacon to go with the liver also, because she knew her father liked that. There was, and baked potatoes in foil wraps just coming out of the oven. She asked for enough to feed three at least and he piled up portions in waxed containers and she told him she'd settle with Merle out of her next check. And back up the hill she went.

Her mother would eat beef liver but was not fond of it.

Ruth was working over the stove, draining fat from the beef, adding the meat to the sauce as well as a drained can of sliced mushrooms. Katey had forgotten about the mushrooms. Ruth had an apron on over her school clothes, her sleeves pushed up. She glanced over her shoulder as Katey came in and said, "What's that?"

252

"Dinner."

Ruth's hair was simple, a shoulder-length bob with the ends curled forward. She said, "In a box?"

"From the Double Dot. Liver and onions and baked potatoes in their jackets."

"Potatoes have skins, not articles of clothing." Then, "Why?"

"I didn't feel like cooking. I'll make a salad, though."

"You will?"

"I said I would."

"You said you didn't feel like cooking."

"It's making a salad, not cooking."

"And what am I to do with this?" Ruth indicated the sauce. Katey noticed there wasn't a pot of water on the stove for noodles. But she'd already recognized the battle joined. Katey said, "Save it for tomorrow night. We can have it then. I just didn't want spaghetti tonight. I didn't feel like cooking."

"Twice a month I ask you to fix supper. Do you have any idea how many days I come home and don't feel like cooking? We have to eat, a fact that hasn't escaped you. Three meals a day, every day of the year."

"I eat cereal for breakfast almost every morning. And fix my own lunches. Peanut butter and jelly. Do you even care that I hate peanut butter and jelly?" This was not true; she liked the combination as long as the jelly was not raspberry with seeds, which lodged in her teeth. This was about the failure to be allowed to eat the hot lunch at school. Which, mostly, was disgusting. Although there were days she wanted tater tots and sloppy joes. And while saying and thinking this she was moving around her mother, laying out the liver in another pan, spooning the onions over it, setting bacon strips on top, covering the pan but not yet turning it on. The food still warm to the touch. The three giant potatoes brilliant in their shiny wraps in the oven.

"For four years now you've made your lunch. And even then, many days your father does it for you. Don't think I don't know that."

"And why not? He enjoys it, often while I'm eating breakfast. We chat about our days. You're already gone."

Then Ruth turned to the fridge and lifted out the head of lettuce and tore the wrapper free, pulled a bowl from the shelf and with a great whomp brought the iceberg down upon the counter and pulled free the core, stripped off the outer leaves and began to shred it into the bowl. As she said, "Yes. Well, it's a paycheck. And if you want to waste your money hard-earned as it is, that's your business. Although next year when you're at college you may regret it. But that's your business. I suppose you need to go put your laundry in the dryer."

"I've got Calculus and also the second act of *Hamlet* to read tonight. I'll do my laundry then."

"I see. And all done and dried and folded by nine o'clock."

"I might stay up until ten, Mother."

And as this is occurring, both women are seething, but each believing themselves clinical and cool, and so thinking on a second level that feeds the first outer, vocal level. As large trout feed upon a hatch of insects. These underwater thoughts.

She thinks her mother is a pinched angry woman who has settled for a life where she is a small god among children, with a quiet distant husband, whom she has allocated to a realm of some version of childhood, a shambling amiable and largely ineffective creature against her own starched efficiency. All those novels she reads—who was she kidding? Besides, of course, herself. She fussed about Vietnam but worried about the communists—look what we walked away from in Korea and how that turned out? And she'd loved Kennedy, or perhaps had loved Jackie, and so distrusted LBJ and worried that the whole Civil Rights business was necessary but perhaps just maybe a wee bit rushed? If you pushed people too hard, too fast, wasn't it human nature to push back? Well, the woman was old and maddening and didn't understand how the world was changing and that was her right but not her right to force her moribund wretched small-town views upon her daughter. Who was an adult. Practically an adult. And while thinking this she pushed around her mother just gently enough to not be reprimanded and turned the heat to low under the pan of liver and onions and lifted the lid and ate a piece of bacon because she wanted to and what was wrong with that, anyway? When she served it onto plates she planned to skip the bacon altogether, just onions for her and more bacon for her dad. But her mother didn't say anything to that. Fine.

She was thinking, Fine then but I won't do her laundry if she doesn't, she can live in a sty if that's how she wants it and felt herself curdle a bit at the thought of what then the girl would wear to school. God knows it was hard enough just getting her, all of them, to adhere to the dress code, as if somehow they all knew someone, somewhere, was instructing them they didn't have to. And of course there were multiple someones, those voices over the radio, through the television, just barely a bit older than these children who walked through the halls of her school daily, strange and alien except for those few who weren't and even she had to admit that those had always been the ones to plod, clopping along until freed back to the farm or their father's garage; to get pregnant and leave school before graduating, setting up house and thus also proving the waste of all those years the town, the state, the country, had lavished upon them, attempting to offer a step up and out, and this galled her even as she knew it had always been this way and even needed, for those few, to be this way. But also how daily she walked through the funk, the odors, the eyes-turned, as these children that her daughter yet walked among turned their eyes upon each other, their jutting breasts and nyloned legs in very short skirts, the boys with their hair popping around their ears, the tumescence in their trousers, some few who wore jeans or striped

255

bell-bottom pants, lounging back in their chairs, openly doodling on their tests or quiz sheets while they ran eyes over the girl in the row beside them, that same girl with a second blouse button opened and how did they not know that she saw all this? The reek of sex hung about them as a fume. And yet she knew, damn it she certainly did know that it had always been this way and always would be and yet— the music from their transistors was ribald and held nothing of romance about it, the urging voices to Get it on, to Do it, to be feeling groovy and she had a pretty good idea what *groovy* meant. Turn on, tune in, drop out. Good God. The sheer wrongness of it all took her breath away.

Thus, together, they jostled the kitchen. Bristling and silent to each other. Both knowing someway the other's pique.

Then Ruth said, "I will not." Her teeth were clenched. "I will not wash your clothes. Do you understand?"

"Jesus Christ, Mom," Katey said. "I already told you I'd do them later."

"Don't you Jesus Christ me!"

"What is *wrong* with you?" Hearing herself, knowing she was pitched too high and angry with herself for it, but more angry with her mother for provoking this way.

"What's wrong with who? My girls." Oliver had opened the door and came in. Shaking his head as if to dislodge snow, not against the temper of the room. He fooled neither of them. But they allowed him to think so.

Ruth said, "Nothing's wrong with anybody, honey. Do you want a beer before we eat?"

His head swung back and forth between them. "No, thanks. I don't believe I do."

Katey said, "Mom's upset because I didn't make her famous spaghetti. But I got dinner ready anyhow. Liver with onions and bacon too. From the Dot. And baked potatoes ready to go. I know you like all that. I needed a break from spaghetti. You ready to eat? Daddy?"

He again looked back and forth at the two of them and drew a deep breath and it seemed he sucked a certain level of air, of tension, from the room. He said, "I could eat."

They sat around the table. Candles lighted, although the small light over the range was still burning. Ruth had candlelight always for meals after dark and all of them liked this softening of the day just passed. The meal was almost over and had been delicious—Denny was a great cook and the liver was browned crisp but pink and rich inside, the onions cooked to a caramel sweetness, the big potatoes flaky white richness with butter and salt. Even the salad added a pleasing crunch and vinegar tang. And during the meal they had talked of ordinary things even within the compressed sense of caution that almost grew to seem an unnecessary precaution. Ruth speaking with candor about the difficulty with the new first-grade teacher, the candor a treasured thing that Katey had long ago understood was a trust to be held and even savored, an entry into the world of adults. Oliver leaned over his plate, sawing apart the emptied potato skin, forking up the folds of rich goodness while somehow keeping his eyes on his wife and nodding at the right places, a small noise of understanding issuing forth. And Katey, Katey only eating and happy to do so, feeling they were all again solid and at ease under this one small roof, a girl who understood the value of such things. And reaching over to pluck the last piece of bacon from her father's plate, because she knew she could.

Then she'd stood to clear the plates as her mother stood also to open the carton of rainbow sherbet removed from the freezer just before they sat to their meal, softened now to be served into the small white china bowls shaped like hollowed-out tulips and Katey was back in her chair as her mother served the bowls out before them and,

257

smoothing her dress beneath her as she sat, said, "By the by, Katherine. Have you made an appointment with Evelyn? You're past due."

So there it was. They were not done. Her mother determined to prevail.

Katey took a bite of the bright lime stripe for time and comfort but the sherbet tasted metallic and slowly she set her spoon down and, raising her head, glanced at her father as she turned to face her mother. "No," she said. "I haven't."

"You need to."

"Oh, I think it's fine. I like it."

"It's not fine. And you know it."

"I'm growing it out, Mother."

"You're doing no such thing. Call her tomorrow."

"No."

"What? What did you say?"

Katey was aware her father was watching this exchange and she did not look at him, trusting that he'd understand and come to her aid when this was clear.

"I'm growing my hair. I want it long. I can trim it myself as I need to. Until it's all even."

Ruth now had tilted her chin toward her, both her eyes firmly upon Katey. She said, "Nonsense. You're doing no such thing, I said."

Then Katey pushed back her chair and stood. She said, "I am."

Ruth sat straight, pushed back her chair but resisted her desire to also rise. She said, "I'm not raising some tatterdemalion. Do you understand me?"

"Oh. A big word. You're not raising anyone. I'm myself and will always be myself. I want my hair long and it will be that way."

Ruth came out of her chair and for the briefest of seconds appeared to raise an arm as if to strike. Then the arm was dropped, hands clasped before her. But she said, "One. You will not speak to me like that. Two. You will do as I say under this roof and outside of it, for that matter. What's wrong with you?" Her voice rose to a pitch near fit. "Are you taking drugs? Are you *strung out*, as you kids say? Why do you argue with everything? You're not reasonable anymore, at all. There's something wrong with you. What is it?"

Katey said, "Jesus Christ. I don't believe this. I don't believe you. What is this crap? Who are you to talk to me like this? You're crazy! Are you even my mother? What, was I adopted or something?"

Ruth was crying and the candles were guttering as Oliver then slowly stood up and became a presence in the room again and Katey thought There, he'll calm her down. Meaning and knowing also that he'd calm her down, as well as her mother. The two of them, daughter and father, had stepped along this path, never spoken of, a few times before. Ruth became overwrought, was unreasonable. Then settled again to her old self. So she stood there, hearing the sputters of burning wax. And waited as he righted himself into the scene between the two women.

Then, his face turned downward to the dying light, he said, "Adopted? I guess, you want to put it that way. Sort of."

In that silence he turned from the table and walked to the door, paused to pull on his red–and–black wool shirt, opened the door and looked back.

"Oh, Katey," he said.

And stepped out into the night and closed the door upon them.

Katey looked from the door that appeared to shimmer, shut so tight, to her mother. Whose face had collapsed upon itself. An old crumpled woman stood in her place. Katey was working her way toward words, a question of some sort, when her mother leaned down and held her palms over the sputtering candles and sucked breath, then lifted those same hands and held her cheeks. Turned to look at Katey, her eyes dark holes in the dimness of the room. She spoke, her voice at a strained level.

259

"He's not angry. Certainly not at you and, despite what he said, I don't believe he's angry at me. Or perhaps he is angry at me but I know your father and he doesn't hide things like that. I made a mistake years ago but it was an honest one. I can't explain this now. You said you are almost all grown up. Well. This is how it can be to be almost all grown up. Now. I'm going upstairs to take a bath. We will talk about this another time."

She turned and Katey said, "Mom?"

Ruth halted, hesitated and then turned. "What is it, Katherine?"

Katey's heart was hammering, her lungs not up to their expected job. She said, "What just happened? What did he mean, *adopted*?"

"That's how it is. Being grown up. You think you know where you stand, but the damned land seems to keep sliding under your feet. Sometimes, the best you can hope for is to not land on your ass."

She turned again and walked from the room into the hall and Katey stood listening to her footsteps up the stairs, then moments later the swoosh of water into the tub, the wallpipes clanking. Stood even worse than moments before; the word *ass* and her mother were not even remotely aligned with each other and this, then, was the moment when Katey understood the enormity of what had just occurred.

She was not a sneaky girl but one wandering through the vast and vague mysteries of childhood, her parents the primary owners of those mysteries. How they'd possibly existed before she had. So, many years before that evening, she'd found the packet of Christmas cards in a shoebox at the back of her mother's closet. Under the tissue that was under the pair of heels that her mother had never, in Katey's memory, worn. And hidden so and discovered so, signaled to the child that found them, a deep, mysterious and profoundly romantic array of scenarios attached to the cards. All of which were wrong, and, as she learned, none of them as central to her own life as the truth. And she kept her knowledge of the cards secret. At least, until the night she stole them. To have them with her.

There was a lightening over the low-slumped hills before her from where she sat in the cab of the truck. This time of year this meant it was about four in the morning, possibly not quite. No birdsong, yet. And abruptly and almost savagely she knew she didn't want to stay where she was. Another day with the sisters and the little boy. Well-meaning and kind people but really only strangers that kept her connected to the incident of the night before. She was tired but not terribly so, given her long sleep through the day yesterday. And she also felt a lurch of resolve, to see through what she'd started upon, and with that the recognition she was, within herself, close to tossing the whole business, the seeking, out the window and returning home. Which she could not do.

Her mother, she realized now, had not been raped. There was nothing in the story she'd been told that even hinted at such a thing. Most everything else about the story she found difficult if not impossible to believe, of her mother, of the man she thought of as her father. Which was the point: to stand before the man who was her father, her other father, and simply see how that felt. And how he might respond to her. Her mother had told her Brian Potter had no knowledge of her existence. But then, she would say that, wouldn't she? Those Christmas cards. Had there been other correspondence, from her mother to him? This, much else, she would learn. Even if the learning was a negative, a void.

So, to press onward. Her suitcase was back in the house. She let herself out of the truck and crossed the yard. The first tentative pipes of birds, a call and then a response. In the kitchen only the same light was on over the stove. Luna was snoring gently on the couch. She went into the study and knelt in the dim light from the window and closed her suitcase, then stood and went back into the kitchen.

261

Laurie stood in a robe at the stove. She looked Katey up and down, nodded. She whispered, "You're taking off?"

"It's the right time. But thanks for everything."

"I can have coffee in fifteen minutes."

"I'm good. Really."

"Sure," Laurie said. Then stepped and kissed Katey's forehead, pulled back and said, "Not all men are dicks. But you take care out there, you hear?"

"I will. I'll do my best."

Laurie then just stood watching as she hitched her suitcase out the door, into the pale morning. With nothing more to say.

Katey laced on her sneakers in the cab of the truck and then drove out, vaguely the way she'd come in. She'd find a place to stop and study her maps and find some more, have food and coffee and figure out what was reasonable to expect from the day. She had the heater on low and the windows open for the birds singing and the radio pulsing music to beat her onward as she came fully into this new day. She glanced at herself in the rearview and her hair was a fright and somehow just right and she grinned at herself and then drove on.

Eight

Oliver

THE SNOW BEGAN during the night, fine flakes that streamed from a low mantle of opaque sky, without cease throughout the muffled day and so when he went to put the chains on the truck in the last light of the afternoon he already knew they weren't going anywhere soon but wasn't terribly concerned; Ruth wasn't expected at Mary Hitchcock Hospital until the end of the week. It was Monday of the second week of March. He shoveled snow away from the doors of the ell shed, backed the truck up there and loaded the bed level with split cordwood, for weight. He did so feeling it was a gesture but then much of life these past strange months had seemed one gesture piled upon another upon others endlessly. And he didn't even know if he was right about that. As he felt about almost everything, his very self most of all. The snow swirled about him as he worked.

Even as he'd sat shocked and silent as she'd told him that August evening that she was having Brian Potter's baby and would wait for his answer if it was immediate or days, he'd admired her courage. And wondered but did not ask, did not need or want to ask, if she'd have told him about Potter if there was not this question now lying before them. Or before him. He'd stood from the table and left the house for his shop where he did not work but perched on his stool, knowing his answer but not willing to tell her so quickly and wondering if this revealed more about himself than it did his wife. Or if that even mattered. When he finally told her they'd have the baby as if it were their own he'd been unsure of his own courage and, secretly he believed, shamed by his doubt.

It was still snowing when the power went out and he filled the furnace and old kitchen range by flashlight and carried one of the old brass lanterns up for bedside come morning but the Baby Ben clock showed quarter to four when she woke him with the quiet news that her contractions had started and when he stepped outside the fine snow was a veil in the beam of the flashlight. The snow in the driveway topped his rubber boots up to his knees. He used an old broom from the woodshed to clear the snow off the cab of the truck and went back inside to tell Ruth the hospital was out of the question and he'd make it to the village to fetch Doc Durgan.

She was perspiring and working hard to keep her breathing even, caught out by sudden clutches. "Do you think," she asked, "you can make it up for my mother?"

"I can sure try."

She opened her mouth, lifted her hand to signal wait. After a moment she said, "No. Don't. I know that hill. If you made it up, you'd never get back down. I can't take the risk."

"Maybe later," he said. "The snow stops."

"Bring your mother." Her eyes steady upon him.

"You sure?" Out there, between them, both of them knowing it.

She nodded. "I want the doctor. I want a woman. I want you."

"I'm not sure I'll be much help."

"Oliver."

"I'm going. I'll be back."

"Be careful."

"I will be."

He had to sweep the truck again. Then, headlights pale in the snow, he drove with a slow steady precision, a greatly heightened caution, a state of mind he'd almost forgotten as he made way down the hill, slipping, wheels churning, the streetlights out, some few windows lit pale as his own. He woke his mother first, left her to dress and ready herself and went on to the doctor's house. That man was already up, drinking coffee made on a parlor stove, unsurprised to see Oliver in his door. The return was easier, following his own tracks, the truck working hard going up Beacon Hill but not slipping, sliding. The doctor and Jennie in their heavy overcoats, the doctor with his oversized case on his lap, Jennie with a small suitcase of her own. It was thin daylight behind the snow.

Ed showed up with one of the road crews, plowing. But for footsteps overhead it was quiet where they stood in the kitchen. Oliver asked his father if he thought he should try up West Hill for Jo Hale. Ed peered out the window and said, "This could be hours." It was unclear if he meant the continuing snow or the arrival of the baby. Both, Oliver guessed and took these words in silence. They were men easy with silence. Ed poured himself coffee and Oliver began a measured pace of the room. The plow truck did not return and the road filled again with snow. A wind had sprung, swirling the snow in white sheets, skimming rills off the drifting tops of the snowbanks. Times, Oliver couldn't see the apple trees from the window over the sink. Jennie came down and filled the canning kettle and put it on the stove to heat. She looked at her son and said, "She'll be all right. Not just now, but soon enough." Out of deference for his father, who disliked tobacco, Oliver stepped out into the woodshed to smoke, careful with his ashes, the butts going into an empty Black Label beer can. The second time he did so, he returned to find his father making grilled cheese-and-egg sandwiches for them both. Oliver was halfway through his when her first scream, a long rising plaint of pain, filled the house, cut off with an abrupt suck.

"They say," Ed said, "If a woman could remember childbirth she'd never have more than one." Then added, "Or even try."

Oliver looked at his father with the unspoken question and his father leaned to open the firebox on the range and add more wood. The water in the kettle was boiling and he pushed it to the back of the stove, to simmer.

It was still snowing when Oliver laced tight his rubber boots and pulled on his red-and-black wool coat and snap-brimmed black wool cap, midafternoon, to leave the house. His father sat at the table reading last week's newspaper. Oliver couldn't bear to remain in the house. From upstairs now came long mounting cries that edged into screams or were cut off in gulps, drained into whimpering moans. He let himself out, aware his father was watching him but unable to meet his eye. In the shed he eyed the shovel but left it be and plunged into the snow and slogged his way across the drive to his shop. The road was unplowed, a mock of effort. He kicked and tramped down the snow from the door of his workshop and let himself in. There he built a fire in the small chunk stove and set upon his stool at the bench, the open frame of a fiddle set up in clamps, tender thin strips of wood glued to the interior, as if the delicate structure was being prayed into place. He sat with his hands caught tight, balled in his trousers above his knees. This past Christmas a card had arrived from Brian Potter and Oliver had no idea if it was still anywhere in the house but guessed it might be. Or maybe not. In any event, he swore in silence that if Ruth died he'd travel to Maine and find the man and slaughter him in some slow and gruesome fashion. And then knew he would not and gazed into the streaming whorls of snow beyond the windowglass.

Darkness fell early with the snow and it was years ago that he lay on his back and put chains on his useless truck, so certain the gesture was empty, which it certainly was, but also sure the gesture was a small halt against bad luck, against misfortune. After a time he dug in his pocket and lighted the dented barn lantern that sat on the bench and sat in the flickering soot-hazed light. The window darkened and threw back a flickering reflection of the bench, himself a vague presence behind the twice-seen lantern. Where he was when some unknown time later his father kicked at the door and then hauled it open and stood, coatless and bareheaded, sprinkled with snow, and said, "You're wanted to the house." Then turned and left, not waiting for him and Oliver did not wait, did not bother with his coat or hat but plunged out, paused and blinked and went quickly back into the shed to shut the flue and damper on the stove and plucked up the lantern to make his way across the yard. The snow still falling heavy as ever, the rough track of his father already filling, edges softening with new-fallen snow.

The kitchen was warm after the modest heat of the shed. Steamed from boiling water. His father was nowhere in sight. The house was quiet but for steps down the stairs. He leaned against the range and waited, for what, he did not know. For what, he could not know.

His mother came into the room, clutching to her breast a bundle of soft blanket. Which she held out to him and he took the bundle into his arms and his mother said, "Isn't she the most amazing thing in the entire world." And turned and went out of the room and back up the stairs. Or, he later assumed, that was what she did.

The bundle was, within the blanket, solid and warm and the size of a cottontail rabbit but only a small pinched red-and-purple face was revealed to him. And as he stood looking down at the face and realized what he was holding, the eyes flickered and popped open and he gazed upon the girl as she gazed up at him, their eyes meeting, locking. Her eyes blue and endless.

And he was flooded. Not only was he the first person she saw in this world, but she entered him at that moment. All ways. Without speaking, for words were outside his heart, he made promises to her. She was indeed amazing, a miracle for a man void of miracles and she was not so much his as he was hers. Newborn and yet solidly herself, her eyes, and he did not know if newborns could see or what they saw—it did not matter—her eyes upon him as if entrusting and she was. He would guide and protect her, carry her when he could, carry her when she needed him to. Carry her always if together or apart. For but then she would never be apart from him. He lifted her close to his face and held his breath and felt her own small breaths upon his face, warm and sweet.

He did not think of the war. He did not think of the blonde Brigitte. He did not think of anyone, for she was not a stand-in for anyone or anything—in those moments she was fully and solely herself and the weight of this understanding was there in the weight of her, more considerable than her actual weight. She seemed to him grave and contemplative and this also felt right, as if there was no other way for a new soul to take purchase in the world, to take measure and find some other soul tending, attentive and given utterly to her care and safety and all things she might ever want or need. How could it be otherwise?

A whisper, meant only for her, ever: "Katherine Anne Snow. Hullo there, you. Katey. Hullo Katey, girl. Don't fret. I've got you now." And she was not fretting, her face ancient and newly made, her eyes almost unblinking upon him. His also, upon her. His heart wild and immensely calm. As the job of his life now lay clear before him, within his hands.

She was moving now within the blanket-swaddle and her face pinched and her bow of a mouth opened but no cry came out as he leaned and loosened the swaddle enough so one small fat arm, tiny fingers clenching, came out and he shifted her along his left forearm and extended his right index finger down to her seeking hand and she wrapped her fingers around his single one.

Her eyes still upon his. He walked the kitchen with her, slow at first, then still slow but certain as her calm remained. He was carrying her. He'd carry her however far she'd let him. And then some incalculable distance well beyond that on into eternity, was how it felt. Was how it was.

Sometime later his mother came into the room and said, "You can see Ruthie now. She was torn up pretty badly but Doc has her stitched up and she's resting but awake. Here, let me hold the baby."

And even more later the story would be told of how he'd handed Katey over and then seconds later taking her back into his arms and leaving his mother so abruptly and dismayed at the sudden snatch but at the moment it seemed too long to be parted from her, and so he carried Katey up the stairs and into the bedroom, now cleaned and freshened which he also didn't understand at the time, Ruth under heavy covers of layered quilts, propped upon pillows and Doctor Durgan tilted back in a rush-seated chair against the wall, his eyelids drooped but awake. Oliver stood against the side of the bed, the girl cocooned in his arms as he looked down upon his exhausted wife and he said, "It's good, Ruthie."

She made a tired smile and pushed the covers down and reached toward him. "Let me have her."

"No," he said. "I've got her."

She studied him a short time, then reached and unbuttoned the top of her nightgown, her breasts hard, nipples protuberant. She said, "But she needs to nurse, Oliver. And I need her to."

"Oh," he said. He turned sideways and settled on the edge of the bed and only then passed Katey over to her mother.

Only once they were gone did he realize how many doubts he'd carried. The girl lifted them away.

*   *   *

Two months later on a flawless May afternoon he carried her high up Beacon Hill to the hayfields beyond the old plane-spotting tower and sat in the new-sprung grass dotted with dandelions like a starfield, and then lying back in the grass with the girl curled upon his chest and shoulder, the warm bake of the sun an almost forgotten pleasure. And lying there he told the girl things he knew. Later, he could not recall what he said but at the moment he spoke to her for half an hour or longer without pause and he did not tell her all he knew, for there were some things she might never need to know, but he told her enough, far more than he'd told anyone else. But, importantly, he told her of the world around them, the world that he knew and that sustained him. He told her of the people she came from, and what that meant to her. Finally, the one thing certain he retained, was he told her of the beauties of life, in the multitudes of that beauty. And telling her these things, he knew his words were entering her and lodging there, somewhere in her formative brain, her mind, her soul. That perhaps he was doing nothing more than putting words to what she already understood. She was silent throughout this account and when he finally rose up to carry her back down the hill she nested against his shoulder and cheek and bobbed along as if she too was calmed and settled, what worries might surround her laid to rest. So he walked downhill this most lovely of afternoons with an ebullient heart, as if indeed there was goodness in the world. For he had just witnessed it, been party to it. And even within hours when he forgot all he'd said, he understood he'd been in a state of grace. And that buoyed him as well. It seemed right and well that his actual words were forgotten. Or not forgotten so much as residing beyond memory—two very different conditions.

Ruth resumed teaching when Katey was seventeen months old— she'd been off two full years, that of her pregnancy and then the next and told Oliver flatly that she couldn't afford to risk losing that job forever and it was unclear to him exactly how she meant those words but he didn't argue with her. They owned the house and he still worked a few nights a week taking inventory, stocking shelves and writing up orders for the mercantile and the fiddle money wasn't great but he passed time in relative contentment and also knew Ruth did not, that she needed her work for reasons well beyond money. They'd reached a harmony within themselves and with each other, or, truly, found the harmony that had long been there, learning it now as adults and thus growing into it, as if it held an existing shape they must discern and fill. If they were seen as unconventional they didn't consider themselves so; they knew everyone and everyone knew them and no one they knew could be considered conventional; it was, in fact, the inconsistencies and eccentricities that delivered character and personality to their neighbors and community members. The gossips were known and thus marked, and all people know themselves distinct. Ruth had pedigree and intellect and the sharp kindness of a good teacher. Oliver held to himself and repaired fiddles and quietly understood that his parents were the principal merchants, wealthy people by the standards of the place. If some saw him as odd it was only so much more truth in his deliberate pace. And the little girl riding bobbing on his shoulders made people smile.

They only ever once had another conversation about Brian Potter. At Katey's first Christmas they received a second card from him, addressed to both and with a handwritten message of cheer and best wishes for the coming year.

"Did you send him one from us?"

"I did not."

"Does he know about her?"

"He has no reason to."

The cards came for several years and Oliver glanced at them and tossed them aside and then one year realized they'd had no card

271

and couldn't remember how long ago the last had come and he didn't ask Ruth. He didn't care.

In her fifth November he drove one afternoon of watery light up into the hills beyond the Williamstown Gulf, the trees bare-limbed but for the curled coppery beech leaves that would hold through the winter, the balsams and hemlock needles a dark, oily green, the sun pale behind thin clouds, low in the west. The truck heater threw the faint tang of old mouse droppings and the radio was turned low to country-and-western songs. Katey was bundled in a corduroy jacket, jeans tucked into rubber boots against the frozen rutted mud, her honey-brown hair pulled back in a high ponytail. Dirty pink mittens dangled from their strings from her jacket cuffs. She was singing very low along with the radio, not the words of the songs but her own words, too faint for him to make out. He was used to this, much as she was used to being bundled into the truck for excursions. She was not a child to pester asking about their destination but content simply to ride, having done so since earliest memory. They passed some other few trucks and cars, with men in wool pants and coats, hunting rifles, now and then with a buck in the bed or lashed over a fender. The sound of gunfire cutting across the stark land. He watched her as he drove, as he often did, his eyes almost furtive with love. This afternoon watching more cautiously, wondering as he seldom bothered to how she would respond at their journey's end.

She was still young enough, a year away from starting school, that he hadn't yet begun to watch her and think of himself in the moment. Of herself in the moment. She was simply there, along with him as she had been all of her life.

There wasn't so much of a driveway as simply the road widening off to one side, a couple of old cars, neither running, before the low one-story house, the swaybacked barn off to one side. The side of the barn hung with traps of all sizes. A pair of big hounds, some part redbone some black-and-tan showing in both of them, stood at the end of chains and roared at his truck. A pack of beagles swarmed out of the barn and also stood, their baying surprisingly deep for such small dogs.

"I think those dogs are more bark than bite," he said. "But why don't you let me get out first."

"All right." She was looking at the dogs.

As he came down out of the truck the door to the house swung inward and a man stepped out and stuck a pair of fingers in his mouth and whistled and the pack of dogs went silent. The big hounds sat on their haunches, the chains still stretched tight, watching.

"Hey, Cap, it's Oliver Snow, here," he called.

Cappy Levesque wore stained wool pants that at least one owner ago had been part of a suit, a pair of flannel shirts buttoned one over the other, colors muted with wear and woodsmoke. His gray-and-black hair was worn long and pulled back behind his ears, touching the collars of his shirts. He peered, setting one hand scout-like above his eyes to shade from the weak sunlight.

"I can see," he said. "Your little girl, she up in the cab there?"

"Yup."

"Bring her in, bring her in. What you want, you?"

Oliver walked forward and shook hands, nodding, then as he turned back to the truck and lifted Katey onto his hip, he said, "I'll tell you, Cappy. I was looking for a pair of snowshoes and I came to think of you."

"Aw, I don't make em no more. Them folks up at Tubbs, they got their big steamers and use precut evert'ing. I got work enough come the winter." He leaned toward Katey and smiled bright white dentures at her and said, "And you, missy? How you be this pretty afternoon?"

"I'm fine, thank you." She was wide-eyed and her hand clenched tight to Oliver's coat.

Cappy said, "Your papa, there. Tell him to come on in the house and we figure out this snowshoe business, okay?" Then he leaned to Oliver and winked and said, "I got me a litter of beagle pups, tickle her pink. Come on."

As they went through the door, Cappy said, "Your snowshoes busted or what? I could make new bindings, that what you need. But why don't you just get em from Tubbs? You get the wholesale anyhow, don't you?"

The kitchen was warm from an old flattopped logging camp stove and smelled of smoke, wood and tobacco, and man, and a braid-stream of other odors, the tang of urine underneath all, from the scents and lures the man cooked up himself to use on his traplines. A pot of stew gently simmered on the back of the stove and Oliver guessed once it was cool enough to keep the fire, the pot likely never emptied but was replenished with meat and root vegetables throughout the winter.

He set Katey down and she stood there, now gripping his pantleg. From a nest of blankets beside the stove came a low growl and then puppies came bursting across the floor. She went down on her knees and the puppies scrambled over her legs and lap, her hands floating among them as she leaned down and they lifted to lick her face and then one nipped and she jerked up and the nipper tried to scramble up the front of her coat. She reached and plucked the puppy up and turned it sideways in her hands and held it against her cheek.

Levesque said, "There. She's set now."

Oliver pointed his chin at her and said, "I was thinking about a small pair of snowshoes. Tubbs, the smallest they make is the bearpaw and I remember as a boy wearing those and struggling through the snow and most all I got was cold and miserable. I quit em for years. I was hoping to start her off better."

"You want a good crust of snow. But hold on, let me see. There's somet'ing to the barn, they ain't rotted or mouse-chewed." Beside the door was a row of pegs hung with wool jackets and sweaters, a mackintosh, a pair of hip boots and various caps and hats. He took down a blue tuque with white snowflakes around the rim, pulled it on and went out into the day.

"Daddy?"

He turned. "Yes, bean?"

She was struggling to stand, a beagle puppy the color of deerhide with one black ear, the black patch crossing over the crown of its head and down its nose, clutched in her hands. He reached for her elbow and she came up as she said, "I want him, Daddy. I want him so bad."

He thought Oh, a hound. He'll break your heart. But said, "I didn't hear Mr. Levesque say anything about their being for sale. How do you know it's a him?"

"He peed on my jacket."

"Well, that's not a very promising start, is it now? What would Mom say?"

"She'd say he's just a puppy and was excited."

"Would she now?"

She was looking at him, blinking slowly. Very serious. "I think so."

"It's about winter. That's not a good time to get a pup. The snow and all."

"But he's here now!"

Levesque came back through the door. He was carrying a pair of very old small snowshoes, the shape of teardrops, with fine delicate lacing. "Who's here? Me?" He looked at Katey and said, "Oh, I see. You found the right one?"

"Daddy said they might not be for sale."

"You wait a minute, you," Levesque said. He held out the snowshoes to Oliver, who took one in each hand and turned them over, looking at them.

Levesque said, "You get your deer?"

"No," Oliver said. "I went a couple times as a boy and it didn't take. You get yours?"

"Oh yuh, I got mine all right." And shot his eyes away the briefest of moments. Cappy Levesque ate deer meat year-round. As did a number of dairy farmers and others up in the hills. Contrary to rumor, the meat in his winter stew never came from the fur-bearers he trapped, although he swore by young woodchucks fat with spring grass. He looked back to Oliver and said, "Those pretty things, they do the job, you think?"

"They're lovely. But so old, they must be worth a fortune."

Levesque shook his head. "They only worth being used. They come down to me. Now I pass em along. But that babiche, that's moose. You don't be putting no shellac or nothing like that on it, you hear?"

Oliver ran his fingers over the delicate lacing. "It's so dry, though."

"Yup. But sound. You got bear grease?"

Oliver almost laughed. "No," he managed. "I don't have bear grease."

"I didn't think so." He pulled a Prince Albert tobacco tin from his back pocket and palmed it over. "There's enough here, get you through a couple winters."

Oliver tucked both snowshoes under one arm and reached for the tin. As he took it, Levesque held his eye and said, "But you run out, good clean lard works fine. Just fine." And he grinned.

"That's good to know," Oliver said, and grinned also.

Throughout this Katey had stood with the puppy cradled between her chest and left arm, her right hand running over the tawny fine teacup of dog-skull, waiting.

Levesque swiveled to her now and said, "Your papa. He's right. Them pups ain't for sale."

"Oh." She didn't move.

"They dam? Mama-dog? She my best rabbit dog. They sire, he my second-best. The rest of that pack out there, barking at you? They all worthless. I'd drown em if I didn't have such a soft heart, that's how bad they be. So these, these pups here, they gone get me back in the rabbit-fur business. That's how it is. So, no, they ain't for sale. But I'm thinking . . ." His voice trailed and he scuffled one hand over his face as if chasing a thought.

"What?" she said, unable to help herself.

"Well," he said. "That little bugger you got there? He all the time be pestering me. Biting at my ankles, my pant cuffs. Trying to climb up me when I'm setting in the chair. That a problem, see?"

Her face was screwed with puzzlement.

"Yup. That's not good sign. You hounds, you want em to be thinking about other things than you. You ain't looking for a pal in you hound. You want the hound to be thinking Rabbit! all they time. It's true. You, all you be good for is to feed em, that's all they think of you. And when you come out with the little .22 rifle, they know that mean Rabbit! You see? That one you got there? He worthless, is what I think. He gonna want to sleep on the bed, follow you to school, that sort of thing. You be setting down he go to sleep on you foot. Oh, no. Now, he might, you go in the field, the woods with him, he might holler and chase off after the cottontail. He might. But you know what else he gone be doing?"

She waited and then, cautious, not sure if she should speak, not sure what charm was being spun, ventured, "What?"

"Why he gone keep turning around to make sure you chasing right behind him. Yes, ma'am. That's what I see there, that pup. So, no. He ain't for sale. Worthless, like that? But, you take him home, take care a him like you will, he gone be a fine little dog just for you. You hear?"

"Oh, my," she said. "You mean it?"

"Why yes. I do. I think so. But you forget one thing, ain't you?"

"I did?"

"You got to ask you papa it be all right with him."

She looked at Oliver.

After a moment he said, "We can discuss the rules on the ride home. But I think it will really help with Mom if you had a name for him before we get there. She'll be home from school."

"Tinker," she said. "I'm going to call him Tinker."

"Now there," Cappy Levesque said. "A good name, that one."

Katey said, "Daddy's always tinkering with something. What Mom says."

The puppy chewed a pair of rawhide laces from a pair of Oliver's boots and while snowshoeing he clambered upon the back of Katey's small shoes and tumbled her headfirst into the snow but they couldn't leave him home because he would not so much howl as bay, a deep-chested roar of outrage and anguish. While still very young he made his way onto a chair and then the table and when Ruth returned from a quick trip out of the room, she discovered he'd eaten an entire plate of cookies. Summers, he would not quit or be dissuaded from digging his own den under one of the apple trees, where he'd spend the hottest afternoons, as well as seek quick shelter from rain if not caught first and brought inside. Except for Katey's bed, he was not allowed on the furniture and he seemed to understand this but protested the policy when left home alone—the opening of the door was accompanied by the loud thump of his jumping down from the sofa or a living room chair. He would bark at night to any passing car; other times the cause was not so obvious but from his daytime patrols the family knew he included all dogs, cats, once a woodchuck in the garden and once—learned hard at dawn by his furious determination to be let outside—as Ruth, for she had been the one to let him out, heard a sound from the dog, somewhere between a cough and gasp and then even before he came crying to her the air carried the dense sour rime of skunk. He had a passion for garbage of any

278

sort and haunted the family of chipmunks that made their home in the barn foundation, killing a few over the years. He snored loudly while sleeping and even with frequent baths carried about him a pungency, the odor of hound. And, despite Levesque's prediction, he was an ardent trailer of rabbits, often of a summer causing them to drive the backroads above Beacon Hill, calling his name and stopping to hike out into fields to call some more. Twice he was gone overnight and while Oliver feared the worst, both times the next morning he come loping and panting back into the yard to bark at the door to be let in, then to sleep for the rest of the day.

When he wasn't a bother he was a plague upon them. But he was a shadow of Katey and once she started school and after his first weeks every year baying over her absence, he'd settle into the workshop with Oliver until midafternoon when he knew she'd be walking up the hill, then whining to be let out to meet her. He seemed to know weekend mornings, although Ruth pointed out this behavior was not brilliance but observation: there was no alarm set and Katey simply slept until she woke. Tinker happily stretched out on his side atop her blankets.

In his third October, two weeks apart while hiking with Katey after school up Beacon Hill, he encountered a porcupine. While Katey tried to hold him, his head flaring bloody slobber from his mouth as Oliver worked over his tongue and gums with tweezers and a fine pair of needle-nose pliers, she asked if he'd not learn better. "Perhaps," Oliver said. "Or perhaps the temptation is just too great. You'll only have to keep him close a couple more weeks, then the porcupines will be hibernating. That's why you run into em this time of year."

Tinker roared with pain and outrage.

"Daddy, you're hurting him."

"Lord, Kate. I'm doing the best I can."

Summers, weekends, and afternoons he went where Katey went, as long as she was on foot or her bike. A friendly dog, he'd growl at strangers and Oliver and Ruth never doubted her safety, in town or in the woods, as long as he was with her. But his life excluded automobiles—he became excited in the car or the truck, slobbering heavy ropes of drool, even coughing up clear bile. When he had to go along, she carried a towel to wipe his muzzle, dashboards, windows.

Despite Oliver's initial silent prediction, it took eleven years for Tinker to break Katey's heart. He began to lose weight although his stomach grew larger. She'd seen photographs in *National Geographic* of sub-Saharan children that reminded her of Tinker. The vet palpated and contemplated and then sat with Tinker, Katey, and Oliver as he explained that the dog had growths in his stomach, likely within his intestines as well. She said, "Can you take them out?"

"I'm afraid I can't."

"Why not?"

"They're everywhere. It would kill him if I tried."

"What will happen, then?"

"They'll continue to grow. I can't say how quickly. But there will come a time when he won't be able to eat. At all. He'll become very bloated and uncomfortable. And he'll be starving, also. His kidneys may fail. It's hard to determine what the course might be—one thing affects another and so on. Do you understand?"

Tinker was on her lap, she was stroking him. She said, "What can we do?"

"Not much. Take care of him, feed him a little bit a few times a day, rather than all at once. As long as he'll do it, exercise is probably a good idea, just don't overdo it."

"I don't want him to hurt."

"Neither do I. When the time comes, and it will most likely be clear, the best thing then will be to put him down."

"Kill him?"

"I can give him a shot. He'll know no pain."

She bent over the dog and a tear struck her hand. Tinker licked the wet from her skin. She remained like that a long pause and then looked up and said, "No. I'll take care of him. I'll find ways to feed him. He trusts me. I won't abandon him."

She didn't see her father and the vet exchange looks. But the vet said, "Of course you won't. And, as I said, there's no way to know how it will be for him. I can help with ideas for food and I'll see him anytime you want me to. All right?"

She'd stood, gathering the dog tight and careful to her chest. She was crying but she looked first to her father, then to the vet. And said, "All right. Thank you. Daddy, can we go now?"

"Of course you can go," the vet said. "But I want you to think about one thing, as you go along. Okay?"

"What?"

"When the time comes, we—you and me, too—hope for him to pass easy. But Katey, if he comes to great constant pain, you have to ask yourself, Is he suffering for you, or is he suffering his own way out of life?"

The last week he'd take no food at all, the hamburger and rice she cooked and mixed with beef broth and mashed with her own hands into a paste. He'd lick her fingers but not eat. He was oddly massive, as if somewhere within him he was resurging. But it had been weeks since he could make the leap onto her bed and so she'd made a nest of blankets and quilts on the floor and slept with him, daytime lifting him onto her lap until she quit that because those efforts broke a painful sharp yelp from him. She missed two weeks of school. She was almost fifteen years old and her eyes were red-rimmed and pouched, as if she'd gained a greater age than was possible.

Oliver and Ruth talked. At night in bed, before and after her school day, passing. After dinner. Talk cautious but gentle. Both agreed this was Katey's time, Katey's choices, Katey's heart. The only question was how, if they had to, would they intervene. For both of them also loved the hound. They agreed they'd know that time when it came.

And she saved them. She came to his shop, still in her pajamas, not even midmorning of a Thursday. He was repairing a crack off an f-hole—a most common job but also one demanding for all things to align properly. He'd just glued in the little temporary blocks either side of the crack when she opened the door. Her face a defiant ruin but also holding a particular glow, she said, "It's Tinker. We need to go see Doc Rodgers. But, Daddy, could you make that call? I can't do it."

He stood and went and hugged her and she clung hard to him and then, the dog in mind, he lifted away and said, "Of course, sweetie. You go back to that Tinker boy. I'll let you know when I get the vet."

She went out and he followed her to the house, his heart bursting all ways, knowing that the most important call had already been made.

When she started work as a waitress at the Double Dot, Friday and Saturday nights, Sunday morning breakfast until noon, she preferred to drive the truck. If he needed it, she used her mother's car but she liked the truck. He attributed this to the many trips they'd taken around Vermont and northern New Hampshire, for fiddle repairs, when she'd been just a few years younger. And a couple of times he allowed her use of the truck for dates; he liked that she wanted to drive, to have some control, although she tended to date well-mannered boys. Best he knew. During the summer, mostly, she walked to work and back. In a rainstorm, he or Ruth would pick her up. So he'd heard her the night she snuck out for her test-drive to Royalton and back. He'd guessed she was meeting a boy, hoped it was nothing more than that. The same way he heard her stealthy creep through the house the night in June when she left. He lay awake a long time waiting for her homecoming. When first light smeared the windows and she had not returned he was still awake. And had a pretty good idea what she was trying to discover. He didn't know about the hoard of Christmas cards but would, within hours. Sometimes, everything in a life feels like a mistake.

To Ruth, he honestly could not say why he'd blurted the news that wretched night. Or, worse, not even news but something wrong thrown down that he then left Ruth no choice but to pick up. And explain. Which, after several tension-stretched days of all three walking around each other, avoiding the others as much as possible, what few meals were taken together in a pitch of silence, Ruth informed him she'd done her best to be honest and open with Katey and had no idea to what extent she was believed. Oliver then went very silent for several weeks. Although he assured Ruth this wasn't a long-held anger; he'd taken her explanation at her word, after all, he'd said, no one knew better than he did how a pitched-high moment could alter a life. He wasn't sure she entirely believed him but then what could she say? And, those weeks after the truth came to Katey, he caught her often looking at him, studying, trying to determine something of him she'd never before contemplated. Or had reason to. He was the silent man and in his silence he continued on as he always had. Certain both women would come to understanding and life would slowly regain what slender compass waver it had long attained. And what he did not tell Ruth, could not begin to tell Ruth, was that on that evening of unintended revelation he was responding to something else altogether: For months, no, spread over the past couple of years, there had been many times when he felt he was not living with mother and daughter but rather two fractious, unstable young girls.

He had no experience to draw upon but certainly his father had never imposed upon him the unreasonable demands Ruth did upon Katey. It seemed to him nothing the girl did pleased her mother and everything, or almost everything she did was a matter of dispute. And he lived within the swirl and on one level knew the girl was attempting to make herself anew and knew also her efforts were tentative, half-formed, idealistic and often angry. As, he thought, was natural. What he did not understand was his wife. She was furious, ferocious, pugilistic. Over small things, things that Oliver understood did not matter to Katey, and things he knew she already understood and would carry forward with her through life. But for this constant harangue from Ruth. How Katey dressed, the state of her room, her failure to do expected chores, how one assignment would be slapdash, the next some deep immersion she would not discuss or share with her parents. All, as he saw, so very petty. All so dreadfully important to both women. But especially Ruth.

He thought these were unfair odds, mother against daughter.

He thought Why in the world is she doing this? Pushing her away.

He never asked. It was a question to be held tight and silent. He understood this much. If nothing more.

Mostly, through this period he worked. His workshop a refuge and over the past twenty years a comfort and locus of his heart, of his life. Although in the past few years the work had fallen off somewhat, or rather the complexity of it. There were fewer old fiddles in need of careful extensive repairs but a greater flow of student violins and fiddles with bridges or tailpieces that needed to be replaced, a crack from carelessness to be re-glued. The children had less interest in the old music, the old instruments—some learned the violin for music classes in school, a very few were taking lessons because parents demanded it of them; children sullen and prone to damage their instruments through neglect if not outright hostility. Most wanted to play guitars, electric or acoustic. Or drums.

But in his shop was a lovely fiddle at least a hundred years old, made by some anonymous master and brought down to the states from Cape Breton by the grandfather of Ross Sutherland, a serious, dark-faced and fine-featured boy from Haverhill, New Hampshire, who told Oliver he wanted to learn the old songs before his grandfather could no longer play. But the fiddle had bad sound; his grandfather guessed the sound post was shot, maybe the bass rib, also. Oliver bowed a few notes and agreed. Perhaps replace the linings, the top nut as well, the ivory worn down with age. Which meant he'd have to open it up. And had the presence of mind to loan the boy one of his own fiddles, not his best but a pretty good one. The boy played bits of a couple of reels, one into the other, not even remotely familiar but sprightly well-made tunes. Ross Sutherland dipped his head and assured Oliver he'd care for it as if it was his own. Oliver had no doubt of that. In the end, the loan was a smart thing to do. Two months after the dinner-table debacle, some weeks yet before Katey left.

And then she was gone and he couldn't work. Every morning he had his coffee and went to his workshop and sat there. He'd go in for lunch. Ruth was home from school of course but was busy, it seemed, with everything and nothing at all: the garden, working with her flowers, reading, cooking something or other for supper, canning rhubarb, taking afternoon naps with the shades in the bedroom down. They spoke to each other, formally and from a great, hidden distance. He was back in the shop for the afternoon. Evenings they'd sit and watch Walter Cronkite as he drank a single beer. Sometimes she'd have a gin and tonic. Many of those evenings he'd go back to the shop and listen to the Red Sox games on the radio. He'd never really loved baseball the way many of his acquaintances did but it was better than television. It took his mind away, a bit.

Mostly he was struck by the profound absence of his daughter who now knew she was another man's daughter, and was seeking that man, heedless, it seemed to him, of the previous years of her life. And of his life.

The Cape Breton fiddle lay on the bench, in pieces. He'd replaced the sound peg, the bass rib. Decided to put in new blocks but hadn't yet. The maple sides and back were lovely, the spruce top also, in the quiet muted way of old wood. And there it sat. He'd reach, those mornings, afternoons, a finger to move one part or another. Then left it be. To reassemble it raised a host of questions, ones that usually he'd be of the mind to sort through and then come to an order and proceed. Instruments, much like people, were individuals and as such called for scrutiny and understanding, a sense gained through observation and touch of their hidden pasts and, importantly, not only what would heal their obvious needs, but also what work might be done to bring them most fully alive. Work that was not what was agreed to with the owner but what the instrument revealed. But this instrument had fallen mute. Or Oliver could no longer hear its language.

He hadn't lost knowledge of the technicalities. Of the woods; maple, spruce, ebony. Of hide glue. Of varnish. Of the multiple ways of fine-sanding coats of varnish. Of patience. Perhaps the most important tool of all.

What he had lost was the girl. Who had come to him almost at the same time as the knowledge. Almost twenty years, the two. Close enough so any discrepancy was meaningless. Music, a language of the soul, the unspeakable rendered to emotional comprehension and expression, at a time when he'd understood all other such attempts to be empty efforts, lies, embellishments, or most often, delusions and so false excuses of the human engine, the impulse toward striving forward, all of these things had been met and leavened, by the delivery into his arms of that fresh-minted soul, intact and fully formed, gazing upon him as his reason for life, her protector but also simply her guide. And he'd accepted that responsibility. And done his very best to see it through.

He'd felt, mostly, to be doing a pretty good job.

And now, nothing made sense. He knew she thought she hadn't rejected him, was simply trying to fill her picture to a wider level. To find another old song that she'd recognize, to add it to the songs of herself. And likely she would.

While he no longer understood anything at all.

He'd known she'd be leaving. And feared and dreaded it but also welcomed it. After all, that was what she was supposed to do. Just not in this way. And he was responsible. What to make of that?

Ruth had told him everything, long ago. He didn't blame her. He didn't blame Brian Potter, mostly. No. He didn't blame Brian Potter. He didn't blame the girl, the first one, Brigitte, offering what she had to offer. So many of the women, girls even, during those days, weeks, and months after the war ended had offered what they had. Many with a great fervor and sense of delight. Welcoming back life. They'd all heard stories of the Russians and these women, these girls, for many of them were little better than children, knew they were lucky. Even with the Brigittes and the gas-siphoning boy among them, knew they were delivered into kinder hands, more gentle hands, even if those hands could slap or find a sudden rip of malice, for this was a release of tension. Those Americans with their chocolate bars and tinned meat, cigarettes. They had no Stalingrad. These women knew they were fortunate. And their own war was ended. Fires raining from the sky. They offered what they had and mostly what they had was themselves. Certainly there was calculation involved but then, there always is. Just more deeply cloaked. When you have nothing, a cloak is a luxury ill-afforded.

And after Brigitte, there had been young women that he tried to help best he could. Small things can be very large. But, because of Ruth, he held himself. He wasn't alone doing so but mostly. Until the afternoon with Emilie up in the hills, in the vineyards, late summer, where they'd walked at her suggestion, hand in hand. She was nineteen she told him. They coupled in vine-spattered shade and then lay back, both smoking his cigarettes, watching the clouds overhead and he thought of Ruth and then also came the image of the blood-soaked blouse of the little girl and he was curling into himself without moving until Emilie caressed him with her hand and then her lips moving down his body and he stiffened and held his breath and gazed at the foreign German sky before he rolled over and fucked her very hard and long, as if he'd drive her into the earth under both of them, all the time seeing Brigitte beneath him. She cried out, her mouth against his shoulder. As Brigitte never would, with anyone.

A year after that he came home. Someone who resembled some version of himself long ago projected came home and everything around him was too loud and moving too fast and senseless to the true cost of being alive. And he walked through that the best he could.

Then the Bienceneaus' fiftieth wedding anniversary which he'd had no intention of attending but needed to, suddenly. For Brian, he thought. Until the girl who was Brigitte, hair braided and curled up, blonde hair so almost white, not deep honey like some French-Canadian girls, had come running up to him and speaking French not German, such a clever disguise that he knew she meant for him to see through, "Oh! There you are. I've heard about you, you fiddle player you. Tell me. Will you play for me?"

* * *

Or perhaps she was Brigitte as Katey, waiting a way to come through, back into this world.

He did not know. He was a sad thoughtful man who owned a great despair over the turbulent engine of life. Which he felt tethered to. And knew that it was the knowing this that tethered him.

And he was lonely, and loved. The love bestowed upon him was also a mystery to him, one he accepted as the grand mystery of life. For he also knew that for all the years behind him, and all that lay ahead he would remain lonely. That he stood, feet planted upon the earth but separate and apart. Alone. A bird in this world.

And Katey out there somewhere. His Katey girl.

Nine

Katey

SHE MADE THE mistake of taking I-95 from southern Connecticut and on through New York City, New Jersey, all the way through Washington, D.C. The truck kept speed but she was taut and hunched over the wheel the entire way, through multiple lanes of traffic, all it seemed with drivers who knew what they were doing, and were doing it very quickly. She hit Richmond a little after noon then, and got off for more than gas. She ate a sandwich at a Howard Johnson's, then stalled before the counter in a gas station before swiftly and without thinking further bought a pack of Old Golds, asked for a book of matches and then asked to buy a map of Virginia, which, as she'd guessed, was free. Somehow it made the purchase of the cigarettes easier. She then drove on to Petersburg, and got off the interstate for good, taking a state highway that led west and then south. She was headed to South Hill and, from the map, her best bet was that from there, on country roads and highways it wasn't more than a couple of hours to Cranston. Or less. She was still struggling with scale, even more so after this wild clenched flight down the eastern seaboard.

Before We Sleep

She had the windows down and the radio loud and the air that
came through the truck was a heat that flowed over her thick and
snug, a humid caul. She drove with one arm slung over the top of the
wheel and smoked a cigarette and watched around her. It was a
different country, yet someways reminded her of home. The roll
of hills, woods and fields interspersed. The hills were much smaller,
more slow rolls of the spread of land. Some barns of a size and
pastures of cattle, all this time of day clumped around the big
trees left to stand in the pastures for shade. But also the smaller barns
of squared logs, chinked with mud and unpainted, the timbers
the color of river-drained driftwood. Fields of corn unnaturally
high this early in the summer and also fields of crops she could not
name. Low bushy rows, or slightly higher even fields of some sort
of grass. Not hay, or at least not any she knew. And fields with rows
of plants of mid-height with broad leaves among which crews of
people moved along the rows and she saw the people were all
black, and were not only men but women and children. Several
times she came up behind slow-moving old cars or trucks and these
she recognized; older people moving along the roads of home.
She passed through a crossroad with a white cinderblock store
with ragged worn tin signs for Cheerwine and Pepsi-Cola, a hand-
made sign of plywood with black lettering that offered boiled
peanuts, fish bait. A pair of old black men sat on the porch in ruined
kitchen chairs, tipped back, watching the road but not seeming to
see her pass by.

In South Hill she found a motor court. It was four in the afternoon and she was done for the day. Twelve hours of driving. The
woman in the office was watching *As the World Turns* on a rabbit-
eared television and was irritated to be interrupted, then looked at
the card Katey had filled out and said, "Vermont," with the accent
on the first syllable as well as some judgment being passed but of an
unknowable kind.

291

She carried her suitcase to the small unit. Inside was stifling hot and she pulled a string for an overhead fan that swirled slowly and began pressing waves of heat down against her. She pulled down the pilled bedspread that had once been white and regarded the sheets. They seemed clean and she ran her hand over them and they were soft and crisp at once. She thought Perhaps it will cool down come dark, then considered the sort of heat outside and inside and doubted it would cool to what she was used to. She didn't want to open windows here but, looking at them she saw the metal box fitted into one of the windows, with louvered metal slats on the front. A cord ran from the air conditioner to a wall outlet and she bent down to study it. She'd never seen one before, outside of advertisements. There was an ON button and beside that a knob with settings for LO, MED, HI. She turned it on and turned the knob to LO. The machine ground to life and a faintly acrid smell came through the slats, a smell that gradually turned to a cooler temperature than the room was. She turned the knob to MED and the air came a bit faster, perhaps a shade cooler. She tried HI but either the knob was broken or someone had jammed it against this final setting. She thought perhaps an hour or so and the room might be bearable.

She locked the door, stuck the key on its metal diamond tag in her back pocket and got in the truck and drove out, turning away from how she'd come, toward the downtown.

It did not strike her as a prosperous place. She passed ranks of one- and two-story buildings, storefronts. A hardware, a ladies apparel store of some size, a barbershop and then a beauty shop. A small department store. A record store with a Ferlin Husky poster in the window. Then, set back to make a good-sized parking lot, busy with cars, was a Piggly-Wiggly, clearly a grocery store. She found herself scoffing at the name, and then caught herself and decided the name was sort of interesting. Better than the Acme store in Randolph. She'd never even thought of that before—the everyday boring sound of it. She went on and passed a long large tin shed that covered most of a block, the sign on this almost missed but over a small door that led into one end of the building that read: BRIGHTLEAF BEST OF THE SOUTH. After that she bumped over railroad tracks and glancing back saw that the rear of the tin shed abutted the tracks, with loading docks and some pickup trucks also parked there.

Then she was in a different place altogether. There were a few stores, all small and rough compared to what she'd just come through. The pavement gave way to packed red dirt and houses cramped back on rough yards between what stores there were—small groceries or automobile garages, another beauty parlor which she only guessed because Aunt Peal offered *Straightening*, *Wigs*, and *Cuts & Rinses*. There were people on the street, people on porches, children on bikes weaving threads around and past her. All of them watching her and all of them ignoring her and all of them black. A bit of cramp of fear struck within her belly and she almost leaned to lock the passenger door when she realized it was too hot to roll the window up and then wondered why she'd felt that need. Beyond that, though, was a deeper sense she was where she shouldn't be. That she was bringing as much discomfort as she felt, perhaps more. As if to answer this a young black man in bell-bottoms and with an Afro had turned at the sound of the truck and spying her in it stood watching her, his eyes offering a challenge of some kind she could not read but also then saw the lifted eyes of the older men, the women especially on the sidewalks and porches, as if to ask What's your business here, strange white girl?

She pulled into an empty lot of withered grass studded with cans and shattered glass and punched the radio on and spun the dial against the static and found a raw keening electric music she didn't know but was already backing around, not wanting to do anything but head back the way she'd come. So she drove back through those streets with delicately scrawling electric guitars alongside the voice of a man who she guessed was also black, that man asking not just her but anyone within sound of her passing truck: Baby, what you want me to do? Fervent and pleading, with an edge of anger. She kept her eyes dead ahead and her hands locked on the wheel.

Back over the railroad crossing she slowed by a restaurant she'd passed earlier, Peanuts, with signs for fried fish, shrimp, sides. There was a pool of cars in the lot and she found a place and parked and locked the truck and paused again, remembering her seafood gluttony in Maine and here again it was clear that America ate fish. As she paused, two couples of indeterminate age came out through the door and all glanced at her, the men running eyes as men did but there was also again the sense that she presented an immediate strangeness. Perhaps it was her jeans. Perhaps it was simply being a young woman alone. Or perhaps it was that those quick eyes had registered all of her in some way she couldn't know. Then they were gone and she blew past her hesitation and pulled open the door and went in.

The walls were a gold foil with embossed bronze fleurs-de-lis and there were four-and six-top tables, with booths along the sides. She was put in a booth but felt all right—the restaurant was about half full. Her waitress was a middle-aged woman with a luxuriant auburn beehive and violent red lips that would deeply stain the filters of the cigarettes she smoked behind her station between working with customers. She handed Katey a one-sided plastic menu. She ordered a shrimp basket because the idea of catfish was daunting. The waitress asked if she wanted sweet tea and she had a vision of bone china, a tea cozy, sugar cubes from tongs, memories of her grandmother. She was deeply tired and said, "Yes, please."

The tea came in a tall amber plastic glass tinkling with ice cubes. And so sweet her one cavity ached from it.

The shrimp were battered and flaky and delicious dipped in the red sauce hot with horseradish. The great revelation was the hushpuppies. She'd had no idea what to expect and almost ignored them as the french fries latticed over them. Then lifted one of the round brown misshapen balls and bit into it. Some kind of corn bread but both sweet and savory all unto itself. An edge of onion, one also of honey or sugar, and the fried crust was delightful in the way a baked johnnycake never would be. Unless you were starving. Of course, she thought, the ham and cheese at Howard Johnson's now was a lifetime ago and perhaps she truly was close to starving. She ate another shrimp and the tail slid off in her fingers and she realized she'd been missing the last good bite of each of the shrimp. So she dug back through the basket and drank more cold sweet tea and thought All right. This place is good, too. See what the morning brings.

She woke cold in the night and pulled the spread up over her and curled up tight and slept until well after the sun was up.

She got a cup of acrid coffee from a machine in the office and sipped that as she studied her gas-station map. She was too antsy to eat. Best she could tell she was an hour from Cranston. By back roads, some red lines with numbers for state highways, some roads thinner black lines which she guessed would be more of the red dirt. So longer or shorter than an hour. And there loomed the question of how, once in Cranston, she'd find Brian Potter. The Trask farm, perhaps. She really didn't know. Perhaps a phone book in a booth in Cranston. Or just asking around. She'd know when she got there.

Once again she was out in the country, rolling along past wide fields and folds in the land where she'd drop down and pass through woods and often there then clattering over a bridge that showed a deep narrow dull brown stream. Not the clear brooks and rivers of home but the boil of red dust that rose behind the truck and the red soil of the fields explained those muddy waters. Again, there were crews of Negroes working in what she now realized were tobacco fields. Brightleaf, she guessed. She passed a white man on a tractor cultivating a field of the long, low-clumped rows and realized, whatever the crop was, it was a job not given over to the Negroes. She had no idea if this was expediency on the farmer's part or if there was a judgment of capability involved. All she knew was the past few years it had often been dangerous to be an outsider-white person in the south, along with great bravery and determination from the black people. And that much violence had occurred in all sorts of ways. As, she knew, violence had occurred without much notice by anyone outside the south for many, many years before that. Those little girls in Alabama. She knew about that. And wondered how many other little girls had perished without her ever knowing of it. And told herself, But that's not why I'm here.

Which was true. Even as at the same time she knew she would be looking and listening and trying her best to understand this place. For all kinds of reasons.

She turned the radio back on, still tuned to the station she'd found the afternoon before. This time there was no music but a man was preaching. She wasn't interested in Jesus on this day, or sin, or being a sinner, or glory and redemption. Though she admired the cadence of his voice enough to not change stations and merely turned the volume down so he was an undertone to her travels. And this felt somehow right and fulfilling. Comforting, or better, calming.

Then she was back on a state highway, blacktop, and the land spread wide around her before of a sudden large trees flanked the roadside and she passed a black-on-white metal sign that indicated the Cranston City Limits.

It wasn't a crossroads but more like two. Not a full village either. There were a few houses leading in and a hardware and farm supply store. The houses were larger homes with well-kept yards, trees along the road throwing a canopy of shade. She passed a newer sprawling two-story brick building with a football field and

playgrounds and a sign that read CRANSTON CONSOLIDATED
SCHOOL, with another sign, the sort that churches used, black letters
on a white field that could be changed, that announced CLASS OF
1967 GRADUATION, MAY 27. Near a month ago.

Then she was among houses again and realized she would shortly
be beyond the town and thought, then turned around in someone's
driveway and headed back. The farm supply store was what she
needed, the best bet.

She was back among big spreading fields and stands of woods when
she saw the modest sign and turned into the driveway. She passed
along the berm of a pond and there, flanked by large trees, was the
house. Some smaller barns and outbuildings clumped along the
extended dirt driveway beyond. The house was white with a roofed
full porch running the front, center steps rising to the porch and first
floor. Three windows behind the porch railing and three more
across the second story. A brick chimney ran up one end and the
roofs of both the porch and the house itself were covered with aged
cedar shakes. It struck her as oddly simple and yet with a settled
grandeur about it. To her practiced New England eye, it was clear
the house was very old and well kept up. There were wooden
rocking chairs on the porch with small tables between and gera-
niums on the tables and the chairs all matched. There were narrow
flower gardens before the porch and taut crisscrossed strings running
up to the railings along which slender vines tendriled and bright
flowers like small trumpets depended. Below that the beds held other
blooming plants and she recognized none except the far edges of the
porch both offered the pruned canes of roses, old-fashioned with
yellow and white blossoms. The shade trees either side of the house
were tall and had thick, dense waxy leaves and held large globes of
white flowers, most near the size of her open hand. Some spread
wide and the edges of the white flowers turning a shade of rust. She

pulled up in the drive across from the steps and got out of the truck. There were no other vehicles in sight, save for down by one of the small barns an old Massey Ferguson tractor. And from beyond there, out of sight, came the clamor of baying dogs. She stood by her open door a moment but whatever dogs they were, they were penned or shut in someway. She turned from that peering and walked along a pea-stone path and started to climb the steps. As she did the door opened and a Negro woman of middle age, wearing an apron over her floral-print dress stepped out and said, "Help you?"

Katey was prepared for the wife, or possibly the man himself. She said, "Well, I hope so." Sliding into her best confused, slightly girlish but also mildly supplicating tone. Which she used with certain teachers, other adults. She said, "I'm looking for Brian Potter. Isn't this his place?"

The woman scanned her up and down and said, "This the Trask place." At the same time turning and calling back through the open door, "Miss Judith? Some gal here looking for somethin. You best come." She glanced again at Katey and went back in the door, a simple screen open to the day, shut it behind her and left Katey, who heard her footsteps going down the hall.

Katey considered all of this and wanted to get in the truck and flee. Instead she went up the rest of the steps so she stood on the porch and waited. Her hands clasped in front of her.

The woman came fully out the door and stood on the porch before Katey. She had sandy blonde hair cut in a neat bob, blue eyes and a graze of freckles over her nose. Wearing a white sleeveless blouse, light blue capris and tan mary-janes with low heels. "I'm Judith Potter," she said as she reached out a hand. "Faye said you're looking for Brian?" Just the hint of upward lilt put that question into his name.

Jesus, Katey thought, I can't do this. Judith was perhaps thirty, a good couple of inches shorter, a small woman with presence and command. And as she thought this she sensed movement and glanced at the screen door where two little girls had materialized behind the dull cast of the screening. But she was taking the cool hand in her own warm damp one and said, "I don't mean to bother anyone. My name's Katey Snow and my dad was in the war with Mr. Potter and—"

Judith had released her hand and at once looked over Katey's shoulder at the truck and then was turning to the door as she spoke. "From Vermont. Yes." And then said, "Phyllis, Diane I want you to go to the kitchen and sit with Faye while I speak with Miss Snow."

"Mama!"

"No sass. Now scat! I mean it."

They went down the hall and for the moment there was a pause and together the two on the porch watched the little girls, perhaps five and six, one with long blonde hair and the other with auburn hair much like Katey's. In mismatched dresses and both barefoot as if the day hadn't truly started for them.

Katey said, "They're cute."

Judith studied her a moment and then said, "They are. They're also sisters. Do you have siblings?"

"I don't."

"Well, I don't know how that is, but I can tell you: Girls. And there's a third. Veronica, who's out with her daddy. If I had to have all girls I'm grateful for Veronica. I love em all, don't get me wrong. But Veronica, she's Daddy's girl. Loves the dogs, loves being outside along with him. Oh, I guess you'll get to meet her. Maybe." Then she paused and said, "Why don't you come in and sit." This time, not a question.

"Oh. I don't want to be a bother."

Judith regarded her with an open face. The trace of suggestion that perhaps Katey already was a bother. Then said, "We'll sit in the parlor. Faye will keep the girls in the kitchen. Come along and give me a minute with Faye. Would you care for coffee?"

Katey felt caught out, as if there was something out of balance, as if this woman had someway expected her. And thought of Maine and Thornton Potter and wondered what message he might've conveyed. She wanted to leave but couldn't. And beyond that, she felt no anger or hostility from Judith Trask. But guessed there might be some hidden. She was finally here, and that meant riding this through and learning what she would.

She said, "I'd drink a cup, if there wasn't any trouble to fixing it."

Judith said, "It's in the percolator still hot. How do you take it?"

"Just black, thank you."

"Come along, then."

They went into the house. A long central hall ran all the way to the door that opened onto the back of the house, with rooms opening off the hall, and a staircase built midway that went up and down in both directions. Judith led her to a room off the right-hand side and Katey could hear the murmur of little girls further ahead down off the hall.

They went into a parlor that was sparely furnished with an old daybed covered in crushed faded green velvet, a set of chairs of a deep cherry wood, with padded seats and armrests, a pair of wing-back chairs placed across from a table holding a chessboard with a game in progress laid out. The walls were old beadboard painted a deep warm mustard color and a pair of oil portraits hung on opposing walls, a man and woman, in clothing from another century.

"Sit where you like," Judith said. "I'll only be a moment." And left the room. She closed the door behind her, which had been open when they entered.

Katey looked about and considered. She chose one of the wing-back chairs because they looked the most comfortable and the chess table gave her a bit of distance from wherever the woman chose to sit when she reentered. She sat forward on the edge of the chair and clasped her hands between her knees. She felt out on a great precipice and wildly uncertain and wanted to be at her best and wished she'd considered more carefully what she'd worn and then simply gave herself over, knowing she'd actually done that once she'd made the decision to come here. Also, she was trying to recall what Brian's father had said about Judith Trask, and while she couldn't recall his words, or perhaps his comparison, she had the distinct impression that Thornton Potter felt Judith to be a formidable woman.

Judith came back in with a tray in one hand with coffee in cups and saucers. She bent and set down the tray and handed Katey coffee, took up the other cup and settled herself, much like Katey, on the edge of the other wingback.

She studied Katey a moment and said, "Good Lord. Ronnie, that's Veronica, will look just like you in a few years. Give or take an inch."

"Ma'am?" Katey managed. She drank some of the coffee but her separate hands couldn't quite manage the cup and saucer, both shuddering. She brought them back together and set them down.

"As you said. You're Katey Snow from Vermont and your father was in the war with Brian. Oliver, is that right? And your mother is Ruth?"

"How'd you know all this?"

Judith smiled. She said, "Well now, you told me much of it, yourself."

"I guess I did?"

"I'm sorry," Judith said. "I suspect it took a bit of gall but a great deal of grit to set out doing this. And I expect you're terribly nervous. You don't need to be. As long as we reach some . . . understandings." And let that last fall slow into the room.

"All right." Katey said this slowly, a deliberate lilt of uncertainty, of possible confusion.

Judith said, "For the moment at least, we don't want the girls to know who you are."

Katey took up the coffee cup, leaving the saucer on the chessboard and using both hands to steady the cup as she sipped and dipped her eyes away from Judith. Then lifted her eyes and said, "But you know who I am."

"It appears that you're Brian's daughter."

The last thing she expected, this bald statement. Then she gathered herself and said, "I guess Brian's dad told you I visited him."

"It was Louise, actually, who made the phone call. She spoke with me, had no choice. And Lord bless her but it was hard. She hemmed and hawed but the end was simple—you take one good look at you, your eyes, that hair, even your frame. Struck from a mold, so similar once you see it, there's no argument. And it was a terribly hard thing for Louise to do and I was kind as I could be. And, yes, surprised but not, oh, you know, not bowled over."

"I'm not understanding this."

Judith nodded. "I'm sorry. It's such an old story for me that it just feels a part of who I am, of who *we* are. Brian and myself. But you see, between when he came to visit your parents, when *those things happened*, there was another thing in his life before he met me. A terrible tragedy. There was a girl he loved—"

"The girl that died in the car wreck. Deedee? His dad told me."

Judith smoothed her hands down her lap. "Debra. Debra Springer. So you know that story. Well. Here's the part you don't know. When he met me. Well, now. I need to get my mind around this. He met me in the summer, I was up in Maine, there's a little place on an island, from long ago, my great-grandmother came from there. And we don't go every summer, there's cousins and all sorts of descendants and it's not that grand sort of place that can fill up with five or six extended families. Anyway, we met there and I saw plain as the nose on my face that this was the man I'd been waiting for but it took him a bit longer. He was still in school, college, I'm talking about. But that fall he almost surprised me by coming down to see me and meet my family and when I got that letter I thought I knew what it all meant. But I recall the moment, the evening after dinner, we walked out past the sheds and down the farm lanes and there was a full moon and a warm night for December and he'd spent that day out bird hunting with my granddaddy. Those two, a small joke, they were birds of a feather. Some good things are hard and hard things are never easy, even if they make your life better. So, we got to this certain spot, an old rail fence by some rundown tobacco sheds and a big old oak strung with dead wisteria, just a pretty spot in the moonlight and we paused there, as a young couple will. He asked me to marry him. I already knew my answer. But he stopped me and told me before I answered, he had things about himself to tell me. And that once he did, he'd understand if I said no. That he'd leave and never bother me again. Well, that was a wallop to my heart. I didn't have the first idea what to expect. He started off telling about Debra, who I already vaguely knew about. Then he told me about the war, things he saw, things he did. A whole pile of it pretty bad stuff and I got a sense of what sort of burden he was carrying. And I did stop him then and reminded him of where he was, and that the old man he'd come so fond of those last few days, how that man's own father had his own war and one piled up with right and wrong so much it can't hardly be sorted but how those things stay with a man and float on down the years, even into the children to come. In ways we can never know, or endings we can never see. Excuse me."

Judith stood and walked to one of the side tables and opened a silver box, took up a cigarette from the box and an oval lighter shaped like an egg, removed the top of the lighter and smoked. She returned to her seat and set a glass ashtray on the chessboard. Katey wanted to ask for one but didn't. She was perched still on the edge of her chair, cramped and hot like a bird on a wire.

Judith said, "It was after I ran off at the mouth, trying to reassure him, that he told me about your father. When he visited after the war. Now, I don't know how much you know of that time, except enough to have come looking for him."

Looking at the floor, Katey said, "My mother tried to explain it to me. The best she could."

"People," Judith said, "are complicated. More so than some of us more fortunate ones can ever know." Then she paused, crushed out her cigarette and gazed toward the window out the side of the house, raised her hands and made a church steeple of her fingertips and rested her chin there a moment. Then made a barely perceptible nod and looked back at Katey. "And how did she come to tell you? No, wait: Oliver Snow? What sort of man is he? I mean, I've heard the stories from Brian. I'm asking, is he a good father to you?"

"Oh. Oh, yes. He was, I mean, he is . . . I love him dearly and he loves me, I know. I never doubted him—he's seen by some as a little odd but never anything but kind and attentive to me. I miss him and I'm terribly worried I've hurt him by running off like I did, but once I knew the truth I just had to . . ."

"What, dear? You had to what?"

Katey picked at nothing on the knee of her jeans. She took a breath and said, "Once I knew, I got the notion into my head, and it wouldn't let go. That I needed to stand before Brian Potter and have him see me and learn what that felt like. I'm prepared to dislike him, to feel nothing at all. I know he might deny me or just ask me to stay fully out of his life, I'm prepared for that. But I felt like, at least for me, I needed that. I needed for him to know I exist."

"Yes," Judith said, although with a certain hesitation. Then, "I can see how that would be. How old are you? Katey? Or is it Katherine?"

"It's both. I'm seventeen."

Judith nodded. "That's a hard age."

"People keep saying that! Why's it so damned hard? Because I think and feel and want to know things? Because I'm figuring out all the little boxes we're supposed to fit things into are almost all false? Because the world is so wrong and everyday we just go along pretending it's not? Is that what you mean?"

Judith dipped her chin and then, eyes full on Katey, said, "I was thinking more about how, in the process of learning those things, the old ground you once walked so sure and certain upon is swept from under you. That's the hard part. Now, then, answer me a question I came upon a bit ago. Why did your mother, Ruth, why did Ruth tell you about Brian? What happened?"

Katey was quiet a moment, drank the last of what was now cold coffee. Her hands were steady as she set cup into saucer. She looked up and said, "She didn't."

"You just told me she did."

"I told you she tried to explain what happened. With Brian and herself."

"All right. But, what happened to cause her to attempt that explanation?"

Katey stood and walked to the side table and took up a cigarette from the box and the lighter and smoked. She went back to her chair and leaned to pull the glass ashtray close and tipped the miniscule ash from her cigarette and said, "I found six years of Christmas cards hidden away. Addressed to both of them and with his Maine return address. Which is how I knew where to go looking."

Judith crossed one leg over the other knee and looked off again. Then she said, "I guess it's how they say. We keep the very things that will hurt us most, for the worst possible reasons. But I don't quite understand. How did those cards tell you who he was? He told me he never heard from your mother after that weekend. So how would he have known about you? What could he have said in a card that alerted you to who he was?"

"Nothing." Katey was suddenly small.

Judith leaned toward Katey and said, "The truth can be a slippery thing. And you learned one of those slippery truths. But how? It's just not clear to me."

"My father told me."

"What? What do you mean, he told you? Why would he do that?"

Katey was now the one looking beyond, out the window. There was a bit of lawn, then a swale of dried tall grasses and a stand of tall pines with long trunks before spare branches. She said, "I don't really know."

Judith paused and again steepled her fingers and frowned. Then she said, "Your mother, when she tried to explain what had happened, what did she tell you? I'm not meaning to pry, and I'm not asking for details. Just a sense of her tone, her words. Because I can't imagine the man you've described, and the man Brian has told me of, doing something so cruel. Which is how it sounds to me."

Katey thought about this and then said, "All right. Mom, when she explained, mostly what she told me was that it was a long hard weekend for all three of them. She ended up learning things Dad had never told her about. And she said she was just struck down with it all and there was a part of the whole story I could never understand unless I was there. But that there was a real bad time when she was listening to all of this from Brian and she sort of broke down and he, Brian that is, did also. And Dad wasn't there. I don't know where he was. But they were alone and she said to me that there are times when life is terrible and raw and precious and people do things that they wouldn't otherwise do. That's almost her exact words. And I knew from the way she told me, she was talking not just about all the things she'd learned but also what happened right then, that afternoon or night or whatever it was. When I was made."

A silence then. Made more so by the whir of a housefly about the room, then up against the windowglass. Also the sound of a vehicle coming past the house, the engine pulsing onward but barely receding before it cut off. Which brought Judith upright in her chair, alert. But she only said, a low voice, "I be damn."

Katey shook her head. "Look, this has all been a big mistake. I think I should just get in my truck and go. Save everybody from any more misery that I never intended in the first place."

"You could do that, I suppose."

"You want me to?"

"Of course I do. But you can't."

Katey stood up. "You watch me."

"Sit down. You can't leave, first of all, for you. Second, for the man who's going to be walking in the door in the next half-hour or so. And finally, finally I think for your mother and your father. The man who raised you. Comes back to that, doesn't it? Now you sit down."

Katey walked over and took another cigarette from the box and lighted it and then, as if it were her own choice, came back and sank into the wingback chair. Her head hurt. She smoked a bit, studying the black and white tiles of the chessboard and then raised her eyes to Judith and said, "Comes back to what?"

"Why he told you that you were not his birth-daughter. Why, after all those years of being, as you said, a wonderful father, would he do that? It doesn't make sense to me. Can you explain it?"

At the time, that evening at the dinner table when her father rose and spoke and left the house, she'd known somehow why he spoke. And when her mother finally addressed the statement two long days later, she also had been candid: "He's tired, Katherine. Of how we bicker, you and me, it seems all the time these days. And it's my fault as much as yours. I don't think he meant to say what he did. But look at us, always at odds with each other. It must wear on him. I think he meant to shock us, both of us, out of our constant harangue with each other. I know he feels dreadful about it. But then, he also has a certain freedom, he's a bit aloof isn't he? From how you disregard me, the all-too-reasonable demands I place upon you. And your utter refusal to comprehend the reasonableness. Goodness, girl, you'd think I was intending you for a life of servitude, the way you react to me." But within days Katey had tossed this aside, seeing only a way for her mother to lay blame upon her. To the point that she'd forgotten this exchange. Best she could.

She looked at Judith and said, "I don't know. Honestly. On the one hand I think perhaps my dad was always really angry at her for what happened but covered it up to keep peace. Maybe even because he loved me. But there's also this: The past few years my mother has not been the cheerful, sunny woman I remember as a young girl. It's like she'd gotten pinched and mean, or maybe just unhappy with her life and doesn't care who knows it. Nothing turned out in her life like she thought it would and she's gotten old and bitter. Why, these last months they haven't even shared a bed! And they never had any kids, the two of them. There was only me and all I was, clearly, was the biggest mistake of her life. It's complicated—she fell in love with someone not quite to her family's standard and she was hot-blooded and sure of herself and then he came home from Germany and it all fell apart as the years went on. That, honest to God is my best guess for how she became the way she is. A tired bitter woman with a wasted life."

Judith Potter had kept her eyes level on Katey throughout this. And held them upon her when Katey stopped. The silence in the room stretched like an old rubber band and Katey felt a headache coming on and wished she eaten something, the pit of her stomach a roil.

Then, abruptly breaking the weight gathered within the room, Judith stood. And looked at Katey and said, "I see. Well, I can't help you with all that. I think what you need to do just now, is walk out the front door and follow down to the barns. You'll pass an old truck with dogboxes in the back. By the kennels. Brian will be there. Go talk to him. That's what you need to do."

She turned and walked halfway to the door and paused just as Katey said, "But what do I say to him?"

And Judith turned out of her pause and said, "Isn't that why you're here?"

Then she was gone.

When Katey stepped into the central hall she saw Judith at the far end by the back entrance leaning and talking to a girl, the older one in overalls and a checked shirt, Veronica. The girl who loved being with her father. Katey turned quickly and walked to the front door and let herself through the screen and down the steps to the pea-stone path.

She walked past her truck and down the farm lane. Beyond the pond there was a big willow and then a long stretch of field. Past the tractor and alongside the row of weathered sheds. Some were open-fronted and held machinery. A couple were of a good size, of two stories and with a window set into the chinked-log walls, a slab-plank door with a wooden latch worn smooth. Behind the second was a wire pen opened out the side and back and she could smell the hogs before she saw them. Three big white- and black-spotted sows with litters of young piglets rooting in the ground, the sows in a muddy patch the far end of the pen, under the shade of tall lank trees with fine spindly leaves. One of the sows lifted its head and grunted at her and the piglets all scrambled toward their mothers. The lane curved right and the blue truck was parked along the curve. There were a few dents and scrapes in the body and the bed of the truck held wooden boxes built-in, with ventilation holes and panels cut out of the doors that faced the tailgate, the panels covered over with fine hard wire mesh. And then she saw the kennels and dog-runs. The kennels were also old squared timber buildings but had many more windows let into them and the runs were broad and long, divided into long avenues onto the grass and under the shade of more trees, these large oaks. Each run had either young dogs or a female with a litter of puppies. And to the side of that were a pair of stand-alone kennels with shorter runs that were raised a couple of feet off the ground, the flooring of the same hard mesh and in each lounged large dogs. The studs, she guessed. All of the dogs had short white coats marked with splotches and speckles of either black or liver color. But for one of the females with puppies, whose spots were more yellow, like lemon drops. Some of her pups had those spots and some were liver-splotched.

And then she heard a door opening in the shed behind her and she turned as a man stepped out into the sun and blinked his eyes against the brightness and they stood looking at each other.

He wore hard leather boots that laced up to just below his knee, with old khaki trousers tucked into them, neatly, so they ballooned evenly about the tops of the boots. A white shirt with the sleeves rolled up above his elbows and open at the neck. A metal whistle hung on a lanyard against his chest. He was wiry but well-muscled, the skin on his arms, neck and face weathered and sunburnt to the color of tobacco. His eyes, like hers, were deeply set and large, dark brown. And his hair was pomaded to a gentle roll off his forehead, cut short, the same thick rich honey-brown. He squinted at her.

She said, "Hi."

"Well, there you are," he said. "Heard you were coming. Then, a course, saw your truck as I came in with the dogs. Oliver and Ruth Snow's girl."

This was not what she expected. She said, "That's right." And he sounded almost as southern as his wife, in ways more so. As if this country had rubbed into him, been absorbed through his skin and changed him.

He said, "Mother called Judith. After you showed up there." And speaking of his home she heard Maine. Muthuh. "I understand you're looking for me on account of your father. That he's been

310

struggling again. Or something like that. I'm sorry to hear it. He was an important person to me. Saved my life. But that was a lifetime ago. I don't see how I could help, now. I'd do what I could, of course. But," he paused and spread his arms wide before bringing them back and crossing them over his chest, "I've got a pretty full plate here, what with the farm and the family and all. Mostly, life rolls on and a man rolls with it. But again, a man can't always call what life demands of him. And so, a troubled man, one so his own daughter chases after another man down nigh half the country, needs help, you pay attention to that. So tell me. What can I do for you?"

She looked about, as if to seek out an answer to all of this. One of the stud dogs had stood in his run and was looking at her. She looked upon the dog and saw how he was muscled and strung, relaxed and alert, all at once. And looked back at the man before her and saw he wasn't so different. She said, "All of that was a lie. My father doesn't need you. You know who I am."

He rubbed one boot against the ground and looked up at the sky as he lifted a pack of Luckies from his shirt pocket and tapped one out, stuck it in the corner of his mouth. Then his eyes came back to her as he palmed a lighter from his khakis and spun the wheel and blew smoke. He said, "That was not my proudest moment. What do you want of me?"

"It's a nice thing to know I'm not a proudest moment."

Again he looked off, smoked, then looked back. "It's not you. I never knew about you. I was never told. Think on that. So, again I say, what do you want of me?"

Without knowing she was doing so she looked down to the ground as he had and kicked one sneaker against the ground and then looked up at the sky and felt the heat of the day drain against her as she dropped her eyes to again meet his. She said, "Nothing."

"Now, that can't be true. After all the work you went to." And his voice was kind.

She blinked and was near tears and she said, "I don't want to make problems for you. Not the first one. Which I guess I already have. Your wife certainly knows who I am."

"But we weren't talking about her, were we? I can handle Judith. Probably. Which is what makes life interesting, tell the truth. So, then." He waited, eyes clear upon her.

"All right," she said. Took a breath and said, "What I'd like, is to know a bit about who you are. Is that crazy? I don't even know how that could happen. And I'm really ready to just get back in my truck and drive off, I want you to know that. And I told your wife that, also."

"I bet you did."

"I did. And I meant it."

"I'm sure you did. What did she say?"

"She said I should come down here and talk to you."

"And here you are. Talking to me. Tell you what. What say we take a ride and talk a bit. Maybe talk as I want also? How's that, for a start?"

"I could do that."

He hitched at the waist of his pants. Then he said, "I got to fill a couple of water bowls first. And then we'll get along."

"Could I see the dogs? I had a great dog, a beagle that died three years ago but he was a wonderful old guy."

He looked at her, again a short and dense study. He said, "Of course you can. What did you say your name was? I can't recall, just now. I'm sure Judith has it nailed, my mother, too. But I have a hard time with names, not sure why. It works against me, the work I do. But I get around it. There's a way to greet a man you already know, who's about to spend good money, and not let on you can't recall his name. And he will reveal it to you, each time. That's the truth." He grinned at her, a wide full smile. Then he said, "Funny thing is, I never forget a dog's name."

She told him her name and then said, "What should I call you?"

"Katey," he said, "I think you should call me Brian. That okay?"

"Yeah," she said.

"Come on, then," he said. He turned and went toward the large kennel building with all those windows cut in. There was a path around to the side and he walked there with her following, to a door. A regular door with glass windows in the upper half and flower beds either side of the path. Beside the door there hung a bell from an iron brace, the bell about half the size of a school bell or the bell in the meetinghouse at home. With a chain dangling from the clapper that if pulled side to side would set the bell to ringing. It was an old bell, dark with age, the bronze gone blue and black and a shade of green like a precious stone, jade or some sort of turquoise. She looked at it and knew she was seeing something that held an importance but didn't know precisely what that was. A farm bell, for alarms or warnings of some kind.

Then they were inside and it didn't seem to be a kennel after all but some sort of office before she realized this was only the end of the building. There was a desk with a telephone and gooseneck lamp, a pair of heavy leather chairs and a leather couch. Along one wall stood a sideboard that held ranks of cut-glass decanters not so different from those at her grandmother's house, and she guessed the cupboard below held tumblers of the same cut glass. On the interior log walls hung a pair of prints of dogs and men out in the woods, the fields, birds lofting up in spectral lovely light. A third of a log with quail lined up atop it. Feathers and bark and autumn leaves so real as to touch. The quail clearly dead. Brian Potter stepped to a rack and took down a short leather thong and bunched it in his hand and glanced at her. He said, "This is the office. Truth is, the business end of this farm is done in the house but when the gentlemen come for the hunt they like coming in here. Where they meet the dogs and we talk what we're going to do and where. Afterward we come back here and

I pour drinks and we talk about what we just did. Because," he went on, "nothing seals a memory better than recounting it. I hope I'm not boring you. What I do is all of a piece, even if the fragments of it, some are more interesting for me than others. But I think most all of life is that way." He lifted his hand and let dangle free the leather thong and she saw it was a short leash that forked at the end into two strips each ending with a D-ring and a small brass snap. He said, "I'm going to run that water and then we'll take a pair of young dogs out and drive around and watch em work. Sound good?"

She nodded, stunned and within another world and hungry for it.

They went through another door and were in the kennel then. The dogs had heard them coming and were piled up at the pen doors, whining and wagging tails, happy dogs. Brian Potter took a coiled hose off the wall and went along the row of pens and swung out stainless-steel water pans and emptied them into a drain and used the hose to fill them and replace them. As he went, crouching and rising and crouching again, he talked.

"They all go back to a dog named Diablo, though doubtless there was some before him. But that's the line. And a bitch, around the same time called Blue—legend is her ticking was so light it faded into the white so it looked blue more than black. My guess is she had some setter blood in her—those days, bird dogs were bird dogs, and setters and pointers came later. This was way back before the war, you understand? My wife's grandfather's father, but more likely that man's grandfather. Or more. A long time, is what I'm saying and no one knows how long before they started keeping paper records. At some point, or points, it was all in one man's head. That's an amazing thing. Both that it happened that way and also some one of those men figured out to start writing it all down. Knowing what he had. Now see here, these are the couple little girls I thought we'd watch work this morning."

He'd knelt down before a pen of young dogs and slipped open the door only enough to slowly work one, then another dog out from the scrambling mess of them all anxious and wanting to go. He ignored the two, who circled behind him and nosed up against him, as he slowly pressed the rest back and shut the door. Only then, crouched on his knees, did he swivel around and run his hands over the two freed dogs and let them bump their muzzles against him, before he clipped the leash on their collars and stood. "All right," he said. "Let's get these girls into the truck and go see we can find some birds."

When he said that final word both dogs turned and tricked up their heads and looked at him. As if he'd just made clear what the morning held. He ignored this as if it was only to be expected and motioned to Katey and they walked out another door into the yard and up the lane to his truck. He dropped the tailgate and popped open one of the doors in the boxes in the bed of the truck as he reached down and unclipped the leash and said, "Up." But both dogs had already launched effortlessly upward into the box. He shut the door and tested the bolt and lifted the tailgate and slapped it into place and looked at Katey and said, "Shall we ride?"

They didn't turn and go back out to the road but instead bumped down the lane and proceeded past fields on both sides until they came to another lane that made a crossroad and turned left there and went on along. Maybe five miles an hour. He fired up another cigarette and let his right hand slop along the top of the wheel as he smoked with the left and otherwise held his hand out the window, or gestured about as he kept talking.

He said, "It's getting to be a little late in the morning to be doing this. A bit warm. Not for the dogs but for the coveys. It's a lot of young birds this early in the summer and I like to leave em be once the sun is up good. We'll ride on to a place I haven't bothered in several days. Just so you can see it but also so the birds we trouble are cool. It's a trick this time a year—the young dogs need the work but the birds need to be left be. But it's also twelve hundred acres and some more and I got it all in my head. It'll work out fine, you'll see."

"Okay," she said.

He glanced over at her. "Now listen: I can putter along and talk about all of what we're seeing and doing because it's second nature. You want a lesson in dogs and birds, by which I mean English pointers and bobwhite quail, I can give it. I've done it a thousand times. Or what all's planted in the fields and why. Or, and you'll see, the different pine plantations we'll pass by and maybe a couple we'll go through. The creeks and hardwood bottoms. Every bit of it makes money, not just for birds, but it's also part of a plan to make a good place for birds. Which, those birds, fall to late winter, make as much money as all the rest put together. Them and the dogs, of course. Outside of Judith, which is not a clear way of speaking, those things are what brought me here and kept me here. So they're a most central part of my life."

Then he paused and tightened his expression and drove and she waited, feeling the silence between them, wanting him to collect whatever he was thinking and bring it back to her. Finally he ground his smoke out on the floorboards, glanced at her and said, "I appreciate how tough it was to learn what you did and even more, take on the job of running me to earth. It doesn't make a lick of difference that I never knew about you. The important thing here, is you learned about me and I want to do right by you. And I won't know what that is unless you tell me. I'm saying, you can have at it."

They bumped along in silence for a few minutes. Then Katey said, "Can I have one of your cigarettes?"

"You hadn't ought to smoke, you know that don't you?"

She looked at him. He then drove with his knees as he pulled out his pack, tapped one out, lighted it and handed it to her. She took it and blew toward the ceiling of the cab of the truck. He turned the wheel and they went down a rutted lane with hardwood trees tangled with vines and thick undergrowth on both sides and labored through a small muddy creek and then up the other side and out again into more fields.

"Can I ask a question?"

"I said you could."

"No. I only have one. That I have to ask."

"All right," he said. "Shoot."

She smoked a bit more. It was hot and still, the fields, the trees, all steady, upright, no breeze to press upon them, no breeze through the open windows. Looking straight ahead she said, "I heard all the stories. As much as most would tell, at least. Including your own 'Not your best moment.' So," she paused and turned on the seat to face him, to read his face as much as hear his voice. And to gird herself for his possible anger. "Did you rape my mother?"

His arms went slack on the wheel and he pressed in the clutch and popped the truck out of gear and let it glide to a stop. The truck wavered and guttered over the rough road some few feet, then was still. He was nodding his chin, his head, up and down, staring straight ahead. Even after the truck was stopped. Then he lifted his right hand off the wheel and wiped his forehead with the back of it and then wiped his hand on his pants. Only then did he look at her, his mouth pursed tight, his eyebrows clenched. A muscle in his neck throbbed with a sudden tension. She held his gaze, and smoked.

Finally he said, "No. It was complicated but to answer your question the only truth is to tell you. No."

"You say," she said and looked away, out her window.

He said, "I do. What happened that afternoon was something neither she nor I expected or wanted but when it happened it was what both of us needed. But it was that certain afternoon. It wasn't any other. You asked her, I'd expect she'd agree. There was indeed force, a tremendous force. But it came from both of us all at the same time. And that's how life is sometimes. It's not pretty. It's how it is. Does that, can that, answer your question?"

She sat a moment looking again out at the day and realized she'd been holding her breath and took in a great gulp of air, released it, looked at him and said, "I believe you. I'm sorry, but I had to ask. Now." She took another breath and said, "Go on, now. Show me your life, best you can."

He nodded and was mercifully silent. He put the truck back in gear and drove on. They came out again between fields, one big one toward the east where the sun was most bright, a field of tobacco and she again saw gangs of Negroes working along the rows and then the lane ended at a red-dirt country road and he pulled onto that and drove a mile or so and then turned off again onto another lane, wending down through smaller fields and ahead another rise of trees, these all pines of a sort unfamiliar to her; with very long clusters of needles arrayed on slender limbs that bowed down with the weight. All uniform of height although the sections to one side of the lane were considerably higher than those on the other side. As they passed through she could see that the trees were planted in rows, either side, and as they went she saw different angles of avenues down through the trees and it was mildly disconcerting, as if some funhouse-mirror version of trees was upon her.

He spoke then. "Those are loblolly pines. As you can see, they're planted. Those ones, they're about fifteen years old—the other side are about ready to harvest, they're around twenty-five years. And when we come up out of here we'll see what's called slash. That's where the crews came in a couple, three years ago and cut all of the mature trees, which means all of em. Right now it's grown up to canes and brush. The thing is, each one of these sections, they serve the birds well, different times of the year. The bigger trees, they're a good place for nesting come March. The younger ones, that's where the current young birds break apart earlier so the males can strut and call and entice the hens in, to mate. Or get eaten by a hawk or owl or possum or skunk or most anything else. A bobwhite has strong legs

318

to run and flies like a rocket but mating makes em stupid. Like, pardon me, many youngsters all the world over. I had to say, I'd hazard mating season is when we lose the most birds. Well, that and the many creatures that will raid a nest and eat up all the eggs. But come fall and winter, they move out into the slash. Plenty other places also, all the bean and milo fields, where there's corn, anyplace there's edges. Edges are key, here. Birds know to keep to the edge, close to the food but hid as best they can. That's why they like the slash. It's all edge but with the berries and seeds and being close also to those food crops, the slash doesn't have edge—it's all edge. Look, see what I mean."

And they were out then into a desolate landscape of piles of brush from the logging, along with rough tracks throughout, huge brambles of red blackberry canes, wound round with vines thick with leaves and blossoms, young thorn trees, and here and there a stunted older hardwood or apple that had been held back by the canopy of taller pines and left behind by the loggers. The sun now a huge blister in the sky.

He said, "This would be a good place to run the dogs, the birds are setting tight deep in the shade. But it's too hot for the dogs, eager as they are. What we're going to do is roll on through here and get back into the farm fields and let em out and drive the perimeters and see what coveys the dogs come upon. That way everyone will be happy."

She was listening to him and only partly understanding but enough so she knew it was pieces that one way or another would all make sense, at some point. So she nodded and said, "Tell me about these dogs. In the back of the truck."

"Oh Lord," he said. "That's Lil-Bet and Jill. Sisters. I keep my litters together after they've been weaned but before I decide who to keep and who to sell. They were whelped out of Lady by Doc, last summer. Ten months old. So I got em started at two months and

319

then had to put em aside for the season and now I'm working em up. They're both pretty good, which is why I haven't had em out in a few days. It's the dogs you haven't got your mind clear about that you pay most attention to. To figure em out."

"That beagle I told you about? Tinker, he was called? Well, he came from a man in Vermont that raised beagles and I got him when he was just a pup. And that man, he was a trapper and a rabbit hunter and he'd already figured out that Tinker wasn't going to be the best rabbit dog of the bunch and so when I showed up he decided I was the best place for that dog to be. And it was, for both of us. He liked to chase rabbits when he had the chance but he was best just being with me. And that man, he's dead now, shot himself over something a few years ago, I never did know what, he saw that Tinker and me, we were made for each other."

"Uh-huh. A dog-man knows his dogs. Before anything else. All right, here we go now."

They'd driven down another lane to the end of the second of two bean fields. Around the perimeters of both fields were stands of hardwoods. Even the grass between the fields and the beginning of the woods was high. And between the side of the road and the bean fields the grass was also high. She was beginning to understand what he meant about edges.

He stepped down out of the truck and she did also. He walked to the back and opened the tailgate and then the dogbox and the two young dogs bounded down and started to mill about him and he said, "Sit," and they did, squirming in the dust of the road. He looked down at them and waited and the squirming slowed and stopped. Their heads up, mouths open, pink tongues licking quickly, eyes upon him.

"Now, girls," he said, and raised his right arm straight above his head. Then dropped it to point to the near corner of the field as he said, "Find some birds."

They broke and were off, but floating back and forth, crossing paths, first working down the edge along the woods until they hit the corner, heads raised as they went. Then they turned and began to quarter the bean field.

He said, "See how they keep their heads up? What they're doing is not looking but letting all those countless ribbons of scent flood through their noses. They're smelling all sorts of things we can't. God knows, they can probably smell earthworms under the bean plants. But all they're interested in is the very hot and rich smell of birds. And I can say that because a dead quail, one just shot, even a man can smell it a bit. And you gut it, right then in the field because the intestines and organs, they hold the most heat and will start to ruin the meat you just stick it in your shooting vest. And that viscera, that's a rich odor, let me tell you. All right, they're not finding anything yet—let's ride up to the opposite end of the field and they'll work their way along." He started along his side of the truck and she stood a moment watching the lovely precision of the two young dogs as they worked and then she saw first one and then the other seemed to almost flip backward and then all motion was arrested, the dogs, one right behind the other locked as if frozen. And Brian saw this also and said, "Well, there we go. My bright little stars. No hurry, walk up here with me."

She met him by the hood of the truck. The dogs still hadn't moved. Their cropped tails were flagged high and she saw each stood on three legs, one front foot raised and cocked back at the knee. He said, "They're staunch. The birds will likely hold unless Lil-Bet, the one in front, starts to creep—young dogs will sometimes do that. Now Jill, what she's doing is called backing. An obvious enough term. So I'm going to circle around so I come up behind the dogs and then move ahead and flush the birds. The dogs should hold throughout. In fact, they shouldn't break point until after the birds are flushed and I've shot and dropped one. But they're young and so once the birds rise, I won't be upset if the girls go after em. They also mark not just birds that go down but where the singles land. The birds will run then, and if there's shot birds the dogs would be busy retrieving em. But, if the gunners miss, they'll go after the singles, quick, to try to point em again before they can run too far. That, anyway, is how it's s'posed to work. But like I said, these are young dogs." Then he paused and said, "But my. Ain't they grand."

Then he walked out slow and easy, striding down rows and crossing over until he was behind the dogs and came up toward them and as he passed her, Lil-Bet raised her head to look at him and he quietly said, "Whoa." With that there was a burst up of birds before him, a rapid, fluid pummeling of wingbeats against air, bodies soaring and planing again outward and the clump was separating as fast as they came up and birds already gliding downward to cover again but at a greater distance than she'd thought possible. And the young dogs were out and trailing after birds that, from the ten or a dozen Katey guessed she'd seen, it seemed each dog had chosen one and marked, now seeking.

Brian walked back over and said, "I was shooting, I'd walk up after each one. But with dogs this young, I want to see em do something else. Get in the truck."

They drove around the field up to the opposite corner and he stepped out and blew a short single blast on the whistle. Within moments she saw both dogs bounding up through the field, heads swiveling until they saw him. He blew again, two sharp tweets this time and both dogs arrested and again he lifted his arm but this time moved it back and forth and the dogs broke apart and began quartering the field, again crossing over each other's trails as they worked.

He turned to her and said, "That's how it works."

"They're fabulous."

"They're little moneymakers, is what they are." Then he couldn't help himself and smiled at her and said, "Yup. They sure are. It's not as easy as it looks. And there's all kinds of aggravation, all sorts of ways. Why, every now and then, a bit of that aggravation is caused by a dog. But mostly, the dogs is what makes it all worthwhile. Come on, now. Let's ride around a little and show them some more fields and enjoy that. And we can talk. Isn't that what you wanted?"

"Yeah," she said. "I guess so. But these dogs. I've never seen anything like this."

"That's because there isn't anything like this. So, you can ask any questions you want. Me, I'm always happy to talk about the dogs. But, as the feller said, we got some more fish to fry. Isn't that right, Miss Katey?"

She pushed back a strand of wet hair that had come down over her face and said, "Damn, it's hot."

"I'd say it's a warm morning. But nothing like August. Shall we ride?"

Now he drove with a clear sense of purpose, as if her understanding something of the mystery of dogs and birds had enabled him to settle himself within the day. And realizing this, she realized he'd been terribly nervous by the news of her, by her actually showing up. And of who, of what, she was. And she also relaxed, understanding that she had more power within the moment than she'd thought she had. Even as she determined not to abuse that power. She wasn't interested in making anyone miserable, in creating problems. And it came to her that she was problem enough for herself, to try and get her mind around, as it was.

For the next hour he drove from field to field where he let the dogs out. While they were working both stood outside the truck and watched and after he decided the dogs were comfortable with her presence he brought her along as he walked up past the pointing dogs and so she was close for the covey rise. This proximity rocked her, the percussive moment where the day was golden and still, and then ripped open with the burst of birds, and their breaking apart to individuals, open and gliding away. A matter of seconds but she felt it within her as if she was connected to the birds, the dogs, the fields, the sky. Like the jolt of an electric fence—a moment where her brain stopped and then the sweetness of the pain, a sort of clarity of existence, came over her and then was as quickly gone, receding to a memory of what was barely witnessed. And she felt also the quickening within, of wanting it to happen again. As soon as it faded.

Between fields he was loquacious: "Tell the truth, I met Judith in Maine and fell in love, fell hard. At a time when I thought love was done with me. Or maybe even life. But then there she was and life was back and I came down here and I fell in love all over again. I'd be lying if I said it was just the country, the dogs, all of what you're seeing. That was a big part of it of course but behind it all was Judith's grandfather. William Llewellyn Trask. Everyone called him Dutch and I never did know why. The hands called him Mister Dutch. I called him Bill, because that was my way. Still is, I guess. I don't stand much with putting on with things. And he seen that, with me. Those first times out together. Or maybe he just saw I understood the dogs and the years and years behind the dogs, the men, all his family, that made the dogs. But also he saw I understood the land. How all those things rolled up together and made a whole. Bill Trask stood about five feet tall when he was wearing boots and he always wore boots. He favored dungaree jeans and boiled white shirts without a collar but he also wore a out-at-the-elbows tweed jacket and a tipped fedora. He was a clean-shaven man with his white hair combed back and cut short, his face burned year-round by the sun but also the wind and rain. He was a banty rooster and there wasn't a person alive that knew him, didn't fear him. The dogs didn't fear him. There's men will kick or wallop a dog that doesn't work right—that of course is on account of the man. There was even a fellow who peppered his dog with birdshot when she broke point but all that fella got was a gun-shy dog and nobody'd ever hunt with him after that. But Bill's dogs loved him and he loved em right back. They have to know who's in charge. But you get that with patience and being firm. Which is not the same as being harsh. Some men never learn that.

"This family was not poor but they were never rich, either. Before the war, and here you have to understand when people say that, they mean the War Between the States, which is the war that defines everything; all those wars since, those have been just a proving ground for young men or a hole those young men disappeared into. Before the war this farm was only half the size it is now. It was after, that Bill's daddy and then Bill, as he was coming up, started buying up pieces of farmland around and added on, and then again, and again. A part of that is they never, from the get-go, had share-croppers but always tenant farmers—"

"What do you mean? What's the difference?"

"Well, now. It's a delicate thing, you might not understand the difference but I'll try. Most Yankees don't."

"You're a Yankee."

He grinned at her. "No. I'm a Damned Yankee. Some say it one way and some another. And how they inflect that *damn* is how you know if they like you, if they hold you in contempt, or if they flat-out despise you. But you're getting me further afield."

"Go on. They were buying land . . ."

"Yup. And farming it and raising bird dogs and at the same time, raising birds. Or letting birds accumulate with the land. There's ways to farm that can maximize both the birds and the money, but only if you count the birds as a cash crop, too. So hear me now: Like I said, they weren't rich but they were *noticed*. And a good bit of that was the dogs. Anyway, Bill's daddy, he was a William Llewellyn Trask, too, I honestly don't know how far back that name went, if Bill was a Junior or a Third or what, but his daddy was Mister

William and he knew everyone in the state worth knowing, which meant he also knew lots of people in Washington, as well as a good handful of other Yankees that had come south after the war to make money where money could be made. Short of it is, again, because of the dogs, people started to show up wanting to hunt. Of course, neighbors, *friends*, had always hunted with him and always did for free, just like he'd hunt with them. But these other fellows, we call em Sports, they'd come down from D.C. or Richmond or up from Raleigh, with their Purdeys or Holland & Holland double-guns in walnut cases and dress up like Englishmen, well, at least some of em did, and still do, to spend the day out hunting birds. And pay cold hard cash money for it. Old William had a boy would meet em at the train station in Doakes, that's the nearest town with a rail-line, with a wagon and a pair of mules and trot em out here. You might not know it but a team of good mules can make a sprightly trot. These days of course they just drive in. There's a pair of men from Minneapolis, one's a college professor and the other owns not only a couple a tire plants but also a rubber plantation in Honduras, they fly in, in that man's plane. He's got a pilot's license. Those two, well, they own the second week of November. Just them, the whole week. I won't tell you what that costs and they're a bit on the high end but not so alone as you might think. There's a bird colonel from the Pentagon who has every Sunday in January for himself and whoever he brings with him and, missy, there's a blue law in Virginia that says you can't hunt on a Sunday. But they can and they do."

"That doesn't seem right."

"You ask me, a law says a man can't go looking for food on any day of the week isn't right. Most of those sort of laws, they're not aimed at the high and mighty, they're aimed at keeping the poor fellow down. On the straight and narrow. In a church pew of a Sunday morning. You think on that a minute, before you condemn a man who doesn't give a damn and knows he can thumb his nose at it."

"It's still about money, isn't it? And power?"

"Girl, everything of this earth is about money and power. Who has it and who doesn't. Now let me finish this up."

"I'm listening."

"Well," he said and went silent a moment. "I guess that's pretty much it. What we do here is farm on a big scale every crop that works and allows us to raise birds, and through the winter we sell quail hunting to people can afford it. Which is a good number. And the dogs. I run the farm but mostly I raise the dogs and train em and work em in the fields with the Sports. There's a colored man, Robert Jay Haskins, everybody calls him Robert Jay, who helps with the dogs and the hunts also. Robert Jay, he's a rare one—there's not a thing I do that he can't do as well. He's got the touch. And the rare Sport what rears back and insists he's paying for me and not a colored man, I just toe up a little dirt or rub my eyes and glance down and tell em what they're paying for is good dogs and good hunting and a man knows how to put him there and for him, that day, it's Robert Jay. Or he can load up and drive on out of here. That most always works. Hell, missy, there's some that when they call, they request Robert Jay. Been out with him and that's who they want again. I take no offense, you understand?"

"Sounds like you've got no reason to."

They were in the midst of another slash of cut-over land. Along with the brush piles and tangles of vines and canes, they were parked by an old house, a small rough-sided house, a story and a half, the bricks from the end-chimney loosened and fallen away at the chimney's top. The house had never been painted and the glass was out of the windows, the shingled roof was curling and the whole house seemed to list toward them, as if the scant front porch was all that was holding it up. The dogs had worked through the slash and pointed three coveys and come back, both of them with red welts raised on their sides from the cane thorns, heaving from the work.

327

He'd poured them water out of a big tin can from the bed of the truck into a pan set on the ground and now the dogs rested in the box in the bed of the truck. It was, Katey thought, brutally hot.

Coming in to the slash they'd passed along between two large tobacco fields and there had been a cluster of Negroes out by the end of one of the fields, gathered around a very old truck, taking a break, drinking water from a similar tin can in the back of the truck, some few with bottles of soda, passing among them food from grease-stained paper sacks. Not only men but women and children too. They seemed to ignore the truck, even though Brian maintained his slow speed, but Katey, looking back, saw a couple of the smaller figures raise their heads and study them as they passed by. And they, all of them, were oddly dressed.

Now she looked again at the old house. It felt sad and lonely, a house given over to some larger plan, some greater need than for human habitation. And knew there was something in all of his talk, all of this place, something key she was missing.

She said, "Those people we passed just now? That were dressed funny? What's that all about?"

"You mean the hands?"

She looked at him. "I don't know. It was men and women and children. Negroes."

"Yup. Field hands." He nodded as if explaining something obvious.

She didn't smile. "You mean people who work in the fields? But you just call them *hands*. Like, that's what they are to you, each of them? Is a set of hands?"

He kind of reared back from the wheel, turning his upper body to face her. He squinted and said, "I know em all. By name, by family, which is what you were looking at. Three different families. And yes, obviously, they work in the fields."

"Your fields."

He held his squint. "Yes. Well, legally the farm belongs to Judith and me. And her two brothers, Eric and Tyler Trask. Eric's a lawyer in Richmond and Tyler owns the tobacco warehouse and auction barn in South Hill, also a string of movie theaters around southern Virginia and a jukebox and arcade business—we joke that he's in the entertainment business although tell the truth I think he makes more money than the rest of us. He won't admit it, though, likes to say he's just another poor dirt farmer trying to get by."

"What do they do? Those people working in the fields."

"Why, they do whatever needs doing. It changes with the seasons, sometimes with the week. Just now they're suckering tobacco. Which explains why, as you say, they were dressed funny."

"Not to me it doesn't. Explain why they were dressed as they were."

"Suckering tobacco is essential at this stage of the plant's growth. It's removing side stems and some leaves, so you end up with a strong and uniform plant. But doing that, there's what we call tobacco tar that gets all over you. It's funny, you can't really see it, but it's there. A thick heavy juice that flows off the plant, where those stems and leaves are removed. It coats a person head to toe and is the very devil to wash off. Which is why when you do that job you cover up with long pants and long shirts, a hat or a poke-bonnet. Doesn't matter how hot it is, the heat's easier to bear than the tobacco tar. Just a part of the job."

"That you don't do."

"No," he said slowly. "I don't do that work. I do other things."

"So, your, hands, as you call them, they do that work. What else do they do?"

"I already told you—whatever needs to be done. And I see where this is going. So let me tell you. You don't know the first thing about how things work here. I said earlier that we have tenant farmers, not sharecroppers, and never did. A tenant farmer has a house and pays rent on it. And gets a fair wage for the work they do. The old share-cropping, that was a bad deal for the Negroes. Everything belonged to the white man, the farmer, and the sharecropper, he and his family was paid, well, a share of the harvest. But those shares never amounted to what the farmer claimed was owed in rent and seed and feed and whatever other ways the farmer could work it against the Negroes. Most sharecroppers never saw but a nickel or two in their pocket at the end of the year and most lived on what little they could grow around their house and a hog killed in November if they were lucky enough to get a shoat from someone. Our tenants pay rent but get a weekly paycheck and know exactly what's expected of them and also know what to expect in return. It's all of us, working the land, together. And we all do the best we can and all know it. It's a fair deal, is what it is."

She gestured out the window at the fallen-down house. "Who used to live there?"

"Girl, I do not know. That pine plantation was planted a long time before I was even born, I'd guess."

"Was it a tenant farmer's house?"

"Might have been. Most likely."

She said, "That weekly paycheck you talked about. Does everyone get that? How does that work?"

"You've lost me now."

"I mean, does every man and woman and child get their own check? And how do you figure out the value of how the work's divided? Can a child do a man's work in a day? Or a woman? I'm just trying to understand how this works."

He looked at her and said, "I'm telling you, you don't know the first thing about this country or the history or how things work here. It's this Civil Rights business you've been seeing on the television. But these are people, these Negroes, that have been part of this land forever. It's families. *Families*, do you understand? That have been living and working together for hundreds of years. We all, all of us, are working together best we can. It's complicated and not always right but most all of us, white and colored, we're doing the best we can to live well, all of us."

She said, "Did you ever sucker tobacco?"

His right hand came up flat and open and swift and then came down on the dash and he said, "No! I never suckered tobacco! Why would I?"

"Yes," she said. "I guess you wouldn't." Then she said, "So, how's that paycheck thing work? You never did answer that."

"I just did. I told you. It's families. Now, up in Vermont, you know plenty of farm kids that work, year-round. Right? It's not so different. It's helping get done what needs to get done. And, also, just so you know, nothing is keeping those families here—plenty of Negroes have gone north: D.C., Baltimore, Philadelphia, New York. Most have stayed but some also have come back. The tenant houses? We keep em up good and tight—if there's ever a problem, and there's always problems, it gets taken care of. All of em have a piece of land goes with the house. There's garden plots and most all have hog pens and chicken coops, not a few of em also keep a milk cow. There's one fellow, he's a bachelor, he keeps hives of bees. And that honey is his to sell and what's more, he gets paid extra to move his hives around to the places where we need bees to pollinate crops. It's all, and by that I mean all the people, part of one big community. Now, there's parts of that which are mostly white, parts mostly black—the churches are a place to start, but it comes down to what everybody, Negro and White, are comfortable with. For the most part, and most of the time, we all get along. And why wouldn't we? It's a hundred years since that damned war and most folks have figured out what's what. Which is we all need one another, we all work together. How I see it, for the most part it's a good thing."

She sat quiet a moment. She was hot and overwhelmed with the magnitude of the day, with the physical presence of the man across the bench seat of the truck from her, with everything that had brought her here. She wanted to push, to ask about the lunch counters, the March on Washington, about the bombings and the Freedom Riders, about the segregated schools, restaurants, movie theaters, about everything she'd been reading and hearing and watching on the television news the last few years. And remembered then her mother, strident and angry, talking back to LBJ and Cronkite or those larger forces out beyond her reach, her grasp. And this memory sharpened her focus and woke her from the long moment she'd drifted into with him and she realized that, as he'd said, she didn't know the first thing about this place. But she was learning, and learning about him, which was her job here. How he fit into some larger picture, she could ponder later, when this encounter, meeting, whatever it was, concluded.

Then he spoke again, his voice kind and low, words drawn out slow. "Katey Snow," he said. "I can't fix the world and neither can you. It's a good thing to try, though. But you, here." And he stopped then and gazed off out his window at the sun-spattered wave of heat. His voice the same, he said, "What world is it, truly, that you are trying to fix, by coming here?" He then looked back to her.

She blinked and thought a moment and said, "I don't think I'm trying to fix anything. All I knew, starting out, was that I wanted to stand in front of you, I wanted to see you, see what sort of man you were." She paused and he didn't speak and she went on. "And, I guess, I wanted you to know I was in the world. That what you . . . that what you and my mother did was more than just what happened that afternoon." She paused again and took a great silent gulp and said, "That there were consequences."

He nodded and again ran his hand over his face. Then he said, "So much of what makes up a life is consequences. Things that happen as a direct result of actions of a moment, that you don't expect would be what they are." And a deep sudden sadness filled his voice and his face closed a bit, a darkness shrouding him.

She then boldly reached out and touched his forearm, the first time she'd touched him and her finger jumped away and he looked at her as she said, "I heard about that girl. In Maine."

"Oh." As if softly punched. Then he made a crooked grin and said, "Deedee. Yes. Well. Tell the truth, Katey Snow, it was another girl I was thinking of when I said that. A girl in Germany, a young girl who died and that death was a powerful and terrible thing. For your dad and for me, too."

"I don't know what you're talking about."

"Well, I'd guess not. And you won't hear it from me. And if Oliver hasn't told you, that's his business. All I was truly trying to say was, be careful where and how you dig, when you're looking at what you call consequences. Because what you find might not be what you hope or expect or want to find."

She said, "I don't want anything more from you. You don't have to worry about that. Once we're done here, I'll be gone. That's the truth, so help me. I've got no interest in bothering you or making trouble for you. Or your wife and those little girls. Maybe especially those little girls." And she hadn't known she felt this or even knew it before she spoke but once out the words were true to her as writ electric upon her soul.

"Well," he said again. "You sounds as if you're about ready to hightail it out of here."

"Like I said, I don't want to make any trouble for you."

He grinned again and said, "Hell, girl, you already did that. But Judith, she's a good woman, she's going to understand this. Probably already has it worked out in her head. Probably did once she got off the phone from my mother. But you need to hold on a minute: You came and saw me and I did my best to give you some ideas about who I am, like you asked. But you know, I'd like to have a little better sense about you. Don't you think that's fair?"

"I don't know," she said. "Maybe. I guess."

"Yes, it is," he said. "And what's more, just to keep things straight, when you do leave, that doesn't mean I want it to be the end of you. Unless, of course you decide you want it to be. And we can determine that after we talk a bit more."

"All right," she said. "What do you want to know?"

He lifted up out of his seat to pull a watch out of his pocket, the watch attached by a fine-lined chain to a belt loop. He peered at it and pushed it back into his pants and said, "First thing, I got to get these dogs back and out of the heat. Then I thought you and me could go get some lunch. A place I like to eat. Means you don't have to worry about bothering my family and so maybe you can relax a bit. Because, girl? Right now you're screwed tight as a lid on a jam jar and there's just no call for that."

Her mouth was dry and she was so very hot and sweaty and couldn't remember when she had last eaten and then did and that was a thousand years ago and she also realized he was not ready to be done with her. And she bloomed warm and then was oddly cooler and she pushed back those wet strands of hair and said, "It's true. I could do with a bite to eat. If you're sure it's not a problem for you."

He fired up the truck and then took his right hand off the wheel and reached to lightly backhand-swat her knee and said, "It's not a problem, girl. It's a pleasure."

They dropped off the dogs and he spent some time in the kennel, taking care of things there, she guessed, as she waited restless and uncertain in the truck. Then he was back and again grinned at her, and backed the truck around. They went past the house without stopping and the girl Veronica was up on the porch watching them go, scowling after them and she thought He's going to have a time with that one, someday. He was silent and so was she as they drove out along the pond's berm and came to the road where he spun the wheel and went out fast onto the road, traveling away from how she'd come in.

They passed more fields planted with beans and corn and tobacco, more grass pastures with black beef cattle clumped up around the big shade oaks and they also passed what she realized were the tenant houses, mostly weathered clapboard but neat and tight, some with chimneys leaking woodsmoke, garden plots fenced with slab wood, some with a woman working in them. Outbuildings, as he'd said. And flower beds along the porches, the garden fences. One with stones painted white lining the driveway. Another yard had, among the flower beds, a sculpture made of automobile parts, of a man, tall and angular with a stovepipe hat and arms that lifted toward the blank mask of a face, holding a real cornet, face and horn tipped upward toward the sky. This last sent a jolt through her as the image formed within her fast-passing glimpse. And it came to her that these were indeed homes, not an idea, but abodes possessed if not owned by the humans within.

They dropped into a river bottom and came out and to the south of them was a lake, or an inlet of a lake, the water stretching far away. To the north of the road was a scrabble of piney woods, not like the plantations Brian Potter had showed her but wild woods with trees of varying size, laced with vines and some few giant hardwoods.

He pointed out his window and said, "That's Simms Lake. Back in the thirties it wasn't but a wide place in the Simms River and a bunch of low-lying land but they made a dam down in North Carolina and flooded over this land. Some was against it but most have changed their minds. There's a pile of good fishing now and people enjoy the lake all sorts of ways, from waterskiing on a hot summer day to duck hunting in the fall. And pret' much everything else people can get up to on a big expanse of water." And he looked at her. As if she would understand all the nuance in his remark and she guessed she wasn't so far from that understanding. She said, "It's wicked big, what I can see."

"Damn," he said. "I haven't heard somebody call something wicked in years. All right, here we are. It's a boat landing and a bait shop and some other good thing. Which is what we're here for."

He turned into a small jut of land out in the lake. There were trucks with boat trailers parked where the water lapped up shallow and beside that was a modern log cabin that had signs for red worms and minnows and such tacked onto the front and he went on past that to a low cinderblock building with a curl of smoke rising from somewhere behind it and three picnic tables under a tin-roofed canopy off one side of the building. And through the windows of the truck came a dense rich and lovely smell. Atop the building was a giant painted plywood pig wearing a chef's hat and across the belly of the pig were the letters B B Q. The tail of the Q trailed on out into the tail of the pig.

He parked and again grinned at her and said, "He does it right. It's whole-hog, snout to tail, cooked in a pit. Come on, girl, let's put some south in your mouth."

He stepped out of the truck and she did also. The smoke was paling about them and the smell of cooked meat rode the smoke and she followed as he walked to the building and together they went through the door.

A large Negro man stood behind a counter of pitted and scarred wood. He wore a pair of bib-overalls and no shirt, with a red bandanna tied like a pirate over the top of his head. His face and powerfully muscled arms were beaded with sweat. Before him on the counter was a heap of glistening charred meat and in one hand he held up a cleaver, the blade thick as an axe along the top but tapering down to a wafer edge.

He said, "Hey, Mr. Potter. How you this fine morning?"

"I'm good, Clyde. How bout a couple jumbos?"

"You got it. Wrapped in foil?"

"Naw, paper plates is fine. We'll eat at the tables."

"Yes, sir."

He reached to a shelf and from a plastic bag took two of the largest hamburger buns Katey had ever seen, pulled them apart and set them on plates from a stack. Using the cleaver he moved meat from the mound and then chopped the big hunks into a finer mass of pieces, then used the cleaver and a spatula to divide the meat and mounded the two piles neatly atop the buns, moving them around with the tip of the cleaver while leveling the meat into even thick circles. He set down the tools and opened a big plastic tub and used an ice cream scoop to place an equal amount of coleslaw on the meat. Then he put the tops on and gently pressed down. As he was doing this Brian went to an old zinc cooler and lifted up sweating bottles of Coca-Cola and set them on the counter. The whole process was fast and neat and not once during it did Clyde so much as glance at Katey and she realized he was deliberately not seeing Brian Potter in his place with an older teenage girl he'd never seen before. And she wondered if Brian was even aware of this.

"Two dollar and dime each for the Co-Colas, you leave the bottles on the table."

Brian paid and picked up a plate in each hand and said, "Thanks, Clyde. It's the best."

"You right it is."

Brian looked at Katey and said, "Grab the dopes, will ya, girl?" And turned for the door.

There was only one thing he could mean by that and so she lifted the bottles of soda and turned, then stopped and glanced back. The Negro man was looking at her and averted his eyes when she turned. She said, "Thanks."

He took the cleaver and slapped the spare trimmings back onto the heap of meat and glanced at her and said, "You welcome, missy."

She went out and sat across from Brian, to where he'd pushed one of the plates. There in the shade a breeze was coming off the lake and

337

while it was still very hot, the breeze felt good. Brian had carefully lifted the top of his bun and took up a small bottle of thin pale red liquid and dribbled some out onto the coleslaw and then handed it to her.

"Some people like to put it on their meat. It doesn't really matter 'cause it all mixes together once you start eating."

She held the bottle. There was no label on it. She said, "What is it?"

"Sauce for your barbecue. Not the ketchup stuff you might be used to. Made for pig meat cooked over hardwood and eaten with slaw. It's mostly vinegar and red pepper. It packs a punch but you'll see, all three go together real good."

She sprinkled some on top of her slaw as he had, glanced up and he said, "You're bold enough so far. Don't overdo it but take a bit more. You'll like the bit of heat, I promise you."

And she did. They ate and it was all good. Pieces of meat and clumps of slaw fell onto her plate and she saw the same was happening to Brian and he looked at her and scooped it up with his fingers and then pulled paper napkins from the dispenser on the table to clean his fingers and she did the same. The food settled into her stomach and she gained a solidity that had been lacking since the beginning of this day and then both were finished and they sat drinking the cold Cokes.

"That was real good."

"I told you it would be. I haven't lied to you yet and I don't plan to start, just so you know. Now, Katey Snow. I told you I wanted to know more about you and I do but there's a pair of questions I'd like to ask first. Fact is, how you answer will tell me some of you, also. Maybe not a bad place to start."

"Go ahead." The food and the Coke were gaining on her and she felt her face turned into the wind, ready for whatever came next.

"I'd like to ask after your father and your mother. How are they?"

And there it was: He wasn't denying her paternity but clearly identifying who her father was. And she knew he was right about that, in fact, once it was out between them, or at least laid before her, she understood she'd never wavered from that knowledge, even come seeking the man who, one way or another, sired her. She sensed as well that within her answers would lie the key to her future dealings with him. And found a burble of respect for him that she hadn't been sure she'd find, and, finding that, didn't want to lose. And once again was all complicated within. But without confusion. Things were starting to make sense.

She traced a finger along the rough planks of the tabletop, then drank the last swallow of her Coke and looked at him across from her, the man relaxed and solid, deep within himself and she liked him. She said, "They're good."

"I'm glad to hear that. But can you enlarge on that a little bit? It's been many years. You should understand what I mean."

"Well. I said, 'They're good.' But truth is, once I took off to try to find you, I wonder how well they're doing."

"They did not know you were doing this?"

She paused then and considered. Then said, "I didn't announce it. I snuck off in the night. But they had to know what I was up to."

"Why's that? Was it a point of contention between them?"

She remembered the night her father had stood from the table and announced that she might as well have been adopted and left the house, left her mother to explain what he meant by that remark. And what her mother finally told her and how she'd then understood the Christmas cards found years ago. How she'd then blamed her mother.

She turned her eyes steady on Brian Potter and found his steady upon her. She said, "I honestly don't know. My mother and I, we don't see eye to eye on much. She's prickly with me and unreasonable with her expectations of me. But that's a recent thing. As a child all I recall of her was kindness—well, that's not true. She always had expectations of me but they were ones I was happy to strive to reach. And Dad—Oliver—he wasn't ever anything but kind and loving with me. You have to understand, he's a man different from other men. Most deeply silent and withdrawn into himself, keeping best he could away from other people. Except for fiddle players. He repairs fiddles and is known for the work he does. But that work, that allows him to mostly be alone. I guess maybe the music, the instruments that make the music, the men who understand how that all works, I guess those are the men he understands best. I spent most of my childhood with him and meeting those few men and watching him at his work. So I'm guessing I'm pretty much right about him. And this, also: He was not only tender and gentle and loving with me, but with my mother, also. Does that answer your question?"

Brian turned and looked out upon the water spread with the sun as a sheet of golden light stretching far away. He tapped out a smoke and struck fire and turned back to her then and said, "Not really. But you wouldn't know. By the time you were old enough, whatever she told him, how he reacted, those moments were long ago. And pret' damn clear, he took you on as his own, even as he also knew the truth otherwise. That says much. About both of them. Tell me. You don't have any brothers or sisters?"

She said, "No." Then she said, "No. I'm it. I do recall in a vague way as a young child there was a time, maybe two, when I thought I was getting a baby brother or sister and then that talk stopped. I was too young to wonder much, or ask questions. So I don't know. I do know, because it's a grand famous family story that I was born in a blizzard and there were problems with all of it. So. Maybe I'm alone because of that storm. Or maybe other reasons. Does it matter?"

"Well, it could. But probably not. Recall what I said about consequences and how we never know truly how they play out? I think this is one of those things. Although I have to say I'm sorry you don't have siblings. For you, for your folks."

Then he fell silent and she knew he was thinking about his other daughters. And oddly felt a stab to her gut, her heart. For him, for her mother and father, for the scowling girl on the porch an hour ago, for Judith, for all the people in the world wrapped up in their own miseries and vales of sadness and regret. At the same time knowing she'd just learned something, a wider net suddenly cast out into the dark.

After a long silence she looked at him and again said, "Did I answer your question?"

He lifted his dropped head and said, "Maybe. Maybe close as it gets." Then he said, "No. Not all of them."

"All right," she said. "What are they?"

"What about you? What are your plans for this life, Katey Snow?"

A flutter of panic. Once she'd set herself on this course of discovery she'd also slammed shut those doors of coming-future. And now all she could think was What would he want to hear? And with that she realized she wanted to please him, wanted, at the least, to have him continue what he'd hinted at the possibility of in some undefined way, their remaining in touch. And with that a bit of surge—he knew nothing really about her and it wasn't her job to make him want to keep in touch. Not even sure he'd meant what he said.

She said, "I'm enrolled at UVM for the fall."

"Good for you."

With great nonchalance she said, "I was an honor student straight through high school. And valedictorian, as well. In Vermont that's a full ride to UVM."

He nodded and said, "Very good. You have a major?"

She paused and took a breath and said, "I'll figure that out if I go."

He lifted his chin a hitch and said, "If?"

"When I set out looking for you, I didn't have any idea what I'd find. If anything. But also, all through high school I waitressed weekends and summers and saved my money. So I brought some along with me. Because I thought, maybe I'd drift about some this summer and see what's out here." She raised an arm and swept it toward a vague horizon, one that had nothing to do with where she was. He was looking at her, his eyes quizzed to almost a squint. She went on. "Frankly, I already have seen a lot, some interesting and some not so much but I'm curious. There's plenty of interesting stuff happening and I'd like to explore it some more. Maybe, once I do get to college, I can learn even more. But for the summer, I was thinking, just go looking, see what comes."

He'd sat up straight and was level and hard-eyed upon her. "You're not talking about the hippies and their drugs, are you?"

"Oh, no," she lied. "I'm more interested in the Civil Rights stuff, also the people against the war. Mostly the political parts." Smoothly she thought, she said, "Strikes me, when I get to college there's going to be a lot of talk about that and I was thinking if I saw some of it up close, I'd be a little ahead of the game. At least at UVM. That's still, you know? Vermont?"

"Don't do it," he said. "Go home. Go back to your job and go off to college in the fall."

"I could do that. But I was thinking, why not drive around and meet some people and see what's happening? I think the world is changing, maybe in big ways and I think maybe that's a good idea. But how can I know if I don't see some of it? I mean why in the world are we in Vietnam? I know people, young men not so much older than me, who are about to be drafted, or might be drafted, to go fight a war that they all know we don't have any business in. Right?"

He stood then and walked off from the table, out past the canopy onto the grass and stood looking out on the lake. Then, swiftly he turned and came back and stood over her and said, "Communism. That's what we're fighting. You think we shouldn't, you go back and read some more history. The Chinese, the Soviets, those are not

342

good people. Maybe once upon a time there was an idea that as an idea, wasn't such a bad thing. But in both those places that idea got all turned around and became a truly terrible thing. I'm talking about how it ended up in life. A few truly terrible people have total control over a great huge number of people. I was there; I saw it. In Germany, to start with. But also, at the end of the war? You know what I heard the most from the Germans? How glad they were that it was us and not the Russians that liberated their town. You know why? Because at the same time we were coming over the Rhine, the Russians were coming in from the east and we heard the same stories the Germans did about those Russians. Khrushchev finally told the truth about Stalin. Millions of people, millions of Russian people died. Because of the terrible power that man held. And how the people around him feared him and so aided and abetted him. Because, they, each and every one of them, knew they could be next. Mao and his bunch, they're no better, it seems. Maybe even worse. And it's that sort of business that your dad and me and so many others went off to fight against, the Japs and the Nazis. Vietnam? You know how I see it? It's like Poland in '39. One little country that the Germans had some claim to. Or so it was said. But then came France. And the Maginot Line crumpled like," he paused and took a paper napkin and closed his fist around it and dropped the balled paper to the breeze off the lake where it then tumbled across the grass and he finished, "it crumbled like that. The Japs bombing Pearl Harbor. Is how those things start. This time, I think, we're getting in there before it goes too far. Because, girl, once the red Chinese get Vietnam, why would they stop there? You want World War Three? With the Soviets having the Bomb?"

She'd heard versions of this before. She feared the atomic possibility, of all life being wiped out. She knew of a couple of summer houses whose owners had paid to have elaborate bomb shelters built and, if those people from New York or Boston, if they felt such fear,

how could she discount it? She also remembered a day the year before when she'd been in her dad's workshop one afternoon after school and Barry Sadler's "Ballad of the Green Berets" came on the radio and Oliver had stopped work, stood from his bench and walked to switch the radio off. Then he'd looked at her and said, "Whatever it is, it's not something to make a sentimental song out of."

To this other father she said, "Of course not. It's just, everything seems so complicated now."

To her surprise he sank back down but this time on the bench beside her and he nodded and paused and then said, "It does feel that way, some days." Then after a bit he said, "I was your age, I didn't have the chance to question anything. We knew what had to be done and we did it. And I still don't doubt the rightness of what we did. But there was a cost, no doubt."

She looked at him and was silent and reached again, for only the second time, but this time let her hand rest on top of his. He nodded and said, "Yes. Oliver. And me, too. Deedee. All of that. Many others, too. I've seen those damaged men, still do. So I understand how a young person could have their questions. Perhaps that's not such a bad thing. To question, I mean. It doesn't change that you still have to do what's demanded of you. But to know enough to think it through, first."

And he looked away. Her hand still atop of his.

After a moment he lifted his other hand and wiped at his face that she couldn't see and she knew it was a tear he was pushing away. Still not looking at her he said, "I heard there was some of those hippies. Up in Vermont."

She'd heard the same, some sort of commune in the southern part of the state, around Putney or Chester, maybe somewhere else. And she felt as if together, the two of them had just walked through some heaving territory and were close to some altogether new territory. And Vermont still felt too close, not only to home but also to what had happened to her in New Hampshire. So she said, "You know what?"

"What's that?"

"Until I got to Maine? I never saw the ocean before. I went to Pemaquid Point and it was amazing and wicked scary at the same time."

He turned back and said, "Yup. Maine's a rocky cold coast." And took his hand away.

She said, "Last night? I stayed in a little motel in South Hill? And there was a brochure from North Carolina, the Outer Banks? Might've just been the pictures but that looked like a coast I'd like to see. Closer to what I had in mind."

"The beach. What we call it here. Because it's not a coast like Maine but beaches. It's all a beautiful place."

"I'm thinking to visit it. Before I do anything else."

He nodded. Then he said, "Do you understand?"

She was quiet a moment and said, "Yes. He's the best father I could ever ask for."

"And your mother?"

"I haven't settled that yet. But I know I've got some thinking to do."

He nodded. Then he said, "Yup. We all do. You know, it never really stops, needing to think about things. I'm glad you're in this world, to use your words, Katey Snow. And I'd be delighted if you chose to keep in touch with me. It's not for me to set limits—it's for you to decide what's best, all the way around. But what I think, just now, is you should go and see a beach."

Again she was struck, knowing this was done. For the time being at least. She tangled her legs trying to quickly rise from the bench of the picnic table and then he was up also, his hand on her upper arm, steadying her and she slowed her flounder. So they came up together, finally, and he took her hand and they walked down to the water lapping among the stones and the oozing red dirt of the shore and stood side by side, gazing out upon the flat expanse of water.

After a long moment she said, "You've been kind."

He let go of her hand and said, "It pleases me you think so. I'm not so certain, myself. We do the best we can, mostly."

"Isn't that a grand thing?"

"It's the best we can," he said again.

Her gut twisted as she understood that he knew nothing more of how to live than she did, that perhaps no one did, ever, those ones honest with themselves. She turned then and quickly kissed him on the cheek and said, "You take care of yourself. And take care of those girls, they need you in all kinds of ways they don't know yet. And thank you, thank you for not running from me. You could've so easy. And your wife, too. But you did not. Now, I'm going to go. It's time. Any more of this would ruin it, isn't that right? And thanks for giving me my dad back, even though he never went away. And finally, finally, I'm off to see a beach. Because that's what I need. To walk at those edges of the world. Where the water meets the land and maybe does so in a different way than I ever saw before. Maybe a way I need to see. Okay?"

He smiled at her then, as if presented with a pure delight. Then he said, "Well, we need to get you back to your truck, don't we? Before you say all your goodbyes and thank-yous."

She felt herself warm with blush. "I'd forgotten about that."

He said, "You're going to be driving around looking at beaches and sunsets and all of that, you don't want to be forgetting your truck." As he spoke he'd stepped off toward his own truck and she followed. As she got in and pulled her door closed she said, "I was never absentminded."

"I didn't think so."

They rode in silence some time but it was an easy silence, as if a space both knew from their own natures and inhabited now by

346

shares. After a time he said, "You don't want to go due east. You want to get a little farther south and then head for Morehead City, Beaufort, that area. You'd like it there. And the beaches are easy to get to, not like far on the Outer Banks. You got a North Carolina map yet?"

"I figure I can pick one up when I stop for gas."

"Dig around in the glove box. There's one there you can have."

She did and found it and unfolded it onto her lap and found where he was speaking of.

He drummed his fingers on the wheel and kept his eyes squinted before him as if he was thinking something over and then finally he glanced at her and said, "I was you I'd run down to Durham, then head east. Come to think of it, Durham, Chapel Hill, those towns might be a good place to stop over, also. Young people. There's Duke University in Durham, UNC in Chapel Hill."

She looked at him but he was driving, not looking at her. Cautious with his message. She folded the map back up and said, "Thanks."

Then, after a bit more driving, he said, "That beagle you were telling me about?"

"Tinker. I miss him terribly."

"Of course you do. But don't be getting yourself a dog now. Wait until you're done with college, settled some place where you know you'll be for a while. You'll know it when the time's right. Otherwise, it's not fair to the dog."

"That's what my . . . that's what my dad said after Tinker died. Said to recall I needed to commit for ten, fifteen years to the happiness of the dog, seeing what the dog was prepared to give to me."

Brian nodded and said, "In a nutshell." Then after a pause he said, "Those English pointers? Now, they *like* to hunt birds, it's bred right into em. But they don't *have* to. Long as they get plenty of exercise and have a good loving home, that's what they really need. And smart? They most nearly train themselves, just by looking at what

347

their person expects of em. They do, they figure things out. A person could look a long ways and not find a better dog."

"Is that so," she said.

He shot a glance at her. "What I'm saying. The time comes you feel you're ready for a dog in your life, and if one of em would be of interest to you, you talk to me. We'd look em over close and get you just the right one. If you wanted."

They then turned and went over the pond's berm and the house and her truck came into view. She turned and said, "I couldn't imagine a finer thing. And it gives me something to look forward to. Thank you."

He nodded and said, "I believe it would be a good match."

She drove back to South Hill and the land rolled along almost familiar and she felt within it, as if someway her blood knew the land, as if she'd been here before—more than just the morning's drive out. She felt light and full of purpose and tilted up toward whatever lay in front of her. And what was just behind her. Once in town she circled around, was confused for a few minutes and then found the motor court where she'd spent the night. She parked midway down the lot and walked up to the office and let herself in. It was midafternoon and no one in sight. Beside the door was a cheap metal rack attached to the wall and from it she plucked a brochure, indeed noticed the afternoon before. Without disturbing a soul she went back to the truck and studied the brochure and it was as promised—the Outer Banks and other beaches of North Carolina. It was a grand moment and also caused her to reflect on what else in life was glimpsed and almost forgotten from the corner of an eye. She put the brochure up under the visor and looked again at the map. The map he'd given her. Now she saw it. Those beaches were a drive, but she could be in Durham by late afternoon. And she smiled even as a ripple ran her spine—how the two of them had come so close to argument and stepped away, how he'd given her more information than she knew she was getting at the moment. It had been a good day. It had been a better and different day than any she'd imagined.

She pulled out of the motel parking lot and drove down toward the highways that would take her to North Carolina, to Durham. Then she had to pee and looked at the dashboard and decided to gas up, maybe get a candy bar and a Coke—what had he said? A Co-Cola, a dope, to get her through the afternoon. She stopped at an Esso station where a banner alerted her to put a tiger in her tank and she filled the truck and bought the drink and a Snickers, used the bathroom, and then was back out and rolling along. She had the radio loud and was pounding the beat on the wheel when it came to her. She slowed and turned into the Piggly-Wiggly and circled the lot and came out and reversed direction, back to the gas station. Once there, she sat a moment, looking at the glass and metal booth in front of the station. It was time to call home. She got down out of the truck and walked across, pulled open the folding doors and snapped them shut. It really didn't matter who answered. It was suddenly and deeply hot in the phone booth. She lifted the phone and cradled it between her ear and shoulder. She took a breath, happy to talk to either one of them. She dug a dime from her pocket and dropped it in the slot and dialed 0 for an operator and held the dial down a long moment before pulling her finger out and letting go. She knew she wanted to talk to her mother. There was a whir, then a dial tone. Then an operator came on the line and said, "Help you?"

She heard the dime chink down into the coin-return slot and said, "Yes, thank you. I need to make a collect call."

Ten

Ruth

SHE'D HEARD HER leave. The furtive steps down the hall and stairs, the soft slap of the screen door. The bedroom windows were open to the June night and there then came a pause and she thought perhaps the girl was reconsidering; then heard the truck door open and moments later the rolling tires' quiet grind against the gravel drive. She rose from her bed and went to stand at the window and watched as the truck rolled silent down the hill and came into sharper view under the first streetlight as Katey popped the clutch and the engine fired and the taillights made small red beacons in the dark, receding. The lemon wash of headlights. At the bottom of the hill the truck turned left, northward and then shortly was lost from sight.

Ruth went back to the bed and sat on the edge for long moments, hearing the slow certain tick of the bedside clock's second hand, and then knew she'd sleep no more this night. After a time she rose and slipped into her light summer robe and also went down the hall in the dark. She passed the guest bedroom where, since the night in March when he'd stood at dinner and split their world open, Oliver had been sleeping. He hadn't truly moved there, his clothes were still

350

in the drawers and closets of their bedroom. She hadn't asked why he'd made this move and he'd offered no reason; neither of them wished to speak of it. Neither of them trusted themselves or, as likely, the other, to not make the matter worse. Ruth held no blame for what he'd done. This was not the same as wishing he'd not done it but she understood, whatever his reasons, the blame always had and always would remain with her. She'd done her best not to repair the damage which she knew was impossible, but to mitigate it within her abilities, as she finally explained herself to Katey. She did so as honestly and thoroughly as she knew possible, with one result being that Katey never asked what had prompted the revelation from Oliver. Which, at the time at least, seemed a great blessing.

In the kitchen she plugged in the percolator by the light from the stove back, then realized she wanted tea and so filled the kettle and turned on the stove burner. She set out a cup and saucer, the teapot, and filled a metal strainer with loose leaves from the tin and waited. Like her mother, she did not use teabags. As her mother had, she ordered tea in bulk from an importer in Boston—the same importer, the same tea. A delicious dark and smoky tea called Hu-Kwa, a blend the company solely imported. It was the tea Ruth had first drank as a child, the tea Jo had made every afternoon of her life, fall, winter and spring. Hot summer afternoons she favored iced coffee, a drink Ruth had never taken to. The small differences between a mother and daughter. Jo took her tea at quarter past three; for Ruth, weekdays, it was forty-five minutes later and poured from a thermos at her desk at school, as she corrected papers or worked on study plans. Jo always had a saucer with a pair of cookies upon it with her tea, taken fireside in the library. She favored butter cookies, or those with a lace of molasses, a single half-pecan pressed into the middle. Ruth only ate with her tea when she was with her mother and then it was the same cookies. At Christmas time there would be a single dense slice of fruitcake for each of them. How it was, how it had been.

351

Katey had learned from both of them. Ruth filled the teapot and turned off the burner. She guessed that someday, perhaps, Katey would find her own way of having tea. It was a small thing but at the moment Ruth understood this was also continuation, how things moved down and along. Guessing that at the moment if the girl should prospect such a thing, she'd see her grandmother's afternoon ritual as being superior, the one to be aimed for. Ruth wondered if it was possible the girl might build a life where afternoon tea could be taken at such leisure, then wondered if that would even be a good thing for her. She put the cup and teapot on a tray and carried them into the parlor and turned on a light behind her chair. She poured out a cup and sat down with it, the saucer balanced in both open palms as an offering. The air was cool enough so slender vapor rose from the hot tea and flooded her nostrils. She had no idea what small rituals would become part of Katey's life, of how that life would accommodate rituals, beyond knowing that it would. As all lives do.

She settled the saucer on the reading table beside her chair and lifted the cup and brushed her lips against the hot thin porcelain of the cup and made a small sip from the surface of the tea. It was hot and dense and filled her mouth with morning life as she sat in the otherwise dark and empty house and waited for the early summer dawn.

Katey had the old packet of Christmas cards. Ruth had no idea how many years ago she'd discovered them but guessed it was likely a long time, that the child had prowled through the house more times than once, trying to learn herself as she tried to learn the secrets of her parents. She, herself, had done much the same as a girl up on West Hill, old photo albums holding the mysteries of those two much older and grown distant sisters, women with children as old as Ruth, the one cousin only months younger, but there then in the dusky maroon leather bindings, the black paper sleeves, the old almost brown-and-white photographs snapped into place of improbably young girls within settings at once familiar and strange, on laps also both familiar and strange. How young her father had been! How young they'd all been. And those found fragments of a vanished life had always left Ruth a bit lonesome, a little cast down, as she held the clear sense she'd missed something. The child unable to see what had also been gained. And now, drinking her tea, her own child off out into the world with a packet of cards saved for no good reason, cards that Ruth also knew she couldn't guess the value Katey placed upon them. Only hoping that value wasn't a brittle thing soon to pall to shards and dust in Katey's hands. She drank her tea and knew she had no idea what to hope for.

She smiled, once. Because Ruth had never worn that pair of heels had Katey not thought or known her mother would detect the smears of fingertips along the dust of the box, the slightly canted lid, at the back of her closet? And guessed also Katey had thought she was taking great care, great stealth in her thirsty theft. Ruth's smile was there and then gone and left a small ache in her jaw. Her breast.

There came the first pipe of birdsong, tentative as if the robin did not yet trust the day. Soon there came another robin. Then vireos, wrens. English sparrows. An ovenbird. Redwings from their nests in the apple trees. Ruth reached and snapped off the light and the windows showed a pearly oyster-shell light. Not dawn yet but nearly so. She sat silent and still and within moments the birds were in full call-and-response outside, no longer a solitary warble and return but a curtain of sound. The eastern windows showed a film of rose light through the morning fog risen off the river. She stood and went through the lightening house, silently back upstairs to the bedroom and dressed in old dungarees and a blouse, then went down to the kitchen. She fried bacon and set the strips on old newspaper to drain. Sliced bread and left the slices in the toaster and then set out his coffee cup and a jar of new tart rhubarb preserve next to the butter where he couldn't miss it.

In the ell she stepped into her boots and took up a basket and placed a trowel and old bread knife in the basket and went out into the yard, not looking at the empty driveway. She went around to the north side of the house where a dense row of hostas grew close to the foundation. She knelt and began to dig them up and separate them with the knife, making many out of few. She planned to plant the new-made clusters along the shady side of his workshop and the garage also. Some few under the spread canopy of ancient apple trees that cast a heavy shade. It was a job long overdue.

She was still there when he came out some good time later. She heard him coming and didn't cease her work. Bent down and digging, now new holes along the side of the shed. She waited and finally he said, "Where's the truck?"

She sat back on her heels but held her tools, twisted about and looked up past him and said, "She's gone." Then turned back to her work.

There was a silence behind her and she knew he'd have to speak again. It was the way of him. She waited.

"Gone where?"

She kept on working. This morning, at least, she would not look at him. Finally, as she felt within her his tension, his rising uncertainty and fear and recrimination, all those things and even more that she couldn't name, and just before she was sure he'd speak again she paused her hands at her work and leaned back and looked at him and said, "Gone where she felt she had to go. Is my guess."

They remained looking at the other, in silence. She saw the wince over his face and he raised his hand and rubbed his eyes, as if to clear his vision. She saw he was about to speak and she turned back to her work. After precious few moments he walked away, back into the house. She was still planting when he again exited the house and went past her to the rear entrance of his shop. She wasn't interested in talking with him just now. She was trying to determine

354

her daughter's mind, trying to determine her own failures with that girl.

All those years ago when she made clear it was best he go, Brian was no doubt grateful to drive off with his own guilt and self-loathing as his accompaniment, or, perhaps simple relief to be gone and knowing he'd never return there, and she'd finally sat alone in the house. Her husband still sleeping or passed out, some deep almost primal withdrawal from the world she now understood he inhabited. She bathed and then dressed simply and sat at the table and made her resolve to tell Oliver, best she could, what she'd learned and what had occurred between herself and Brian Potter. But Oliver remained in bed until late in the afternoon when he called for her in a voice of lurching distress and she raced up the stairs to find him in the bathroom with a pool of rank vomit one side of the toilet. She cleaned him up and helped him back to bed. Where he passed through the night. She'd remained downstairs and fixed a grilled cheese sandwich and then made herself a gin and tonic. And then as dusk came on she poured another and turned on the Philco and listened to a litany of sad songs while she drank. She slept on the couch and in the morning made coffee and carried it up to Oliver, yet again steeled for the truth. She had to urge him awake and he sat up in bed, clammy with rank sweat, his skin the color of an old candle dug from a drawer. He vomited the coffee and then begged her to drive downtown and bring him a vanilla milkshake. Which she did and he sipped that down and slept again and woke and asked for another. And only after that was consumed did his apologies begin. And she realized she could not tell him. This silence was not for herself, not for safety or hidden indiscretion but only because his own despair of himself was too great to burden further. And so, the third afternoon on, as finally she was poaching eggs and making dry toast did she realize she held a secret she would always be bound to. A silence that was the necessary kindness called for, for both of them. Much as he'd kept his secrets of damage from her, she owed him to hold her own damage close and silent. And it was only then that she understood how much greater such burdens can be, how the worm turns and chews from within, denied the light of confession. An ugliness of self, sliced into a permanent chamber of the heart. At the time, she felt this was also gaining maturity. Of the two of them, side by side with their secrets, their strangeness, both close and forever distant. Of this then, she thought, is the true business, burdens, joys, of love. They went along, both with their own secrets.

She missed her period. She tried to count back but the last weeks had been of such befuddlement and distress, and her own fear surged over her to the point where she couldn't make sense of time. She waited and felt sick and convinced herself this was only anxious response to those events. Until it didn't come again. She'd had enough sense to place a small dash with a red pen on the calendar and for days before and some few after, she studied that date with growing dread and also a growing certainty.

Finally she went to see her mother.

Who said, "You have to tell him."

"What if he leaves me?"

Jo thought a moment and then said, "When I first realized I was pregnant with you, I was horrified. At my age! I thought. How would I ever manage? Then, of course, when you were born I wondered How did I ever doubt? You'll see. Things are never how we expect, babies perhaps most of all."

"You didn't answer my question."

"I don't need to. But, one piece of advice?"

"Yes?"

"Wait another month. First trimesters can be very tricky. Whatever he says, if you lost the baby, neither of you would ever be the same. I know of so many women who've miscarried in those first months."

A pause and then Ruth said, "You?"

Jo rose. She said, "Go home and wait. I'd say August would be about right. We're not talking about me, are we?"

She studied him carefully during that next six weeks. And nothing she saw allowed her to discern how he might respond. He went about his days much as always. Although she did reflect, once his terrible hangover had passed, once he'd slept through much of the week and then regained himself, he'd studied her a few times in a way that felt new, but he'd never questioned her in any sort of detail about Brian, about what had been reported or explained to her. It was as if he didn't want to know. It was very much as if Brian Potter had never been there at all. And as the weeks passed with her growing certainty and imagining of what she'd tell him, she understood that however she divulged her news, she must do so in a way free of the details of the stories Brian had told her. It would be up to Oliver to ask, or not. So she had to draw upon the essence of that very long day and still remain true to Oliver's privacy. She wondered if he would understand that of her. And she had terrible visions of his flaring righteous anger and her failing then, and rising and spilling the details of all she knew that he'd kept from her and the absolute rupture between them this would bring, beyond any hope of repair. And daily she knew she was pregnant and the baby would stick and felt aimed like a missile toward some uncertain day in August. She lay sweating at night, locked herself in the bathroom to cry during the days. Burned food. She was not herself and knew she was not and during all of this Oliver seemed to float through his days much as he always had. But she couldn't even be sure of that. Perhaps he was watching her the same way she was watching him. Her mind was a terrible twisting wheel of broken spokes and over-greased gears. And on top of all of this she was pregnant and lacking all joy in that wondrous fact, except in those rare calm moments alone when she'd rest her clasped hands over her belly where she felt the slightest of swellings and spoke her mind, not words but her mind to the child within her and promised every kind and good thing she could promise. And stood, strengthened, and walked a little way back fully into the day.

It happened by accident. She'd planned to tell him Sunday, the twenty-first, after breakfast. She planned to make waffles, which he liked, and sausage and fried eggs. A good breakfast but not elaborate or special, except that it was a Sunday. Which she thought would allow them as much time as was needed. And had resolved to tell him whatever he might ask—she owed him that, even if it meant opening subjects, issues, that he'd obviously chosen to keep from her. But she would also be strong and make clear her position, her solidity within herself, regardless of his response.

What happened was at supper Friday night, beans and franks, applesauce and sweet corn, sliced tomatoes, an ordinary meal for the season, he'd mentioned that on Sunday there was an auction in Cornish New Hampshire and possibly some tools he'd like and would she care to come and she sat across the table from him and took a breath and drank from her glass of water and then said, "Oliver? I'm pregnant. And the baby is from when Brian Potter was here back in the spring. I'm not proud of it at all and I'll answer any questions you have. But however you feel, I'm going to have this baby. So, whenever we get done talking about all the things you might want to talk about, the question you have to answer is Are we going to have it together or am I going to have it alone." And held her level gaze upon him as she also began to cry. And watched as he rocked back and forth in his seat and then after a very long silence he stood and left the house. A few minutes later she heard him drive off.

She'd never known where he'd gone, those two days. That evening she'd cleaned the house top to bottom and went to a sleepless bed after midnight, then crashed to wakefulness with the sun well up. She was making furious and unbelieving and frightened plans for her life as a single mother throughout the day. Still, midmorning Saturday she drove down to the village and passed by his parents' house and then slowly all about the village but could not spy his truck. Finally she went into Snow's Mercantile and bought a case of canning jars that she needed and, since it was a Saturday had the chance to chat with her mother-in-law who was the same as ever. Or hiding her son from the harlot wife. Anything and everything was possible. She went back to the house and gathered bushels of tomatoes from the garden and made a cauldron of sauce and canned that and then thought of going to talk to her mother but would not do that yet—the step seemed final and premature at once. She slept that night but not well and was up early Sunday, with coffee, a single poached egg on toast, the yolk-rimmed plate still before her when she heard the truck and he walked back in and looked at her and said, "It's our baby. Do you understand? That's how it has to be."

Now the girl she'd fought for was gone. And she knew it was her fault. When, days after his unexpected outburst, days after she told Katey what truth she could allow herself, she'd finally had the moment to ask Oliver why he'd said what he said. And he'd looked upon her with a weary set to his face as if long awaiting this question. His eyes skittered away from her quickly, then back again. "I don't know, Ruth. Honestly, I don't. It was just . . . I'm sorry. I love you both so much. I do."

She noted he didn't ask her forgiveness, didn't ask how Katey was. He knew how Katey was. The girl ratcheted up high, going through her days, studying at night, cordial but cool to her mother, tender and kind to Oliver as ever. Bending to offer her cheek for a good-night kiss from him. Their morning banter as Ruth was rushing out the door to be at school the half an hour before Katey needed to be there. Almost as if everything was the same, as if nothing had changed. And, to her shame now, she'd wanted to believe it, almost had been able to believe what he'd said.

Because in that moment, in the immediate moment, she'd been struck with why he'd revealed this news. Meant to shock of course and shock it was. But not for Katey. For her. She'd spent several days quietly taking stock of herself. And what she realized was that the adolescent girl had tired of Ruth's constant battles, of the daily, weekly insufferable prodding over expected chores and over school-work and all of the ways that Ruth was trying to help press her daughter into assuming responsibilities around the house, as well as her academic achievement, all the while as Katey was excelling at school and also dismissive of the need to make her bed each morning, to do her own laundry, to pick up and hang towels wet from the shower. To turn down her record player as she studied in her room. And Ruth had realized she'd been frightened by the news that was flowing into the house of this new generation, of the rebellion and rejection that was everywhere it seemed, in a way she didn't understand or comprehend and this pushed her even more and her daughter had, at some point over the last year but well before Oliver dropped his own bombshell, come to see her mother as the embodiment of all that was good reason to rebel against, to refute, to refuse. And carried that knowledge within herself daily, a knowing placed in silent stockade against those things she found most unreasonable that issued from her mother. As if her mother was living proof of all Katey was hearing and, most importantly, feeling, all that resonated within her.

To what point, truly, Ruth's relentless hectoring? Katey was an excellent student and always had been. In short months she'd be vale-dictorian of her class. Though sworn to secrecy until it was announced during Commencement, she already knew she had the Green & Gold full scholarship to the University of Vermont. And, within all of this, doubtless, was the girl's knowledge that her time here, in this house, was shrinking very fast. And then she would be gone, out into the world. Out into her world.

And Ruth realized that Katey, once she'd learned the truth of her parentage, had turned a different eye altogether upon her mother. That—and Ruth had poured herself a stiff gin and tonic with this understanding—Katey was aloof and pleasant and distant because she had come to pity her mother. Not to dislike her, or spit bitter against the unfairness of Ruth's demands upon her. But to pity. She'd come to see Ruth as a woman who had settled. Who had not made the life for herself that she wished and all the noise she heard from her mother was less about what her mother hoped and expected for Katey, but was a blind and unreflected purge of anger over her own life, the failures of her own dreams and ambitions. Whatever, Ruth conjured the girl thinking, those might once have been.

Fire to smoke to ashes.

Endings and beginnings are often intertwined, which is not something a girl of fourteen might understand but a woman almost forty certainly does. For the survivors, death is less an absence than an unraveling.

Jo Hale pulled a coat on over her heavy flannel nightgown one February morning and still in her fleece-lined slippers walked out to get the morning paper. The weather had warmed the previous afternoon and there'd been sleet in the night before the sky cleared and the mercury fell almost to zero by dawn leaving a glaze of ice cracked like an old mirror over the flagstone walk. Jo went down and was not found until some hours later when the rural-delivery mailman's truck paused beside her box, seeing what he'd first thought was an old blanket humped halfway to the house. At the hospital in Hanover it was learned she'd broken a hip, had a fracture of her pelvis and bruise on the back of her head which indicated a probable concussion. When admitted she had a temperature of almost 104, pneumonia from the exposure, and it was a full day before she regained consciousness. Ruth had been with her throughout that first long night, sitting bedside holding her mother's hand, a hand grown slight and waxy, fingers of knobbed arthritic bones under skin spotted brown and bright red. A pale yellow light was thrown through the tipped-open door, the intravenous bag held by a ceiling hook, the tube wending down to where the needle was buried in her mother's arm. Earlier the doctor had told all of them that the morning would be a new day and they should hold hope—that Jo was strong and otherwise in good health. Ruth had sent Oliver and Katey home for the night, wanting to be alone with her mother. Who had not yet once stirred and Ruth somehow doubted she would. In the pale light she studied her mother reared high on hard pillows, the bed cranked up to ease her breathing, to help allow the drip into her arm, and she had never seen her mother this way. The folds under her chin sagged tired, her hair was loose and wispy on the pillow. Her chest rattled as she slowly drew in and then slowly released each breath. And Ruth sat and held her mother's hand and leaned forward from the hard plastic chair and rested her head against her mother's hand and for some long moments closed her eyes. A nurse woke her when she came in to check the IV bag.

In the morning Jo was awake and lucid. Oliver and Katey had returned barely after sunrise and they were all together in the room when the doctor returned to check Jo over. Somehow during the night the drip needle had been removed from Jo's arm, which was the arm she raised to pause the doctor before she sent her family from the room. "Go have breakfast," she told them. "While I talk with this young man, here." Her voice dry, shredded, as if so many corn husks lodged deep within her throat.

The family huddled in silence in a small waiting room. Katey sat apart, tissues balled in her fist, rubbing her eyes. An older man appeared, in soft gray flannels and a tab collar, white hair cut neatly short, the ruddy just-shaved face of health and righteousness and introduced himself as the chaplain on call and asked if he might assist them. Both Ruth and Katey looked at him and then both away and Oliver spoke softly and thanked the man for his concern but No, they were fine. Then again, they were alone in the room.

The doctor returned and announced that Jo was again sleeping, which was the best possible thing for her just now. She'd suffered a series of great shocks to her system and they must be patient. He spoke in terms of a long haul to regain her full health and suggested it might be best if all of them carried on with their day, that Jo needed rest and was under the best of care. When Katey stood and announced she'd not leave her grandmother, the doctor, a young man who carried his fatigue handsomely upon his face, allowed his eyes to settle on Ruth and she saw his message was a partial one, that perhaps he wanted some help to discern all her mother had said.

She'd stood and told Oliver to take Katey to school, that her mother needed rest and certainly for the time, only one of them was needed. Katey protested but Oliver was quick and gentle with his arms upon the girl's shoulders. Though none of them knew it, it was the last time there would be such simple solution toward harmony for the next couple of weeks.

The doctor, once they were alone, said to Ruth, "She's fuddled. I'd have to say with good reason, all she's been through. But still it's a concern and so you should know."

"What do you mean, 'fuddled'?"

He shook his head. "I gave her morphine, for the pain and to help her sleep. She needs rest to clear her mind."

"There's never been a thing wrong with my mother's mind."

"That may be a problem."

"How so?"

"She's refusing to sign off on any further treatment. Any at all."

Jo had a single window in her second-floor room that looked out the rear of Mary Hitchcock upon a pair of tall hemlock trees. The boughs held clumped snow and a blue jay flew onto the branches to worry the cones and then away. Ruth couldn't hear the harsh call of the bird and wished she could. From an angle late-afternoon sunlight pooled against the ranks of needles, lighting up their dark oily stiffness. It felt a long time toward spring. Her mother spoke from the bed behind her, addressing her back which Ruth had turned upon her. Not from the words but to hide her slide of tears, her vacant yet oddly tight focus upon the coming and going of the brilliant winter bird.

Jo said, "The past few years have not been kind to me and I've hidden that from you because I've hidden it from myself, much as I've been able. Which I see now, was quite a good job. I've had shingles three years running and can't tell you the last time I had anything one could call a night of sleep. Much less an afternoon or morning free of pain. Most evenings a toddy or two allowed me to forget all that and have a blessed short hour when I felt my old self. But there's little in life more wretched than falling asleep at eleven only to wake at one and know that for all intents and hope, the night is done. Think about the long hours from then until dawn. And the day stretching ahead. And now, then. I'm broken to pieces. What would you have me do? Lie here and hope to heal enough to be taken home and live in a wheelchair? My house as good as lost to me—sleeping God knows where? And people, strangers, in and out throughout the day? I wouldn't have it. And No, you nor Katey can do that sort of work and I wouldn't have you—think now if I managed through another year or two and became even more ill, less able to tend myself. Even insensible. We both know it happens. I will not have you grow to hate me and hate yourself for wishing me to finally die. I'd loathe myself and loathe myself ever the more for finding myself without the ability to change a thing. Which, you see, I still have. And intend to use that power while I do."

"What?" Ruth turned then and faced her mother. "What are you saying?"

"I'm in terrible shape. And I won't allow them to do a thing to, what? Humpty-Dumpty, put me back together again? Because I'm also in a place where that young man, Doctor Jensen, can help me. Gently. And you must never ask him, because I plan to fool him as much as he needs fooling in order to help me with what I need. Which is, my dear, to not go gentle into that good night. 'Rage against the dying of the light.' That fool, Thomas. I've already raved and burned aplenty with old age."

Ruth wiped her face and suddenly stalked to the bedside and did her best to loom and leaned in. "How can you say this?"

Jo was suddenly crumpled against the pillow, her silver hair shot with thinly washed gold from the last of the sun and Ruth could hear clearly through the shut window the proud and raucous call of the jay. "Perhaps he had the right idea," Jo said. "At least he drank himself to death before the passage of years could catch him. And now they've caught me. No matter, you see, poetry is all that's left of life in the end. Perhaps God lurks somewhere behind it, the closest place he might be found, I think. It's simple really, my lovely girl. I'm done eating. Simple as that." Then her eyes closed for a time and the sun crossed the rest of the window and rose pale above and the jay didn't return and the slice of sky was a blue so brilliant it was almost green and then it went to black and the overhead lights showed her mother sleeping or so it seemed and Ruth had almost turned to go when once more Jo opened her eyes and as if only seconds had passed said, "Do you know the last thing I ate that I truly savored? Not a holiday dinner or oatmeal in the morning but the true last thing?"

Ruth suddenly wanted to flee the room, to be away from all this, to not have any of it happening, but she only swallowed and said, "No, Mother. I don't."

Jo writhed upright in her bed, higher against her pillows and then she said, "It was a Heath bar. I had to break it into pieces and hold each piece in my mouth while first the chocolate dissolved and then slowly the toffee, those lovely tastes all the way down. Oh, my. That was delicious."

"Yes," Ruth said. "You always liked them."

Jo looked at her and then said, "That was three years ago. An August afternoon. I'd go back there in a heartbeat if I could but it's gone. It's all gone."

After a moment Ruth said, "Mother?"

"Promise me."

"I can't."

"Oh, yes. You can. You have to."

Ruth held her hands clenched tight before her, twisting her fingers until they ached and she could not feel that pain as she said, "Oh, God. Mother. Don't you see? It's not only about you."

"Yes," Jo said. "That's the problem. It's not all about me but what I fear most of all is when it will be about nothing except me. But without my being able to take part. Or be a part of myself. And that is what I'm not willing to be. And not only for myself."

As it happened Jo recovered from the pneumonia with a vigor that surprised them all, not least herself. The broken hip and fracture of her pelvis were more difficult, the old bones not so willing to mend, the techniques for replacement of her hip were complicated and finally abandoned because of severe arthritis and calcification of the surrounding joint. Her plan to simply stop eating failed from the simple and surprisingly strong urge of appetite. She was home in time to see the snowdrops and crocus blooming and then the daffodils and the astounding bed of multihued tulips beyond the library window. Where a rented hospital-style bed had been set up, along with a set of tables drawn close, a reading lamp, a bell to summon whoever would be in the house and, finally and against her strong argument, a second telephone had been installed. Incongruously, once she'd agreed to that phone for the rare times when she was alone, she'd insisted on a pink pastel princess phone otherwise popular with certain teenage girls. "Why not," Jo said. "Everything is frivolous at this point. And perhaps when I do die, it can be a gift to Katey."

"Not if I have anything to say about it, it won't," Ruth had said.

"I'll put it in my will, then."

"For God's sake, Mother. You last wrote a will after Father died." She was clearing away a mostly full bowl of now-cold beef consommé, dry toast and a bowl of applesauce.

"I can write a codicil," Jo said. "All I need is a witness. I'm sure for a five-dollar bill passed her way, Mrs. Greene would happily serve that purpose of an evening."

"I'm sure she would. Mother, won't you eat the applesauce? It's your own, you know."

"Don't trust it—how old are those jars? Bring me a bowl of ice cream if you would. Coffee, please."

"You can't live on ice cream, Mother."

"Well," Jo said. "I seem to be. Aren't I?"

Katey went up afternoons after school and warmed the hopeful supper left by the day nurse, visited with her grandmother when she was awake, did her homework. Ruth came at eight and stayed until midnight when the overnight nurse came. Jo was awake it seemed most of the time but then would slip to a deep staggered sleep, daytime or night. Friday and Saturday nights Katey stayed over with her grandmother—after a determined, almost stubborn discussion with her mother, the girl insisting that when the two of them were alone her grandmother seemed to rouse and would tell old stories or query Katey about her own world, her plans for her life. Ruth had no doubt this was true but nevertheless felt a bit of a pang—it had been so many years since Jo had spoken to her in those sorts of ways. Ruth found herself studying the girl, not only wondering what she shared with Jo but also wondering if in the distant day when Ruth was in need of such care, would Katey offer such kinship and love so freely given? And if Katey would lead a life that would be as close to her mother, as Ruth had with Jo. There was no way to know but somehow Ruth doubted it. There were only hints at the coming changes for the children of this generation so it was the spirit of the girl herself that Ruth studied. Her own daughter, but how unlike her she was, bold and restless, a tucked-in chin of determination yes but eyes that flared also with a fire hidden by placid tones. Or, more recently, not. Ruth had never talked back to her mother this way, never this taut nerve of defiance, as if there was something mildly distasteful that Katey couldn't name or even voice, perhaps only a dreadful but accurate appraisal of Ruth's own character. How a child so well known can suddenly seem to become a stranger.

In the end, which came just as the lilacs were rusting, it wasn't her lack of eating or the secretly planned overdose of hoarded medications she'd secreted in the mudroom drawer but a clot that built within her bedridden body and traveled one afternoon to her brain. The day nurse was with her when the stroke seized her and Jo was dead by the time the ambulance arrived, as much as dead by the time Ruth was there; a slack gray face and body failing response to any touch or voice, any reach from the living. Oliver stood behind Ruth with his hands on her shoulders as the body was wheeled out on the gurney. Katey had stood before the window that looked out on the apple tree, hunched, silent, her face when she finally turned toward her parents a mask of bright anger and sorrow, as if this were all somehow someone's fault.

Before We Sleep

The service in the Congregational Church was overflowing which was almost a surprise to Ruth; her mother had been a quiet and retiring soul the last decade of her life and so this abundance of mourners at first felt unseemly, as if people were making an appearance. This impression was strengthened by the new minister, a man on the job for half a dozen years. Ruth sat rigid through the first part and then it came to her that while her mother might've grown hidden to the town, the town always had known exactly where she was, who she was, something surely of what she and her family meant within not only the history of the place but its ongoing fabric and Ruth understood this fabric was something she was very much a part of. Now, after all, the bearer of whatever standard, whatever torch, the Hales had ever held and ever would. Jo was buried in the cemetery on West Hill next to Nathaniel and as Ruth stood before the graves on that early summer late morning she understood for the first time that the span of years, just shy of twenty, between the deaths of her parents had not been so great after all. It was her own life that made it seem so.

Ed and Jennie, Jennie probably, had rented the Grange for the reception after the committal and there was an abundance of food, far beyond the usual carried-in hot dishes and cold platters and Ruth felt now as if she were sleepwalking as person after person approached her and leaned to press her hand and speak close to her face, as if these somber and dulcet tones were some strange and lovely tonic. At one point she saw Katey clumped with some other young teenage girls and then the next time she looked for her she was gone. Later, on the short drive up Beacon Hill to home she asked Oliver if he knew where she'd gone and he'd only said, "Likely where she needed to be." Ruth let that go, not even wanting to probe but then an earlier thought returned and she said, "All of that, back there at the Grange. That was lovely of your parents. But it seemed so much."

He drove, his jacket sleeves a bit short so his white cuffs protruded. He said, "It's what people do, Ruthie."

At home she made a pot of tea and then was suddenly deeply exhausted and went upstairs to their bedroom and, still formally dressed, removed her shoes and stretched atop the covers in the bright afternoon. When she woke it was late evening and the sun was streaking low bars of gold down the wall across from the bed and for long moments she had no idea where she was or what she was doing. And then it all came back to her.

The great shock was that there was no money. Not that Ruth had been expecting it, in the sense of having plans for an inheritance. Simply she'd assumed there would be something beyond the house. But as it turned out, in important ways there was even less than nothing. Not only were there the hospital bills and the home-health nurses to be paid but the house itself was a bit of a shell, a facade of something resembling what it once had been. After meeting with the lawyer and learning these bare bald harsh facts, Ruth had sat with Oliver of a late evening in the garden. Katey was in her first summer working at the Double Dot and would be walking up the hill soon. Oliver had a can of Narragansett, Ruth a gin and tonic that she nursed, her brain firing hot and not yet wanting to let the drink soften her. Oliver said, "It's sad but makes sense—your father died almost twenty years ago which is a long time to live, modestly as she did, on whatever money he'd put aside. And the house, well, you have to consider there were another four or five years, during the war, when he probably didn't have much work done, if any at all, on the house. That's near on to a quarter-century of, I don't know. What? Benign neglect? Perhaps that's the best way to look at it. Nothing intentional. For that matter, I imagine Jo might not've even truly seen the issues. A place gets into ill-repair slowly unless there's some major event—an ice storm or somesuch. The important thing was she was able to live out her life there, the life, as she saw it, that she'd always had."

Ruth felt a ripple of unease and lifted her drink and swallowed. She said, "We'll need to get a man in to go over everything and determine what must be done and what it will cost. Who would you think would be best?"

Oliver was quiet a long moment and then said, "Why, Ruthie. That's a pile of money you're talking about. And the property taxes, well, you know, with so many folks from Boston and New York buying up those old hill places for summer houses or to retire. We don't have that sort of money, Ruth."

She was not looking at him. "That's my home," she said.

He nodded and looked off into the greening evening slowly fading to black. In the sky dome to the east a planet hung bright. He then looked up at her and said, "I know it was." Then he paused and she knew he was almost about to remind her that this was now her home, the home he'd made for her. But he didn't. Instead he said, "Even if we were able. What would you do with it?"

"Hold on to it for Katey. It should be hers. It's a grand place to raise a family, you know that's true."

He nodded and said, "Ruthie, Katey's a dozen years, maybe more from such a time. And we'd be assuming she'd want to return here." He paused again and squinted off and then said, "She'll leave you know, even if just for college but whatever happens with her in those years, even when she's ready to make a home and family, how can we be sure this is where she'll want to do it?"

Ruth stood. She was suddenly atremble and angry that she was. She said, "I'd want her to have that choice, that chance to make her home here."

He said, "I understand. But say we found a way to hold on to it for her? What burden would we be placing upon her? Would that be fair?"

"Why can't you see what this means to me?"

"I do. But that doesn't mean I can make it happen. Even if I agreed with you."

"So there's not only no money, or you're not willing for us to find it, but you think it would be wrong anyway. That's what you're saying."

He was silent and again looked off at the darkening sky.

After a time of holding herself against the twirling wrong world she managed to break out her question. "So what do you propose?"

He waited and then said, "There's a man from Westchester, New York, who last year was poking around and found the lawyer. He made an offer then, a good one that he said would stand as long as needed."

"So you already sold it."

"Of course not. But Ruthie, think about what you were saying. A place for Katey in the future when she's ready to have a family. The money gives her a choice, is what I'm thinking."

The ice cubes had melted in her drink and there was a scant inch or two of liquid in the glass and she threw it in a hard arc of splash in his face. "You bastard," she said and turned and stalked toward the house. Where she'd put fresh ice in the glass and a pour of gin, find cigarettes and go on out the seldom-used front door to sit in the tangle under the old apple tree and drink and smoke and be alone with her molten core. And as she approached the shed she saw the dark form of her daughter coming into the drive and walking toward where Oliver still sat, outlined against the night. Then as Ruth reached open the screen door she heard Katey say, "Dad? Was that Mom? Is everything okay?"

It was now a week to the day that Katey had slipped out of the house and Ruth was trying to hold herself steady. Surely, if she'd had success finding Brian Potter, it wouldn't have entailed an entire week. It was

372

all of the other possibilities that had Ruth so worried. The many ways Brian Potter, in whatever his life now was, could've reacted upon learning of this girl. Of what their chance encounter had brought forth—not just upon himself but for Oliver, for Ruth herself. She calmed herself; however short her time had been with him there had been nothing but pained kindness and genuine concern for Oliver, as well as his own deep mortification over how it ended. It wasn't Brian she feared but what else was out there in the world that might snag her girl.

Katey was moving into the life she saw for herself, not the life they'd envisioned for her. However much Ruth knew this was true, she also knew how much pain the world could give. And also, on top of walking so quiet through her June days, knowing how Katey had come to see her, these past years. As a fearful person of crushed dreams, of one who had settled for less. When nothing truly could be further from the truth.

On this, the seventh day, she'd spent the morning at the school, completing the last of the paperwork for the year, routine work she could barely make her way through for thinking of her daughter. Finally a bit before noon she gave up and drove home. She made egg salad and ate a sandwich and set out another on a plate for Oliver, who, it seemed was in his workshop. Perhaps finally working on the fiddle he'd been unable to undertake. She understood in some ways he was more devastated by Katey's departure than she was. Or, perhaps, simply differently. That she could understand. She cast about in her mind and knew, whatever she did, she wanted to be in the house, felt that within her. She determined to dust her books. This was not a simple job but one she undertook each year—working her way along the shelves, taking them down and using a cloth to clean them, replacing them and moving to the next shelf. It was a slow process, laborious even, but in the end as worthwhile as owning the books themselves.

And, importantly, she'd hear the phone when it rang. Some part of her knew it would, this day. Some other part also understood that this was a fevered mother's urge, close to a dream. A quiet pleading to the universe for relief from her worry.

As she worked she considered again how her daughter had come to think of her, of how she was viewed. And the wry humor was not only that Katey was wrong, but how close she'd come to being right. Only late by about three years.

By the time winter came again after Jo died Ruth felt she'd come to terms with it all—peace certainly wasn't the right word. By autumn the house was sold and she, along with Oliver's tender and quiet presence, had worked her way through the furniture and art, books and household goods, long lifetimes of items and oddities, all, it seemed known to Ruth—even those surprises and things she didn't have a clue of their purpose; the goods and items gathered over time and held for possible use. Even if those uses were uncertain. In the end about half of the major items made their way from the house on West Hill to the house on Beacon Hill, replacing similar things of lesser quality or simply lacking the luster of the long-held and precious. The little Shaker-made cherry bedside tables with their dovetail joints and single drawers. The two-century old dry sink with its fading ancient red milk paint. The dining room table and chairs, the old china and older silver. The Seth Thomas eight-day clock. Her father's shaving cup and brush simply because it had been his. Books. And finally, in late October on a Sunday morning Ruth had driven up alone and avoiding the empty house had carefully dug parts and sections of certain plants, even a few she had much older transplants from already. Iris and lily, bleedingheart, another slip from the smokebush. Masses of spring bulbs already dormant. And finally, from along the fence that separated the gardens from the adjoining fields, fields that long ago had also been part of this property, she dug a clump of wilted goldenrod and another of purple asters. Common, abounding everywhere. But these, these were from here and therefore would bloom now on Beacon Hill forever. From here.

That day she never once stepped inside the house although she still had a key. The fact that she had a key and the house was locked was enough itself to stop her but beyond that everything left inside was grouped into lots for the estate sale to take place the following weekend. She had no intention of attending that event. She'd heard workmen would be in the house through the winter. Men hired by the lawyer from Westchester who had bought the property. She'd met him, had to meet him, at the formal closing of the sale. He'd been pleasant and solicitous and she'd disliked him immediately, with his deep suntan and argyle sweater vest. But she'd stood outside the house that afternoon with the backseat of the car loaded with plants, technically stolen, and took a shiver of pleasure in knowing this and yet she still held a spark, hidden well, she thought, that Oliver had been so unable or unwilling, she truly didn't know which, to have let her hold this property. To understand what it so deeply meant to her. She drove down the hill with the car filled with the rich smell of dirt and tubers, seeping tears. She didn't know it at the time but it would be years before she'd drive again up West Hill, to drive past the house she no longer recognized that nevertheless held within it the shapes of memory, the walks and rooms of childhood, the footfalls and voices of the dead.

She'd planted those stolen plants and envisioned them growing the next spring, had walked through her house now with those older familiar items, had taught school, been tender as she could with her husband, and daily bickered with her daughter over learning the necessary work of daily life. It wasn't all bad, she thought. Katey laughing with her when both forgot the final batch of Christmas cookies as they finished trimming the tree, standing in the kitchen with the dark hard lumps steaming rank smoke. From the radio a suddenly hilarious solemn version of "The Little Drummer Boy." Pa-ROM-pa-pa-POM.

It was about this time that almost nothing seemed to make sense. She held to this as a secret—even from Oliver. Afraid if she tried to articulate she'd only further discover the madness that seemed to burble along inside. She walked through her days as if inhabiting another body. She woke in the night with her heart racing, her mind a tumbling turmoil.

She wasn't herself but didn't know what that self might be. In constant panic invisible to those around her. Not just Oliver and Katey but everyone. For the first time in her life she was confronted with issues she couldn't share with her mother.

She started to walk the streets of the village at night. She began one evening in February after a day of snow. It was much later she realized this was a year to the day that Jo had fallen. They'd all eaten together, a supper of pot roast with potatoes and carrots and onions in brown gravy and salads of iceberg lettuce and Oliver had excused himself to his workshop. Katey did homework at the cleared table while Ruth washed the dishes and put them away and then the girl had watched television in the next room while Ruth sat in the one soft chair next to the old wood range and read without much care for the story. After a while Katey had come to kiss her good night, before going up to shower and go to bed. Ruth read some more and then closed the book and stood. She put her hands in the small of her back and stretched, opened the firebox and filled it—she liked a wood fire in the kitchen in wintertime, even with the wood furnace down cellar. Then, as if she'd planned it, she went to the row of outdoor boots by the door, the pegs above holding coats and hats and stepped into her felt-lined gum boots, pulled on her dark gray wool coat and belted it snug and then took down her navy scarf and made a triangle with it over her head and wrapped her neck, twisting the ends under her chin and tucked them down into the coat. She let herself out into the woodshed ell and then into the driveway. Oliver had shoveled the driveway sometime in the afternoon but before the snow had stopped. There were tire tracks that disappeared into the garage where her car sat. She walked out the tracks to the road which had been scraped mostly clear by the plow trucks an hour ago and she walked down into the village.

The air was still and chill but not bitter and the streetlights threw light upon the freshly made banks of snow. She kept to the side of the road going down Beacon Hill and turned into the village proper where the squares of lit windows reflected out onto the snow. She also passed winter trees, the dark balsams with boughs pulled low and outlined by the weight of new snow, the bare fingers like ink stains of the maple crowns, the ash trees and the inverted wineglass shapes of the elms. There was disease killing the elms although not yet in this village but as she looked at the big elm at the corner of the North Common and Creamery Row she understood one year soon the tree would look like this in the summer, bare of leaves, standing dead, until it was cut down and removed and forever gone.

Everything was closed for the night in the block of business, although the windows were lit in her in-laws' store, the four ranks of plate glass that flanked the steps leading in and each window held goods specific and arrayed neatly; kitchenware and crockery, winter clothing and folded blankets, tools and snow shovels and a pair of Tubbs snowshoes and in the last, a small pyramid of round wooden cheese boxes, with an open round of cheddar on top, along with coffee grinders and small sacks of roasted beans. And along the bottom of that window was a line of brightly colored packets of garden seeds. To remind that winter was not forever.

The only other light was up at the top of the block where the small VFW post had a naked bulb over the door and a red Schlitz neon sign in the high small window. There was an older truck parked there and a Studebaker sedan. She recognized the truck but not the sedan and walked on, for a few moments trying but failing to pull from her memory the name of the owner of the truck. Then she was up the other side of the Common and walking again along residential streets. Some people had shoveled their sidewalks and others had left that job to the morning. For themselves or the boy who would be paid to do so, early. The snow had only stopped sometime after dark.

She wasn't sure what she was doing but knew it was the best thing she'd done in a long time. She walked at a brisk pace and passed house after house with their lit windows. Some few fully dark and these mostly homes of older people. Some houses all dark but for the one gray flickering window where a television was on. Kitchens bright as someone worked inside. An upper room throwing its light out, perhaps a child studying, someone reading, listening to the radio. She passed a house with a bright window just yards away from her and an older man sitting in his chair, seeming to gaze out upon her or perhaps only lost in his own mist of reflected light in the glass and whatever memory he was enraptured by. Also the second-story window where she briefly saw a girl come before it with a towel wrapped like a turban around her head and another around her torso, her shoulders and arms bare and then Diane Tucker lifted her hands and pulled away the towel and stood bare-breasted looking out into the night. Ruth back under hemlock shade from the streetlights and so invisible and she stood, wondering who the girl intended or thought might be waiting outside for this vision and then understood most likely it was no specific person but the idea of someone. Then Diane went away from the window and a few minutes later the light went off and Ruth walked on. After a time she circled around and made her way back up Beacon Hill and let herself in to a quiet house. The lights were all off but for the one that burned all night in the

378

kitchen and she knew the stoves were banked. She took off her boots and scarf and coat quiet as a whisper. In sock-footed silence she made her way to the side cupboard and poured a small measure of gin into a glass and looked at the fridge but didn't want to risk the noise for an ice cube and so sat in the chair with her feet up on the warm ledge of the stove in the near dark and slowly sipped the gin and felt the warm flush through her and didn't know much more than when she'd started out earlier except that she was not so frantic, that her heart was calmer. Or she was only tired. Even that, she knew, was enough. She went up to bed only after she was fully warm.

This went on. Not every night but a couple of times a week. Weeknights. She was a bit shocked how easy it was to leave the house at a certain hour and have no one miss her. But not so shocked—she was calculating and careful, as she wandered. After what, she still did not know. But it was good that she did, she knew that.

There were no strangers that she passed in the dark. But she did wonder what was hidden, when she passed houses with front windows lit and no one in sight—what might be occurring in the rooms away from the streets. What arguments or fights were hidden in those darkened back rooms. Mike and Rita Howell. Word about town was they were having a hard time, that Rita had been spotted in the Acme in Randolph in a scarf and sunglasses grocery shopping on a cold and cloudy day. Twice passing by their house on High Street she'd glimpsed them in the front room with the lights on. Sitting in their chairs side by side facing the television. Then again on a Tuesday night but still early the lights in the house all damped and dark. Their one car in the drive. A faint flicker from a second-story room. Fighting or fucking or, she understood, both. The widow Madge Garnett who sat in her kitchen every time Ruth passed by, at her table with her back to the window but clearly dealing cards to an empty chair across from her. Some conversation was occurring in that room. Once standing again far back in tree shadows as she watched Chuck Morton just come out of the VFW and trying and failing to open the door of his truck, slipping and falling, hauling himself upright, steadying himself, then reeling away, pitched off in fast stumbling steps into the night, unable to find equilibrium. From the looks of him, a stumblebum drunk but also the owner of the sawmill up on Kipling Hill and as such a buyer of loads of logs, an employer of a crew of men, one known for delivering lumber cut true and fair, always behind his men. How to explain this, she thought?

She was caught twice. The first time she walked back into the house toward the end of the second week of her stealthy hikes, had gotten comfortable with the stove and her glass of gin when Oliver padded in on sock feet and mildly said, "What're you up to, Ruthie?"

She looked at him and raised her glass but didn't yet swallow and said, "I'm walking. Is that all right with you?"

"I guess." He reached and gently rubbed the back of her neck. "Is it good for you?"

"I don't think I'd be doing it, if it wasn't."

He paused a moment and then said, "All right, then." And turned and padded away up to bed. She took her time with her drink and again, when she went to bed her feet were warm and he was sleeping soundly.

The other time she was coming on toward home on a late April night and the air had been switching between warmish and chill all day and into the evening. There was a moon and scuds of clouds passing between the moon and the earth and she walked from shade to shadow, more so than simply the pods of yellow light from the streetlights. As she walked along she heard the hum of a motor coming up slowly behind her and she kept her head held up and straight, her shoulders squared. Her posture almost martial. This had happened a couple of other times and she'd never given them so much as a glance but strode on with purpose and defiance in her walk and they'd always drifted by and then pressed the gas a bit and moved along, taillights fading in the dark.

This night however a deputy sheriff in his prowl car glided alongside her and came to a stop in the street just ahead of her. The driver door opened and the deputy stepped out and turned to look at her under the streetlight. His cap was pushed up on his forehead and she saw that it was Merle Howe. She was bareheaded that night and so stepped forward so he could see her clearly. "Good evening, Merle. What can I do for you?"

His face was broken into planes of light and dark and he said, "Oh, my. Is that you, Missus Snow?"

He'd been a student of hers, years before. She realized that he was already mortified but trying to do his job. Which matched her memory of how he was as a boy.

A moment passed. Then he said, "I got a report on someone walking about the village."

"I guess that would be me. I thought I was free to do that. It's where I live."

He pushed one boot up the side of the other and then did it again as he watched himself do it. Then he looked back at her. "Yup," he said. "Is everything all right?"

"Everything is fine," she said. She considered a moment and added, "I'll get along then. Thanks for checking on me, Merle. You have a good night." And set off walking again, making her way slowly down the main street, the state highway, then around the South Common before finally crossing the road and heading up Beacon Hill. Beyond the scraps of clouds and the moon she could see Orion and the Sisters lowering toward the top of the hill. The streetlights were too few, too dim and widely spaced, to choke out the stars.

She continued one or two evenings a week as the spring came on. She knew people were aware of her walking and guessed those that did, or those that talked about it, likely thought her strange. This didn't bother her, she knew she was strange. She just didn't quite know why. But she changed her route, walking up the narrow street beside the courthouse where it doglegged past a few houses and opened into the ranks of the Hillside Cemetery and here she found peace and solitude among the memorials to the dead. And was alone. The evenings were growing longer and so she found herself there in the remainder of the day's light. From the higher part she could look across the narrow valley and just spy the front side of her own home, the back of the barn and Oliver's workshop. This rambling almost satisfied some unease within her. She also spent days that spring feeling as if she were making do, putting on a shadow play of her own self, as if her real self lingered a half-step behind her, and that self a muddled, mute and perturbed one. Looking at her husband and daughter and knowing they had no idea what dark land she inhabited. She was skillful at that. Maintaining her disguise of normalcy, her facade of mother, of wife. Katey, fifteen in January, within her own confusions, would hug and kiss her mother spontaneously, bursting through with her own need for comfort and consolation, turning to where she knew safety to be. Oliver humming a tune over his soup, then reaching out to pat her hand before rising from the table and back to his shop. And, in his way, still coming to her in the night.

It all came to a stop on a Sunday night the end of April, the evening of the full moon as she stood in the cemetery. The stones around her were white in the moonlight, the older dark slate stones almost the soft color of bones. She'd stood looking down upon the village and then lifted both hands together just below her chin, her elbows joined before her and without a clue she would speak before she did, found herself saying out loud, "I'm not going anywhere. There's nowhere else I want to be." And only understood then that she was still grieving her mother and stood for a time silently weeping.

Then a great well of peacefulness came upon her and tension drained out of her, down from her neck and shoulders and arms to flow from her fingertips and into the ground. She stood so for a time, washed in the moonlight and then walked slowly but easily down out of the burying ground and back through her town and home. As she made her way up Beacon Hill in the soft night she heard the first broken cries of northbound geese beating on through the night and thrilled to that sound, as if, the world turning once again, she'd not only made her way home but had linked herself to something greater than herself.

Now, two years later working on her hands and knees along the shelves of books, lifting and glancing at titles, some making her smile, others just a job to be done, wondering where her girl was now, knowing how foolish was her certainty that Katey would call. And knew again that jittering uncertainty of mind, wondering if this strange and accommodating measure of her life, if that was all she got. And knew that question had come truly from her but also from those around her. A rift it seemed opened and demanding an answer. As if she might have cast it all away and gone off into the world after something else, as indeed so many had. And, indeed, as so many still were doing. Including her daughter. But beyond Katey, as if the world were pressing on all sides, demanding a need for more. Since clearly more was offered, why settle for less?

Yet here she was. And this was good. There were far worse things than to prepare youngsters for the world that would lie ahead of them. To prepare them for the day when, inevitably, that world would not make sense. She couldn't save Katey or anyone. She had barely saved herself. And she knew her daughter saw her as a woman settled so, and knew also her daughter didn't yet know what peace she'd earned in that settling. To do work in the world. To be loved by a good and kind man. As it moved between both of them, so often not spoken of. For that, then, she knew was the most important thing of all: not the words but the greater love. The one constant through silence and darkness, through doubt and fear. Of knowing the other understood, that lived within that very same world, not exact, but parallel. Running along, side by side, the two of them down through life.

She'd just dusted and put back Hemingway's *Old Man and the Sea* and lifted down *A Farewell to Arms*, had held that book a long moment, recalling that when she first read it in high school she'd thought it to be a tremendously passionate story of love, and then rereading it a few years ago it seemed on a whim and had been struck by what a tremendously terrible and tragic tale it actually was. And how lucky she'd been in her own life, then dusted it and set it back on the shelf, paused before *A Moveable Feast*, her fingers dirty and her nose filled with dust, thinking she should pause and take a break, wash her hands, perhaps brew a pot of tea. There was no great hurry. It took a couple of days to dust the books and she also needed to make a call about the strawberries. They should be ripe now and she didn't want to miss them. She'd almost forgotten all about it when the phone rang. She turned and looked at it. It rang again. She set down the rag and thought It's going to be Jennie wanting Oliver for something. Or anything else.

She crossed the room and waited for the third ring and then lifted it to her ear and took a breath and, her voice rising toward a question, said, "Hello."

She listened a moment and then said, "Of course."

When she hung up the phone she stood serious for a long moment. Then smiled. She went into the kitchen and made tea and sat thinking about all she'd heard while the tea steeped. Then drank a cup as she mulled other things. When she finished she rinsed her cup and saucer and left a cozy over the pot and went upstairs. She went into the guest bedroom where Oliver had been sleeping since he'd broke the news to Katey. It had been his choice and she'd accepted that he was doing what he needed to do. She stripped the bed and carried the sheets and pillowcases downstairs and washed them. She went back up and remade the bed with fresh sheets and a blanket, then from the cupboard a chenille spread, all tucked down tight and square. She popped up the shades. On the top of the bureau she found a bottle of Old Spice and she returned it to the bathroom by his shaving mug and razor. She returned to the room and looked around. It was the guest room again.

His place was with her.

Acknowledgments

For friendship and support in all forms: Henry & Noele Lyman, Dan & Karen Morgan, Sally Hostetler, Jean & Wendy Palthey, Michaela Findeis, Rob & Petra McCarron. For Richard & Susan Walton.

For, among so much else, still riding her bike at eighty-eight, my mother, Patricia Adams Lent.

For stories of being a child in Germany during World War Two, that led me to more stories, Iba Lent.

For the staff at the Elliot Pratt Center Library at Goddard College, where sections of this book were written in peace and solitude.

For the staff at the Gifford Medical Center, particularly Dr. Ken Borie and Dr. Sandy Craig. For stepping into the breach, Diane Walton, Ben Wolfe, Anita Abbot, Liz York, and, again, Jean Palthey.

For all of my Mississippi friends: John Evans, Jamie & Kelly Kornegay, Richard and Lisa Howarth, as well as Cody and Lyn at Square Books; for Ron Shapiro.

For the hole in the world that is the memory of Jim Harrison.

For Anton Mueller and George Gibson and the entire crew at Bloomsbury.

For the setters of my life, thus far: Jill, Rose, Bella, Franny.

And, as this book opened, so it closes, with my loves, Marion, Esther, Clara.

A Note on the Author

Jeffrey Lent's first novel, *In the Fall*, was a national bestseller and a *New York Times Book Review* Notable Book for 2000. His other novels are *Lost Nation*, *A Peculiar Grace*, *After You've Gone*, and *A Slant of Light*. Lent lives with his wife and two daughters in central Vermont.